HADLEY
&
GRACE

OTHER BOOKS BY SUZANNE REDFEARN

In an Instant

No Ordinary Life

Hush Little Baby

HADLEY
&
GRACE

a novel

SUZANNE REDFEARN

LAKE UNION
PUBLISHING

Text copyright © 2021 by Suzanne Redfearn
All rights reserved.

Published by Lake Union Publishing, Seattle

www.apub.com

Amazon, the Amazon logo, and Lake Union Publishing are trademarks of Amazon.com, Inc., or its affiliates.

ISBN-13: 9781542014380 (paperback)
ISBN-10: 1542014387 (paperback)

Cover design by Kathleen Lynch/Black Kat Design

Printed in the United States of America

For Skipper Carrillo:
the original Mr. Baseball

1

HADLEY

Her watch says 12:52, which means eight minutes remain to get the cupcakes. Plenty of time, yet Hadley feels her pulse ticking. She looks at the two women in front of her and wills the line to move faster. She doesn't like to be late.

The woman at the counter is struggling to make her decision. "So, the special today is strawberry cheesecake?" she asks for the third time. She is older, with silver hair and a bend in her spine.

The salesgirl, perhaps sixteen, offers a patient smile. "Yes, but if your granddaughter just wants plain strawberry, we have that as well."

"She told me strawberry," the woman says, her voice unsure as she clutches her purse tight against her, a frayed black bag possibly as old as Hadley.

Impatience bleeds from the woman directly in front of Hadley, midforties and professional, her arms folded across her chest and her Prada wallet held at the ready, the blush-painted nail of her index finger tapping against it.

Hadley's phone buzzes, and she looks down to see a text from Frank.

Truck ok? Mercedes will be dropped off this afternoon. How u holding up?

"The cheesecake one is very pretty," the grandmother says. "She's six. Did I mention it's her birthday?"

The Prada woman rolls her eyes. The grandmother did mention it is her granddaughter's birthday. She also mentioned she is turning six and that they're celebrating with a picnic in the park beside her daughter's apartment. Her daughter is bringing pizza, and the grandmother is supposed to bring a Sprinkles cupcake for dessert.

Hadley wants to tell her she should buy the original strawberry cupcake, not the special. If it's what her granddaughter asked for, then it will be what she's expecting, and anything other than strawberry will be a disappointment.

Strawberry has always been Mattie's favorite as well. "Stwawbewwy, pwease," she used to lisp when asked what flavor she preferred for cake, ice cream, or Jell-O. And Mattie would have been terribly let down if she'd been given strawberry cheesecake, especially on her birthday.

"The cheesecake is really good," the counter girl says, trying to be helpful. She holds up the special. The pink frosting is decorated with red sprinkles and has a ruby-red candy in the shape of a strawberry on top. The strawberry cupcake literally pales in comparison—cream frosting, no sprinkles, no candy on top.

Hadley returns to her phone and pecks her answer back to her husband.

Truck is fine and I'm ok as long as I don't think about it.

She feels the lie in her chest as she presses send.

Frank's text is instant. Hang in there. Love u.

Prada woman lets out an audible groan, and the grandmother glances back to see her laser glare.

The grandmother returns to the salesgirl and stutters, "F-fine. That's fine. I'll take the special."

She shuffles to the register as Prada woman shakes her head and steps to the counter. Succinctly and rather loudly, she rattles off her order as if demonstrating how cupcake ordering should be done. The

2

grandmother stands a few feet away, her face pinched, clearly uncertain of her decision.

Hadley's phone buzzes. Love u!!!

"Can I help you?" the salesgirl says.

Hadley feels Prada woman watching, judging her on her cupcake-ordering ability. She tucks her phone in her pocket and recites sharply, "Two dozen chocolate marshmallow, two dozen strawberry, one dozen red velvet, and one dozen vanilla." She just stops herself from looking at Prada woman for her approval.

The grandmother is counting out the exact change from her purse as the girl at the register smiles patiently, and Hadley thinks kindness must be the number one job requirement for applicants, and she wants to commend the manager on her hiring. *This would be a lovely first job for Mattie,* she thinks at the exact moment she realizes that, God willing, she and Mattie won't be anywhere near this place when Mattie is old enough to work.

Hadley whispers to the girl at the counter, "Please add two strawberry cupcakes, each boxed separately."

Her phone buzzes again, but she ignores it. She doesn't want to slow down the cupcake-purchasing flow by not being ready when it's her turn to pay. She imagines Frank staring at the screen of his phone, gripping it in both hands, his thumbs poised and his brow creased as he waits for her reply.

Prada woman marches past with her cupcakes, her nose in the air, and Hadley takes a small measure of delight in the smudge of lipstick on her collar, knowing lipstick, especially red lipstick, is very difficult to get out.

Hadley pays quickly, glances at her watch, and hurries from the store. She is now two minutes behind schedule, but she can make that up if she cuts through the minimall instead of waiting for the light.

As she scans the parking lot, she sees the grandmother just climbing into her car.

"Excuse me," Hadley says, hurrying up to her.

The woman looks up, and Hadley startles at the remnant of beauty in the old woman's face. Her vivid blue eyes are framed by magnificent cheeks that still glow pink, and for a flicker, Hadley is reminded of her mother.

"The girl in the store asked me to give this to you," she says, holding out one of the strawberry cupcakes. "She wanted to make sure your granddaughter got the cupcake she wanted, and she felt bad that you had to choose."

The grandmother's remarkable eyes grow large. "She did?"

Hadley nods. She has always been a marvelous liar.

Relief floods the woman's face to the point of her eyes growing misty.

"I hope your granddaughter enjoys it," Hadley says and then hurries away, her heart filled with the wonderful feeling you get when you know you've done something right.

Her phone buzzes again, and she pulls it from her pocket as she races to Frank's truck, the bags of cupcakes thumping against her legs.

LOVE U????

Where the hell are u?

I said I LOVE U.

LOVE U. LOVE U. LOVE U!!!!!

With a deep breath, she types, Love you too. I just needed to pay for the cupcakes.

He emojis back a happy face and a heart, and she closes her eyes, lets out a slow exhale, then climbs into his truck to drive to Skipper's school for his going-away party.

2

GRACE

Yes. Yes, yes, yes!

A man of his word, Jerry promised the contract would arrive before the end of the day, and three minutes ago, at exactly 1:28, the fax machine whirred to life and began spitting out the golden pages.

Grace kisses the contract, twirls, then kisses it again. She looks at the photo on her desk—a picture of Jimmy, Miles, and her in front of Angels Stadium—and gives a thumbs-up.

It's hard to believe the photo was taken only two months ago, Miles so small he practically fit in the palm of Jimmy's large hand. Jimmy is in his army uniform, a proud smile on his face. It was Presidents' Day weekend, and all military families had gotten into the game for free. Jimmy was home to attend his mother's funeral, an event that was both sad and a relief. His mother had been suffering a long time and had been unable to remember him or his brother, Brad, for far longer than that.

As she dances the contract to Frank's office, the heel of her left shoe slaps against the carpet. The sole came loose a week ago. She mended it with superglue, but this morning, it came apart again. Maybe tonight, after she picks up Miles, they'll stop by Walmart and she'll buy a new pair in celebration. Perhaps she'll even treat herself to a meal out—pizza or fish tacos. Her mouth waters with the thought. She hasn't eaten since the hurried english muffin she stuffed in her mouth on the way out the door this morning. She didn't want to risk leaving the office for lunch and missing the contract coming through.

Her rap on the door lifts Frank's head.

"Done deal," she says, walking in and then slapping the contract down on the desk in front of him.

"What's this?"

"The contract to sublease Jerry Koch's downtown lot," she says, working hard to keep the glee from her voice. "Took a bit of persuasion—actually, a lot of persuasion—but here it is, signed, sealed, delivered." She almost singsongs the last line to the tune of the Stevie Wonder hit and just stops herself from adding, *It's yours.*

Three months. That's how long she's been negotiating, cajoling, and back-and-forth flirting with Jerry Koch, owner of the business mall in downtown Laguna Beach. The sublease of his parking lot in the evenings and on the weekends will bring in two to three grand a week for Aztec Parking, and 10 percent of that will be hers—at least a grand a month, twelve grand a year, and the answer to her prayers.

Frank's eyes pulse once in surprise. "Well, I'll be. The old bastard finally came around."

"He did. The entire lot. Evenings, weekends, and holidays."

Grace feels like her heart is going to explode. When she proposed the idea of subleasing Jerry's lot, Frank told her she was wasting her time. He had already tried, and the guy wasn't interested. She said he was probably right but asked if she could pursue it just the same. He told her to knock herself out and agreed to a 10 percent cut if she managed it.

And now, here she is, three months later, contract in hand. Her mind spins with what the money will mean to her and Jimmy, a million ideas tumbling through her head: First, pay off Jimmy's gambling debt so they can stop looking over their shoulders; second, get new tires for her car; next, move Miles out of the crappy day care he's in. Then, perhaps, in a few months, once all that has been taken care of, they can consider a nicer apartment, one with a tub so Miles can take baths, since he is now four months old and starting to sit up.

Frank stops on the last page of the contract, and as she watches his eyes scanning back and forth, her excitement turns slightly nervous. Frank is what her grandmother would have called a righteous slitherer—a fork-tongued charmer who preaches the gospel but whose own word can go either way. Her grandmother wouldn't have much liked Frank Torelli, and she would have liked less the idea of Grace working for him. But then, she wouldn't have much liked most of how Grace's life turned out after she died.

Frank sets down the contract and lifts his face to Grace's. Frank's eyes were the first thing Grace noticed about her boss—deep brown, piercing, and slightly misaligned, as if he's looking at you, but not. He leans back in his chair and steeples his fingers in front of him. "Grace, this is good work," he says. "Mary said you were smart."

Grace tenses at the mention of her previous boss. When Jimmy's debts caught up with them, and they needed to leave LA in a hurry, Mary called Frank and asked if he would hire Grace after Miles was born. It was extremely generous, especially considering Grace was leaving her in the lurch.

"I'd say things have worked out pretty well," Frank goes on. "Baby's healthy. Husband's doing better."

Grace says nothing, the nervous feeling growing.

"The past is behind you, and the sharks don't know where you are."

She tries not to react but knows she has by the smirk on Frank's face, the threat in the not-so-veiled statement plain. The people Jimmy owes money to are dangerous, and getting mixed up with them was the biggest mistake of his life.

Frank picks up the last page of the contract, the commission agreement that promises her 10 percent. After folding it neatly in half, he slides it toward her. "I'm glad things are going so well for you and your family," he says.

Grace doesn't move, her unblinking stare the only challenge she offers, but even that small defiance is enough to cause Frank's features to darken. Holding her gaze, he pulls the sheet back, crumples it in a ball, then banks it into the wastebasket beside his desk. When he turns back, Grace lowers her eyes. She's been screwed over enough times in her life to know when she's been beaten.

3

HADLEY

The truck beeps, making Hadley realize the door is ajar, with the keys still in the ignition. She pulls them out, and the beeping stops.

She stares at the low-slung brick buildings in front of her. It's hard to believe that today is the last day she will ever drive here, the last day she will ever park in this parking lot, the last day she will ever pick up one of her kids here after their day at school.

"Coming?"

She turns to see Melissa Jenkins smiling from the sidewalk, a platter of sugar cookies decorated with smiley faces in her hands.

Hadley blinks, then blinks several more times. "Yes, of course," she says, painting on a smile as she climbs from the truck.

Melissa and Hadley have known each other since Melissa's daughter, Katie, and Skipper were babies, and she is Hadley's closest friend.

Years ago, when they first met, all Hadley saw was Melissa's rose-tattooed arms, long nails, and goth black hair. Now, all Hadley sees when she looks at her friend is the biggest-hearted, hardest-working woman she knows.

A wealthy widow, Melissa inherited her husband's three Harley Davidson dealerships, and she runs them with an iron fist and a soft spot for ex-felons. She also raises three foster kids, along with her own daughter and son.

She wraps her arm around Hadley's shoulder and gives an encouraging squeeze. "Hang in there, kiddo," she says. "Today is not forever. It's just today."

Hadley almost manages a smile. Despite having a month to get used to the idea of Skipper leaving, she is no more ready to accept it than she was the day her sister called with the news she was getting married and therefore ready to take on the responsibility of being Skipper's mom.

They're greeted in the school's courtyard by a hand-painted banner that reads, *Good Luck Skipper!!! We're Going To Miss You!* A hundred handprints of varying colors surround the words, along with the signatures of the kids who belong to those handprints.

She and Melissa set the sweets on the table that's been set up for the celebration, and a moment later, the bell rings. Kids spill from the second- and third-grade classrooms, and Hadley scans over the heads for Skipper.

He is the last to leave Mrs. Baxter's room, ambling behind the others in the slow, distracted way he has. Her heart swells at the sight of him, the way it always does when she sees one of her kids after not seeing them for some time.

"Hey, Blue," he says as he walks into her outstretched arms and wraps his skinny ones around her hips.

"Hey, Champ." She kisses the top of his honey hair. He smells as he always does, of brown sugar and sweat, the result of eating maple Cream of Wheat for breakfast and of being an eight-year-old boy.

For an extra-long moment, he holds her, perhaps realizing the moment is precious or perhaps not. With Skipper it's hard to know how much he understands and how much he doesn't. His IQ only measures seventy-five, but despite that, Hadley often thinks he's the wisest person she knows, blessed with insight and intuition far beyond his intelligence.

Releasing her, he walks to the table, picks up a chocolate-marshmallow cupcake, his favorite, and carries it to the bench beside the playground. Today he wears his Dodgers uniform—always number forty-four, regardless of the team, a tribute to the great Hank Aaron, who is his hero.

As he eats, he looks at the other kids playing. An ordinary playground with ordinary kids, but the way he gazes out at it is as if it's the most extraordinary place in the world. And as often happens when Hadley watches him, she finds herself envying him, wishing she could see the world through his eyes.

The pants of his uniform have ridden up on his knees, and Hadley makes a mental note to buy him new ones. Then she checks the thought. *Vanessa* will need to buy him new ones. Her throat tightens as her emotions rise again.

Mrs. Baxter lets out a wolf whistle and claps her hands three times, signaling for the kids to gather around. She leads them in a chorus of "For He's a Jolly Good Fellow," then lines them up so each can hug Skipper goodbye.

He is extraordinarily well loved. Some of the girls even cry. One kisses his cheek, then giggles and runs away. Katie fist-bumps him, snatches his baseball cap, and then puts it back on his head backward. He smiles. She's been doing that same thing to him since they were in preschool together. Skipper's really going to miss her. She is his "bestest friend," as he likes to say.

4

GRACE

The Honda grumbles but mercifully starts, and Grace pulls from the parking lot onto Laguna Canyon Road, her headache picking up steam as she merges into the bumper-to-bumper traffic.

Deal with the devil, and you're gonna get burned. She imagines her grandmother shaking her head as she says it. *You knew who that man was. Don't know what you were expecting.*

She sneers through the windshield at the darkening sky, wishing her grandmother would leave her alone and stay out of it. Of course she knew who Frank was. She had just hoped that maybe, just this once, things would work out.

She looks at the gas gauge, then at the line of cars in front of her, and her stress ticks up a notch. Miles's day care allows a grace period of fifteen minutes before they begin tacking on exorbitant late fees in ten-minute increments. She is well into the grace period, and the needle on the gauge is moving faster than the traffic.

With no choice, she pulls to the shoulder and ekes past the cars in front of her to pull into the gas station on the corner. The left island is down for repairs, and the forward pump on the remaining island is cash only, leaving only the back pump available.

Grace maneuvers toward it and is a few feet away when a motorcycle swerves in front of her to claim it. She slams on her horn, and the biker turns as he dismounts and gives a shrug, along with an infuriating I-don't-give-a-shit grin. She is about to blast her horn again when three more motorcycles pull past to park beside him.

The first biker begins to fuel up as the last one saunters toward the minimart. Steam blows from Grace's nostrils, and it's all she can do not to slam down on the accelerator and mow over the three bikers who remain, along with their four Harleys.

She rests her forehead against her knuckles on the steering wheel as her eyes fill with her frustration and anger. *Crying don't help nothing.* She looks up again at the sky.

In front of her, the bikers goof off, throwing trash at each other and smoking cigarettes. They're probably around her age but, unlike her, don't seem to have a care in the world. They are decked out in leather touring gear, and their bikes are loaded with saddlebags and sleeping rolls. They are probably on a road trip, and she hates to admit it, but looking at them, they remind her a little of Jimmy.

Had Jimmy not met her and enlisted in the army, this might have been his life, hanging with his buddies and goofing off. He was always happiest when he was on the road, roaming the country with no particular place to go. Their honeymoon was a monthlong trip on his Harley, traveling up the coast, then down through Utah and Las Vegas, possibly the same trip these guys are taking. The thought softens her anger toward them.

The pump clicks off, but the bikers aren't paying attention, so she taps her horn, a friendly beep to let them know it's time to stop screwing around so she can get her gas before she goes bankrupt from the late fees she's racking up with each precious second they are wasting.

The first biker looks up, squints to see her more clearly through the windshield, then offers three hip thrusts and a tongue waggle worthy of Miley Cyrus. Her anger flares, and she decides these idiots are nothing like Jimmy, and she lies down on the horn, pressing it so long and hard her battery is in danger of going dead.

The attendant glares at her, as do the people on the sidewalk. The biker, on the other hand, laughs, and then his friends join in, all of them having a riotous good time at how angry she is.

The biker from the minimart strolls out, an energy drink and roll of chocolate doughnuts in his hands. He moves the pump from the first bike to his own, and he must feel Grace's rage because he lifts his face, cocks his head when he sees her gaze skewering him, and then, deciding it's all in good fun, smiles and winks. The small gesture nearly pitches Grace over the edge, her foot leaping to the accelerator as her hand reaches for the ignition, the desire to bulldoze him almost irrepressible.

A second before ignition, her hand and foot stop, the small voice of reason she almost always regrets not listening to screaming that running over four bikers along with their motorcycles is probably not the best course of action at this juncture in her life. With a deep, shuddering breath, she forces her hand from the keys and her foot to the mat.

After what feels like an eternity, the second bike is finally filled, and the biker puts the pump back in its cradle, and all four get on their bikes and ride off.

Grace pulls forward, jams her ATM card into the machine, and enters her PIN.

CARD DECLINED.

She blinks. Stares. Then blinks again as a feeling of dread creeps over her.

She reinserts the card, slower this time, irrationally thinking or praying that a gentler approach might change things, her chin quivering as her disappointment trumps all the other emotions of the day, knowing, even before the machine rejects her again, that Jimmy has let her . . . them . . . himself . . . down. Again.

CARD DECLINED.

"You going to start pumping?" a middle-aged man says impatiently from the open window of his BMW.

Grace swallows, grabs her purse, and rummages through it to scrabble together four dollars' worth of coins. She hands it to the attendant, and as she walks back to her car, she wonders how he lost it—poker, dice, a losing spread on a boxing match?

Not that it matters—gone is gone.

5

HADLEY

Hadley chops onions and tries not to think about tomorrow and everything it will bring. Prince Charles lies at her feet, a heavy, warm dog blanket draped across her toes.

Frank named the dog Prince Charles as a joke. He loved the idea of ordering royalty around. "Fetch, Prince Charles." "Sit, Prince Charles."

It's actually very funny. "Stop farting, Prince Charles," Skipper loves to say when the dog passes gas, and the laughter it creates never grows old.

Even Mattie gets in on it. "Prince Charles whizzed on the neighbor's mailbox," she will declare when she returns from taking him on a walk. "Very unbecoming for the future king."

Hadley wriggles her toes to give the old dog's belly a rub. *Sorry, buddy, I wish we could take you with us.* She stops chopping, sets the knife down, and rubs her knuckles against her chest, massaging the knot that's formed there.

Her eyes catch on the strawberry cupcake on the counter, still in its pretty brown box with the colorful Sprinkles sticker, and her resolve stiffens. There's no choice. Fifteen years she's waited . . . prayed for this chance, and now, here it is. "This is it, Prince," she says. The dog looks up. "Now or never, and never's not an option."

She sighs heavily and sets the onions aside. As she pulls the pizza dough from the warming drawer below the oven, the front door opens.

"Hi, honey," she says as Mattie walks past the archway.

No answer. Footsteps travel away and up the stairs. Prince Charles pushes his old body up and lopes away to follow.

"I got you a cupcake!" she hollers after them. "Strawberry, your favorite."

Mattie's voice is so quiet Hadley almost doesn't hear, but her hearing has always been exceptional when it comes to her kids. "I haven't liked strawberry since I was twelve. You'd think she'd know that."

Hadley looks at the box. She did know that, or at least she used to. *Too sweet.* Her daughter's tastes evolved when she started middle school and acquired a taste for coffee—chai latte and Cuban coffee the only flavors she likes.

How did Hadley forget? She's losing it. She really is.

She moves the cupcake to the fridge and returns to preparing the pizzas. She rolls out the dough and adds toppings to each: spicy red sauce, sausage, and pepperoni for Frank; peppers, onions, sundried tomatoes, and marinara for Mattie; Sweet Baby Ray's BBQ Sauce and pineapple for Skipper.

She smiles at the finished creations, the familiar satisfaction of cooking for her family washing over her. Making home-cooked meals is a tradition carried on from her mother and one of the few things she is proud of.

She walks to the backyard to start the fire in the pizza oven so it will be heated by the time Frank gets home—and freezes just outside the door. Her eyes fix on the gaping hole beneath the oven, the space where the wood is stored, and her pulse ticks up as her mind spins with the memory of Frank telling her they were out of wood. "Wanted to see how hot it could get," he said a week ago. "Damn thing cranks. Took all the wood, but I almost got it to eight hundred."

She forgot.

How could she have forgotten?

Pulse pounding, she returns to the kitchen, turns on the top oven as high as it will go, then slides the prepared pizzas into the lower oven so they are out of sight.

She scrubs the counters until they gleam, dims the lights so they are more flattering, and hurries upstairs to change. Frank expects her to look good when he gets home.

Frank expects a lot of things.

6

GRACE

Miles is screaming and Grace is close to losing it, her breakdown barely held in check as she carries Miles and his diaper bag toward their apartment. Her head pounds as she climbs the stairs, and she is nearly faint from hunger.

Mrs. McCreedy, the only neighbor in the complex whose name Grace knows, peeks her head out her door. "Oh my," she says. "Do you need some help, dear?"

Borderline eccentric, Mrs. McCreedy is somewhere between fifty and a hundred, and her hair varies in color from magenta to blue, depending on the alignment of the stars. She has at least four cats, makes a living selling things on the internet, and goes by the name Mrs. McCreedy, though there's no sign of a Mr. McCreedy or evidence of there ever having been one. Jimmy made friends with her when they first moved in. Of course, Jimmy makes friends with everyone.

"No, Mrs. McCreedy. Thank you, but I'm fine."

This isn't the first time Mrs. McCreedy has offered to lend a hand, and Grace wonders if Jimmy might have asked her to keep an eye on them while he was gone. A few weeks ago, when Grace was at her wits' end, afraid she might break something, possibly her skull against the wall, she considered asking Mrs. McCreedy if she could watch Miles for a few minutes so she could run to the store. She decided against it. In Grace's experience, it's best to take care of yourself.

The problem with this thinking is that parenting is the hardest thing she's ever done, and doing it on her own has turned out to be far more difficult than she ever would have thought. Until Miles came along, Grace considered herself tough. She'd survived years in the foster care system, then juvenile hall, even jail, but the moment the nurses placed an eight-pound helpless, wailing baby in her arms, all that toughness ran right out of her, and she turned into a trembling pool of putty, constantly on the verge of losing it and so tired she couldn't think straight—a very disconcerting state that now makes her certain she's blowing it and failing Miles miserably.

"Okay, dear," Mrs. McCreedy says hesitantly, clearly not believing Grace is even close to fine. Miles howls and flails, clearly not believing it either. "I'm here if you need me."

No wonder parenting is supposed to be a two-person job. Jimmy worried about it when they talked about him reenlisting, but Grace brushed it off. At the time, she believed she would be fine. Plus, there was really no choice. Reenlisting got Jimmy away from the trouble that was chasing him and kept him away from the temptation that had gotten him into trouble in the first place.

Or so they thought.

She shakes her head, trying to clear away the thought of his betrayal and to keep the tears she's been holding from spilling out. It won't do to have both her and Miles crying.

Swallowing back the emotions, she pushes open the door, drops the diaper bag to the floor, and pulls Miles against her. "Shhh," she says, holding him tight. "You're okay. Hang in there. We're home now."

He continues to scream, and she grits her teeth against it.

"Colic," the pediatrician explained when Grace brought him in at three weeks old, distraught that her baby would not stop crying.

"Nothing to do but weather the storm." The woman said it with a smile, as if having a screeching, inconsolable child were no big deal, a delightful rite of parenthood to be embraced and celebrated like first steps or learning to ride a bike. Grace left the appointment more distressed than when she'd arrived.

She's wanted so badly to love motherhood, to cherish each moment and relish her time with her son. But she can't. Since Miles came into the world, it's been such a struggle, so overwhelming and exhausting, that it's all she can do to survive one moment to the next.

And she feels like Miles knows it, and that is why he cries. He realizes she is going through the motions with no real joy, that when she comes for him at the end of the day, she is so done in she has no energy left to play or read or sing, and that he knows that what she wants most is for him to fall asleep so she can fall asleep beside him.

"That's it, buddy, let it all out," she says, pacing back and forth as she pats his back and as he continues to howl, screaming at the top of his wee little lungs and working himself into a lather until they are both damp with sweat.

This is his pattern. The moment she lifts him from the car, it starts—a whimper, like he is uncomfortable, making her believe he is hungry, has gas, or needs his diaper changed. So, she sets about trying to remedy all those things, only to discover his misery has nothing to do with any of them. And by the time she is done, her nerves are frayed and he is wailing—uncontrollable sobbing that no amount of cuddling, cooing, or pacing can soothe.

The doctor assured her that's what colic is, a frustrating condition where healthy babies cry for no reason, and she told Grace many times that she wasn't doing anything wrong. But knowing this doesn't help. Grace just wants her baby to be happy, and each time he cries, it rips her heart anew.

Her neighbor pounds on the wall. "Shut that damn kid up."

The three-hundred-pound tub of wasted carbon moved in a week after Jimmy returned to Afghanistan, and Grace knows, when Jimmy gets home, there's going to be hell to pay. Jimmy might be a hundred pounds lighter than their neighbor, but he's also at least two hundred pounds tougher, and he doesn't take to people not treating his family right.

But at the moment, Jimmy is seven thousand miles away. So each night, in addition to dealing with Miles's inconsolable crying, she needs to put up with her jerk of a neighbor screaming at her through the walls.

Ignoring him, she continues to soothe Miles as best she can, stroking his back, rocking him, and telling him it will be okay.

She can't believe it was her idea to have a baby. What was she thinking? She remembers the thought process, dreaming how wonderful it would be to bring something wholly hers and Jimmy's into the world. They'd been married five years, and Jimmy was doing well. He had made it through sniper school and hadn't gambled since enlisting. So, she figured it was time and that they were ready.

"Damn it!" the neighbor screams. "I'm calling the landlord. Every goddamn night. Shut that damn kid up."

What a horrible miscalculation. She wasn't ready. She might never have been ready. And now, here he is, this little human, totally dependent on her, and she is completely screwing it up.

She kisses his flaming scalp. "You're okay. You're okay, you're okay, you're okay."

She carries him to the kitchen and rummages through the cabinets, so hungry she feels like she might pass out. She opens door after door—salt, pepper, vanilla extract, two cans of expired tomato paste. She considers the tomato paste, looks down at Miles screaming, and decides against it.

With a sigh, she returns to the living room and pulls out her phone. It's nearly seven, and Jimmy hasn't called. He always calls on Fridays.

She imagines him in his barracks trying to work up the courage and trying to figure out what he is going to say. He is hungover; she is sure. His slipups always involve alcohol. It was probably a friend's birthday, and he lost sight of his promise not to drink. Then he got drunk and was suckered into a bet. His downfall is always the same: he drinks, he gambles, he loses—a pattern that destroys him and destroys them, but that he seems powerless to stop.

She looks around their apartment, at the stained ceiling and chipped counters, at the threadbare futon that serves as their couch, at the crate that holds the old television Jimmy's brother gave them. She's been poorer, but never has she been so broke, crushed by her disappointment in Jimmy and in herself.

She looks at the photo on the counter of her and her grandmother taken six months before her grandmother passed away. In that moment, they were smiling, nearly twins for how much they looked alike, though her grandmother was near seventy and Grace only fourteen—same copper curls and hazel-green eyes. How disappointed she would be. *People don't change, Spud, and only a fool believes they do.*

The tears she's been holding back leak from her eyes, and she blots them away. Her grandmother was right. Grace is a fool. Look what believing in people got her—a snake-in-the-grass boss like Frank, and a sweet-talking loser husband like Jimmy.

Another thought strikes, and she looks down at Miles, then at the cabinets that hold no food, and a shiver runs down her spine. Come Tuesday, she is going to be out of a job. Sure as the sun will rise, Frank is going to fire her. All her life she's dealt with men like Frank Torelli, and men like him don't keep people like her around. He'll blame it on something other than Jerry's contract, but it won't change the fact that that's the reason, the reflection he sees when he looks at her discomfiting and creating an undertow of distrust.

Her hollow stomach growls.

No money. And come Tuesday, *no job.*

She feels her grandmother watching. *Only person you can count on, Spud, is you.*

She looks again at her son, still wailing, then juts her jaw out, hoists the diaper bag from the floor to her shoulder, slides the photo of her and her grandmother into it, and pivots for the door.

7

HADLEY

Hadley stands in front of the full-length mirror in her bedroom frowning. Gone are her comfortable skirt, soft cotton tank, and ballet flats. In their place: linen slacks, a silk blouse, and beige Jimmy Choos. Beneath it all, her pair of thigh-to-waist Spanx digs into her flesh.

Even with the added four inches from the shoes and the super-girdle, she looks fat. She smooths the pooch of her belly and sucks it in, then, with a resigned sigh, releases it and turns from the mirror to brush out her hair. She pins it into a loose chignon at the base of her neck with a gold clip, a style Frank likes because he thinks it makes her look like Sophia Loren, a comparison Hadley finds flattering, though she herself has never seen the resemblance.

First off, Sophia is Italian, while Hadley is French and German. Sophia has soft chocolate eyes set over a long nose and plump lips, whereas Hadley's most defining feature is her green eyes, and her nose is small and her lips wide, like Julia Roberts.

But, Hadley supposes, if you only compare her and Sophia from the chin down, the heights and curves are similar. Of course, Sophia was young in a time when curves were appreciated, while Hadley lives in the era of Jillian Michaels and Heidi Klum.

She glances at the clock, and her irritation grows along with her hunger. Having dinner as a family is one of Frank's rules, a sentiment she used to believe was sweet, naively thinking it showed Frank's commitment to the family spending time together. But over the years, she's learned to see it for what it is: another way for him to control them, making them wait to eat and rarely showing the consideration of telling them when he'll be home.

She looks forlornly at her bedside table, where she keeps a stash of peanut M&M'S and, stomach growling, chooses the less caloric option of sneaking a cigarette on the balcony instead.

Lighting up, she takes a deep drag and closes her eyes as the heady buzz of nicotine seeps into her blood. She ignores the niggle of guilt that accompanies it. Frank hates when she smokes, and she gave it up for the sixth time four weeks ago. But she supposes today is a day for breaking promises.

The breeze is light and warm, a hint of summer in its breath, and she watches as it carries the smoke away and thinks about tomorrow. Frank has planned their trip to her sister's down to the smallest detail. It will take them three days to get to Wichita, three days to get Skipper settled, and three days to drive back. The hotels are reserved, and he's listed all the places along the way where they can stop for meals and gas.

Everything is all set.

Or it was.

Until three days ago, when Vanessa called wanting to know if Hadley could bring Skipper to Tom's hometown of Omaha instead of Wichita so she and Tom could extend their honeymoon in Belize. Tom wanted to get scuba certified, and that required them staying a few extra days.

Hadley never told Frank about the call, and her heart has been beating out of rhythm ever since, the smallest window of opportunity opening at the exact moment she most desperately needed it.

Her phone rings, causing her to jump.

"Yoda-lay-ee-hoo," her sister says when Hadley answers.

"That's how you greet people?" Hadley says, returning to the role of well-adjusted wife and mother, an act perfected for everyone except Mattie, Skipper, and Frank.

"Sometimes," Vanessa says.

"What if I was someone important?"

"You're not. You're you."

Hadley nods and, despite the current state of her life, smiles at her sister. Though Vanessa is twenty-six, it's hard for Hadley to imagine her older than six, the age she was when she and Hadley last lived together.

"You were supposed to call yesterday," Hadley says.

"Yeah, sorry about that. Tom and I got distracted." Giggle. "If you know what I mean." Hee, hee, hee.

Wisely, Hadley didn't tell Skipper about his mom's promise to call. This isn't the first time Vanessa hasn't followed through on a promised call, promised gift, or promised visit. "Ness, when Skipper is living with you, you can't get *distracted*."

Hadley feels Vanessa rolling her eyes. "Yeah, yeah. I know. Blah, blah, blah. Skipper needs to be watched. Skipper can't be left on his own. I've got it. You've repeated it like ten billion times. Stop worrying."

But Hadley can't stop worrying. As much as Hadley loves her sister, responsible and reliable are not Vanessa's strong suits, and taking care of Skipper isn't easy. It requires constant vigilance and care. Handing him over to Vanessa feels a little like handing a live grenade to a known sufferer of seizures. It is a very bad idea, and Hadley very badly wishes she could somehow stop it from happening.

"I'm calling because I forgot to tell you Skipper's passport came the day before we left, so we're all set," Vanessa goes on. "He's so cute. Looks just like me."

"Modest," Hadley says.

"Modest is for people who don't know how great they are."

The statement is pure Vanessa. Hadley's dad used to say Vanessa was 50 percent spunk and 50 percent sass, a combination that suited her well until around high school, when spunk and sass were no longer cute and lovable and instead came off as ditzy and spoiled and landed her in a crowd of wealthy losers, one of whom got her pregnant and never even knew it.

"I still don't understand why you need to go to London," Hadley says. "You're already honeymooning in Belize, and this much change is going to be a lot for Skipper."

"He'll be fine. Skipper loves sports. It will give him and Tom something to bond over. Tom's been going to Wimbledon since he was a boy. He says it's a total blast and that there are tons of kids running around."

Hadley grits her teeth to stop herself from screaming at her sister that Skipper doesn't "run around," that he can't "run around," and that if she lets him "run around," he will end up lost, or worse, duct-taped to a tree by some kids who think it's great fun to torture a defenseless, guileless kid like Skipper.

"Listen, Had, Tom's here. I've got to go. I just called to tell you I got the passport."

"Ness . . . ," Hadley says, but the phone's already gone dead.

She squeezes her eyes shut but then pops them open at the sound of tires turning onto the road. A second later, the silhouette of Frank's brother's car comes into view, the windows on Tony's muscle car tinted so dark that, even in broad daylight, you can't see through them. Hadley snuffs the cigarette into the planter beside the door, then hurries inside to tell the kids Frank's home and that it's time for dinner.

The sign on Mattie's door reads, **MOVE ON**. Hadley ignores it and steps inside. Mattie is on her bed, a pair of headphones strapped to her ears, noxious music that sounds like dying cats caught in a rotor squeaking from the speakers. On her lap is a book, the cover maroon and old, like one of those books you would see in a lawyer's office or in a library at Harvard.

Strewed on every surface are other books. It's the one thing Mattie really cares about, and every minute she's not in school is spent buried in the pages of a story. Dozing on the bed beside her is Prince Charles. Mattie must have lifted the old dog onto the bed, Prince Charles's jumping days long over.

Mattie is so engrossed in the music and her book she doesn't realize Hadley is there until Hadley is standing right in front of her. When she notices, she startles, then stiffens, her hate like a fist that knocks the wind from Hadley's lungs.

Prince Charles lifts his head and thumps his tail three times.

Hadley hasn't told Mattie the plan, terrified that either Frank will pick up on his daughter lying to him, or worse, that Hadley will chicken out and her daughter will hate her even more than she already does.

Mattie continues to glare through her kohl-lined eyes, her white-blonde hair draped across her face.

It's still difficult for Hadley to get used to her daughter's new look. When the school year started, Mattie's hair was natural dark auburn and hung in long layers to the middle of her back. Now, eight months later, she is albino blonde, her hair cut severely to the middle of her neck, and the tips painted pink, blue, or green, depending on her mood. And she has a dozen piercings in her ears. The latest addition, a custom-designed silver serpent, winds in and out of several of the holes as if slithering through her skin.

Hadley has to admit the earring is bizarrely mesmerizing, though she can't understand it. What girl wants to have a snake worming through her ear?

Mattie narrows her eyes, waiting for Hadley to say something, and Hadley is about to tell her Frank is home when something creepy-crawly moves beneath one of Mattie's notebooks on the floor.

Hadley falls back, and Mattie leans sideways to see what's caused the reaction. Then she goes on her knees and, using the edge of her book, scoots the notebook aside. Mother and daughter recoil together as the spider scuttles beneath the bed.

"Well, do something," Mattie says, the most words she's spoken to Hadley in a week.

Right. Do something. The problem is Hadley *hates* creepy-crawly things. Tentatively, she steps forward, then kneels on the carpet and lifts the bed skirt. The spider—shiny, black, and bloated like an overripe olive—stands frozen a few inches away.

"Here," Mattie says, holding out a magazine she has rolled into a spider-smashing club.

"I don't want to *kill* it," Hadley says.

"Well, I don't want it *living* under my bed."

Hadley peeks again beneath the bed skirt, where the spider remains frozen with fear. She takes the magazine and sneaks it beneath the fabric. Squeezing her eyes shut, she clenches her grip . . .

"I can't. You do it," she says, pulling away and sitting up. She holds the magazine back toward Mattie.

Mattie's eyes grow wide, her bluster dissolved into an expression that exactly mirrors Hadley's. Then it hardens, and her brow furrows into a deep V. "*You're* the mom."

"And *you're* the one who doesn't want a spider living under her bed."

They glare at each other, a standoff of cowards. Then the door opens and Skipper walks in. "Coach is home," he says. "Time to load the bases." The phrase he uses for having a meal.

Stepping closer, he tilts his head. "What you doing?"

"There's a spider," Mattie says. "Under the bed. And Blue doesn't want to kill it."

"And First Base doesn't want to kill it either," Hadley shoots back.

Skipper's head angles a little more, then straightens. He walks to Mattie's nightstand, takes an empty Starbucks cup that's there, carries it to where Hadley is, kneels on the ground, and lifts the bed skirt; then, with extraordinary care, he coaxes the spider onto a magazine-subscription card he found on the floor. He puts the cup over it, then slides both from beneath the bed.

"Where'd you learn to do that?" Hadley asks, amazed.

"Mrs. Baxter doesn't like to kill spiders either."

Mattie has joined them on the floor, the three of them looking at the upside-down cup. Her daughter wears fuzzy Cookie Monster pajama bottoms and a Maroon 5 T-shirt from a concert she went to two years ago, when she was twelve.

"I'll take it outside," Mattie says, patting Skipper on the head as if petting a dog. And if Skipper were a dog, he would be wagging his tail, his face lit up with pride.

Mattie slides the notebook beneath the card to give it extra support, then carries it out the door.

"Time to load the bases," Skipper repeats.

"Go on down, Champ," Hadley says. "I'll be there in a minute."

Skipper ambles away, and Hadley falls to her butt and drops her face in her hands. She can't even deal with a spider. How is she going to do this?

Prince Charles grunts as he climbs from the bed to flop beside her. He sets his heavy head on her lap, and she strokes his neck.

"What am I going to do?" she says quietly.

He rolls his chocolate eyes up at her.

Her whole life, Hadley has been taken care of, first by her father, then by Frank—all life's difficult choices made for her. And now, here she is, thirty-eight, facing the most important crossroads of her life, and she is terrified.

At the sound of Mattie's footsteps returning, she takes a deep breath and pushes to her feet.

One foot in front of the other, she tells herself as she heads down the stairs. *Repeat as often as necessary to finish.* Someone famous said that. She can't remember who.

Frank is at the table showing Skipper the new pack of baseball cards he's brought home. At least three times a week, Frank stops by Target to buy a new pack. He's been doing it since Skipper was a toddler, and their collection is now in the thousands.

She leans down and kisses his cheek.

"Hey," he says, taking her hand and looking up with concern. "How you holding up?"

"Okay," she says.

"Hang in there." He turns to smile warmly at Skipper, then reaches out and tousles his hair. "Blue and I are going to miss you, Champ."

Skipper nods, then returns to studying the cards. It's been this way since Hadley explained to him that he was going to live with his mom: an unsettling avoidance of the topic that concerns her, unsure how he's going to handle it once he realizes it's real.

Hadley gathers the ingredients for the salad and, when she's sure Frank's attention is fully back on the cards, carefully moves the pizzas from the bottom oven to the top.

Safely back at the island and chopping the lettuce, she says, "How was work?"

"Home run day," Frank says brightly, then high-fives Skipper, who coined the phrase. "Finally got that old bastard Jerry Koch to sublet his lot to me."

She offers a supportive smile. "Jerry? The man we met last year at the fundraiser for the Boys & Girls Club?"

"Yeah. The old geezer with the bag for a wife."

Hadley nods as if agreeing. Frank doesn't like unattractive women. She remembers liking the couple. Jerry's love for his wife, Sandra, radiated as he talked about her many achievements. He bragged about her as if she were the most accomplished woman in the world and gazed at her like she was still the prettiest girl in the room.

Frank pushes from the table and walks to where Hadley is. He wraps his arms around her waist, and his wide gut presses against her ribs as he pulls her to him. Instinctively, she sucks in her stomach, causing the Spanx to contract and dig into her flesh.

"I saw the Mercedes was delivered," he whispers.

She nods as she continues to chop the vegetables.

He leans in closer so his lips are against her ear. "All day, I couldn't stop thinking about you driving my truck." He rubs his groin up and down against her. "God, how it was driving me wild."

She turns and smiles as if she likes it.

"Mmmm," he says with another rub, then pulls away to pour himself a glass of wine.

When he returns to the table, he says, "By the way, I think I need to get rid of the new girl."

"Really? I thought you liked her," Hadley says.

"Turns out she's useless. That's what I get for doing someone a favor."

"Didn't you say she was the first assistant you've had with half a brain?"

Frank doesn't respond. He does that a lot: offers up what seems like a conversation, only to ignore her when she takes part.

She returns to tossing the salad.

Half a minute later, he says, "Jesus fucking Christ!"

Hadley's head snaps up. Mattie is in the archway, Prince Charles beside her.

"Wipe that shit off your face," Frank says. "You look like a goddamn whore. And what the fuck is that in your ear?"

Every fiber in Hadley's body tenses, and she watches as Mattie's face darkens; then she turns to Hadley, her glare challenging her to say something. When Hadley remains mute, she storms away.

"What the hell?" Frank says. "Why do you let her go around like that?"

Hadley says nothing, her blood pumping wildly. She always reminds Mattie to remove her makeup and earrings before her dad sees her. But tonight she was distracted: first by her daughter's hate, then by the spider, then by Skipper. She always remembers. "Mattie, your dad's home. Make sure you wash your face and take off your jewelry." *Jewelry* being a polite euphemism for her bizarre piercings.

Frank went nuts when Mattie dyed her hair. He raged, grabbed a pair of scissors, threatened to shave her head as punishment. The only thing that stopped him was Hadley begging him not to. She was literally in their bedroom on her knees blocking the door, and then her mouth was on his cock, and because of that, he let it be. The memory sickens her. That is how she protects her daughter. She feels the pain in her scalp as she remembers him yanking her hair as she went about it, the searing pain of having her hair wrenched from its roots and the deeper hurt of the cruel things Frank said, words she prayed Mattie would never hear.

Of course Mattie knows none of this. She believes Hadley is a terrible mother who does nothing to stand up for her. She's right about the first part; no good mother would have allowed things to go this far.

She stops chopping and leans against the counter, the knife trembling in her hand. *And now Skipper is leaving.* Without Mattie knowing it, Skipper is the one who has protected her.

Yes, Frank yells, says horrible things, has a temper, and throws things. He might even have gone so far as to chop off Mattie's hair. But he's never physically hurt her—a mercy bestowed on her by Skipper simply being who he is.

Shortly after Skipper started preschool, his teacher called Hadley and Frank in because she was concerned about something Skipper had said—a strange story about a coach locking someone or something named Blue in the bathroom and not letting them out. Coach of course was Frank, and Hadley was Blue, but the teacher had no way of knowing that.

Frank sweet-talked his way out of it, blaming it on a nightmare and the overactive imagination of a four-year-old, but it was enough of a scare for Frank to realize that, unlike Mattie and Hadley, Skipper couldn't be controlled—his artlessness as much a part of him as the color of his hair.

From that day on, Frank constrained his violence to the master bedroom, a place children weren't allowed, which has spared Mattie from the worst of his rages.

When Vanessa called, it was Hadley's first thought. *No! You can't take him. How will I protect Mattie?* She straightened the thought immediately, realizing how wrong it was. She was the one who was supposed to protect Mattie. She just had no idea how she would manage it without Skipper.

Then, suddenly, as if some guardian angel had been listening, the chance she'd been praying for was in front of her, the smallest sliver of opportunity opening with Vanessa's change of plans. The only question: Was Hadley brave enough to take it?

"So, Freeway Series tomorrow?" Frank says, bringing her back to the moment. His tone is light, as if nothing's happened, but she knows by the way he shifts in his seat that he's uncomfortable, worried he's upset Skipper. "Wilson versus Kershaw," he goes on when Skipper doesn't answer. "A good matchup. Definitely don't want to miss that."

Skipper turns, his saucer eyes unblinking.

Frank smiles warmly. "Blue can stream it for you on her iPad so you can watch it in the car."

Skipper tilts his head, absorbing the words a beat late; then his mouth twitches with a grin as he nods. Frank relaxes, and Hadley exhales as well.

She carries the salad to the table as Mattie slinks into her chair, her face scrubbed clean and the earrings gone. She folds her arms across her chest and looks at her plate.

Hadley sits across from her, and Frank bows his head.

"Bless us, oh Lord, and these Thy gifts, which we are about to receive from Thy bounty, through Christ, our Lord. Amen."

"Amen," they say together.

Frank grabs the salad, and Hadley returns to the kitchen for the pizzas. She sets them on the table, then goes back for the drinks.

She is pouring Skipper's milk when Frank's wineglass whizzes past to smash against the wall. "Are you fucking kidding me?"

Her face snaps up, and the milk sloshes out of the glass as her hands fly in front of her.

"What the hell is this?" He holds up a slice of his pizza. It sags from his hand like a limp rag. "I work my ass off so we can have a nice life, a nice home, a goddamn world-class pizza oven, and this is the thanks I get, oven-baked shit?"

Hadley's heart scatter-fires in her chest as she continues to cower. "I'm sorry," she stammers.

I should have remembered to buy wood.

I shouldn't have made pizza.

I should have . . . I should have . . . I should have . . .

He drops the slice back to the pan, then hurls the entire pizza at her as well.

She coils her arms over her head as it smashes into the cabinets behind her.

Beside her, Prince Charles pushes to his feet, and Hadley lunges for him with her free hand, getting hold of his collar as he goes for the pizza, worried he will lap up glass. She tugs him back as her mind continues to spin with regret . . . and confusion. Frank never behaves this way in front of the kids. Only a moment ago, he was worried he'd crossed the line with Skipper.

She looks through her brow at him, then at Skipper, and with a jolt, realizes what's happened. In the time it took for him to regret blowing up at Mattie because it might have upset Skipper to the time she set the pizza in front of him, he figured it out. *Skipper is leaving*, and the power he has over Frank is leaving with him. And already, it's started, the self-control Frank has maintained for over four years gone and his newfound freedom intoxicating.

"I've got him," Mattie says, taking hold of Prince Charles, her voice trembling.

Hadley looks up, and their eyes lock, and Hadley knows, as long as she lives, this moment will never be forgotten, the moment her daughter realized just what a coward she is.

"I'll make something else," Hadley manages, her heart hammering so hard the words echo in her ears.

She turns toward the cabinets, terrified of what else Frank might throw. Amazingly, it is Skipper's voice, small and tight, that breaks in to save her. "Coach, do you know how many games Kershaw pitched this year?" Hadley glances back. Skipper's face is sheet white and his pupils reduced to pinpoints, but he pushes the words out. "He pitches like all the time."

Frank's glare continues to skewer her, and Skipper tugs at his sleeve. "Coach, did you hear me?"

Frank turns. "Yeah, Champ, I heard you. Kershaw? All the time? How much is all the time?"

Hadley nearly whimpers with relief as she turns to fill a pot with water for spaghetti.

As she makes a second meal, Skipper continues to talk, rambling on about the Dodgers' pitcher and talking in a way Skipper never talks, the words tumbling out. Not all of them make sense, but on and on he goes in a heroic effort to distract Frank, and her heart swells with his gallantry, tears of love mixing with those of her terror and shame.

～

"I'm going to watch the game," Frank says, pushing away his empty plate.

The kids skulk off to their rooms, and Hadley sets to work cleaning the kitchen.

When she is done, she packs the car.

She closes the hatch on the final load, then leans against it and runs the plan through her head one more time. When she's certain she hasn't forgotten anything, she returns inside and stops outside the home theater. Behind the door, she hears the game playing, and for a long minute, she listens.

Finally, with a deep steeling breath, she steps inside.

Frank sits slumped in the middle recliner of the eight-seat theater. The TV flickers in front of him, the sound muted for a commercial. He looks up through drunk eyes, and she glances at the whiskey in his hand.

"Hey," she says.

"Hey." He reaches for her hand.

She takes it and sits beside him. He takes a sip of his drink, then looks at her, deep regret etched on his face. It's the part of the sickness she has never understood, how genuinely sorry he feels after, like he didn't mean it at all and has no idea why he acted the way he did. He says it's because he loves her—as if his fury and devotion are interwoven like raveled poison vines.

He brings her hand to his face and holds it to his cheek, the whiskers thick and rough from the day, and for a long moment, that is how they remain, silent, his eyes closed as he holds her hand against his skin and as she gives him the acceptance and forgiveness he has come to expect.

"I'm going to miss you while you're gone," he says finally, opening his eyes and looking at her. He brushes a kiss across her knuckles before letting their hands drop to the armrest between them. "The house is going to be lonely without you."

"You'll still have the dog."

"Great. Me and the prince."

"You know," she says, careful to keep her voice even, "I was thinking you might have been right about it being better for us to leave tonight instead of in the morning."

His eyes squint, looking for a manipulation or some sort of deception, and she lowers her gaze, praying he believes her and doesn't see the fear that is driving her. "But only if you think it's a good idea."

He looks back at the television and turns on the volume, and she sits beside him, silent.

The game comes back on, Astros versus the A's, the A's ahead by a dozen runs in the bottom of the eighth.

At the next commercial, he says, "The pasta was good."

"Thanks," she says. "I probably should have just made that in the first place."

He watches the flickering screen awhile longer before finally saying, "You have the itinerary?"

She works hard not to react as her heart jumps in her chest. "I printed it, and I also have it on my phone."

"Don't take the 5. It's under construction."

"No. I'll take the toll road."

He turns to her. "If you get tired, pull over."

"Of course."

"You need to watch out for big rigs. They can't see you."

"I'll be careful."

He nods, finishes off his whiskey, then, with pure devotion in his eyes, looks at her and says, "Nine days. I don't know how I'm going to live without you."

She leans in and kisses him softly. "Somehow you'll manage, and before you know it, we'll be back."

At the door, she stops. "Do you want to say goodbye to Skipper?" she asks.

He shakes his head. "I think it will just make it harder on him." He glances down, then back at her. "He knows I love him, right?"

"Of course."

"And he won't just remember how I acted tonight?"

"He will remember what a great dad you were to him."

~

Five minutes later, they are on their way. She glances at Mattie beside her and Skipper behind her, unable to believe it, stunned that it is happening. For fifteen years, she's been searching for a way out, and now, just like that, she is doing it, driving away with the kids. Her heart pounds with adrenaline and a small sense of pride.

"We're not going back?" Mattie says, startling Hadley from her thoughts.

"You packed your mom's apron," she says to Hadley's surprised expression.

Hadley swallows hard, wondering if her last-minute decision to shove the keepsake in her bag will tip Frank off as well. The apron is hand embroidered with daisies and stained in a dozen places; her mother wore it almost every day of Hadley's childhood, and it is one of the few things of her mom's she has left.

"Don't worry," Mattie says, reading Hadley's fear. "Dad never goes in the kitchen drawers." And all the pride Hadley felt the moment before deflates, knowing how much she has failed her daughter all these years.

A minute later, Mattie asks, "Who will take care of Prince Charles?"

"Your dad," Hadley says, and Mattie turns away. It's not a good answer. Frank will not love him the way Mattie does. He will not look after him the way Hadley does. He will not play with him the way Skipper does.

Mattie's almost silent tears twist Hadley's heart. She had no choice. They couldn't stay for the dog.

~

Half an hour later, they pull into the parking lot of a hotel beside the freeway.

"Why are we stopping?" Mattie asks.

"There's something I need to do before we leave," Hadley says. "We'll stay here tonight and get an early start in the morning."

She uses cash to pay for two rooms, gets the kids settled, then returns to the car and drives back the way they came.

Twenty minutes later, from the loading area behind Frank's office, she calls the Hilton in Victorville, the hotel they are supposed to be staying at tonight, and she books a room.

When she hangs up, she looks again at Frank's itinerary, checking it carefully for anything she might have missed. For her to pull this off, she needs to consider everything and not make any mistakes. Frank is paranoid, neurotic, and brilliant. One misstep and it will be over. Fairly certain she hasn't screwed up yet, she slides the phone into her pocket and climbs from the car.

The lot is empty and the buildings around her dark and buttoned up for the long weekend. An American flag flaps from the flagpole near the street, left flying in honor of Memorial Day.

Using Frank's spare keys that she still has from driving his truck, she opens the back door and quietly steps inside.

8

GRACE

Grace cuts the engine and looks back at Miles, who is sound asleep in his car seat behind her, his chest moving in steady rhythm with his breath. She watches him for a long time. It's nearly ten. God willing, he will sleep until midnight.

She turns back to look at the entrance to Aztec Parking. Other than the light beside the door, the business park is dark. Through the window, she sees the faint glow of her computer monitor, and she stares at it until her eyes blur, waiting another long minute to roll the decision around one more time in her head.

If she does this, there will be no turning back.

Again and again, the answer circles back. If she doesn't do this, then where will she be? She looks again at Miles, thinks of Jimmy and what he's done, and squeezes her eyes tight. As much as she loves him, this is no longer about that. She can't continue to risk her future and Miles's future and to live with the uncertainty of whether they will have rent money or food.

Her stomach rumbles, weighing in on the decision, and yet she waits a minute longer, knowing what she needs to do but dreading it just the same. *One of those moments,* she thinks, *the fork in the road you recognize, knowing it will irrevocably change your life.*

Finally, with a deep breath, she lowers the window an inch and eases from the car. She locks it, scans around her one more time, then walks to the door and lets herself in.

The contract for Jerry's lot is still on Frank's desk. She tucks it in the empty diaper bag slung over her shoulder. If Frank wants to make a deal with Jerry, he can make it himself.

She opens the door that connects Frank's office with the hall leading to the common areas of the building—the storage room, lockers, restrooms, and employee lounge. It clicks closed behind her, and she squints to adjust her eyes to the darkness, the only light borrowed from the thin halo of moonlight that shines through the window in the door that leads to the back parking lot and a sliver of fluorescence glowing beneath the storage room door because someone forgot to turn off the light.

Though her heart pounds, she is not scared. For the past three months, she's spent more time inside these walls than she has her own home.

She reaches for the light switch when a noise freezes her. Her face snaps to the storage room door, and her eyes fix on the strip of light beneath it. She stares so long and hard her eyes buzz but, after a long moment and nothing, wonders if she's only imagined it.

With a deep sigh, she reaches again for the switch, her fingers finding it at the exact moment a shadow crosses the sliver of light.

Her heart lurches into her throat, and she falls back and spins. She fumbles with the keys and, finding the right one, jams it into the lock. It sticks, and she wrenches it free with too much force, and the ring flies from her hands and sails over her head to land impossibly loudly on the ground somewhere behind her.

9

HADLEY

There's a noise. In the hallway. The sound of metal clanging. Hadley stands stock still, a box of paper towels in her hands. Perhaps the building has a security system and she's triggered the alarm. Though, if that's the case, the response time is horribly slow. She's been here nearly an hour and has been through every room in the building twice.

Her ears strain, listening for more. After several seconds, she sighs and slides the box back onto the shelf.

She leans against the rack and closes her eyes. She is not made for this—deceit and deception, plotting and lies. She was so sure she had this part figured out. She knows Frank hides money, and she was certain this is where he stashes it. He paid for his truck with cash, and he paid the contractors who worked on the yard under the table. Before he bought the truck, he stopped at the office. On the days he paid the contractors, he came straight from work. He has mentioned a safe, so she knows there is one, but she's combed every inch of this place and can't find it. All her search has yielded is a petty cash drawer in Frank's desk with less than a hundred dollars in it.

Something moves in the hall, and she opens her eyes, the sound very slight, more like a shifting than a noise, but Hadley's hearing has always been exceptional.

She listens closer, then pushes off the rack, nudges open the door, and pokes her head out. She looks left toward the back door, then right. At the end of the corridor, a shadow crouches, petite, with a wild head of hair.

"Grace?" she says, squinting into the darkness, confirming that she is, in fact, looking at Frank's assistant.

The figure bolts upright. "Mrs. Torelli?" Grace says.

Both look at each other curiously. Hadley last saw Grace this morning when she was dropping Frank off so she could use his truck. Grace was heading into the office wearing the same outfit she has on now, a plain white blouse and baggy gray slacks, loose on her thin frame.

"What are you doing here?" they say in unison, both their voices pitched high.

Hadley holds Grace's stare. After all, she is Frank's wife, and that gives her the right to be here. There are a dozen reasons she might have needed to stop by the office. Frank left something he needs. She's taking some of the commercial cleaner for her driveway. Frank asked her to stop by and pick up traffic cones for one of the lots.

Meanwhile, she can't think of a single reason why Frank's assistant would be skulking around the office on a Friday night in the dark.

She looks at the light switch to Grace's right, easily within reach, then thinks of the gap in time between the first sound and the second.

"Why are you here?" she repeats.

"I wanted to check on the uniforms," Grace says. "I think the order might have been shorted."

Hadley looks at her watch. "At ten o'clock on a Friday?"

Grace shifts her weight, and that's when Hadley notices the bag over her shoulder, a large striped thing, deflated and frayed.

She cocks her head; then a smile spreads across her face. "You're here to steal from Frank."

10

GRACE

Frank's wife is smiling and accusing Grace of being a thief.

The two options of how to respond tick quickly through her brain: *Deny it and make up a more viable lie*, or *Make a break for it*.

The first is impossible. Mrs. Torelli is not going to believe anything Grace says. She can think of absolutely no plausible explanation for why she's here. The second is equally impossible. The keys are still lost somewhere on the floor, and Miles is *locked* in the car. All this processes lightning fast as Mrs. Torelli continues to look at her with that bizarre grin.

Finally, after a long minute with no revelation, Grace surprises herself by blurting out the truth: "I came to get what Frank owes me."

Mrs. Torelli tilts her head.

Grace has only met Mrs. Torelli a couple of times. She's not the kind of woman to get involved in her husband's business. Tall, elegant, and impossibly beautiful, she's the kind of woman who spends her days getting her nails manicured and ordering the help around, not meddling in the inner workings of parking garages and asphalt. Even now, at ten o'clock on a Friday, in the dingy hallway of an industrial building, she looks like a million bucks—her makeup freshly applied, her hair twisted in an elegant knot like a queen's, and her outfit probably worth more than Grace earns in a month—tailored slacks, a black silk shirt, and beige stiletto heels with pointy toes.

"He owes you?" she says.

Grace explains what happened with Jerry, embarrassed to confess what a fool she was in believing Frank would actually honor his word and give her a commission.

"Sounds like Frank," Mrs. Torelli says when she finishes. "It also explains why he was going to fire you."

Grace flinches. Though she suspected that was the case, having it confirmed still strikes like a blow. For three months, she has worked her butt off for Frank Torelli, going above and beyond because she felt she owed it to Mary for calling in the favor to get her the job.

"So you know where the safe is?" Mrs. Torelli says.

The question catches Grace off guard, and she looks at Mrs. Torelli curiously, taking in the clothes, the makeup, and the intensity with which she is looking at Grace. "That's why you're here?" she says as she realizes it. "You're here for the money?"

"Ironic, isn't it?"

An icy shudder tingles Grace's spine. She has never been a big believer in coincidence. Her grandmother used to say moments like this were straight up God messing with mortals, which is exactly how it feels.

And Grace wants nothing to do with it.

"Yeah, well, good luck with that." She squats down to resume looking for the keys.

She finds them a few feet away and snatches them up as Mrs. Torelli steps in front of her, the tips of her shoes directly beneath Grace's nose. "You know where it is?" she repeats.

Grace stands slowly as the new choices of how to answer spin: *Deny it and leave with nothing*, or *Admit it and possibly get what Frank owes me, but end up with my fate tied to Mrs. Torelli's*. The third option is out of her mouth before she has fully considered it. "I might," she says, her blood growing warm with the brilliance of it.

"You *might*?" Mrs. Torelli says.

"I might," Grace repeats brightly. "And for a finder's fee, I *might* be able to show you where it is."

"A finder's fee?"

"Yeah," Grace says. "Like a commission."

It's a complete stroke of genius. Without breaking the law or the vow she made to the judge who showed her leniency when she was nineteen, she can walk away from this with enough money to give her and Miles a fresh start.

"How much does Frank owe you?" Mrs. Torelli says.

"That's not really relevant," Grace answers, her insides lit up.

"Of course it's relevant. You said Frank owed you; that's the reason you're here."

"It was the reason I'm here," Grace says. "But now, you're here, which means I no longer need to *take* what Frank owes me, and instead, you and I can work out a deal."

Mrs. Torelli squints in distrust. "What kind of deal?"

"Like I said, a finder's fee. I show you where the safe is, and you cut me in on a percentage."

"A percentage? How much of a percentage?"

"Fifty," Grace says—fifty-fifty always a good place to start.

"Fifty percent!" Mrs. Torelli says, her hands flying with her words. "That's not a finder's fee. That's half. Forget it." She waves Grace away as if shooing a fly.

Grace smiles like it's no big deal, then lifts the keys in the thin light and flips through them. Purposely, she chooses the wrong one and inserts it in the lock. She pulls it out, squints at it, then searches through the others.

Choosing the right one, she slides it smoothly into the keyhole and is about to turn it when Mrs. Torelli blurts, "Fine. Five percent."

Grace gives a silent cheer and turns. "Fifty," she says.

"It's *my* money."

"Technically, it's only half your money."

"Ten."

Grace turns back to the door. "Good luck finding *your* money." The key turns, and she pulls down on the handle.

"Twenty, but that's my final offer."

Grace considers it. She has no idea how much Frank has. It could be twenty grand, or it could be a hundred. Twenty percent of twenty grand isn't a lot, but it would be enough to get her and Miles out of Orange County and, hopefully, would be enough to hold them over until she finds a job.

"Twenty-five," she says, "and only because I'm being nice."

Mrs. Torelli glowers at her, clearly not agreeing. "Fine," she says. "Twenty-five."

Grace pulls the key from the door and walks past Mrs. Torelli to Frank's private bathroom.

"I already looked there," Mrs. Torelli says. "It's the first place I checked."

Grace ignores her, and Mrs. Torelli's heels clack on the floor behind her as she follows Grace in.

Grace figured out where Frank was keeping his money a month after she started working for him. He asked her to call a plumber for a clogged sink, and she told him she could probably fix it herself. As she snaked the drain with a coat hanger, he hovered beside her, making her curious.

Later that day, when Frank went to lunch, she returned to the bathroom and, just like she is doing now, lifted the lid to the tank of the toilet.

"Oh," Mrs. Torelli says, peering over Grace's shoulder.

Grace agrees. It is impressive: a solid cast-iron safe disguised as a toilet tank and bolted to the wall, making it impossible to steal.

"But how does he do his business?" Mrs. Torelli says.

"This is a commercial toilet," Grace says. "The water supply comes directly from the wall." She smiles to herself at the irony of her juvenile-hall vocational training being used to rip off her boss.

Mrs. Torelli looks at her curiously, probably wondering how Grace could possibly know such a thing, but she doesn't ask. Instead she looks back at the safe and says, "Darn."

"Problem?"

"I thought it would be a keypad," Mrs. Torelli says. "You know, the kind where you enter numbers, like our safe at home. I know all Frank's passcodes and passwords, but this is one of those old-fashioned dial kinds of locks."

"So, you don't have the combination?" Grace says as her insides light up like the Fourth of July.

11

HADLEY

"Well, open it," Hadley says, wondering what Grace is waiting for.

The girl sets the lid to the tank aside so it is resting against the wall; then she straightens, a thin smile on her lips. And when Hadley realizes why she's grinning, her blood boils and she starts to shake her head.

"Fifty percent," Grace says.

"Absolutely not." She really doesn't like this girl. No wonder Frank wanted to fire her. She's nothing but a low-down, scheming thief. "The deal was twenty-five, and even that's a rip-off."

"The deal was twenty-five to *show* you where the safe was," Grace says. "Not to open it."

"Screw you."

"Look, Mrs. Torelli, I get that you're upset. I would be too. But the fact of the matter is I have the combination and you don't, and that puts you at a distinct disadvantage."

Hadley feels like steam is blowing from her ears. She doesn't get angry often. But this is her and Mattie's future this girl is messing with.

"Twenty-five," she says. "That was the deal."

Grace looks at her calmly, her expression as relaxed as if they were discussing the weather, perhaps a bit sympathetic, as if to say, *It looks like rain*, and it's all Hadley can do not to swat the look from her face.

"I could call the police," she spits. "Tell them I caught you trying to rob us."

Grace doesn't laugh out loud, but Hadley hears her laughing.

"Fine," Hadley huffs. "Thirty percent."

"We're not doing this again," Grace says as she pulls her phone from her pocket to glance at the time. "Fifty percent. Take it or leave it."

"You have someplace you need to be?"

"You could say that. So, what's it gonna be?"

Hadley thinks of Mattie and Skipper at the hotel. She thinks of Frank. She thinks of the car loaded with their belongings. She thinks of how angry she is. All this while looking at Grace, who stands relaxed in front of her as if she hasn't a care in the world. Which she doesn't. If Hadley refuses, she'll simply come back when Hadley is gone.

"Fine," Hadley huffs again, though nothing about this is fine in the least.

Hadley feels Grace's silent cheer, and never has she hated someone so much.

Grace spins the dial one way, then the other, and a moment later the lock falls into place, and Grace turns the lever and lifts open the door.

"Huh?" Hadley says.

Grace looks surprised as well, her hand frozen on the safe's door and her mouth hanging open. She shakes her head and takes a step back, backing away as if the neatly stacked bundles of cash piled to the rim of the tank are a ticking time bomb and not the answer to her prayers.

"That's a lot of money," Hadley says as Grace continues to move away from it.

On top of the money and slightly to the left is a small handgun. Without thinking, Hadley snatches it up, whirls, and points it at Grace.

"Put the money in the bag," she says, sounding like a bank robber in a B-rated movie.

Grace's eyes move from the safe to the gun, then back to the safe, then back to the gun; then she lifts her eyes to Hadley's and, with no protest at all, starts to fill the bag, and Hadley feels a small burst of pride. That will teach this girl to mess with her. Maybe she'll throw the girl a bone, toss her a bundle of hundreds as a tip.

Hadley tries to keep count as Grace pulls the money from the tank, but it's impossible. So instead, she wonders where it came from. Skimming is one thing, but this is more than the business makes in a year, and it's not like Frank doesn't spend. He spends plenty.

Before Hadley can puzzle it out, Grace is done, the bag so full the last bundles are stuffed in the outer pockets.

"Hand it over," Hadley says, holding out her left hand while keeping the gun trained on Grace with her right.

Grace rolls her eyes, shakes her head like Hadley's an idiot, then hoists the bag onto her shoulder and walks toward the door.

"Stop or I'll shoot," Hadley says, following her with the gun.

Grace turns and, without an ounce of fear, snatches the gun from Hadley's hand and jams it into the diaper bag. The butt sticks up through the bundles of cash.

"Next time, check the safety," she says, and she turns again for the door.

Before she can take a step, Hadley lunges and gets hold of one of the straps of the bag, spinning Grace around with so much force she nearly yanks her off her feet. With catlike reflexes, Grace recovers and grabs hold of the other strap.

Money flies everywhere as they pull against each other, threads popping as the bag stretches between them.

Hadley wishes she had thought to change her shoes. The Jimmy Choos slip on the slick tiles and make it impossible to get traction. The good news is Hadley outweighs Grace by at least fifty pounds. Finally an advantage to being fat. Loading up with everything she has, she puts all her weight into a final colossal pull, only realizing her mistake after it's too late, when she is already flying backward, the bag flying with her and money tumbling everywhere.

Her shoulder slams into the wall first; then she crumbles to the floor, her ankle twisting painfully beneath her.

Grace picks up the gun, then begins to collect the money. And all Hadley can do is watch as her and Mattie's future is gathered up in front of her.

Her chin quivers as she thinks of Mattie in the car and the hope in her voice when she asked if they were going back. Now it is only a few short hours later, and already, before they've even begun, she has failed.

When Grace is done collecting the money, she closes the safe and puts the lid back on the tank.

At the door, she stops. "I was actually trying to be fair," she says. "Offering to share. I could have just waited for you to leave, then taken it all."

"The money isn't yours," Hadley spits, the words trembling with her misery and rage.

Grace pats the bag. "It is now."

She opens the door, starts to walk through, then stops. She shakes her head, then looks up at the ceiling as if thinking about something.

When she turns back, there's a look of irritation on her face.

"What?" Hadley snarls, pain shooting through her ankle.

Grace sighs heavily and walks back to where she is. She squats down. "Put your arm around my shoulder. Come on, I'll help you up."

12

GRACE

Grace helps Mrs. Torelli out the back door, then locks it behind them. As they hobble toward her SUV, parked in the loading zone, her ears strain for the sound of Miles crying, and she is relieved to hear nothing but night noises and the slight rustling of the wind.

The diaper bag clunks against her thigh, heavy and bloated with far more money than Grace ever could have imagined. She tries not to think about it. She came to get what Frank owed her, but he didn't owe her this much—not even close.

The problem is she's not sure what to do about it. *Leave it? Give it to Mrs. Torelli?*

The woman pulled a gun on her. If the situation had been reversed, Grace knows that Mrs. Torelli wouldn't have hesitated to take all the money and leave her with nothing.

Beside her, Mrs. Torelli hops on her bare left foot, her heels held in her free hand.

Grace stops.

"What?" Mrs. Torelli says. "You planning on stealing my car now?"

Grace sighs through her nose. She didn't *steal* anything. She made a deal, and just like her deadbeat husband, Mrs. Torelli tried to renege on it. But this is *a lot* of money. Her brain spins as she tries to figure out the right thing to do.

Mrs. Torelli unwraps her arm from Grace's shoulder. "I've got it from here."

"You're not going to be able to drive," Grace says.

"I'll be fine." As if to prove it, Mrs. Torelli takes a step that nearly buckles her; then she takes another and ends up on the ground, her face twisted in pain as she hugs her injured leg to her chest.

"Like I said," Grace says, "you're not going to be able to drive."

Mrs. Torelli glares. "I hate you."

"Yeah, well, you're not exactly on my Christmas list either."

Mrs. Torelli's face drops, and though she's at least ten years older than Grace, at the moment, sitting barefoot on the pavement, holding her leg, she looks like an oversize toddler whose favorite toy has been broken.

"Come on," Grace says, crouching beside her. "Upsy-daisy. I'll drive you where you need to go."

Mrs. Torelli doesn't move; instead she continues to hold her leg and look hopeless.

"Look, Mrs. Torelli, you don't have a lot of options here. Either you let me help you, or you call an Uber and invite someone to pick you up at a crime scene."

Mrs. Torelli tilts her head, then tilts it the other way, her eyes narrowing before growing wide, as if she's just realized she might be in trouble for what she's done. Then she looks at the ground, shakes her head, and starts to cry.

Crap.

"Why?" Mrs. Torelli mumbles through her tears as her head continues to shake.

"Why what?" Grace says, losing patience. Miles is in the car, and now that things are what they are, she really wants to get as far away from this place as possible.

"Why are you helping me?"

"I have no idea," Grace says, thinking she should have just left her on the bathroom floor. She's about to tell Mrs. Torelli to forget it when the woman pushes onto her haunches and holds out her arms. With great effort, Grace lifts her to her feet, then helps her the rest of the way to the SUV.

A minute later, they are parked beside her Honda.

Grace nearly cries with relief when she finds Miles exactly as she left him, peacefully asleep in his car seat.

She carries it to the SUV.

"You brought your baby to a robbery?" Mrs. Torelli says as Grace straps him in behind her.

"You wore stilettos to a robbery?" Grace shoots back. Then she slams the door and walks back to the Honda.

13

HADLEY

Hadley stares at the baby, watching him as he breathes. She is alone in the passenger seat of her own car at the scene of a robbery with a stranger's baby.

She shakes her head. Of all the ways she's imagined this night could have gone, she can honestly say she never imagined this.

She flexes her ankle, and fresh tears fill her eyes. She can't walk. She can't drive. She has no money. She's not even out of Orange County, and any hope she had of escape has been quashed. Her best option now is to follow Frank's plan and hope he never finds out she was a part of this.

She bites her lip to keep her emotions inside, knowing babies are very sensitive to the emotions of others, even when they're asleep.

The door opens, and Grace climbs in, her cheeks flushed from walking from wherever it is she's stowed her car and from carrying the bag with the money.

"Where to?" she asks.

"The Ayres Hotel on El Toro," Hadley mumbles.

Grace glances back at the loaded trunk.

"We're leaving," Hadley says. "Or at least we were."

Grace says nothing. Without a word, she starts the car and pulls onto the road.

After a few minutes, Hadley says, "That's why I was taking the money. To get away."

"I'm not giving you my money," Grace says flatly.

"I wasn't asking you to." Hadley huffs and folds her arms across her chest. "I was just trying to explain what I was doing tonight, why I was trying to get *my* money."

The car turns suddenly, cutting right so sharply Hadley slides sideways and needs to catch herself with her hand.

"You want anything?" Grace says as she pulls into the drive-through for In-N-Out.

"I have no money," Hadley snipes.

"My treat," Grace offers without an ounce of pity.

"No, thank you."

Grace orders two cheeseburgers, an order of fries, and a chocolate milkshake, and Hadley hates her a little more. If Hadley ate like that, she'd be the size of a walrus in a week. Meanwhile Grace can't weigh more than a hundred pounds.

Grace sets the food on the console between them, and the smell of grease and salt wafts seductively past Hadley's nose.

"You sure you don't want something?"

Hadley shakes her head as her stomach groans in protest.

Grace pulls back onto the road but a block later veers to the curb and stops. Her hands grip the steering wheel, and her eyes are fixed on the black sky through the windshield, looking at it so intently Hadley wonders what she's looking for.

Finally, with a great exhale through her nose, she turns. "We need to split it," she says.

Hadley blinks.

"The money," Grace says. "The deal was fifty-fifty. So, you need to take half."

Hadley squints in distrust. "Why?" she says.

"Karma," Grace says plainly. "I believe in it. It might make me a fool, but I feel like if I don't give you your half, I'm going to regret it, that it will come back to haunt me, so you need to take your share."

14

GRACE

Grace is huffing and puffing by the time she gets back to Mrs. Torelli's room, carrying Miles in his car seat, the diaper bag full of money, her bag of food from In-N-Out, and the grocery bag with Miles's diapers, bottles, and formula.

Mrs. Torelli sits in the chair beside the bed, her foot propped on the mattress, the ankle already swollen and blue.

Grace sets Miles on the bed, climbs up beside him, and dumps the diaper bag onto the quilt, creating a mound of cash—bundles of twenties, fifties, and hundreds. And the gun.

Her eyes slide from the gun to Mrs. Torelli.

"Sorry," Mrs. Torelli mumbles. "I wouldn't have actually shot you."

She appears really upset, and Grace feels a little bad for her. Mrs. Torelli looks like the kind of woman who would have a hard time squashing a bug, and before tonight, she's probably never even touched a gun.

Grace slides the gun back in the bag, where it's out of sight, and turns back to the money. She stares at it, a queasy feeling in her gut. In her whole life, Grace has never had more than a month's rent in her account, and now, inches away, is enough money to buy a whole new life. Money that isn't hers.

She looks at Miles, asleep in his car seat, his mouth hanging open and his little fists balled on top of the straps; then she reaches into the In-N-Out bag, grabs a burger, unwraps it, and sinks her teeth into it. Her eyes close as the salty deliciousness touches her tongue, and she feels a little like Scarlett O'Hara in *Gone with the Wind* when she declares, "I'll never be hungry again."

Sensing Mrs. Torelli watching her, she opens her eyes and says, "Want some?" She holds out the bag with the fries.

Mrs. Torelli shakes her head, but her eyes track the bag like a dog following a bone, and Grace nearly laughs. Mrs. Torelli is probably one of those women who starves herself to stay thin, constantly counting calories and how many steps it takes to burn them off. Though Mrs. Torelli will never be skinny. She's far too curvy for that. A woman with boobs and hips, something Grace has neither of.

When half the burger is gone, Grace looks back at the money, takes a deep breath, and starts to sort the bundles into piles—hundreds, fifties, and twenties. There are only a few bundles of fifties and twice as many bundles of twenties, and the remaining bundles are hundreds.

She counts the bills in one of the bundles of twenties, then does the same with a bundle of hundreds. There are one hundred bills per bundle.

She points to each pile in order. "Two grand. Five grand. Ten grand."

"Each?" Mrs. Torelli says, clearly stunned.

Grace nods; then she looks at the bundle of hundreds still in her hand. She tests its weight, which can't be more than a few ounces. *Ten grand*, she thinks. Childcare for a year, a new car, half a year's rent. It seems impossible that so little could be worth so much.

Sitting back on her heels, she starts on the french fries and sips her shake.

"You sure you don't want some?" she says to Mrs. Torelli, part of her enjoying the torture she's causing. Grace has never understood the diet mentality. Her grandmother used to say the first three letters in *diet* are a warning, and Grace agrees. Her grandmother wasn't five feet tall, and she died a content 180 pounds, and if she were still alive, she'd tell you she'd enjoyed packing on every ounce with the kind of southern cooking that made Paula Deen famous.

When the fries are done, Grace counts the number of bundles in each pile, then counts them again before letting out a long, slow whistle.

"Well?" Mrs. Torelli says.

15

HADLEY

Hadley hears the number, but it doesn't register. She repeats it to herself: *One million, eight hundred seventy-two thousand.* She attempts to see it in her mind: a one, a comma, three digits, another comma, three more digits. She rounds it. One point nine million.

She shakes her head. "That can't be right."

It can't be. She and Frank do well, but they don't have *that* kind of money. She thinks about Frank—the stress he's been under, the late-night phone calls, his extravagant splurges over the past couple of years—then she pushes the thoughts away, a bad feeling in her gut.

She glances at the door that connects her room with the kids' room. She checked on them when she got here. At some point Skipper had climbed in beside Mattie, and they were curled together like a pair of kittens. Mattie probably wasn't even aware of it, believing the warmth beside her to be Prince Charles.

A million dollars. Tears spring to her eyes as she thinks of what it means. She looks at Grace slurping her shake, and she wants to kiss her, plant a great big smacker on her forehead or cheek. She wants to whoop and holler and throw the money in the air and dance a jig around the room.

Instead, her voice cracking with emotion, she says, "Thank you."

Grace looks up, then quickly looks away, her face pink.

She sets the shake down and starts to divide the pile of twenties—one for Hadley, one for herself, one for Hadley, one for herself . . .

Hadley drops her leg from the bed and pulls the bundles of hundreds toward her to do the same.

As she counts, she thinks how unimpressive it looks. Nearly two million dollars, and it barely takes up a quarter of the bed. Some people work a lifetime to earn this much money; how disappointed they would be to see how measly the result of all that effort is.

When they're done, Grace begins to put her share back in the bag. She's almost finished when the baby starts to stir. First, he yawns; then he turns his head and makes hopeful sucking motions with his mouth.

Beside Hadley, Grace freezes, her body rigid as if stunned with a Taser. Her hands are suspended in front of her, a bundle of money clenched in each.

The baby lets out a small whinny, and Hadley watches as Grace squeezes her eyes shut, takes a deep breath as if steeling herself for battle, then snaps them open. She drops the money to the bed, then scrabbles off it to undo the straps of the car seat. She lifts him into her arms as he starts to cry, and she hugs him tight against her and jiggles him up and down.

He cries harder.

"Maybe he's hungry," Hadley suggests.

Grace shoots daggers at her, and Hadley clamps back her next suggestion that he might also need his diaper changed.

A piercing howl shatters the air, followed by another, then another, until the baby is screaming at the top of his wee little lungs and Hadley's skin is on fire, his wailing at a specific bloodcurdling decibel level that implores you to take action and do whatever is necessary to stop it.

"Here," Hadley says, "give him to me while you make a bottle." She holds out her arms.

Grace shakes her head, more reaction than response, her brain clearly overwhelmed with distress nearly as severe as her son's. Her jiggling is almost frantic now, the bouncing causing the baby to flop up and down.

"Grace," Hadley says firmly as she pushes to her feet. Pain shoots through her ankle as blood rushes into it. "Let me take him."

Grace blinks as if just remembering Hadley is there, and her head almost shakes again, but Hadley's stern look stops her. "Grace, give him to me and go make a bottle."

The baby howls louder, and Grace's nostrils flare; then she practically throws him into Hadley's arms, frantically rummages through the grocery bag to retrieve a bottle and formula, and races to the bathroom.

Hadley places the baby over her shoulder so his belly is pressed against the round bulge of her muscle—a position Skipper was particularly fond of—then she lowers herself back to the chair and gently rocks him back and forth. "Shhh," she soothes as she pats his back.

He chews on his little fist, and his crying softens to whimpers. "That's it. You're okay. Your bottle's coming."

She hums softly, no particular song, just a gentle sound to let him know she's there, and he quiets. He's a solid baby, thick and strong. His chubby legs climb against her chest, and the fist that is not in his mouth tugs at her hair. She buries her nose in the sweet folds of his neck, the smell spiraling her back to when Mattie and Skipper were babies, that miraculous time when they needed her so much it was as if they were a part of her.

Grace races from the bathroom, a woman on fire. She thrusts the bottle at Hadley, then pulls it back. "How'd you do that?" she says, staring at the baby, who now snoozes peacefully on Hadley's shoulder.

"What?"

"Get him to stop crying?"

Hadley gives her a thin smile. She's always had a way with babies. "Why don't you get some rest? I've got him. Leave the bottle."

Grace's head starts to shake.

Hadley rolls her eyes. "Rest. You're exhausted. You helped me; now I'm helping you. If you don't trust me, sleep with the money. But you're tired and he's tired, and there's nothing you can do tonight that can't be done in the morning." It's something her mom would have said, and she likes the way it sounds coming from her mouth.

"You're very bossy," Grace says.

"And you're a pain in my ass."

For a long moment, Grace looks at her, searching for the lie. Finally, not finding one, she says, "Fine, but wake me if he wakes up again."

"Go. To. Sleep."

Grace lies down on the bed, distrust still in her eyes as she fights to keep them open, but eventually exhaustion overtakes her and she falls into a deep, still sleep.

Hadley stares at the striped bag beside her filled with Grace's half of the money, and again she thinks of Mattie and Skipper in the room next door, and about the past and the future and about what she needs to do.

16

MARK

Senior Special Agent Mark Wilkes wakes to buzzing he thinks is in his head. He squints into the brightness streaming through the blinds, then at the clock beside him: 7:32.

Saturday? Yes. Last night was Friday. The song "Yankee Doodle" from Shelly's spring recital still plays in his head. His six-year-old was a sunflower, then a chipmunk; then, in the finale, she was herself.

He almost smiles, but the buzzing still vibrates somewhere to his right, so he gropes around on the folding chair that serves as his night-stand to find his phone. The ticket stub from the recital falls to the floor, along with an empty taco wrapping from his dinner. After finally unearthing his phone, he brings it to his ear and grunts into it.

"Boss," Kevin Fitzpatrick says in way of greeting.

"Fitz."

"We've got a problem."

Mark's mouth tastes like a sock coated with athlete's foot, so he pushes to his elbow and takes a swig of the half-empty beer also on the folding chair as he waits for Fitz to continue.

Fitz is Mark's deskman on the Torelli case, a two-bit racketeering case Mark's been coordinating for a year. Frank Torelli is a small-time hustler running a gambling and drug operation out of his parking business in Orange County, California. It should be a regional case handled by the LA field office, but because Torelli has a cousin running a similar racket in Chicago, it's multijurisdictional, and since it also involves multiple agencies—FBI, DEA, local law enforcement—Mark was assigned the job of coordinating a task force.

The case isn't complicated and should have been wrapped up months ago, but they hit a snafu when the marked money they'd put in circulation never showed up in Torelli's accounts. Not a big deal: it simply meant Torelli was stashing the money somewhere other than the bank.

Mark set up surveillance cameras outside Torelli's office and his garages, and now they're just waiting on a search warrant. As soon as they have it, a team will go in and find the money, and Torelli, his brother, and his cousin will be sent away for a nice long stay at their local federal penitentiary, compliments of the US government.

Mark rubs the bridge of his nose as Fitz says, "It's the tapes from last night." He hesitates, mutters an "uh," then an "um," then stops again.

Fitz is a good kid, smart and hardworking, and Mark genuinely likes him. But his dream is to someday be a field agent, and Mark has his doubts. While the kid has a great criminal mind and good instincts, being on the ground means making life-and-death decisions and, more importantly, being able to live with the consequences of those choices after they're made. There can't be any second-guessing, and with Fitz, everything the kid says seems to come out a question.

"Fitz?" Mark says, trying to conceal his irritation. A hazy hangover has formed behind the front of his skull, the thrum of his pulse in his brain, and he presses his fingers against it, regretting the beer binge he indulged in last night after the recital.

"Maybe you should take a look for yourself?" Fitz says.

Mark grunts and hangs up, then for a long minute sits where he is, staring at the fan as it pulses back and forth beside the window. Even at seven in the morning, the heat that's descended on the capital this week is suffocating, and again, he is reminded of how much he misses Boston.

Finally, he pushes from the bed and shuffles to the bathroom, his left shoulder and right knee creaking—the first from his football days, the second from the shrapnel of a grenade that blew up too close to his team's Humvee during his second tour in Iraq.

As he walks, he turns on every light in the small apartment as well as the television. He pays no attention to what's on. He does it for the noise so the apartment is not so quiet and so he'll miss his kids a little less. He scans the empty space as he goes and tells himself, as he has every morning for the past two months, that he needs to get some furniture. Someday, the kids will want to visit, and this is no example of how to live.

As he shaves, he thinks about Shelly and her performance. She was smack in the middle of the front row, her curly blonde hair held up in a large white bow. She got the center stage position, she told him, because she sung with the "most emfusiasm." And she did. Head held high and shoulders pulled back, she belted out the song with gusto. *Yankee Doodle went to town, riding on a pony . . .*

He rinses his face and pulls a towel from the box Marcia neatly labeled *Bath Stuff* in her very precise handwriting.

He stuck a feather in his hat, and called it macaroni . . .

Stan the Insurance Man was there, at the recital. He, Marcia, and Ben, Mark's nine-year-old, sat two rows in front of Mark. A delightful little family enjoying the show.

Mark had arrived a few minutes late. Probably a good thing. Had he arrived on time, he might have made a scene, told Stan the Insurance Man to go to hell, that *he* could sit two rows back . . . *by himself*. That this was *his* family and that Ben was *his* son and therefore should be sitting beside *him*.

But getting out of downtown was a bitch, so Mark showed up late and, broiling mad, took his seat two rows behind them, his eyes shooting daggers at the back of Stan the Insurance Man's gray-haired, slightly balding head.

He steps into the scalding water.

Yankee Doodle, keep it up, Yankee Doodle dandy . . .

Shelly looked out at the audience, saw Mark, and, for a moment, forgot to sing, her hand waving excitedly. And that's when he saw it: the gap in her smile where her two front teeth had been.

He slams his fist against the tiles, his shoulder protesting. *Damn her. Damn her. Damn her. Damn her.*

Had Marcia called to tell him Shelly had lost her teeth, he would have told her what she needed to do, where the gold dollars, purchased specifically for Tooth Fairy-ing, were kept. He would have told her about the silver Sharpie in his desk and explained that she needed to leave a rhyming note along with the coin, the penmanship curly so it looked like a fairy had written it.

But his ex-wife didn't call to tell him that their daughter had lost her first tooth. Or her second. It probably didn't occur to her. Marcia is busy these days, running her business and "raising two kids on her own," as she likes to say. She has no time to keep her ex-husband informed about small insignificant details like their six-year-old losing her teeth.

He is the Tooth Fairy—also Santa Claus, the Easter Bunny, and Saint Patrick. He should have been there, been a part of it.

After stepping from the shower, he wraps a towel around his waist and returns to the front room. In a single gulp, he finishes the remainder of the stale beer, then, with a heavy sigh, opens his laptop. Fitz has sent four video clips, two from each of the surveillance cameras outside Torelli's office. He looks at the ones from the entrance camera first, then at those from the back lot; then he looks at them again, this time in sequence.

He calls Fitz. "What the hell?"

"Exactly."

17

GRACE

Grace is dreaming of food. Bread, mostly, warm from the oven, the crust breaking open in her hands to reveal its soft, steamy insides. Jam and honey and butter waiting to be spread in great slathers across it. Grapes and apples. Blueberry muffins in a basket. A plate of thick waffles beside it. She holds the torn loaf, its heat spreading through her fingers as she reaches for the knife, her mouth watering as her nose fills with its yeasty smell . . .

Her eyes blink open as her mouth continues to water. The ceiling above her is smooth, entirely unlike the popcorn ceiling of her bedroom, and for a precious second, she thinks she is in her old apartment, the one she and Jimmy moved into when they first got married, light flooding in through the window as it always did in the morning. She loved that bedroom and that bed, the way the golden light would stream in each day to wake them. It was such a hopeful way to greet the day.

She can almost smell the pancakes Jimmy would make in the morning, fluffy as air, a special recipe made with lemon-zest ricotta, warm maple syrup on top. Her stomach rumbles, and she realizes something is baking nearby. Stretching her arms over her head, she inhales the heady scent, unable to remember the last time she slept so well or the last time it was so quiet.

Quiet!

She bolts upright as she realizes where she is. *In a hotel room. Alone. No Miles. No money.*

She leaps from the bed and runs for the door.

"Morning," Mrs. Torelli says as she bursts into the brightness.

Grace spins to see Mrs. Torelli sitting in a plastic chair beside the door, Miles cradled in her arms. He stares up at her, his fists waving.

Grace blinks.

"Sleep well?"

Grace swallows back her panic as her eyes slide to the diaper bag at Mrs. Torelli's feet. The bag has been neatly repacked, the diapers, bottles, and formula organized in the outer pockets, the money bulging in the zipped main compartment. Miles's car seat is beside the bag. It looks freshly scrubbed, the lining cleaned of crumbs and several of the stains gone.

"Where's your stuff?" Grace says, noticing that Mrs. Torelli has changed into a cotton skirt the color of plums and an ivory tank.

"Packed in the car. My daughter loaded it for me."

As if on cue, a teenager with white-blonde hair with half an inch of dark roots walks from the door on the other side of Mrs. Torelli. She looks at Grace with dark-brown eyes the exact color of Frank's, then turns to Mrs. Torelli. "Can we go now?" she says, her arms folded across her chest in a silent, trademark teenage harrumph.

The girl is edgy cool. She wears black leggings and a rock T-shirt from a band Grace has never heard of, and an awesome snake earring spirals through her left ear.

"Mattie, this is Grace," Mrs. Torelli says.

"Hey," Mattie says, not bothering to look at Grace again, and Grace nearly smiles, remembering being like that when she was a teenager, completely caught up in her own world while trying to figure out how she fit into the bigger one.

Mrs. Torelli sighs, lifts Miles so he is standing on her lap, and nuzzles his nose, apparently in no rush to give him up.

"Mo-o-om," Mattie says, rolling her eyes.

"Mmmm?" Mrs. Torelli says, nuzzling Miles again, clearly enamored.

"Well, I guess we should be going," Grace mumbles. "Thanks for, you know, looking after him." She steps forward to take him at the exact moment the door beside them opens again and a boy in a Dodgers uniform walks through.

He steps between her and Mrs. Torelli, looks down at Miles, places his hands on the baby's cheeks, then squishes them to make Miles's lips into a fish mouth. "Hey, Rookie," he says; then he proceeds to play Miles's cheeks like an accordion, smooshing them in and out.

Grace steps forward, slightly concerned. The boy is around eight, slight as a rag doll, and there's something different about him, a slowness that speaks to viewing the world through an altered lens.

She reaches around to take Miles just as Miles lets out a squeal that startles her. She stops, straightens, looks at the boy, then looks back at Miles, who is waving his pudgy arms and kicking his pudgy legs in what can only be described as delight.

The book Grace has on baby development says babies start to laugh at three months. But though Miles's four-month birthday was two weeks ago, Grace has never seen him so much as crack a grin.

The boy removes his hands, then looks at Mrs. Torelli. "Time to get on the road, Blue," he says, and Mrs. Torelli smiles at him with so much love Grace's heart swells.

Grace takes Miles, and Mrs. Torelli pushes to her feet with a wince.

"You need to get that looked at," Grace says. The ankle looks worse this morning, bulging, blue, and misshapen.

"Yeah, I'll get right on that," Mrs. Torelli answers with a sarcastic grin. "Mattie, give me a hand."

Mattie steps up, and Mrs. Torelli wraps her arm around her daughter's shoulders. The girl barely breaks five feet, and it's obvious the arrangement is not going to work. They attempt a step, and Grace lunges, catching Mrs. Torelli by her bicep as she stumbles and yelps in pain. The lurch causes Miles to practically tumble from Grace's arms, and he cries out, letting out a bloodcurdling wail.

Grace releases Mrs. Torelli and hugs him to her. "Sorry," she says, holding him tight. "I'm so sorry."

He continues to scream and rails against her, his little fists pushing against her shoulders as he arches his back to break loose. She reaches for his car seat on the ground, but he's flailing so hard she's afraid she might drop him.

"Mattie, help her," Mrs. Torelli says.

"I'm fine," Grace says, attempting to reposition him so he's more secure as she continues to reach for his car seat.

"Mattie, now!" Mrs. Torelli practically screams.

Mattie lifts the car seat onto the plastic chair, and Grace pushes Miles into it as he continues to shriek. "Thanks," she mumbles, her heart pounding.

She feels Mrs. Torelli watching her, and heat rises in her cheeks. Miles flails, his face purple with his hysterics as he kicks and screams, the crown of his head pressed painfully into the headrest.

"Oh, for Christ's sake," Mrs. Torelli says, hopping on one foot to where Grace is. "Hand him over."

Grace hesitates.

"Now!" she snaps.

Grace's hands fly over the harness, releasing and lifting Miles in a single panicked motion, and Mrs. Torelli takes him and flops him over her shoulder.

"Shhh," she coos. "You're okay." She sways back and forth on her single foot, her left hand holding him as her right pats his back, and immediately he starts to calm, gulping air and grabbing onto Mrs. Torelli's hair for comfort.

Grace bites her bottom lip and looks at the ground, her eyes filling. She sucks at this, sucks so bad it hurts. It's one thing to suck at cooking or sewing or making small talk, but to suck at being a mom, that's got to be the worst failing in the world. And so not fair to Miles. He deserves so much better.

Miles gnaws on his fist, his other hand still holding tight to Mrs. Torelli's hair, and over his back, Mrs. Torelli says, "Grace, you don't look so good; maybe you should sit down."

Grace doesn't feel so good, but she shakes her head. Mrs. Torelli is the one balancing on one foot. "I'll take him now," she says, holding out her arms as she swallows back the acid that's risen in her throat and thinking she shouldn't have eaten that second burger last night.

With a concerned frown, Mrs. Torelli hands Miles back, and mercifully, he does not cry. His body lies limp against her, sweaty and spent from his hysterics.

"Do you want us to give you a lift back to your car?" Mrs. Torelli offers.

"How? You can't drive."

"I thought I'd try driving left footed."

"You're kidding, right?" Grace says, certain she can't be serious.

"How hard could it be?"

"Really hard. You're going to kill yourself."

Mrs. Torelli's expression tightens, clearly not pleased with Grace's opinion. "Well, I suppose we'll see about that."

Grace rolls her eyes, and Mrs. Torelli glowers at her. Then she lifts her chin, extends her hand, and says, "Well, I guess then this is goodbye."

Grace shakes it, surprised by the well of emotions she feels. After all, she's known the woman less than a day.

Mrs. Torelli hops away, using the wall for support, and Mattie shuffles behind her. The boy takes up the rear, loping after them with his face lifted toward the sky as if examining the clouds for rain.

And because Grace really isn't feeling well, she lowers herself into the chair and closes her eyes, hoping the nausea will pass.

She keeps her eyes shut when the car door slams, but when she hears the SUV reversing, the herky-jerky sound causes them to snap open. She watches as the Mercedes backs up haltingly, the brake lights blinking like a warning signal; then suddenly they stop blinking and the car shoots backward, skipping over the curb to run over the sidewalk before slamming into a planter beside the stairwell.

Grace leaps up, slings the diaper bag over her shoulder, and, holding Miles with one hand and his car seat with the other, races down the stairs.

She throws open the driver's door. "You okay?"

Mrs. Torelli blinks rapidly. "Yeah. Fine." She cranes her head back to look at Mattie, then the boy; then she looks back at Grace. "I don't know what happened."

You're an idiot. That's what happened, Grace thinks, but she says instead, "You hit the gas instead of the brake."

"I did?"

Grace nods. "Get out."

"Why?"

"Because I'm driving."

"Where?"

"To the hospital. You need to get that ankle looked at, and I'm not having your death and your kids' deaths on my conscience."

Mattie moves to the back, and Mrs. Torelli hops around the car and into the passenger seat. Grace buckles Miles into his car seat between the two kids, then climbs into the driver's seat.

As she starts to drive, a strange vibration buzzes in her veins, the feeling a bit like vertigo, dizzying, like she is free-falling—plummeting and tumbling toward a destiny over which she has no control.

18

HADLEY

Grace agreed to take the kids to the cafeteria, so Hadley is alone in the emergency room as she waits for her discharge instructions. Her ankle is badly sprained but, thankfully, not broken. It's wrapped with an ACE bandage, and the doctor has given her strict instructions to stay off it for several weeks and to keep it wrapped, iced, and elevated—no driving.

As she waits, she considers her options. She could ignore the doctor and try to drive anyway. She flexes her ankle to test the theory, and tears fill her eyes, letting her know driving is not an option.

They could take a bus or a train, but that would mean ditching the car and most of their belongings, and it would leave a trail for Frank to follow, which would be far too dangerous.

She looks at Skipper's backpack on the floor, which has her share of the money, and wonders if it would be possible to pay someone to drive them. *Maybe Grace?* she thinks, then just as quickly dismisses the idea. Grace has close to a million dollars of her own; why would she want to drive them?

Which means she would need to hire a stranger, an idea that makes her hair stand on end—a single woman on crutches with two kids and a boatload of cash asking a stranger to drive them halfway across the country. Even she's smart enough to realize that's not a good plan.

She hates life-altering-decision moments like these. She's never been good at them: always so terrified of making the wrong choice, inevitably she ends up hemming and hawing so long the decision gets made for her.

She needs a cigarette. She looks at the backpack again. Along with the money, it holds the contents of her purse—Skipper's backpack the only bag they had, which would leave her hands free so she could grab onto things for balance.

She never smokes in front of the kids, so this might be her only chance.

She's still thinking about sneaking outside when, through the slit between the curtains, she sees two men approach the nurses' station. Both wear dark suits and have the rigid bearing of military men. One is white, the other black. They look like they're here on official business, and Hadley leans in to listen, wondering who's in trouble and why.

"Yes, Torelli, Hadley Torelli . . . ," the white one says, nearly causing Hadley to fall off the table.

Heart pounding, she slides to the floor, slings the backpack onto her shoulders, and then grabs her new crutches and hobbles quickly out the back of the exam bay. Her brain spins as she races for the elevators, wondering how Frank figured it out so fast. Maybe he went to the office? He wasn't supposed to. He was supposed to play golf. She called him before they left the hotel, and he said he was getting ready. He was excited. He had bought new clubs.

Irrationally, she pats herself down as she jabs the down arrow, checking for a bug or a tracer or some sort of homing device.

The elevator opens, and she races onto it and presses the button for the basement, then presses it again and again until finally the doors close.

When she reaches the cafeteria, she scans the large room and spots Grace and the kids in the corner, trays of empty plates in front of them. Grace holds a cup of coffee, while Mattie and Skipper play on their handheld PlayStations. The baby is in his car seat on the table, the striped bag on the ground at Grace's feet.

Grace looks up, sees Hadley's expression, and says, "What's wrong?"

"Frank," she stammers. "He found us."

Before Hadley has finished the sentence, Grace is standing and moving so fast Hadley falls back a step. The coffee is no longer in Grace's hand; the striped bag is over her shoulder; the car seat is being lifted; then she is racing for the door.

"Wait!" Hadley says, but Grace is already halfway across the room. "Mattie, grab Skipper and make him keep up."

Hadley whirls and race-hops after her, instinct more than thought telling her it's important not to lose her.

"Grace!" she yells when she reaches the corridor, Grace now thirty feet ahead, the car seat and bag clunking against her legs and making her slow.

"Please." Hadley hops faster, throwing the crutches out in front of her and propelling herself forward. She catches up as Grace pushes through a set of double doors with a sign above them that says EMPLOYEES ONLY.

"Do you know those guys?" Hadley says, breathless.

Grace's face snaps sideways. "Guys? You said it was Frank."

"Yes. Frank's guys, but . . . please, Grace, slow down."

Grace doesn't slow down; instead she continues to race forward, lugging the baby and the heavy bag as fast as she can. Hadley works hard to keep the arm-leg rhythm of the crutches in sync as she chases after her. The room they've entered is some sort of mechanical space, machines and computers whirring. A man in a workman's uniform looks up from a clipboard and watches as they race by.

"Grace, they might not be Frank's guys," Hadley wheezes.

Grace stops so suddenly Hadley nearly crashes into her. "You just said they were Frank's guys."

"Yes, I thought they were. I mean, they have to be. Who else would be looking for me? But I don't know. I think . . . it's just . . ."

"Christ, Mrs. Torelli, spit it out."

"One was black," Hadley says.

Grace's eyes squint, then tick side to side, and then she frowns.

"Exactly," Hadley says. Grace knows as well as Hadley that Frank would never hire a black person.

"Blue?" Skipper says, racing up with Mattie beside him and looking up with worry.

"It's okay, Champ," she says.

"What did they look like?" Grace says.

"I don't know. One white. One black. Both big and athletic and dressed in suits. They kind of looked like jocks dressed as businessmen, except for their shoes."

"Their shoes?"

"Yeah, their shoes were . . . I don't know . . . practical. The kind a restaurant manager might wear. You know, made for comfort, not style."

Grace's face blanches, the color draining clear out of it.

"What?" Hadley says.

Grace doesn't answer; instead she pivots away and starts running again, even more frantically than before.

Hadley hurries after her.

"Please, Grace," she says as Grace pushes through a door with blue sky blazing through the glass. "At least tell me who they are."

The door starts to swing closed, but Mattie races past to push it open before it shuts. She holds it for Hadley, and Hadley hops through. In front of her, Grace has stopped and is scanning around her. They are in the back lot of the hospital, most of the spaces empty, a few ambulances parked off to the side.

Grace's eyes dart left, then right, and Hadley watches as she tries to switch the car seat to her left hand, but the diaper bag gets in the way, so she returns it to her right.

"Please, Grace, who are they?"

Grace's head snaps sideways to look at her. "How would I know?"

"Because you do. You freaked out when I mentioned their shoes. You know something."

Grace's nose flares once; then she exhales and says, "I can't be sure, but if I had to guess, I'd say feds. Business suits with ugly shoes is kind of their trademark. They were probably watching the money."

"The money?"

"What money?" Mattie says.

Hadley ignores her. "Someone was watching the money?"

Grace rolls her eyes. "It's probably dirty. We stole dirty money, and they were watching it."

"You stole money?" Mattie says, her eyes flicking between Hadley and Grace.

"Blue?" Skipper says, not following the conversation but confused just the same.

"It's okay, buddy, hang in there." She looks back at Grace, trying to make sense of it. *Dirty money?* She's never even had a speeding ticket, and now the FBI is chasing her because she stole dirty money?

"But how?" she says. "How did they find us?"

Grace considers the question, then looks down at the diaper bag. She pulls her phone from the front pocket, walks to the trash beside the door, and drops it in the hole; then she turns back to Hadley. "Now leave me alone."

She hurries away, racing quickly as she can toward the mall on the other side of the street.

19

GRACE

Mrs. Torelli, Mattie, and the boy are racing behind her and gaining ground. Miles's car seat, along with the diaper bag, makes it impossible for her to outrun them. Her arm trembles from the weight of the car seat, and it feels like it's going to snap off. The day is scorching hot, making her hand slippery, and she struggles to hold on as she races toward the Nordstrom across the street.

"I've got it," Mattie says, hustling up and lifting the car seat before Grace can react.

She wants to grab it back and scream at the girl to leave her alone, but Mattie is already racing away, carrying the car seat with surprising strength and speed.

Mattie glances back over her shoulder. "Come on, Champ, keep up," she says. "Run like you're rounding third and heading for home. Fast, fast, fast."

Awkwardly, the boy pumps his arms and clomps his feet to catch up. He passes Grace and leaves Mrs. Torelli huffing and puffing as she crutch-hops behind.

Grace's heart pounds. She's desperate for this not to be happening. She looks at Miles in his car seat and prays she has not just made the biggest mistake of her life.

20

HADLEY

It takes all Hadley's focus not to miss a landing that will send her sprawling onto the asphalt. Mattie is forty yards ahead carrying the baby, Skipper right behind her.

After Hadley dumped her cell phone in the same trash in which Grace dumped hers, Mattie pieced things together. She ditched her own phone and took off after Grace, intuition or logic telling her that sticking with Grace was their best option.

Hadley doesn't disagree. Grace seems oddly adept at this, whatever *this* is—knowing toilets conceal safes, knowing you need to flick off the safety before you shoot a gun, knowing bad shoes with nice suits add up to the FBI.

The cool air of the store smacks Hadley as she races after them into the Nordstrom. Grace has retaken the lead and now weaves in and out of the makeup department.

The heel of Grace's left shoe flaps against her foot like a flip-flop, the sole unglued, and Hadley finds herself staring at it, the defect having a profound effect on her and making her very angry at Frank.

They dart through the shoe department and then the purses and finally into a family restroom. As soon as Hadley is through the door, Grace locks it behind them.

Hadley collapses against the wall, her breath coming in gulps, and silently she swears that if she gets through this, she is going to quit smoking for good.

She slips the backpack from her shoulders, and it thumps to the floor.

Mattie sets the car seat on the changing table and places her PlayStation console beside it; then she kneels beside the backpack and unzips the main pouch. Her eyes grow wide when she sees the bundles of cash, and she looks up at Hadley. "You robbed a bank?"

If the situation weren't so awful, Hadley might laugh. But there is nothing funny about what is going on, and no explanation is possible, so all Hadley manages is to shake her head.

Mattie turns to Grace. "You're a bank robber?"

Grace glances at her, then ignores her, her eyes flicking side to side as she paces. The room is small and crowded with the five of them, but Grace takes two steps, pivots, then takes two steps back, her bottom lip sucked in like she is thinking.

The baby stares wide eyed; then his mouth skews sideways, and Hadley pushes off the wall, unhitches the harness, scoops him up, and drapes him over her shoulder.

Absently, Grace hands her a half-full bottle from the striped bag, and Hadley lowers him into the crook of her arm and pops it in his mouth.

He sucks on it greedily, entirely content, and Hadley wishes she could trade places with him.

Skipper squats in the corner on his heels and rocks back and forth, his eyes narrowed on the black and white tiles at his feet.

"Hey, Champ," she says.

He doesn't look at her, but she feels his stress. Slow and steady is the only pace that works for Skipper, and she knows this must be terrifying.

Awkwardly, being careful not to jostle the baby or put weight on her ankle, she lowers herself beside him. His eyes shift from the floor to the baby.

"Would you like to feed him?" she says, forcing the quake from her voice.

His eyes grow wide, and she watches as his stress dissolves into a look of awe at the prospect of being entrusted with such an important task.

"Sit crisscross," she says.

He scoots onto his butt, then stares in wonder as the baby is placed in his arms.

The baby looks up at him, still contentedly sucking on his bottle, and Skipper's face melts into an expression of pure love. Hadley adjusts his left arm so it supports the baby's head; then she shows Skipper how to hold the bottle so there's no air in the nipple.

"Got it?" she says.

He nods, his eyes still fixed on the baby, his gold hair draping across his forehead.

Mattie shifts to squat protectively beside them, there if Skipper needs her, but Hadley knows he won't. Skipper's incredibly trustworthy when it comes to being responsible.

Grace continues to pace—two steps, pivot, two steps—her brow furrowed. On her sixth rotation, she stops an inch from the wall and screams, "Fuuuudge!" the word ricocheting off the tile.

All of them freeze.

Grace spins to face Hadley. "What was he into? Frank? Why are they following you?"

"I . . . I . . . I don't know," she stammers.

"Dad?" Mattie says. "It's Dad's money?" She almost sounds disappointed to discover they're not bank robbers.

Hadley nods as Grace runs her hands through her hair in frustration. "What now?" Hadley says.

"I think he's done, Blue," Skipper says, and Hadley looks over to see the baby smiling up at Skipper, formula dripping from his mouth.

She places a burp rag on her shoulder and lifts the baby to drape him over her shoulder so she can burp him.

"What happens now," Grace says, her eyes on the baby, "is that *you* are going to take *your* kids, and *you* are going to leave *me* alone."

Hadley blinks at the harshness of her words.

"Right. Of course," she says; then, without meaning to, she starts to cry. It's not intentional. She's always cried easily. Any emotion can do it—sorrow, fear, happiness . . . stress. She tries to blot the tears away with the hand not holding the baby, but they stream down her face faster than she can wipe them away.

"Christ," Grace says.

"I'm s-sorry," Hadley stammers. She uses the corner of the burp rag to dab at her face. "Of course you should go. Here." She holds the baby out to her.

Grace doesn't take him. Instead she glares at Hadley, her arms folded across her chest. Hadley pulls him back, cradling him against her as she sniffs back her emotions.

"Blue?" Skipper says, unsure what is happening.

"It's okay, Champ," Hadley manages. "We're okay."

"For criminy's sake," Grace says; then, with a huff of aggravation, she adds, "Fine. I'll help get you out of here, but then, after that, that's it. You're on your own."

21

GRACE

Grace has always had a weakness when it comes to crying. Whether it be Miles or a grown woman, tears set off an alarm in her brain that floods her with a crazed need to do whatever it takes to stop them. So now, instead of her and Miles being safely on their way to freedom with close to a million dollars in her pocket, she is in the bathroom of a Nordstrom arguing with Mrs. Torelli, which is making her seriously regret her impulsive, stupid offer to help her.

"No." Mrs. Torelli shakes her head back and forth to emphasize the point, her black hair swaying in front of her face.

"We *need* a car," Grace says, irritated beyond belief that this woman, who she is putting her neck on the line for, is giving her a hard time.

"I also need a smaller ass, but I'm not going to steal one."

"We're not going to *steal* one," Grace says. "We're going to *borrow* one. They'll get it back in a day or two."

Mrs. Torelli shakes her head harder. "We are not pointing a gun at someone and *borrowing* their car. Not for a day, not for a minute."

"You have a better idea?" Grace seethes.

Mrs. Torelli's green eyes snap wide. "Actually, I do," she says, sounding surprised. She reaches into the backpack at her feet and pulls out a bundle of hundreds. "Catch more flies with honey than vinegar." She waves the bills back and forth so they fan the air.

The statement catches Grace off guard. It was one of her grand-mother's favorites.

"You okay?" Mrs. Torelli says, stopping her money waving.

Grace manages a nod, the disconcerting feeling of free-falling returning.

"Better idea than a gun, right?" Mrs. Torelli says.

Grace blinks and nods again, a bit amazed that Mrs. Torelli, who doesn't seem to have a sensible thought in her head, has had not only an idea but a rather good one—a very obvious, very sensible idea. They have money, a fact Grace keeps forgetting. Like june bugs bouncing off a windshield, the idea simply won't stick. She has money. Lots and lots of money. Which means they can *pay* someone to borrow their car. Which is actually a great relief, since Grace really doesn't want to stick a gun in some poor unsuspecting person's face.

Mrs. Torelli smiles a smug see-I-told-you-I-had-a-good-idea grin that Grace very much wants to swat off her face.

"Come on, tell me I did good," Mrs. Torelli prods.

"I'll tell you you did good when you actually manage it," Grace says. "We still need to find someone willing to loan us their car for that bundle of cash, which is a whole lot easier said than done." In Grace's experience, strangers aren't exactly trusting of other strangers.

"Follow me," Mrs. Torelli says, grabbing her crutches and hopping confidently out the door.

She follows Mrs. Torelli across the store and out the opposite exit from where they entered. Mattie carries the car seat and the diaper bag, and Grace holds Miles, who is sound asleep on her shoulder.

"Wait here," Mrs. Torelli says when they're outside but still beneath the canopy of the entrance. She sets the backpack on the ground at Grace's feet and slides a bundle of hundreds into her skirt pocket. She hops on her crutches into the parking lot, where she stops beside the handicap spots, both of them empty.

For several minutes, nothing happens. It's steamy hot, and sweat pools beneath Grace's shirt. She hasn't showered since yesterday and is still wearing the same clothes she wore to work yesterday. Aware of her stench, she takes a small step away from Mattie.

A few shoppers come and go, and Grace watches as Mrs. Torelli smiles sweetly at them but lets them pass without a word.

What's she waiting for? Grace thinks. If it was the FBI at the hospital, they're probably studying the surveillance tapes at this very moment. She imagines them clicking frame to frame until they spot the five of them leaving through the back parking lot and heading toward the mall.

A car, circa before-Grace-was-born, makes a wide turn into the parking lane, then an even wider turn to pull into the handicap spot nearest the entrance. It takes an eternity, but finally, the driver's door opens and a woman with white cotton hair, a brightly colored blouse, and black sunglasses that wrap all the way around the sides of her head steps from the driver's seat.

The woman is frail, white, and dotted with liver spots, and Grace tenses, worried that, if Mrs. Torelli approaches her, either she will give the woman a heart attack or the woman will scream bloody murder because she thinks she is being mugged.

Beside her, Mattie shifts her weight, nervous as well. Together they watch Mrs. Torelli hop forward, a smile on her face as if she has run into a neighbor or an old friend. She lifts her hand from her right crutch to offer a wave, and the woman stops. She looks up from her stoop and tilts her head curiously, like perhaps Mrs. Torelli is someone she might know but has forgotten.

Mrs. Torelli says something that causes the woman to smile, and Grace relaxes. At least the woman doesn't think she's being mugged.

"What do you think she's saying?" Mattie whispers.

"I have no idea."

Mrs. Torelli's hands move with her mouth as she continues to talk, very animated as if she is telling a great story. The woman listens and several times reacts in surprise. Then she turns toward the entrance, her black glasses aimed at Grace and the kids.

Grace, not knowing what else to do, waves, and Mattie does the same. Then, before Grace realizes what's happening, the boy runs from her side. He crosses the street and crashes into Mrs. Torelli's hip. His arms wrap around her, and the old woman looks down at him. The boy pushes off Mrs. Torelli and tilts his head one way, then the other, and then he reaches out to touch the woman's shirt.

It's an odd gesture and one that, coming from anyone else, might be offensive, but coming from this curious kid in a Dodgers uniform, it's nothing but sweet.

She points to the spot he's touching, and Grace squints to see that the pattern on her blouse is of birds, a colorful print of parrots and toucans. The woman says something, and her expression softens into a smile; then she moves her finger to another spot on her shirt and says something else.

The boy nods along, his eyes wide and his grin mirroring hers, and as Grace watches the strange exchange, she notices how remarkable the boy is. There is something almost ethereal about him. Though he's awkward, he is also beautiful—his eyes oversize and the soft color of worn blue jeans; his lips pink, small, and perfectly formed; and his skin so pale it glows.

When the woman looks back up at Mrs. Torelli, her face is transformed, still serious but more open and welcoming. Mrs. Torelli says something as she tousles the boy's hair; then she points to Grace and Mattie, and Grace and Mattie wave again.

"Do you think she'll do it?" Mattie says.

"I have no idea," Grace says, unable to believe Mrs. Torelli's gotten this far and that the woman is even considering it.

The exchange goes on for another three or four minutes, the two women now chatting and laughing like old friends, and Grace feels her pulse rate rising with each passing second, certain that, at any moment, the feds are going to descend on them. She considers throwing something at Mrs. Torelli, like a shoe, but decides against it. *Ask to borrow her car. And let's get the hell out of here.*

And Mrs. Torelli must hear her because suddenly the money appears, and in the next second, the woman is holding out her keys.

Mattie nudges Grace's shoulder excitedly, and Grace nudges her back, her insides lit up with relief and disbelief, unable to believe Mrs. Torelli has done it, managed to convince the woman to loan them her car.

She picks up the backpack, and she and Mattie walk toward the car.

As the woman passes them, she lifts her raisin-skinned face to Grace's and says, "I hope you get there in time."

Grace has no idea what she's talking about and frankly doesn't care, her focus entirely on hightailing it out of there.

22

MARK

"Tell me you're joking?" Mark says as he pulls his shirt from his skin, the cotton soaked through with sweat.

It's one of those weeks where the humidity chokes you, each breath so cloying it's like inhaling mold into your lungs. Though he has lived in DC almost two years, he still thinks of it as his temporary home, like he is a foreign organism surviving in an unsuitable environment. The weather is always either too hot or too cold, and always too wet. Boston has weather, but it has a more clear opinion of it—fall, winter, spring, summer—all of it crisp, clear, and breathtaking.

"Sorry, boss," Fitz says.

Mark closes his eyes and clamps his mouth around the expletives that threaten to escape. In front of him, Shelly holds on to the wall of the pool. Around her, half a dozen other six- and seven-year-olds cling to the edge as well, all of them watching the swim instructor, who is teaching them how to blow bubbles underwater.

If Mark were a cartoon character, steam would be blowing from his ears. "You're telling me that two women, one on crutches, who are traveling with an infant and two kids, first managed to evade two highly trained FBI operatives at a hospital, which has a thousand security cameras, and have now slipped past the entire Barstow police force, along with half the agents from the LA field office?"

"We missed them by minutes," Fitz says.

"And you have no idea where they went?"

"There's video of them driving past the McDonald's, where they left the old lady's car in the parking lot, but nothing after that. Agents are canvassing the area but so far have come up empty. No one's seen them. The roadblock on the 40 is solid: no way to see it coming and no place to hide. The highway patrol's checked every car for the past three hours, and nothing."

Mark feels like his head is going to explode. "So, you're saying they just disappeared? Into thin air?"

Wisely, Fitz remains silent.

After three long breaths, Mark sighs and says, "What's the connection between them? Between Herrick and Torelli?"

"It's strange, boss. There doesn't seem to be one. From what I can tell, the women barely know each other. I looked at their phone records and even looked at the old tapes. Torelli hardly ever went to the office, and Herrick hardly ever left it."

"What's the sister say?"

"She hasn't returned my calls. She's in Belize on her honeymoon. I contacted the local police, and they're sending a couple officers to her hotel to talk to her."

"And Herrick's husband?"

"I feel bad for the guy. He didn't even know his wife had left, and the news really hit him hard. He kept going on about how it was all his fault. I guess he has a bit of a gambling problem, and last week he lost their rent money betting on the Marlins."

"The Marlins?"

"Yeah, I know, right? Guy's obviously not real bright."

Mark closes his eyes. So, Herrick's motive for leaving and ripping off her boss is clear. Her idiot husband bet on the Marlins, a team his softball team could beat this year, leaving Herrick and her baby high and dry.

Torelli left for the same reason most women leave: Frank Torelli is a grade A jerk. Mark's been watching him for almost a year, and the whole time he's wondered how a guy like that has ended up with a wife like Hadley Torelli.

But why team up? It makes no sense, and something about the way the whole thing went down doesn't add up. Torelli showed up first, and Herrick arrived an hour later. Torelli parked in the back and Herrick in the front. Herrick left her kid in the car. Torelli left hers somewhere else.

Maybe Torelli ran into trouble. She couldn't open the safe, so she called Herrick and made a deal. There's no record of any calls between the two, but they could have used burners, which would mean it was planned.

And somewhere along the way, Torelli was hurt. So maybe that's why she called Grace. The plan was for Torelli to bring the money to Grace, but Torelli sprained her ankle and couldn't drive. Perhaps a hostage situation—Herrick holding Torelli's kids hostage?

Okay, so if that's the case, then why stick together? Torelli and her kids were chasing after Herrick in the hospital parking lot, and Herrick looked like she wanted nothing to do with them.

So what's the connection?

Mark pinches the bridge of his nose.

"The note was kind of nice, don't you think?" Fitz says, breaking the silence.

"The note?"

"The note they left for the lady whose car they borrowed. It was kind of nice."

Again Mark clamps his jaw shut. Shelly grins at him from the pool, and he gives her a gritted grin back, along with a thumbs-up. The note was not *nice*. It was infuriating. These two women have turned into an incredible thorn in his side. Not only have they hijacked his case and embarrassed half the agents west of the Grand Canyon, but they actually took the time to tape a very sweet thank-you note to the steering wheel of the old lady's car.

"By the way," Fitz says, "she's pissed."

"Who?"

"The lady who loaned them her car. She's saying we violated her constitutional rights."

"What constitutional right? To be stupid and loan her car to criminals? To aid and abet fugitives?"

"Technically, Hadley and Grace aren't criminals," Fitz says. "They're only wanted for questioning. Which means she actually couldn't have aided and abetted them."

"Hadley and Grace?" Mark snaps, his voice so sharp the swim instructor looks over.

"I mean Herrick and Torelli," Fitz corrects, but Mark can tell he doesn't mean it. Already the kid is rooting for them, confirming once again why he is not cut out for the field. An agent cannot get emotionally involved. Whether a suspect is a thug or a sweet, gray-haired grandmother, the job is black and white—gather evidence and arrest the suspects, regardless of the circumstances, the crimes, or the victims. It's up to the courts to figure out the gray.

"She says she's going to sue," Fitz goes on. "And I've gotta admit: she kind of has a point. She's like ninety, and she made a fair deal. Taking her money feels a little like we're mugging Betty White."

"We aren't mugging anyone. That money is evidence."

"Right, boss."

Mark exhales slowly through his nose and reminds himself this isn't Fitz's fault. He's not the one who screwed up.

"Is the file updated?" he says.

"Yeah, it's all there."

"Okay. Thanks, Fitz. Go home and get some rest. Thanks for staying late."

"Sure, boss."

Mark slides his phone into his pocket, and Shelly flashes a gaping grin, now that he's done with the call, which makes her forget to paddle, and the instructor lunges to catch her a second before she sinks.

Across the pool, on the opposite deck, as far from the action as possible, Ben sits on a bench reading. With a deep breath, Mark walks around the edge to join him.

"Hey, buddy."

Ben ignores him, his eyes fixed on the page in front of him.

"What are you reading?"

Ben lifts the cover for Mark to see. *The Lightning Thief.*

"Didn't we read that one together last year?"

A year ago, before Mark's life was yanked out from under him, he and Ben would read books together, and *The Lightning Thief* was one of their favorites.

Ben gives the slightest nod, his jaw slid out.

"Might help," Mark says, "if you told me why you're so mad."

Ben says nothing, his eyes still fixed on the page.

Since Mark moved out, Ben has refused to talk to him. At first, Mark thought he was just angry in general because of the divorce, but lately, Ben's made it clear that his anger is specifically targeted at Mark. But no matter how many times Mark asks, Ben refuses to tell him what's wrong.

Mark sits beside him a minute longer, feeling like this is an important moment, one of those critical parenting junctures where he is supposed to say or do something profound. But he has no idea what that something might be. Parenting often leaves him feeling this way: like he is floundering in the middle of the ocean with no compass or oars.

Mark's dad was brilliant at it, and he made it look easy. He always knew just what to do and say with Mark and his brother. Of course, his dad and Mark and Mark's brother were all cut from the same cloth, hard boiled and tough, while Ben is a different animal altogether, sensitive and thoughtful, introspective in a way that is difficult for Mark to understand.

With a sigh, Mark pushes to his feet and walks a few feet away to review the updated files, which include the surveillance videos from the McDonald's, the interview with the lady who loaned Torelli and Herrick her car, and the note Torelli and Herrick taped to her steering wheel.

Mark clicks on the note. The first image shows a scan of the outside of the card. It says *Thank you*, with butterflies floating around the words. The second image is of the inside. In loopy cursive it reads:

> *Dear Nancy,*
> *Your car was wonderful. Skipper nicknamed her Pujols (after Albert Pujols who plays for the Angels) because, while she's not fast, she's reliable and gets the job done. Thank you for loaning her to us. Trust and faith are often difficult to find and even more difficult to give. I'm glad our paths crossed however briefly.*
> *Stay kind, stay you.*
> *Best,*
> *Hadley, Skipper, Mattie, Grace, and Miles*

Mark practically groans. Fitz is right, the note is *nice*, and a horrible thought hits him, the idea of what will happen if this story gets out and the media gets hold of it: two women on the run with their kids, eluding the FBI, giving money to old ladies, and leaving thank-you notes with references to beloved baseball players. If the press gets wind of this, the FBI is going to be crucified.

"Dad?"

Mark startles at Ben saying his name.

"Yeah?" he says, trying not to look overly anxious as he sits back down beside him.

Ben's head is still bent over his book, and the book is still open to the same page it was five minutes ago.

"You promised," he says, the words hitching and barely above a whisper.

Mark's mind spins, his thoughts pinging around in his brain, searching for the promise he made and hasn't fulfilled. Mark prides himself on being a man of his word, and he hates himself for breaking a promise, especially to his son.

Perhaps he promised that he and Marcia would never get divorced? He dismisses the idea before it fully forms, knowing he never would have promised that. From the day he married Marcia, he knew there was always the very real possibility it would end.

Maybe he promised he would never leave, and that's what Ben thinks he's done: left him.

"You said," Ben mumbles.

Mark looks at him, desperately trying to decode the riddle. Ben's skin is pink with emotion, his ears heated red, signs of how difficult this is for him.

"You said once we were settled, and when Mom wasn't so stressed."

Mark's thoughts spiral back to two years ago, when they first moved to DC, and a thought tumbles forward through the stressful milieu of that time, his throat closing as he realizes why Ben is upset. Not anger but disappointment—Ben's persistent silence a result of deep disappointment he's kept buried for two months now, and heat creeps into Mark's skin that matches his son's, his rage so fierce it makes him want to lift the bench they're sitting on and smash it against the wall.

That's the thing about divorce, which he tried again and again to explain to Marcia: it's not just about them; it's about the damage it does to the kids, to the unit, to the foundation, and to their future. To goddamn everything.

"The dog," he mumbles to himself out loud. "I promised we would get a dog."

Ben nods, his nose pinched as he holds back his emotions.

They joked about it, how they would go to the shelter and pick the ugliest mutt they could find, one that no one else wanted. Since Ben could talk, he's been asking for a dog. Mark was going to get one for Ben's birthday this year, then again for Christmas. But the timing was wrong both times. Marcia was threatening divorce, making things far too tense to bring a dog into the mix. Ben turned nine, Christmas came and went, and three months later Mark was no longer living at home.

"I know it's not important," Ben says, the words quivering. "It's just . . . you said . . ."

Mark scoots so he is right beside him and wraps his arm around Ben's shoulder. "It is important. Very important. And I should have remembered."

Shelly bounds up to them, dripping wet. "Whassup?" she says in the sassy talk she's been using lately.

Ben straightens and pulls away from Mark so his little sister won't see his tenderness. "Nothing," he mumbles.

Mark takes a towel from the bag Marcia packed and holds it open for Shelly to walk into. As he rubs her down, he tickles her through the terry cloth until she begs for mercy; then he releases her to go to the locker room to change.

Mark turns back to Ben. "I'll look into getting a new place," he says. "One that allows pets."

Ben looks up at him through his brow. "Really?"

Mark has no idea how he's going to afford a place with a yard, but he'll figure it out. Lately, Mark hasn't had a lot to be proud of, but he has always been a man of his word, and that's not going to change. "Really."

Shelly returns, and together they walk toward the exit, Ben walking a little taller, which makes Mark feel a little better himself.

Marcia and Stan the Insurance Man are waiting at the curb when they walk through the door. Mark loads the kids in the back of Stan the Insurance Man's Volvo, and when the car is out of sight, he sits on the bench beside the door and drops his face into his hands, the heels pressed against the sockets of his eyes.

When spots begin to swim, he lifts his face, pulls out his phone, and pulls up the Torelli file. He stares at the small screen and scrolls through the pages until the words blur into black blobs on a field of pulsating white.

He's missing something. He can feel it. There's always something, a loose thread that, when pulled just right, unravels the whole damn mystery.

Leaning back, he closes his eyes, and Shelly's gap-toothed smile fills his mind, making him smile. Then he thinks of the note Torelli and Herrick left and the love he felt in it toward the boy, Skipper. Torelli has raised him since he was born, a special-needs child who isn't her own. It takes a special kind of person to do that. She's certainly not your typical mobster's wife or criminal.

Herrick, on the other hand, is another story. Her record of trouble with the law stretches back to her teenage years.

Mark toggles back to her file and opens it, scrolling through page after page of her rough history.

Reading it boils his blood. The system has failed her on so many levels it makes him want to strangle each and every person who's had a hand in it.

Orphaned at fourteen, she was shuffled from foster home to foster home for the first year, then finally placed with a distant relative who was never properly screened and who turned out to have a drinking problem. He saw Herrick as his ticket to the easy life and kept her out of school so she could work flipping burgers for a paycheck.

When social services discovered what was going on, they moved her to a group home, but group homes don't usually work out too well for cute, nice girls like Herrick, so not surprisingly, she hightailed it out of there the day after she arrived.

A few months later, she was arrested in Savannah during a homeless sweep. They locked her up in juvie, and from what Mark can gather from the records, social services tried to get her out, but Herrick wanted to stay. When they said she couldn't, she did small things to extend her sentence—stole things from the commissary, scratched her name in the warden's door. She probably figured it was safer than another group home or the streets, and she was probably right. When she turned sixteen, she took the GED and then, for the next two years, took vocational classes and online courses. She even got an online associate's degree in accounting.

He looks at the photos of her through the years. The fresh-faced freckled teenager with the bold glint in her eye evolved into a tough young woman with a poker-faced fierceness glaring defiantly into the lens for the mug shot that was taken of her three months after she left juvie. She had been arrested for a crime she never should have been arrested for: trying to help another homeless girl, who, through no fault of Herrick's, ended up dead.

He thinks of Shelly. He thinks of Ben. He thinks of his own mom and dad and the home he grew up in with his brother. It must be very lonely becoming an orphan at fourteen, to lose your family before you've had time to create a new one to replace it.

Herrick spent six months behind bars before a merciful judge commuted her sentence to time served; then she moved to California and has been flying straight since. A husband, a baby, a job—the American dream. Then her husband screws it up. He gambles away their rent money, and Herrick takes the baby, rips off her boss, and goes on the lam.

With Torelli?

Again, this is the part he trips over every time, the part that doesn't make sense. By all accounts, Herrick is a lone wolf. Everything in her record points to her being independent to a fault. Her juvenile-hall counselor repeatedly wrote that Herrick's biggest obstacle was her trust issues. She didn't like to ask for help or to rely on anyone.

Mark toggles back to Torelli's file. Compared to Herrick's, the file is remarkably thin. Thirty-eight, she was born and raised in Los Angeles.

Skipper's mother, Vanessa Valla, is her only sibling, a half sister from her father's second marriage.

Her mother died when Torelli was in college. Her father passed ten years ago. The only blemish on her perfect record is a traffic ticket she got a dozen years ago for rolling through a stop sign.

Torelli's not a criminal, which means Herrick is the key. The question is whether Herrick knew the money was dirty and if she knew the feds were watching it. Interfering with a federal investigation and tampering with evidence are federal offenses, and with her prior record, that could put her away for a very long time.

It doesn't feel right. Herrick's not stupid, and she's been living on the right side of the law for more than seven years. It's hard to imagine her jeopardizing the life she's built.

He thinks of the baby and what he would do to protect his own kids, how far he might go to provide for them if things became desperate. She must not have realized the feds were watching, believed she was only stealing from her boss, dirty money he couldn't report stolen—the perfect crime, so long as he never found her.

So why involve the wife? Maybe Herrick didn't know where the safe was, or she didn't have the combination?

Mark shuts down the window and starts again, reopening the case file from the beginning. *Two moms. Three kids. What's the connection? What am I missing?*

According to the nurse in the emergency room, Torelli was on her way to drop Skipper off with her sister, who had gotten married. The story jibes with what he already knows. The elementary school confirmed that Torelli had taken the boy out of school because he was returning to Wichita to live with his mom, and a credit card search showed that hotel rooms had been reserved at Hiltons in Victorville, Lake Havasu, and Albuquerque, all three cities en route to Wichita.

Mark looks at the notes he has on the sister. Vanessa Valla, twenty-six; lives in Wichita, Kansas; occupation, server.

So, Torelli packs up her nephew and her daughter under the pretense of dropping her nephew off and returning nine days later, but instead, she rips off her husband with her husband's office assistant, and the two set off together. They drive to Barstow, which makes sense, but then disappear, not taking the 40, which is the only route to Kansas. So where did they go?

He looks away from the screen, stretches his arms over his head, and rolls out his neck.

The sister. Something niggles at him. He toggles the screen back to life and clicks on the sister's file. She's ordinary to the point of boring. Other than Vanessa's getting pregnant when she was seventeen, her life has been completely unremarkable.

He scans the itinerary for her honeymoon. She and her husband are spending three weeks in Belize. On Wednesday they fly home.

A smile creeps onto his face, and if he were a fist-pumping kind of guy, he would be punching the air. Instead he gives himself an invisible pat on the back and zooms in on the three glowing letters he hadn't noticed before.

OMA.

The thread he's missed until now. The pull in the fabric and possibly the key to unraveling the whole damn mystery.

The sister lives in Wichita, and that's where she and her husband flew out of for their honeymoon, but on Tuesday, they will be returning to Omaha, the city where her husband lives.

Torelli has led everyone on a wild-goose chase, leading them to believe she is going to Wichita, when the entire time her plan has been to go to Omaha.

So who is she trying to fool? Frank? The FBI? And how does Herrick factor in?

He pulls up Google Maps, punches in the new destination, then hits redial. "Fitz, I need you back at the office. Call off the roadblock and get me on the next plane to Las Vegas."

23

HADLEY

Hadley's ankle is killing her, and she is bored and irritated—the drive so far a tedious, torturous journey of worry and pain.

They've been driving for three hours, and Grace hasn't spoken a word other than to ask Hadley where she preferred to eat, McDonald's or Jack in the Box, to which Hadley replied neither, to which Grace rolled her eyes and chose McDonald's, then proceeded to inhale thousands of calories in a matter of minutes as Hadley picked at an undressed wilted salad and cursed her mother's wide-assed genes.

The lack of conversation is deafening. They are in a small confined space; the least Grace could do is make polite conversation to help pass the time. But anytime Hadley starts something, Grace answers with a monosyllabic response and a glare that makes it clear she has no interest in chatting.

She's probably upset she's involved in this, and Hadley does feel bad, but what was she supposed to do? The FBI was chasing her. How was she supposed to know they would follow them to Barstow? She figured that once they were out of Orange County, they would be fine.

She glances back at Mattie and Skipper. Skipper stares out the window. Mattie has her eyes closed but opens them when she feels Hadley looking at her. Hadley gives her a reassuring smile, and Mattie offers a thin one back.

Then she shocks her. "That was cool the way you talked that lady into giving us her car. I didn't think it would work."

"You didn't?" Hadley says as a strange ballooning fills her chest, and it takes a second for her to recognize the feeling. It's been a long time since she's had anything to be proud of.

Grace chimes in, "How'd you know to wait for someone old?"

Hadley's pride grows. Grace doesn't seem easily impressed. "I don't know. I've always liked old people. They're less uptight about things, so I figured my chances were better."

Grace nods her approval, and a small smile curls her lips. "I think you're right. My grandmother would have loved to have been given ten grand to loan her car to someone. She'd have talked about it for years."

"Were you close with your grandmother?" Hadley asks.

"We'll stop in Baker," Grace says curtly, the smile dropping from her face to settle into a tight line. "Less chance of us being spotted there than in Las Vegas."

Hadley tries not to be hurt by the abruptness.

"Make sure you call Dad," Mattie says.

Hadley glances back at her.

"He'll get suspicious if you don't call him."

Hadley nods and turns back in her seat, disturbed that Mattie has been thinking about Frank. Mattie is right to worry, but Frank is her dad, and Hadley can't help but wonder about the damage it might be doing for her to be conspiring against him.

"Do I need to pull over?" Grace says.

"No. I called him this morning from the hotel, and I'll call him when we stop for dinner. He knows I turn my phone off when I'm driving."

"What will you tell him about your phone?"

"I'll tell him I dropped it in the toilet. I've done it before."

"You can use my burner," Grace says, "so he can't trace the area code."

"Your burner?"

"I bought one when we stopped at Walmart."

"Oh," Hadley says as her heart sinks, realizing she should have thought of that, and also realizing that, had Grace not said something, she would have made the catastrophic mistake of calling Frank without thinking about the area code.

"Thank you," she says, meaning it to only be for the offer of the phone, but it comes out thicker than that.

Grace gives a curt nod, but Hadley watches as her jaw twitches, then sees her slide it out to still it.

"So, where are you from originally?" Hadley says. "Do I detect the hint of a southern drawl?"

Grace sighs through her nose. "Look, Mrs. Torelli, we're in this together because I said I would help you, and I am, but we're not friends. This doesn't make us friends."

Hadley tries not to be stung, but it's hard. She's always hated when people don't like her, and she likes Grace. Last night, when they were counting the money, she actually thought they kind of were friends, or at least friendly.

She turns toward the window and looks out at the same beige scenery they've been driving through for hours—beige desert, beige scrub, beige hills in the distance.

"Can you stop that?"

Hadley looks at Grace, then down at her leg, which is jiggling up and down in rhythm with her hand, tapping impatiently on her thigh.

She forces her leg to be still and slides her hand beneath her thigh to stop its twitch, and she decides it's a good thing she and Grace are not friends because, if they were friends, Hadley would have something very unfriendly to say at the moment.

She turns back to the window with a huff, then quickly straightens. She can't really blame Grace for being pissed, especially after what happened in Barstow. The cops arrived minutes after they'd left Nancy's car at the McDonald's. They could see the police cars from across the street, dozens of them with their lights swirling. She thought Grace might have ditched them right there, but she didn't. Instead, she growled, "Get in," and they all scrambled into the van Grace had bought from Craigslist when they were still in Orange County.

At the time, when Grace insisted that they stop at the Walmart so she could buy a car online, Hadley thought she was being ridiculous. Hadley suggested they go to a car lot when they got to Barstow so they could pick the car they wanted.

It turns out Grace was being cautiously brilliant. She wired the money to the seller from the store and instructed him to leave the van at the Motel 6 across from the McDonald's, with the key hidden behind the bumper. It was like she suspected that what happened in Barstow might happen, and again, Hadley can't help but wonder how it is she's so good at this.

"Stop."

Hadley's head snaps sideways; then she looks back down at her leg and realizes it's bouncing again. She folds it beneath her to quell its jitter.

They were on their way before the police were out of their cars, and there's been no sign of trouble since. She wishes Grace would just relax. They're safe. They made it.

She feels her leg wanting to bounce.

24

GRACE

Grace pulls the van beside the office of the Wills Fargo Motel in Baker and kills the engine. She leaves the others in the car and is relieved when the kid behind the counter accepts her cash for two rooms without any questions.

She returns to the van and parks it out of sight; then all of them walk toward the strip of restaurants they saw on the way in. The choices are limited—Dairy Queen, Pizza Hut, or Denny's. They settle on Denny's because it's closest.

They wait at the front for the hostess, who also appears to be the waitress and the manager. The sign on the register reads **NO CHECKS**, and Grace watches Mattie looking at it, her brow creased, and she wonders what she finds so interesting.

"This way," the hostess/waitress/manager says.

Mrs. Torelli leads with the boy, and Grace follows, holding Miles tight against her and breathing him in. He has been amazing through all this. Four hours in the car and not a peep. She's so thankful she feels it all the way to her toes. She's not sure she could have handled any more stress.

She's realized she's made a horrible mistake. Whatever Frank is into is bigger than skimming cash and not reporting it to the IRS. Her heart hasn't stopped hammering since they left Barstow. A battalion of cop cars raced into the McDonald's moments after they left the old lady's car there. They don't send that much firepower for fudging on your taxes.

She should have ditched Mrs. Torelli at the hospital or even in Barstow, jumped in the van with Miles, and taken off. Whatever this is, she wants no part of it. She has Miles to think about. She nuzzles the soft folds of his skin, unable to believe the danger she's put him in.

In the morning, she and Miles are leaving. She got Mrs. Torelli out of Orange County like she promised, and from here on out, they are on their own. With a little luck, the FBI will forget about Grace altogether.

She glances over her shoulder and realizes Mattie is not with them. She stands at the hostess desk, an amused smile on her face as she places a pen back in the penholder.

~

Dinner is quiet. Several times Mrs. Torelli attempts to start a conversation, but Grace refuses to engage. This relationship is over, and Grace sees no reason to make it more difficult than it already is.

As they shuffle toward the door, Grace glances at the hostess desk, and despite herself, she smiles. The **NO CHECKS** sign has been altered, and now, beneath the original message, in parentheses, it reads, *Czechs welcome.*

Grace looks at Mattie, and color rises in the girl's cheeks, though her expression remains poker straight. Grace gives her a small nod, then turns away. She likes the kid; she really does. She's funny and has a rebellious streak Grace can relate to.

When they get to the motel, Grace changes Miles into his pajamas, then gets changed herself, shoving the disgusting clothes she's been wearing for two days in the trash.

At the Walmart, where they stopped so she could buy the van, she restocked Miles's supplies and bought a few supplies for herself, including jeans, sweats, a couple of T-shirts, and a new pair of shoes.

She smiles at the broken sole with its dried superglue gaping at her from the trash can. *A million bucks.* She will never have to superglue her soles again.

She carries Miles outside, to find Mrs. Torelli lounging beside the motel's sorry excuse for a pool, a hole of water ten feet long and eight feet wide. Mattie and the boy wade hip deep, talking about baseball, a topic that seems to be high on the Torellis' conversation list.

The desert air still holds a remnant of the day's warmth, though soon it will be cold.

Mrs. Torelli holds her arms out for Miles, so Grace hands him over and sets down the diaper bag, which holds Miles's baby supplies along with the money.

"You okay?" Mrs. Torelli says.

"Still kind of hungry," Grace says. "Do you mind watching him a minute? I'm going to check out the vending machine."

"You just ate."

Shrug.

Mrs. Torelli rolls her eyes like there's something wrong with Grace, but hungry is hungry, and Grace has always had a healthy appetite.

She walks to the vending machine and stares at the selection. None of it sounds very good. As a matter of fact, now that she's in front of it, staring at the bags of chips and cookies, her stomach roils and she feels a little sick.

"You okay?"

Grace looks up to see the motel clerk looking at her with concern, and she realizes she's been staring at the machine for a while.

The kid is probably a few years younger than she is, acne peeking beneath a half-grown beard that only sprouts in earnest on his chin and lip. He reminds her of Shaggy from *Scooby-Doo*, or maybe of Scooby-Doo himself.

"Do you have anything stronger than soda?" she says, realizing what it is she's really craving.

His smile screws up at an angle. "Follow me."

They walk past Mrs. Torelli, who holds Miles in the crook of her arm. She's looking down at him, making little pucker noises as he sucks happily on his bottle. The woman is like a baby whisperer, a serious miracle worker. If Grace were the one holding him, he would be screaming his head off, the bottle being swatted away as he shrieked.

She's read about certain people having a gift when it comes to soothing away colic. Some experts hypothesize it has to do with a particular scent; others say it's acoustic, a particular tone of voice. Whatever the case, Mrs. Torelli has it in spades. Grace has never seen Miles so happy.

Mattie and the boy are now out of the pool, wrapped in towels and playing with the handheld electronic devices they seem obsessed with.

She follows the clerk into the office, then behind the counter and through a door that leads to a small room with a desk, a bed, and a chair. He gestures to the chair, then opens the bottom desk drawer to pull out a bottle of Johnnie Walker Red and two Dixie cups. He pours them each a shot and holds hers out to her.

"What were you in for?" Grace says with a nod toward the crude tattoo on his forearm of an *X* with a line through it.

"Stupidity."

Grace smiles. "Me too."

"You were in prison?" he says.

"Didn't quite make it. Six months in jail, and the judge commuted my sentence."

"Lucky."

Shrug. At the time it didn't feel lucky. At the time it felt like Grace's life had ended.

They raise their Dixie cups to each other and knock back their drinks. The whiskey burns as it goes down, and she coughs. It's been a long time since she's indulged in anything stronger than beer, and even scrounging together enough money for that has been difficult.

He lifts the bottle, offering another, and she nods. He refills her cup, and this time she nurses it, sipping it slowly.

"Rough day?" he says.

"You could say that."

"Hunter."

"Grace."

The alcohol takes effect quickly, swirling warmly through her body before seeping into her bloodstream and wrapping softly around her brain.

Hunter pours himself another as well but just holds it, staring at the liquid as he swishes it around. He barely looks old enough to drink, and Grace wonders what he could have done to land him behind bars so young. He doesn't look like the dangerous type. Probably drugs. That's what most young people are in for. His tattoo is a popular one among inmates. It means strength, something you need a lot of when you're counting your days to freedom.

"Got caught stealing a car for a girl," he says, reading her thoughts.

"You were going to give your girl a stolen car?"

He shakes his head. "No. I stole a car so I could go see her."

"Wow, that is stupid."

He toasts her with his Dixie cup. "You?"

She gives him the abbreviated version. "I broke into a church." She leaves out the part about her best friend being with her and about it being the coldest winter Georgia had ever seen and that Virginia was sick.

"Really needed to pray?" Hunter says with a cockeyed grin.

"Really needed to get out of the cold."

She sees a small shudder run through him and knows he's spent some nights in the cold himself.

"No big deal," she says. "I went in. I got out. And now, here I am, living the dream."

None of it is that simple, but he raises his cup to toast her anyway. "To second chances."

"To second chances." They both shoot back what remains in their cups, then for a long moment sit quiet. That's the nice thing about ex-felons; they know how to be still.

Grace rarely thinks about Virginia, that distant night like a dark hole that sucks the light from the present each time she remembers it. They say she fought the police when they tried to take Virginia away. She doesn't remember that part, but it was included in the charges: breaking and entering; destruction of property; negligent homicide; resisting arrest; assaulting an officer.

She blinks away the memory and looks around the small room. The space is worn but not unpleasant. In the corner is a guitar, and on the bureau, a harmonica. She imagines Hunter whiling away his nights playing wistful romantic melodies for the girl he stole the car for.

"So, what happened to the girl?" she says as she sets the cup down and stretches her arms over her head.

Hunter's eyes drop to the carpet, a tell of how much he cared for her. "Moved on. A guy serving time without a dime to his name wasn't exactly the winning combination she was looking for. Plus, while I was inside, I lost a couple teeth." He pulls back his lip to reveal a hole on the left side in the bottom row, explaining perhaps why he always grins to the right. "Went from ugly to real ugly real fast." He half grins, concealing the gap.

Grace actually doesn't find him ugly at all: a bit mangy with his untrimmed hair and scruffy half beard, but his eyes are a warm bronze, and he has an easygoing way about him that is very attractive, and again she is reminded of Jimmy.

"You okay?"

She shakes the thought away and says, "You should get those fixed."

"Yeah, I'm working on it. Should have enough saved for implants by the time the rest of my teeth start falling out from old age."

His sideways grin breaks her heart. She really likes him. He's got what her grandmother called moxie. After all, he stole a car so he could see his girl. There's something incredibly romantic about that.

"What time are you off?" she asks, an idea forming.

"Eight."

"Perfect. Then I have a proposition for you."

His left eyebrow lifts in curiosity as he squints with distrust through his right.

"I need to cut out of here with my baby but without the others." She stops, waits for his reaction, and, when he gives none, continues. "The lady I'm with can't drive on account of her ankle, so I'm thinking you might be able to give them a lift. I'll pay you."

"Where would I need to drive them?"

"I'll leave that up to her."

Reaching into her pocket, she peels off five one-hundred-dollar bills from the roll she placed there this morning and holds them toward him. "The beginning of your new-tooth fund."

He gives her another lopsided grin as he takes the money, and as Grace makes her way back to the pool, she wonders how things might have turned out had Hunter not been caught, if he had gotten away with his joyride to see his girl, if his life might have turned out happily ever after, or whether guys like him and girls like her are destined for lives that simply don't work out.

"Where have you been?" Mrs. Torelli says as Grace plops into the seat beside her.

Miles is now on Mrs. Torelli's lap. He is bundled in his jacket, and she is clapping his hands in front of him, a game he seems to enjoy, and Grace wonders why she's never thought of doing that.

Mattie has disappeared, and the boy is back in the pool. He stands on the step in his boxers and a sweatshirt, his face tilted up at the stars and his hands raised above his head as if trying to catch them or lift them.

"He's special," Grace says.

"What's that supposed to mean?" Mrs. Torelli snaps, and Grace realizes she's taken the comment the wrong way.

"I didn't mean it like that. I mean he sees things in his own way. Jeez, you're prickly."

"Me? That's hilarious coming from you, Miss Warm and Fuzzy."

"What did I do?"

"Nothing," Mrs. Torelli huffs, still clapping Miles's hands together but with so much force Miles is no longer smiling.

Grace blows out her breath and shakes her head, unsure what she's done to piss the woman off other than to save her butt yesterday, this morning, and then again this afternoon.

Hunter walks from the office and into the courtyard to take down the umbrellas. One by one, he carries them to the shed beside the parking lot.

"Do you have a pen?" Grace asks.

"Front pocket of the diaper bag. Why?"

Grace ignores her. From the now very organized diaper bag—even the burp rags are folded, making Grace wonder if Mrs. Torelli suffers from OCD—Grace takes out the pen and one of the bundles of hundreds.

She hesitates, her eyes catching on the gun, whose muzzle is sticking out between the diapers. She pulls Mrs. Torelli's backpack closer and moves the gun from the diaper bag into the front pouch of the backpack.

"What are you doing?" Mrs. Torelli says.

"I don't like guns."

"Well, neither do I."

"Yeah, well, if you get caught with a gun in your husband's name, it's no big deal. If I get caught with it, it is. Did you call him?"

"Yeah. He's fine. He has no idea the money's gone. He played golf all day."

Grace nods. It makes sense. The office is closed until Tuesday, and there's no reason for him to go in. The FBI hasn't arrested him, which probably means they can't without the money.

She angles herself away from Mrs. Torelli.

"What are you doing?" Mrs. Torelli says again, bending to try to see.

Grace shifts to further block her view.

"And you're the one calling me prickly," she says with a harrumph.

"You are prickly, and this is none of your business."

25

HADLEY

Hadley watches as Grace sneaks quiet as a burglar into the motel office with the bundle of cash. She disappears into the back room, then returns a moment later, the bundle gone.

She doesn't get this girl; she really doesn't. At McDonald's, Grace ordered two Extra Value Meals instead of three combos to save money, and now she's giving ten grand to a motel clerk who looks like a drugged-out felon.

Grace returns to her chair.

"Why'd you do that?"

Shrug.

"That's ten thousand dollars."

Nod.

"That's a lot of money."

"Not really. Not for a second chance."

That's all she says, as if that explains it.

Hadley stands the baby on her lap so he can try out his legs. He pushes against her with determination, and she smiles at his strong little will. *A lot like his mom,* she thinks with a glance at Grace.

She wants to ask Grace who gave her a second chance and why she needed it, but Grace has turned away, her gaze on the pool, making it clear, once again, she doesn't want to talk. But then, a minute later, she surprises Hadley by saying, "Why did that woman we borrowed the car from say, 'I hope you get there in time'?"

Hadley smiles. "I told her your husband's unit was passing through Barstow and that he had never met his son. We were supposed to take your car, but the transmission blew, and we couldn't rent one because your credit is bad and I don't have a license."

"You told her all that?"

"I had to tell her something."

Grace nods, and again Hadley feels proud. It was pretty quick thinking, considering she'd needed to make it up on the spot.

"So, you're heading to see family?" Hadley says.

"No family," Grace says flatly. "Just him." She thumbs her hand at the baby.

"What about your parents?"

"I never knew my dad, and my mom died when I was two."

"Oh," Hadley says, feeling bad for her. Hadley knows what it's like to be alone. She's lost both her parents, but at least she had them until she was an adult.

"Who raised you?"

"I'm going to bed," Grace says, standing and holding out her arms for the baby.

"What about your husband?" Hadley says.

Grace practically wrenches the baby away as she says, "No longer in the picture." There's hurt behind the words, and Hadley bristles with anger at the man who caused it. She doesn't know Grace well, but she knows her well enough to know she deserves a good man.

Grace stops at the edge of the pool. "What were you doing?" she says to Skipper, who's now sitting on the steps making circles in the water with his fingers. "Earlier, when you were holding your hands up to the sky?" Grace holds the arm that isn't holding the baby above her, the palm stretched toward the stars in imitation.

Skipper lifts his face to look at her, the moon reflecting off his skin and making it glow. "Reaching out to my friends," he says. "Coach says, no matter where we are, we all sleep under the same stars, so I figure if I reach out and they reach out, it's almost like we're touching."

"Hmmm?" Grace says thoughtfully; then she tilts her face upward and closes her eyes, and Hadley wonders who she is thinking of.

"Who's Coach?" Grace says when she stops.

"Frank Torelli," Skipper says. "He's not my dad, but he's always kind of been my dad anyway."

Hadley startles, the words piercing her heart as she is reminded of what she has left behind and that not all of it was bad.

26

MARK

Mark's plane lands at two thirty in the morning. He considers driving to the field office, but driving there will take time he's concerned he doesn't have. These women have slipped past them twice, and he doesn't intend for it to happen again.

Fitz called a few minutes ago with good news. The group was spotted at a restaurant in Baker, California, a blip on the map a couple of hours outside Las Vegas.

Fitz might not be cut out to be a field agent, but he's a hell of a deskman, and when this thing is over, Mark is going to recommend him for a promotion. While Mark was in the air, the kid called every hotel and restaurant from Barstow to Las Vegas, astutely deducing that, with kids in tow, the group would have to stop. And he was right. The manager at the Denny's in Baker served the group dinner; then she delivered pay dirt when she told him that, after they'd finished, she'd seen them walk to the motel down the street.

This case might be salvageable yet. The money's been gone just over a day, and the chain of possession is still intact and should hold up in court. It was a good decision to fly out here. No more mistakes. Bring the women in, recover the money, get sworn affidavits from them that the money was taken from the Aztec Parking offices, find out whether they're involved in any way, and case closed.

As he pulls from the rental car lot, he calls the Las Vegas field office and requests backup. By the time a team is assembled and mobilized, they should be about an hour behind.

He checks his watch. That shouldn't be a problem. The women are probably asleep. He'll keep an eye on things until the team arrives, and then they'll wrap this up. He should be on a plane and headed back to DC by tomorrow afternoon.

He presses the accelerator, feeling a rush in his veins. These days Mark's position makes him mostly a strategist—an academic who approaches investigations from behind a desk, almost as if solving a puzzle, figuring out the most efficient strategy for extracting justice, then organizing a task force to carry out his game plan. But before he took this job and moved to DC, he'd been a field agent, and he'd been good at it. And there are times when he misses it, his pulse ticking one notch faster as he closes in on his prey.

If they try to make a break for it, he'll take them in himself. He feels himself almost wishing for it, already hearing the congratulations and feeling the pats on his back as he marches them into the field office. Of course he'll act like it's no big deal, like he does this sort of thing all the time.

He could use a morale boost. It's been a rough couple of months. He thinks of the dog he's promised Ben. Maybe he'll even get a promotion out of this, with enough of a raise to afford a house of his own, one with a yard.

He opens the window to let in the cool desert air, the night full of promise and the exhilarating rush of things about to change.

27

HADLEY

Hadley stands in the shadows at the edge of the motel, her arms wrapped around herself to ward off the chill. The smoke of her cigarette drifts into the predawn light, and she watches as it spirals away.

She couldn't sleep, worry and guilt plaguing her thoughts. She's concerned about herself and Mattie, but mostly it's Grace that had her tossing and turning and unable to close her eyes. Finally, she gave up and came out here to sneak a smoke.

Who helps someone they barely know? Risks her future for no reason other than out of the goodness of her heart? Hadley thinks of all the people she knows, wondering who else would do that, and the only person she comes up with is her friend Melissa. Melissa is good like that, but she's the only one.

Knowing Grace has no one makes her feel that much worse for the danger she's put her in. She is all Miles has, and none of this has anything to do with them. Hadley never should have asked for her help.

She blows out an angry stream of smoke. Hell, she shouldn't have taken the money in the first place. This is what she gets for trying to take control of her life: a great big kick in the teeth.

Tomorrow she's going to straighten things out. Grace and Miles need to take the van and go, get as far as possible from Hadley and whatever or whoever is chasing her. Hadley will figure her own way out of this mess, or maybe she won't. Either way, she's not going to put Grace in any more danger. Enough is enough. This whole thing has gotten way out of control.

She wonders if she should turn herself in, throw herself on the mercy of the FBI, and if there's a chance they'll put her and Mattie in witness protection if she testifies against Frank. The problem is she doesn't know anything. She didn't even know the money they took was dirty or, truthfully, what that even means. Each time she thinks of the words *dirty money*, it makes her want to take out a scrub brush and go to work washing off the bundles of cash.

She grinds her cigarette into the dirt with her crutch, then lifts her face and sees a car approaching from the direction of the Denny's. She's been out here an hour, and it's the first car she's seen.

She glances at her watch: 4:26. The car drives slowly, its tires barely moving, and she thinks it must be a weary traveler looking for a place to stay. But then, a few hundred yards from the driveway, the headlights go out, and she watches as the car glides silently to a stop in front of the motel's office. Hadley's skin prickles as a man steps from the driver's seat. He is dressed in slacks and a sport coat, his tie loose at the neck, and he doesn't look weary in the least. Medium height and broad like a bull, he walks boldly through the door, like a man used to being in charge and who is on a mission.

Through the glowing window, she watches as he rings the bell on the desk. A second later, the kid who manages the motel walks from the back, rubbing his eyes. The man pulls something from his front pants pocket and holds it out for the kid to inspect, and the kid's shoulders sag as he nods.

Hadley glances sideways at the door to her room, then beyond it to Grace's. There's no way to get to either without being noticed.

Heart pounding, she looks down at the backpack at her feet.

The man returns to his car and pulls it beside the pool so he's in the shadows but directly in front of their rooms. Then he rolls down his window, reclines his seat, and stares. Waiting.

28

GRACE

Grace slept like a rock. Despite her stress, her exhaustion was so complete her eyes closed before her head hit the pillow. Miles woke once for a bottle, then, mercifully, went back to sleep, and so did she.

She rubs the sleep from her eyes and considers again leaving a note for Mrs. Torelli and again decides against it. There really isn't anything to say, and she doesn't need to leave behind any more evidence that might incriminate her. The FBI is after Mrs. Torelli, not her, and hopefully, it stays that way.

She glances at the clock and is surprised to see it says 4:32. She set the alarm for 5:00. A second later, she realizes the ringing that woke her isn't coming from the clock but rather from the phone beside it. She snatches the receiver.

"Grace?"

"Hunter?"

"An FBI dude showed up a few minutes ago," he hisses. "He's out front, in his car. He's alone, but I think he's waiting for others."

Instant panic freezes her, like she's fallen through the ice and is suddenly drowning in frigid water. She looks at Miles on the bed, his arms flung over his head, and her regret chokes her.

"Thanks," she manages before hanging up, knowing the risk Hunter took in calling.

She creeps to the window, careful to stay out of view, and peeks through the slit in the curtains, blinking once before charging for the door.

"Mrs. Torelli, what are you doing?" she says, stopping short of the parking lot, her hands raised as if the gun Mrs. Torelli is holding is aimed at her. Which it's not. The gun is pointed through the driver's side window of a small black car, a car she assumes has a federal agent in it.

"Grace, go!" Hadley screams, the gun wobbling dangerously with her frantic words. "You and Miles. Go. You need to get out of here."

"Okay, Mrs. Torelli. It's okay."

"It's not!" Mrs. Torelli screeches. "None of this is okay. You shouldn't be here. None of this has anything to do with you. You have to go."

Mrs. Torelli is twenty feet away, but Grace can see the tears and mucus running down her face, drips of wetness streaking her cheeks.

Grace takes a tentative step toward her as a man's voice from inside the car says, "Mrs. Torelli—"

"Shut up!"

Grace freezes.

In as calm a voice as Grace can manage, the words sounding like they're coming from outside her body, she says, "What do you say we put him in the trunk while we figure this out?" It's the only idea she can think of, panic running through her as she watches Mrs. Torelli's body convulsing and the gun hiccuping with it.

Mrs. Torelli doesn't exactly nod, but her head twitches around her eyes, and Grace takes that as consent. Slowly, hands still up, she moves toward the car.

Pebbles dig into her bare feet, and her sweats ride low on her hips, in danger of falling down because the tie has come loose, but her focus is entirely on not making any sudden movements that might get the man shot.

Through the window, she can just make out his silhouette, a burly shadow sitting like a statue. When she reaches the passenger door, she says, "I'm going to reach in and grab his keys."

Mrs. Torelli gives another twitch of her head, and Grace creaks open the door.

The man keeps his face turned, his eyes on Mrs. Torelli. His hair is light, and Grace can tell by the lines around his neck that he is not young. She would guess middle aged. Which is good. It means he is not a rookie and has been around long enough to know what's what.

Her heart beats out of her chest as she crawls inside. He tenses, and she freezes, willing him not to be stupid and get himself shot, and he must draw the same conclusion, because a second later he relaxes. She reaches across the seat and pulls the gun from the holster clipped to his belt, then pulls the keys from the ignition and backs out slowly.

After checking the safety on the gun, she clicks it off, then moves to the rear of the car and opens the trunk.

A door behind her opens, and she whirls to see Mattie standing in the frame. "Mom?" she says, her eyes surveying the scene and growing wide.

Grace looks back as Mrs. Torelli looks up, and everything else happens in a microsecond: The car door slams open, knocking Mrs. Torelli to the ground. The man is out of the car and lunging for the gun. Grace fires. The bullet strikes a foot in front of the man's hand, and he freezes.

Time stops, and the world closes in on Grace as she stares at the patch of asphalt that's exploded and realizes what she's done. She's just fired a gun at a federal officer, and her life as she knows it is over. Her heart clatters so hard she feels like it's going to shoot from her chest.

The agent straightens slowly, his hands raised.

Mrs. Torelli scrambles to her feet and points the gun at him, her body quaking violently, the gun waving with it.

"It's okay, Hadley," Grace says, working hard to keep the tremor from her voice and using Mrs. Torelli's first name in hopes of calming her. "He's getting in the trunk now. He's not going to hurt you. He's walking toward me."

The agent backs up cautiously, his movements slow and his eyes on Mrs. Torelli, who continues to spasm and shake.

"In," Grace says when he reaches her.

He looks down at her, sizing her up. "In," she says again, sharper this time, amazed how in control she sounds despite her brain being on fire.

With a sigh more of mortification than fear, he climbs into the small car's trunk and folds his thick limbs into a fetal position so he'll fit.

Grace slams the hood shut and nearly crumbles to the ground, her knees buckling beneath her.

Mattie runs toward them. "Mom, are you okay?"

Grace straightens and steps in front of her. "Mattie, get your brother and your things from the room and from the van," Grace says.

Mattie hesitates, her attention still on her mom, who is convulsing with sobs, the gun still held out in front of her, pointing at the spot where the agent was.

"Now," Grace orders.

Mattie runs off, her face white with fear.

"Mrs. Torelli—"

"Hadley," Mrs. Torelli mumbles, her voice huffing through her panic. "My name is Hadley."

"Okay. Hadley," Grace says, stepping toward her carefully and taking the gun from her trembling hand.

She secures the safety and slides it into the waistband of her sweats; then she does the same with the agent's gun, cinching the drawstring tight around them.

"I need you to sit tight. Do you think you can do that?"

Mrs. Torelli's pupils are small as pinpricks, and tears still stream down her face.

"Hadley," Grace says, taking hold of Mrs. Torelli's shoulders and forcing her to look at her. "I need you to stay here and wait for me. I'll only be a few minutes."

A small nod.

"I'm going to grab Miles, and I'll be right back."

Her head reverses direction.

"Mrs. Tor . . . I mean, Hadley, I promise, it will only be a minute."

Her head shakes harder. "No," she says, her bottom lip trembling. "You need to go. You and Miles. It's not fair. You shouldn't be here."

And as Grace walks toward her room, she thinks Mrs. Torelli is right. She needs to take Miles and go.

29

MARK

Mark is in the trunk of his own damn rental car, bumping around like a sack of potatoes, his body crashing into the hood, then slamming down again each time the car hits a bump. He wraps his hands around his head to protect his skull, swearing and cussing at the pain and his stupidity.

Carjacked by a woman on crutches. It might have been better had she shot him. If he survives this, it's going to follow him to his grave.

She sneaked up on him like a burglar from somewhere off to the side and popped up beside him waving a gun in his face before he could even react. She stood on one foot, no crutches, and he realized she must have crawled there.

From where? He has no idea. Not from the motel rooms. They must have been standing watch, taking shifts. These women are a hell of a lot more savvy than he's given them credit for.

"Hands where I can see them," she said, sounding like a bad actress in a poorly scripted movie.

And what choice did he have? She was waving that gun at him, and his gun was in his holster, clipped in tight, safety on.

Get shot? Thinking back on it, it might have been the better option.

Uuuuugh! he screams in his head; then he yelps out loud when his knees slam hard against the front wall of the trunk.

The backup agents were minutes away. They'd called half an hour earlier to confirm their ETA. The agent in charge had sent two cars, each with two agents. Double backup. No one wanted a repeat of what had happened at the hospital or in Barstow. Five agents to pick up two women in a motel in the desert was overkill, or so they thought.

The hotel was dark except for the light on in the office. He was foolishly relaxed, not a care in the world as he watched the rooms.

He keeps his arms clasped tight around his head and tries not to think how mortifying this is, focusing instead on the fact that at least it will be over quickly. The backup agents will arrive, figure out what happened, and set up roadblocks on the 15, the only artery into Las Vegas. A few more minutes of bouncing around and a lifetime of humiliation, and the women will be in custody and it will be over.

They go around a bend, and he's thrown sideways, his damaged shoulder hitting hard against the wheel well. He grunts with the impact as pain radiates to his spine. He curls tighter, bracing for the next blow; then suddenly the car slows, bumps from the asphalt onto dirt or gravel, then drives a few more feet before stopping.

Through the barrier of the seats, he hears the women arguing, a baby crying, and a boy hollering something about not having his uniform.

"He's getting knocked around back there like a set of bowling pins." The voice sounds like Torelli's, husky and deep. "You're going to kill him."

"Yeah, well, what do you suggest?"

"I suggest not killing him."

"Yeah? Well, maybe you should have thought about that before you decided to pull a gun on an FBI agent."

"What was I supposed to do, let him arrest us?"

A door opens, then slams. The baby still cries. The boy still hollers.

"Champ, we'll get you a new uniform. I promise," Torelli says.

"I left it at the pool. We need to go back."

"No, buddy. I'm sorry, but we can't go back."

The baby screams.

"I need my uniform," the boy sobs.

"Mattie, hand me the baby. Champ, we'll get you a new uniform. Mattie, also a bottle and a can of formula."

"I want to go back." A thumping starts, the whole car bucking with the pounding, and Mark imagines the boy kicking the seat.

"Hey, Champ," the girl says. "What do you think about getting a Rockies uniform instead? I think we're driving through Denver."

"No. No. No."

The pounding continues, and the baby cries louder, and Mark grits his teeth against it.

"I need to go back. I left it by the pool—"

"What if we also go to a game?" Torelli says. "Mattie, check if the Rockies are playing at home this week."

A pause. The kicking suspended. The baby no longer wailing.

"Are they?" the boy says, his voice quaking.

"They are," the girl says brightly, making Mark wonder how she's looked it up. Fitz traced all their phones, along with Torelli's iPad and laptop, and they'd all been abandoned when they'd fled the hospital.

"Number forty-four?" the boy asks.

Forty-four, the great Hank Aaron, one of Mark's favorite players of all time.

"We'll try," Torelli says. "Mattie, hand me a burp rag."

Another door opens and closes, this one on the right.

"Should we check out the roster?" the girl says.

"Wolters. I like Wolters," the boy mutters, still sounding distressed.

"That's the catcher?" the girl says, and Mark is impressed she knows this.

"Yeah. He's really good."

Arguing outside the trunk distracts him from the kids' conversation. Muffled voices that sound like Torelli and Herrick bickering, the words too garbled for him to make out.

The trunk opens, and he blinks his eyes to see Herrick standing over him, his Glock in her right hand. "Get out."

He unfurls himself, his muscles creaking and his shoulder pulsing.

"What are you doing?" Torelli says from beside her, the baby slumped over her shoulder, her injured leg held up behind her.

"I said get out," Herrick says. "Unless you'd rather continue riding in the trunk?"

Mark watches a thin smile break on Torelli's face, and he knows that's what they were arguing about: Torelli's worries about him banging around in the trunk.

He climbs out, and wisely Herrick steps back, keeping herself out of range.

He is impressed by her. She doesn't rattle easily, and she knows her way around a gun. That was no lucky shot she took in the parking lot. Her husband is Army Special Forces, sniper division, and it's obvious he's taught her a thing or two about shooting a gun.

She's different from her photos. Though in her pictures she's pretty, she's fairly unremarkable. While in person, Herrick is anything but ordinary. Her hair is a fiery mane of wild rust curls that swirl around hypnotic hazel eyes, her brain ticking rapidly behind them as she figures out her next move.

Meanwhile, Torelli is exactly like her photos—glamorous, like she belongs on a runway in Paris or on a yacht in Greece. Ink-black hair, catlike eyes, and curves designed to make men go to confession.

"Mattie," Herrick says, "I need your help."

The girl steps from the car. She is a strange combination of her mom and dad. Her hair is bleached white blonde but has a wave to it like her father's, and her eyes are the same chocolate brown as his. But her other features are like her mom's, with the same wide lips and slightly upturned nose. Winding up her left ear is some sort of silver piercing.

"Take off your tie," Herrick says to Mark.

He does as she says, his humiliation mounting as he realizes what she intends to do with it.

"Get down on your knees and put your hands behind you."

He frowns, and Torelli frowns with him.

"Do it," Herrick says, lowering the gun to aim at his knee, letting him know exactly where she intends to shoot him if he doesn't comply.

"Grace," Torelli says, "is this really necessary?"

Herrick glares at her. "No, Hadley, this isn't necessary. I'm just doing it because this is how I get my kicks."

Torelli turns away and continues to coddle the baby, swaying back and forth and nuzzling her nose into his neck. Unlike Herrick, who seems to know exactly what she's doing, Torelli is as unlike a criminal as Winnie the Pooh is a grizzly.

His tie in his left hand, he lowers himself to the ground, and it is only then that he notices the direction they're traveling, the car parked behind an abandoned jerky stand with the sun rising behind them. And his stomach sinks, his hopes for a quick ending to all this obliterated. Baker is on the way to Las Vegas and the women's final destination of Omaha, but Herrick has driven the opposite direction, back the way they came.

Goddamn brilliant.

She must have realized east is a bottleneck, while driving west has too many options to set up roadblocks along each one.

"Mattie," Herrick says, "make sure you stay behind him and out of reach. Do you know how to tie a strong knot?"

"I took a sailing class last summer," the girl says.

"Good. Make sure the bind is at the smallest part of his wrists and that there's no space."

The girl steps in a wide circle around him and pulls the tie from his grip.

He considers whirling around to take her hostage, but Herrick has the gun trained on his chest, and while she doesn't strike him as violent, she does strike him as protective, and he feels her worry for the girl, making him unwilling to risk it.

The girl is surprisingly strong, and Mark feels the circulation being cut off as she cinches the tie around his wrists. When she's done, she tugs on it to be sure it's secure.

"Up," Herrick orders.

He struggles but manages to get to his feet.

Herrick looks him up and down, her brain ticking.

"Take off his shoes," she says to the girl.

"Really?" Torelli protests. "Grace, have some decency."

"Mattie, take them off," Herrick orders.

"Why?" Torelli says.

"So he can't run off if he gets the stupid idea in his head." She holds Mark's eyes as she says it, letting him know she knows he's considering it and that it would be, in fact, stupid.

Mark sighs and then, to spare himself further humiliation, slips the shoes off himself.

"Mattie, put them in the trunk, then take his socks off as well."

"His socks?" Torelli says.

"Would you want to walk across hundred-degree desert in your bare feet?"

Mark's insides go cold, wondering if that's what Herrick intends to do—drive him into the middle of the desert and leave him there.

30

HADLEY

Mattie and Skipper share the front seat, and the agent sits in the middle of the back seat between Hadley and the baby. His bare feet are on the hump between the seats, and his hands are tied behind his back, forcing him to bend forward, his chest practically on his knees. It looks very uncomfortable, and Hadley feels bad for him.

Because of his folded position, there was no way to get the seat belt around him, so Hadley left it off. Hadley has always been a stickler about seat belts, and she really hopes they don't get in an accident.

He doesn't look like a bad fellow. He's somewhere in the midst of middle age, perhaps a few years older than she is, and has a wide, open face; sandy, almost cinnamon-colored hair; and light-blue eyes that remind her of Skipper's.

He keeps glancing over, like there's something he wants to say, but then he reconsiders and looks away.

She wants to reassure him it's going to be okay, but since she has no idea whether it's going to be okay or not, she says nothing. All of this is so crazy; she can't get her head around it. Everything's happened so quickly. One minute she was smoking a cigarette; the next she was crawling across the parking lot with a gun in her hand.

Until yesterday, she had never even touched a gun. Now, in a matter of days, she has pointed one at two separate people on two separate occasions.

She considers apologizing, explaining to him why she did what she did, but each time, she glances at Grace and knows it would piss her off, so instead she says nothing, feeling awful for how uncomfortable he must be.

The agent glances over again, concern on his face, and Hadley realizes she is crying, tears streaming down her face. Embarrassed, she wipes them away, then turns so he can't see her.

He scoots forward on the seat so he's leaning over the center console and closer to Grace.

"Grace?" he says.

Grace ignores him.

He scoots forward another inch and tries again. "Grace?"

The car stops so abruptly all of them fly forward. Seat belts hold those who are tethered in, while the agent slams into the console with an oof.

"Grace!" Hadley snaps as she helps him back to his seat.

Grace glares at her in the mirror, then returns her foot to the gas.

The agent doesn't talk again. He sits with his head down and his shoulders hunched, his left folded more than his right.

When they've been driving for almost an hour, Hadley says, "Grace, do you have a plan?"

The sun is up now, and the kids will need to eat soon, and all of them need a restroom.

"I'm looking for a sign," Grace answers absently.

Hadley swallows, not sure what that means: *A sign from God? A sign from the great beyond?* Hadley wonders if maybe Grace has lost it, if stress has pushed her over the edge, so she is now putting their fate in the hands of the Almighty.

"There," Grace says a few minutes later; then she turns sharply from the highway onto a narrow dirt road that shoots straight into the desert.

The sign they pass reads:

CALICO EARLY MAN ARCHAEOLOGICAL SITE:
OPEN TUES.–SAT.
9:00 AM–4:30 PM
PUBLIC WELCOME
←2 MILES

Today is Sunday. The site is closed and won't open again for two days. Hadley looks at the agent, whose face has turned pale.

"Grace, this isn't a good idea," Hadley says.

"You have a better one?"

"Yeah," the agent says. "Turn yourselves in." He turns his shoulder as he says it, in case Grace slams the brakes again, his arm positioned to take the brunt of the impact instead of his chest and face.

Grace doesn't slam on the brakes; instead she says, "Yeah, that's a swell idea. I've been thinking how I could use a vacation. Three squares a day for the next ten to twenty years. Free room and board. Only two small problems with that plan. First, I'm particular about the thread count of my sheets. And second, the itsy-bitsy issue I have with not seeing my kid grow up."

"Look," the agent says, "at this point, you ladies haven't even been charged with a crime. You're only wanted for questioning."

"So," Grace says, as if seriously considering what he's saying, "what happened this morning—the minor incident with the guns, the carjacking, the kidnapping—if we turn ourselves in, all that will be forgotten?"

The agent hesitates, and Hadley looks at him, her heart pounding as she waits for him to reassure them that this morning was, in fact, not a big deal, a misunderstanding that could easily be straightened out if they turn themselves in and explain what happened. After all, Hadley was just reacting to the circumstances. She was scared and worried about Grace.

Mattie cranes her neck to look at her, her brown eyes wide, and Hadley swallows as she turns to Grace, then back to the agent.

Carefully, as if measuring his words, he says, "It's not up to me, but I'm sure a prosecutor will take the circumstances into account—"

The car slams to a stop so violently Hadley could swear the back tires lift off the ground. Hadley's seat belt chokes her, and Mattie and Skipper lurch forward, Mattie's arm flying in front of Skipper to protect him as the agent crashes with incredible force into the console. His chest takes the blow, and it knocks the wind clean out of him.

He wheezes and gasps as Hadley helps him back up. She pats his back, not knowing what else to do, fresh tears escaping and running down her face. Miles squeals and kicks his legs, thinking it is all great fun. The agent glances at him, then drops his face to look at his lap.

They drive the rest of the way in silence, except for Mattie, who whispers almost silently to Skipper that it's going to be all right as he rocks back and forth with his hands over his ears.

Hadley stares out the window at the thin road winding its way through the desert, her mind catching again and again on the words *prosecutor* and *take the circumstances into account*, her brain unable to process what is happening and that she is the one who caused it, that because of what she did, she and Grace are now criminals.

The agent shifts his leg to touch hers, a small comfort but the only one he can offer. It is kind but does little to quell her panic. She wishes she could click her heels three times and reverse time, find herself back in her warm bed at home, with Skipper and Mattie safe in their rooms down the hall. She wishes she had never decided to leave, that she could have a redo or an undo, return to the time before she and Grace ever met. But, she supposes, that is the lesson in life, the one she trips over again and again. There is no going back. One decision leads to the next and then the next, a continual stumbling forward over each past mistake until you find yourself someplace entirely different from where you started or from where you ever intended to go.

The car rolls to a stop. Beside them is a trailer that serves as the ranger station for the archaeological site. Across from it is a hole the size of a basketball court and deep as a two-story building.

Before Grace can open her door, Hadley blurts out, "We can't just leave him here. They don't open again until Tuesday. There's no food or water."

"We're not going to just leave him," Grace says, and Hadley sighs in relief. "You're going to stay with him."

31

MARK

The trailer is oblong, with a door on the short side and two high windows on each of the long sides. It is warm and musty and full of artifacts—maps and photos, rocks and fossils, spearheads and ancient tools, and a yellow human skull, the bottom jaw missing.

Mark sits on the floor, hard gray carpet with a blackened path worn around the displays. A hall opposite the door leads to a restroom, mechanical space, and storage room. His pants are tied by the back belt loops to the ranger's desk through the hole for the computer cables by the ACE bandage that was on Torelli's ankle. And his hands are still bound by his tie but are now in front of him.

Herrick and Torelli fought about where to tie his hands, Torelli arguing it was horribly uncomfortable to sit with your hands behind your back, and Herrick spitting back that she didn't care, that they weren't running a spa, and the reason you tie the hands behind the back is because it makes it more difficult to escape.

Herrick was right, but thankfully, Torelli won. She threatened that, if Herrick tied Mark's hands behind his back, she would release him the moment Herrick left.

The women glared at each other for a full minute before Herrick finally backed down. "Fine," she said, "but I'm taking the guns." Then she muttered, "Not that I'd mind terribly if he broke free and shot you."

They are an odd pair, the two of them, and Mark wonders again how they partnered up. Like twins separated at birth, then reunited, they are like squabbling siblings with nothing in common except a fierce loyalty to each other.

Herrick is scrappy and cunning like an alley cat—wily and defensive with guile and toughness that speak to her rough history. Torelli is the opposite. The woman belongs in the society pages of a magazine, not sitting in a trailer in the middle of the desert hiding from the law.

"Hadley," he says.

She looks up from where she sits at the desk, her leg propped on top of it, her ankle blue and swollen.

"Please, you need to listen to me."

Her face drops to look at her hands in her lap as her head shakes, her black hair swaying with it.

Not wanting to make her cry again, he softens his tone. "This is all a misunderstanding."

Her head switches direction, nodding with his words.

"You're not a criminal."

It returns to swaying, and though she's nearly forty, she looks like a little girl who's been caught doing something she wasn't supposed to, and he finds himself feeling bad for her. She so obviously doesn't belong in this situation. She is a good person whose only real crime was making some bad choices, the worst being marrying Frank Torelli, a two-bit crook.

"Which is why you need to turn yourself in," he says. "Before this gets any worse."

A tear falls from her chin and lands on her lap, and his heart twists as he realizes he's failed. He has a debilitating weakness when it comes to women and children crying. Tears destroy him.

He tries to block it out and soldiers on. "At this point, there's still a case to be made that you didn't know I was an agent. You could've thought I was working for your husband."

Her face snaps up, her expression slick with tears and guilt, the confession that she knew perfectly well who he was written all over it.

He looks away, unable to take her sad green eyes.

After a long minute, she mumbles, "What did he do? Frank?"

"You don't know?"

"I thought he just ran a parking business," she says.

She either is a very good liar or genuinely has no idea what Frank was into. He believes it is the second. He sighs, irritated and angry, frustrated that women so easily put their trust in men, and angry that men like Frank Torelli take advantage of that trust. When Shelly gets older, he is going to set her straight on how a marriage should work—two people who take care of each other and respect each other. He and Marcia might not have had much passion, but they damn well respected each other. He's surprised when he feels a twinge of appreciation for his ex-wife. It's been a long time since he's felt anything but hurt and rage.

"Frank was laundering money," he says. "Along with running an illegal gambling operation and dealing in some small-time trafficking."

"Drugs?" she says.

"Cocaine. Ecstasy."

Her eyes drop again, and her arms fold across her stomach like she has a stomachache.

"The money you took was evidence," he says. "So we were trying to get it back."

A long beat passes as she considers this; then she says, "So, at the hospital, you weren't trying to arrest me?"

"Nope. Just trying to stop you from destroying our case."

"So, if I'd have just talked to you and given you the money, that would've been it? You would've arrested Frank, and I would've been free to go?"

"Assuming you knew nothing about what your husband was doing."

She shakes her head again and cries harder. "I didn't. I hate drugs. Frank knows that. I can't believe he . . ." She hiccups, and her voice gets swallowed by her emotions.

"Okay," he says gently. "I believe you. Then, yes, you would have been free to go."

She squeezes her stomach tighter, rocks back and forth. "But now, because I did what I did, Grace and I are going to go to jail?"

Prison, he thinks, but he doesn't correct her. Kidnapping a federal officer, firing a deadly weapon during the act, hijacking his car—even with extenuating circumstances, these are serious charges that will draw hard time. He thinks of Herrick's baby gumming a smile at him in the car, of the little boy who loves Hank Aaron and was upset over losing his baseball uniform, of the girl who took sailing lessons last year, where she learned how to tie knots, and his guilt stabs him, knowing had he just waited for backup or gone to the field office first, none of this would have happened.

"Hadley," he says.

She shakes her head like she doesn't want to hear any more.

"How well do you know Grace?" he says carefully.

She doesn't answer, but he can tell by how quiet she is that she is listening.

"Did you know she has a record?"

Her head is bent so far forward he can't see her face, but he hears the small catch of her breath. She had no idea about Herrick's past. He feels terrible for what he is doing, but it might be his only shot at turning this around.

"How'd the two of you pair up?" he says.

More rocking and a full beat of silence; then finally she answers, "We didn't. Grace just happened to show up when I was trying to find the money. I didn't know where the safe was, and she did, so I told her I would split the money with her if she showed me."

"She just happened to be there?" Mark says, not buying it for a second. He has never been a big believer in coincidences, and the likelihood of the two of them accidentally showing up at Frank's business at the exact same time is too impossible to be true.

Sensing his doubt, Hadley adds, "She thought the uniform delivery had been shorted, and she wanted to check it."

"On a Friday night?"

"She was a really good employee. And she said the baby had been crying, and driving with him was a way to calm him down."

Torelli's face is entirely earnest, but he still doesn't trust it. "So, you offered her *half*?"

"I had no idea it was going to turn out to be so much."

"How much was it?" he asks, as if he has no idea. By Fitz's estimation, Frank was pulling in somewhere in the neighborhood of a hundred grand a month from his side racket, and the operation, as far as they could tell, had been running for a couple of years. So Fitz figured he had close to two million, give or take.

The slightest hesitation, her eyes flicking up and to the right before settling back on his. "Around nine hundred grand," she says.

He reveals nothing and says in a steady voice, "That's a lot of money."

She nods. Looks back at her hands.

"Weren't you worried Frank would come after you?"

"Of course," she says. "That's why I ran at the hospital. I *did* think those guys worked for Frank."

She looks small and defeated, and he feels terrible for her. In his line of work, he's seen a lot, and unfortunately nothing matches the cruelty of those closest to their victims.

She sniffles, wipes the tears from her face, then hugs her arms around herself as if she is cold, though the trailer is impossibly warm.

She is right to be scared. Mark has watched Frank Torelli for a year. The man is ruthless, erratic, and mean, and there's no way a man like him is going to let his wife waltz away with a million dollars of his money, along with his daughter, and not come after her.

"Which is the other reason," he says, "why you need to let me help you. Frank is dangerous, and you and Grace are in trouble—"

"Stop," she croaks, clearly on the brink of losing it.

So he does. He clamps his mouth shut around the next words he was going to say, unable to take the distress he's causing.

For a long time, they remain silent, his heart heavy and his mind spinning as he tries to figure a way out of this, for him and for them. Finally, he says, "How'd you end up hurt?"

"I tripped over the toilet lid that had been concealing the safe."

"The safe was inside the toilet?"

"The tank."

He nods. He's seen a lot of creative hiding places for safes but never a toilet.

"And Grace knew where it was and had the combination?"

"No. I had the combination."

Does he detect another lie? It's impossible to tell. He thinks it through. Torelli goes to the office to pilfer money for her escape. She searches for it but has no idea where it is. Then, by some wild coincidence, Herrick shows up and just happens to know where the safe is, but without Torelli, she can't open it because she doesn't have the combination.

Not a chance. Coincidences like that just don't happen in real life.

Torelli continues, "I stepped back, and my heel caught on it, and my ankle twisted when I fell."

The bag. The image of Herrick walking into the building flashes in his mind. She walked in carrying a bag, the same bag she carried from the hospital, so bulky it made it awkward for her to walk. Why would she need a bag to check on the uniform order? Herrick was there for the money, so the question is: Does Torelli believe the story she's telling, or is it a lie?

"I couldn't drive," Torelli continues, "so Grace ditched her car and drove me to the hotel where my kids were. We were supposed to split up the next morning, but instead Grace drove me to the hospital, and that's when your guys showed up, and the rest you know."

He nods as if it all makes perfect sense. "Why didn't she leave you at the hospital?"

Torelli shakes her head and lets out a heavy sigh. "I have no idea. She should have. None of this has anything to do with her."

Bullshit, he thinks, and he wonders what Herrick has on Torelli to make her weave this story to protect her.

"Well, it does now," Mark says.

Torelli's head shakes harder. "It doesn't!" she wails. "She was only trying to help us."

"Hadley," he says, his voice firm, "you need to listen to me. If you don't turn yourself in, this is not going to end well. You need to think about your daughter."

Torelli's jaw slides out, and she doesn't answer. Then, after a long time, she says, "What did Grace do? You said she has a record. For what?"

"She made some bad choices when she was young."

"But it's not like she killed someone?"

Mark remains silent, his heart pounding with guilt, hating himself for using Herrick's past against her, but also knowing it might be his only chance of convincing Torelli to turn herself in.

Torelli looks up. "She killed someone?"

Herrick didn't actually kill the girl. She died from pneumonia, and the charge was negligent homicide, but homicide nonetheless. He gives a small nod.

Torelli swallows, then looks back at her hands and shakes her head, either not believing him or choosing not to let the revelation change things.

"Hadley, a good lawyer, and you could walk away from this."

Her hands twist in her lap, and he watches as a shadow of uncertainty crosses her face.

He tries to capitalize on it. "Grace is the one who pulled the trigger. The one who ordered me into the trunk. The one who drove me here."

She looks up, her brow seamed, uncertain what he's saying.

"Hadley, she's the one with the record," he says, keeping his eyes steady on hers.

He watches as slowly his meaning becomes clear, her eyes widening before turning dark and hard as stone, and he realizes his mistake.

"This isn't Grace's fault," she hisses, a growl that reveals a tiger hidden beneath her kitten exterior. "The only reason Grace is here is because of me. She risked everything to help me."

And just like that, the door of possibility slams closed.

Torelli returns to studying her hands, and Mark returns to contemplating his options, feeling infinitely worse for what he has done and wishing he had just waited for backup and that none of this were happening at all.

32

GRACE

They stop at Walmart to buy supplies. Grace loads up on formula and diapers and buys provisions to tide the agent over until Tuesday: water, food, blankets, a pillow, a flashlight, several magazines, and heavy-duty cable ties. The choice to take the agent with them was a risky one. It adds kidnapping to her list of crimes. But it's also given them the best chance for escape. And truthfully, with all the other charges she's facing, adding another felony to the list won't make a difference. If she's caught, she is going away for a very long time, long enough that Miles will be grown by the time she's released, so getting out will no longer matter.

She can't believe she is part of this. The thought sickens her. It's as if her worst nightmare has come true, the past repeating, as if she is destined to be a criminal, no matter what.

As soon as she fired that gun, everything changed. Until that moment, she and Miles had had a shot at a new life. But now, her only chance to raise him is on the run, looking over her shoulder and hoping she never gets caught. So, while she feels bad for the agent, there was no choice. Taking him gave them the smallest advantage. The backup team would show up, and they'd be confused before panic set in. The agent and his car would be gone, and the van would be parked outside her and Hadley's rooms.

Hunter had posted a sign on the lobby door that said, BACK IN AN HOUR, wisely disappearing to avoid getting involved after he'd called to warn her. Which meant that no one witnessed what happened. No one saw her shoot the gun or saw them drive off in the agent's car. With luck, the backup team would assume the plan was still in place, that the agent was taking a break to relieve himself or to grab a bite to eat and that she and Hadley were still asleep in their rooms.

Only after precious time had passed would they realize something was wrong—the agent not returning their calls and the hotel too quiet.

"You okay?" Mattie says beside her.

"Huh? Yeah." She forces a reassuring smile to her face as she tosses a package of socks into the shopping cart. She feels Mattie's stress, and Skipper has been on the brink of losing it all morning.

She leads them to the computer department, where she logs onto the internet and researches hotels that accept cash deposits, along with possible routes into Canada. She doesn't have a passport, but she knows there are other ways to cross the border.

When she's done, Skipper says, "Can I get a uniform now?"

"I can take him," Mattie offers. "They probably have baseball pants and team T-shirts and hats."

"We'll all go," Grace says. She grabs a burner phone from the end-cap, since Hadley's been using hers, then follows them toward the boys' department.

"Is there anything else you need?" she asks Mattie.

"Do you mind if I buy a book?" she answers shyly.

The answer surprises Grace. "Of course not."

They don't have any Colorado Rockies stuff, but they find gray baseball pants, blue socks, a Dodgers T-shirt, and a matching Dodgers hat, which Skipper proudly calls his travel uniform.

In the book department, Grace expects Mattie to choose something from the Young Adult section or from the display featuring the *Game of Thrones* series. Instead she goes to the tiny "Timeless" section and smiles when she spots a book with the image of a frizzy-haired man wearing an ascot on the cover. She tosses it in the cart.

It takes Grace a second to remember why the book looks familiar, and the answer comes to her along with confusion. She can't fathom what a fourteen-year-old, twenty-first-century girl could possibly find entertaining about the story of Candide, a book Grace CliffsNoted in high school in order to pass ninth-grade English.

Mattie smiles again when she puts the book on the conveyor belt, clearly excited.

"Really?" Grace says. "It's that good?" From what Grace can recall, the story is about a depressing series of misadventures in which everyone dies.

"So good," Mattie says, her face lit up. "The main character, this guy Candide, he's hilarious. It's like he doesn't get it. His life totally sucks. It sucks and it sucks and it sucks. Everywhere he goes and everything he does turns out bad, but he just keeps trudging forward with this stupid, ridiculous optimism, convinced that it's all happening for a reason, when really it's just happening because life sucks. It's completely moronic, but you've gotta love him for it. He just totally doesn't get it."

Mattie returns to putting things on the conveyor belt, a smirk on her face, and though Grace has never read a book for pleasure in her life, she thinks she might at some point read that one.

They leave Walmart and go to Peggy Sue's Diner to "load the bases," as Skipper says.

Afterward, her stomach bloated from inhaling a tall stack of pancakes, two eggs, and half a slab of bacon, Grace is so tired she's afraid she might collapse. The temperature is now in the hundreds, and the combination of the heat and their early-morning start is making her woozy.

She decides to take a short rest before they continue on. She parks in the shade and moves Miles to the front to give Mattie and Skipper more room. The air conditioner whirs at full force and makes it almost comfortable. Mattie opens her book. Skipper plays on his computer game.

"First Base?" Skipper says as Grace's eyes grow heavy.

"Huh?"

"Can you help me make a trade on my fantasy team? I want Wolters, and Coach has him."

"Sure. Is he catching on Tuesday?"

"I think so."

On and on they talk about Skipper's fantasy team and the trades he wants to make before the game, and Grace drifts away to the strong wish that somehow they'll make it to the game and that somehow it will all work out.

She and Miles won't be with them. Her plan is to ditch this car for another, then drive them all to Bakersfield. From there, the Torellis will be on their own. She and Miles will head to Canada and then, God willing, find their way to a nonextradition country. She and Virginia talked about it once, hypothetically discussing becoming jewel thieves and where they would escape to with their riches. They decided on either Indonesia or the Maldives, though Virginia argued for Dubai or one of the countries near South Africa, since almost everyone in those places speaks English.

Forty minutes later, she wakes to Mattie leaning forward, staring at her.

"What?" she says, self-conscious of how she must have looked sleeping. She raises the seat and wipes her mouth for drool.

"Teach me to drive," Mattie blurts.

"What?"

"Think about it. It makes sense. My mom can't drive, and you being the only driver is too much. In nine months, I'd be getting my permit anyway—"

Grace holds up her hand, stopping her, and Mattie swallows back the rest of what she was going to say as she looks at Grace through her eyebrows.

Grace feels her stress. She remembers all too well what it's like to be fourteen and to have your life ripped out from under you and to be terrified of what is to come. Fourteen, a strange age, almost fully formed, but not quite, still young enough to be at the mercy of others, even when they don't necessarily have your best interests at heart.

Mattie looks like she is going to burst an artery, her eyes bulging as she waits for Grace to answer.

"What would your mom say?" Grace says.

"She's not here," Mattie answers, almost making Grace smile, the remark a lot like something Grace would say.

She swallows back her grin as she thinks about it, the idea not entirely terrible. If Mattie could drive, it would definitely give the Torellis more of a chance.

"Okay," she says, and Mattie nearly yips, then grabs for the door.

"Not so fast," Grace says. "Learn by listening and watching, and if you do good, I'll consider letting you behind the wheel."

Mattie's mouth opens to protest; then wisely she snaps it shut, and again Grace smiles to herself. She likes this kid. She really does.

Mattie moves Miles to the back, then climbs into the passenger seat.

"Foot on the brake when you're in park," Grace says. She points to her foot. "Middle pedal. Driving is a one-footed affair. Got it?"

Mattie nods.

"Two hands on the wheel. Ten and two, like a clock. Mirrors. Three of them. You use all three, and you use them twice."

Mattie nods again, her brow furrowed in fierce concentration, and Grace straightens in her seat, feeling a great responsibility for what she is doing—teaching something to someone, something Grace has never done.

33

HADLEY

For the first hour, Hadley was upset. For the second, she was nervous, her energy buzzing and her heart lurching with every move the agent made. He had given up on trying to convince her to turn herself in, and she was certain he was going to try to escape.

After the third hour, her adrenaline petered out, and her injured ankle, which had been throbbing, fell asleep, the pins-and-needles sensation almost as uncomfortable as the pain. Then, in the fourth hour, she became hungry, her stomach growling as her temples throbbed with a headache.

The hour after, the agent fell asleep, and now he is snoring lightly, his mouth hanging open and his head bent uncomfortably against the wall.

She hates that he is so nice. It makes her feel that much worse for what they're doing. He seems genuinely concerned about them, like he really wants to help, but she can't go to jail. Neither can Grace. It's simply not possible.

She stares at the skull in the display case. She has named him Fred. She makes up stories about his life and his wife and his family. She has decided he was a good man and very funny. After all, it looks like he is smiling despite only a few of his teeth remaining.

The agent stirs and shifts position. She watches as his head lolls to the other side. He is not terrible looking, a bit gruff, but also rugged—broad shouldered with thick, Popeye-like forearms. The shadow of beard that lines his jaw is two shades darker than his cinnamon hair, and his long nose is slightly bent—broken from being an athlete, a fighter, or both. His hair is cut short and sticks up straight, a style probably left over from his military days.

Overall, he looks like a good all-American man—the kind who grew up calling his mom *ma'am* and his dad *sir* and who always holds the door open for a woman and says *God bless you* when someone sneezes—and she likes him very much for that. He's the kind of man her father would have approved of and her mother would have loved. A man completely different from the one she chose.

She looks away and toward the clock above the door. It's nearly noon, and she's worried. Grace and the kids have been gone a long time.

The agent shifts again, mumbles something that sounds like "dog," then resumes his heavy breathing, and she returns to her worrying and staring at the clock.

When it reaches one, her concern gives way to intense focus on her bladder. She really needs to pee. She looks again at the agent. His eyes are still closed, but something has changed, an altered rhythm to his breaths.

"I need to pee," she says.

His eyes snap open, and a smile of relief crosses his face. "Me too."

34

MARK

They are laughing. It's very comical. Torelli was so concerned Mark would try to make a break for it that she's insisted on tethering them together as they go to the bathroom.

She managed to release him from the desk and tie herself to him with the ACE bandage, but when they tried to walk, her crutches made a holy mess of things, and he ended up carrying her like a bride over the threshold into the bathroom, his hands bound together beneath her.

Breathless, he sets her down carefully, concerned about her ankle, and she leans heavily on him as he untangles them.

She smells like soap and sweat and something floral. Realizing he is breathing her in, he pinches his nose closed to stop it.

She holds on to his shoulders as she hops over the bandage on her good leg, then lifts her injured ankle for him to duck beneath. He crouches and swoops, but before he's through, she loses her balance and ends up toppling over on him, his shoulder between her legs and her arms clinging to his head.

"Stop making me laugh," she squeals, "or I swear I'm going to pee my panties."

"Don't you dare," he says. "This day has been humiliating enough without being peed on by my suspect."

He manages to set her back on her good foot and come out the other side.

"Technically, I'm your captor, not your suspect," she says as she leans on him to regain her balance.

"Like I said, totally humiliating."

Her forearms are on his chest, her breath on his neck. It's the closest he's been to a woman in months, and before he can stop himself, he finds himself breathing her in again.

He shifts his focus to his full bladder, hoping to distract the other organ that's treacherously sprung to life. Until this moment, he was fairly certain the most mortifying experience of his career was being hijacked by a woman on crutches, then being driven away in the trunk of his own rental car, but getting a boner while she helps him take a whiz would definitely top that.

She hops around him in a circle to unwind the final tangle, then says, "Got it. Now, turn around so I can pee . . . and put your hands over your ears."

He does as she asks, a smile filling his face, and he wants to wipe it away because he knows he shouldn't be smiling and should instead be assessing the situation and considering his escape.

The problem he's having is not whether he can escape but rather whether he should. Even with his hands bound, now that he's untethered from the desk, he could easily overpower her. But each time he considers it, he decides against it. The best chance for resolving this without anyone getting hurt is to convince Torelli to turn herself in. Which means remaining her "captive" for as long as it takes.

And, of course, there's also the not-so-minor consideration of Herrick returning at any moment. There are two miles of open desert between him and the highway, and if she catches him, she'll either bring him back and tether him more securely or shoot him, neither option particularly appealing.

"Your turn," Torelli says as she hops up beside him and leans on the sink.

"Run the water," he says. "And put your hands over your ears."

"Wow, you must be a loud pee-er."

"I'm a guy."

She giggles like she's genuinely having fun, then turns on the faucet. He watches as she squeezes her eyes shut and presses her hands against her ears. She looks like a little girl playing hide-and-seek, a little like Shelly, and he swallows as his guilt and concern grow.

35

GRACE

Miles needs his diaper changed.

"Turn wide," Grace says. "Go out, then come in sharp." She uses her index finger to draw in the air what she means.

Mattie nods, then haltingly pulls the truck into a spot at the far end of the parking lot of the rest stop.

The truck is not easy to drive. It's a Chevy Silverado king cab with oversize tires that they bought off a man named Wade who'd been parked beside them at the Starbucks where Grace stopped to get a coffee.

Fortunately, Mattie is a natural and a good listener. She has paid careful attention to everything Grace has said, and Grace is impressed by how quickly she's caught on.

"You came in too tight," Grace says. The front tire is on the line. "Back up and do it again."

Mattie checks her side mirrors, checks the rearview mirror, checks them again, then looks over her shoulder, backs the truck up, straightens it, pulls in again.

She did it perfectly, but Grace doesn't say so. The only acknowledgment she gives is to climb from the truck. Like her grandmother used to say, "Compliments need to be hard earned, else they don't mean much at all."

Skipper and Mattie head to the vending machines as Grace carries Miles to the restroom.

Miles kicks and smiles as she changes him, then laughs when she raspberries his tummy after. He reaches to snag the wipe, and for a minute, she plays with him, dangling the cloth and snatching it away, feeling guilty for how little time she's spent with him the past couple of days.

Since they started this wild ride, Hadley has done the lion's share of the mothering—the pampering, the feeding, the coddling—things that seem to come much more naturally to her. The woman is seriously gifted when it comes to babies, or at least when it comes to Miles. She just picks Miles up and he quiets. It infuriates Grace but also makes her incredibly grateful. For two days, Miles has not cried for more than a minute, Hadley mystically able to soothe him each time he starts.

She looks at him lying there, smiling and kicking, and she marvels at how quickly he's changing. He laughs all the time now and looks more like Jimmy because of it. She smiles at the small dimple on his right cheek that twitches when he's determined, a trait that makes him look a little like her. It amazes her that five months ago this little guy didn't exist. How is that possible when her entire world now revolves around him, this erupting bundle of life?

"You and me, kiddo," she says, stroking the smooth skin of his forehead with the back of her hand. "Somehow we're going to get through this."

He bats her away and tries again to snag the wipe, making her smile. She taunts him by waving it just out of his reach, and his face grows fierce, his little hands flailing.

She chuckles and dips the wipe low enough for him to grab, and his face lights up in triumph as he snags it from her grip.

She knows she should get going but doesn't want to step from this moment and into the next, reluctant to face the uncertainty of what lies ahead. Finally, with a deep sigh, she gathers him up and walks back outside.

The sun is high in the sky now, the heat sweltering. Skipper and Mattie stand near the vending machines. In front of them is a kid perhaps Mattie's age and beside him another kid a year or two younger.

The first is tall, thick, and lumpy; the other, short and thin.

"Give it back," Mattie says.

It's then that Grace notices that the large boy has Skipper's hat and is waving it in the air, out of Skipper's reach. Skipper leaps at him, trying to grab it. The boy easily swings it away as he says, "Retard."

Grace's vision goes red.

"I told you, give it back," Mattie says, stepping toward the kid.

He stares her down, not budging as he continues to wave the hat in the air.

Grace takes a step toward them, then reconsiders. She scans around her, and her eyes catch on the salt flat behind her; then she looks in the trash can beside her as a plan forms in her mind.

Grabbing an empty Jack Daniel's bottle from the trash along with a half-empty Coke cup, she carries them back the way she came.

A moment later, she is back. Without hesitation, she walks behind the boy and swipes the hat from his hand before he can react. As she passes the younger boy, she says, "Don't follow your brother," and her eyes slide to the salt flat beyond the restroom and the bottle of Jack Daniel's, now half-full with watered-down Coke, glinting a few yards in.

Mattie and Skipper follow her, Mattie's anger pulsing in waves.

"I'll drive," Grace says when they reach the truck.

"I hate jerks like that," Mattie mumbles through clenched teeth as she climbs into the passenger seat.

Grace takes her time strapping Miles in the back, climbs into the driver's seat, then reverses from the parking spot. When she turns to look back through the windshield, a smile creeps onto her face and she points through the glass.

Mattie follows her finger, and together they watch as the large boy tests the crusted mud of the salt flat with his toe to see if it's safe to take a step. Deciding it is, he steps forward, and his right foot sinks to his ankle. He tries to pull it out, but the suction pulls him off balance and he falls forward, his left foot plunging into the muck to his knee.

Mattie laughs, and Skipper yells, "Look. Look at him. Look, look, look," his finger pointing as he bounces in his seat.

The boy flails his arms to hold his balance, then yells something to the younger boy, who still stands safely on the bank. The boy shakes his head, and the bully screams at him, losing his balance in the process. He nearly falls backward, then overcompensates and falls forward instead, his arms disappearing into the cesspool to his elbows.

Mattie laughs harder, and Skipper bounces so hard the whole truck bounces with him. Grace puts the truck in gear and drives toward the exit. She lived in Georgia until she was nineteen, and she knows a mud bog scorched dry when she sees one, the crusted surface disguising the muck that lies below.

As they roll past, Mattie lowers the window and yells, "Look, Skipper, a pig in the mud!"

The boy looks over his shoulder, a grief-stricken expression on his face, the desert mountains behind him—a truly majestic sight.

"Home run," Skipper says. "Way to go, Trout. Home run."

"He's calling me a fish?" Grace says to Mattie, who's still smiling ear to ear.

"Trout, as in Mike Trout," she says. "Your nickname is now Trout. It's an honor. Skipper doesn't just give anyone a nickname, and he definitely doesn't give out names like that."

36

HADLEY

They have hobbled back to the office and are again tangled, the ACE bandage caught on Hadley's crutches and forcing her to cling to the agent as he tries to unsnaggle them. He is trying hard to be a gentleman, and she is very naughtily making that impossible, a recklessness brewing inside her she hasn't felt in years.

Purposely, she stumbles into him, landing in such a way that his bound hands are forced to catch her by the waist, his palms burning against the exposed sliver of skin between her blouse and skirt. Quickly, he shifts them away, which makes her giggle for what a Boy Scout he is—a man the opposite of Frank, respectful almost to a fault.

She has no idea what has come over her. She feels a little crazy. Perhaps from hunger. Is that a thing? Or perhaps it's the prospect of being arrested that's sent her off the rails. She has no idea. All she knows is she is done being good, playing by the rules, and hoping, somehow, it will all work out.

"Stay still," he orders, and she obeys, staying put as he weaves the bandage in and out, lifting her arms and moving her legs, his face screwed up in intense concentration.

She braces herself on his shoulders and hops over the ACE bandage, moving in such a way that her breasts brush beneath his nose, knowing this is a part of her anatomy he has been trying very hard to avoid, his eyes catching and then snapping away, which she finds very amusing.

A boob man. She has always liked boob men, or she used to. They're usually very appreciative of a woman's curves and are willing to spend lots of time admiring them.

He bends down to unwrap the bandage carefully from her ankle, and she laces her hands around his neck as if needing the support, her breasts pressed to his ear.

"You know," he says, "I could overpower you right now?"

She giggles, a high, girly laugh. "I dare you," she says.

"To escape," he clarifies, flushing red. "I could overpower you to escape."

She leans in a bit closer. "Of course, if you did, and Grace came back, she might just shoot you."

"True," he says, "but at least I'd go out in a blaze of glory."

He maneuvers around her, and she maneuvers with him, undoing the progress he's just made.

"Stay still," he orders.

"What's your name, Mr. Blaze of Glory?"

She feels him hesitate, unsure whether to give his first name or last. "Mark," he says, and she gives a silent cheer.

Marcus? Markham? Or just Mark? she wonders. *Spelled with a* c *or a* k? *Mark Wahlberg. Mark Twain. Mark Sloan from* Grey's Anatomy— *Mr. McSteamy.* She smiles.

"There," he declares, stepping back to admire his work, the ACE bandage now draped like a loose snake between them. He smiles triumphantly, believing he has done it and is therefore now safe.

She hops toward him.

He steps back.

She hops with him.

"Hadley—" he says when he runs into the wall.

"Mark," she interrupts, the recklessness bubbling over and making her feel drunk.

He opens his mouth to go on, but her lips on his stop him. It's an awkward kiss, his bound hands pressed to her sternum as her neck cranes to keep them connected, his mouth frozen open as hers clumsily pushes against it.

He forces space between them. "Hadley—"

"No," she says, shaking her head.

"But—"

"No," she says again, tears filling her eyes and causing him to drop his to the floor between them.

Then something extraordinary happens. She is on the verge of losing it, her emotions teetering somewhere between despair and desperation, when his hands rise to cradle her chin, and he leans in and brushes his lips against hers. She knows it is only meant to be a kindness, a consolation to soften the blow of his rejection, but beneath the touch, hunger pulses. She feels it, ache and neediness that match her own, and when she wraps her hands around his neck to pull it closer, he loses the battle and his mouth molds to hers.

When he pulls away, shame blazes in his bright-blue eyes.

"It's only us," she says, setting her fingers against his lips to stop his protest. "And it's only this moment."

She has no idea where the words have come from, but they feel right, too much terror behind her and in front of her to think about, creating a vacuum in time and space so all that exists is him and her and now.

She sets her hands on his chest, then kisses him again. And when she slides her hands down and begins to unbutton his shirt, he lets her. She pulls it from his shoulders, and it falls halfway to his elbows before getting stuck because of his binds.

He looks down, and she looks down, and they laugh.

He bucks like a lunatic in a straitjacket trying to break free, and she laughs harder, and he laughs harder, both of them cracking up until they're doubled over with their fit.

"I've got it," she says. "Bend over."

He does as she says, and she grabs his shirttail and yanks it over his head, turning the shirt inside out and causing it to land in a tangle on his wrists.

"Brilliant," he says, flapping his elbows like a duck to show off his freedom.

Then they are kissing again, but having more fun with it now, the shirt dangling between them and reminding them of the humor. Awkwardly, they remove the rest of their clothes as best they can, and she is aware how ridiculous they must look, his shirt stuck on his hands, her shirt and bra dangling on the ACE bandage between them, his pants and boxers bunched at his ankles, and her skirt gathered at her waist. But frankly, she doesn't care. For fifteen years, the only love she's known has been from a man who terrorized her, and now she is with a man she's known less than a day but who is caring, gentle, and kind.

When they come together, it is strangely ordinary, and yet both of them are aware how remarkable it is, like it is the most natural thing in the world.

It ends too quickly, and she feels how disappointed he is in himself, though she is not disappointed in the least. He was hungry, like she was hungry—two people starved so long it was impossible to show restraint.

It was beautiful, she wants to say, but she knows how corny that would sound.

He rolls off so he is on his back, his chest heaving. "Sorry," he says. "I guess I'm a little out of practice."

She shifts so her head is on his shoulder. "Really?" she says, tracing circles on his chest. "You're a little out of practice making love to a woman in a sweltering trailer in the middle of the desert with your hands tied?"

He chuckles and leans down to kiss the top of her head. It's such a strangely familiar thing to do, and again she's surprised how comfortable she is, like she has known him her whole life, or more like she was meant to know him her whole life but they have only just now met.

"Well," he says, "I can honestly say I've never done *that* with a suspect before."

"Captor," she corrects.

"Right. Captor."

It should be funny, but something in the word deflates the moment.

She runs her finger over the scar on his left shoulder. The broiled skin trembles beneath her touch. "The war?" she asks.

"Football."

"Linebacker?"

"Mascot."

She smiles, then pushes onto her elbow and leans over to brush a kiss across it. When she lies back down, he wriggles closer and takes her fingers in his.

"So, you live in Las Vegas?" she says.

"DC. I moved there two years ago."

He tells her about his life, and she tells him about hers. He grew up in Boston, played football for Notre Dame, served in the marines, then started with the FBI. He beams when he talks about his kids, Shelly and Ben, his love so big it fills the room, and she feels his hurt when he talks about his marriage, like somehow its failure is a reflection of his character.

He tells her he's supposed to see them tomorrow, and that he and his son are going to pick out a dog. She tells him about Prince Charles and how bad she felt about leaving him behind. She knows she should not be upset over such a trivial thing as a pet, but Prince Charles was with her most of her marriage, and he helped her through the worst of times, and she can't help but feel like she's abandoned him after a loyal life of service.

He asks about Mattie and Skipper and a little about Frank, though it's obvious he already knows a lot and has very strong opinions about him.

"Why didn't you leave before?" he says when she finishes telling him about the pizza incident the night they left, a confession that felt like both a betrayal and a relief. It's the first time she's ever told anyone the truth about her marriage.

"I believed in love," she mumbles, feeling foolish. "In marriage." She shakes her head. "We were a family, and . . . I don't know, I guess I just sort of believed in the idea that you stick it out—you know, through thick and thin—and that love is permanent, flaws and all."

He tenses, and she wonders which part offended him, the fact that she stayed so long or that she could be so naive.

"Hadley," he says after a long minute, "I need you to listen to me—"

"Don't," she says. "I just want to lie here. Please."

She feels his reluctance to let it go, but mercifully, he stays silent and they return to quiet cuddling.

She drifts off, and when she wakes, he's looking at her. "Now Grace is really going to shoot me," he says.

Hadley laughs, a blush of pride blooming at the thought of Grace discovering what she's done, almost hoping she does, feeling a little like a gladiator after a conquest in the arena. Then she thinks of Mattie and Skipper, and the thought is obliterated.

Suddenly panicked, she pushes herself up and grabs for her clothes. Her shirt and bra are tangled on the ACE bandage, and she has no idea where her panties have gone.

Mark manages to pull up his pants, but he is completely at a loss as to how to get his shirt back over his head. She gets her bra on, then scrambles to help him flip his shirt right side up. She is still tugging it over his shoulders when the sound of tires on gravel rolls toward them.

"Shit," she says, abandoning his clothes and focusing on her own.

She's buttoning the last button on her shirt when the car stops. Forgetting she's tied to him and that her ankle can't hold her, she leaps for the door.

Mark dives, and his body lands between her and the ground with a grunt. Before she can right herself, the door opens, and she looks up to see Grace, her arms loaded with bags.

She looks down at them and sniffs the air, and her eyes grow wide. "Are you kidding me? Tell me you're kidding me?"

"Kidding about what?" Mattie says, stepping up behind her, Miles in her arms.

"Mattie, wait outside," Hadley says quickly as she pushes off Mark and stumbles to her knees.

Grace closes the door, locking Mattie out; then she storms to the desk. "You do realize he is trying to arrest you?" she says, setting down the bags. "His job is to lock you up, put you behind bars, incarcerate you."

Hadley staggers to her feet, Mark helping her as best he can with his bound hands.

"An eight-by-ten cell," Grace continues, "with a cellmate named Bertha." She practically bounces the water bottles off the desk as she slams them down. "A woman who bites the tails off rats and who names her toenail clippings. You do get that, don't you?"

Hadley looks sheepishly at her through her brow, her cheeks warm, and Grace looks like she wants to slam the flashlight she's holding over Hadley's head. Then her frown deepens, and she shakes her head and harrumphs, but the harrumph lacks oomph, and Hadley thinks she might actually be a little pleased for her. Then she harrumphs again and returns to unpacking the groceries.

Hadley unties her wrist from Mark's and, with apology in her eyes, reties the loose end to the desk, double and triple knotting it.

His eyes hold hers, pleading with her to reconsider, and she quickly looks away.

Grace pulls a Subway sandwich from the bag and holds it out. "I figured you must be hungry. Turkey and swiss on italian, lettuce only, hold the mayo."

"Do I really come off that boring?"

Grace's eyes slide to Mark. "Not anymore."

Hadley smirks, and Grace flicks an annoyed look at her, which only causes Hadley to smirk wider, a grin she can't seem to wipe away, unable to believe she did what she did.

Grace carries a second sandwich to Mark. He opens his mouth to say something, but Grace cuts him off. "Open your mouth for any reason other than to eat this sandwich, and so help me, I'll leave you with nothing but water and granola bars."

He snaps his mouth closed, and Hadley mouths, "Sorry."

While Hadley eats, Grace rebinds Mark to the desk using zip ties, twining them together in such a way as to form a thick rope that chains his right wrist to the desk and leaves his left hand free. Then she moves the supplies she bought so they're within his reach.

She bought enough food for a week, along with two dozen bottles of water, magazines, an air mattress, a sleeping bag, a pillow . . . and a bucket. Hadley looks at the bucket curiously; then, when she realizes what it's for, she cringes and looks away, unable to face Mark, knowing she is a part of this.

"This isn't going to end well," Mark says as they're leaving.

For a moment, Hadley is concerned Grace might make good on her threat and leave him with nothing but granola bars. Instead, her back still turned, she nods and says, "You have kids?"

"A boy and a girl."

"Then you understand," Grace says, and she continues out the door.

37

GRACE

The only station they can get on the radio is country, and Mattie is in pain, her hands pinned to her ears as Grace and Hadley belt out "Save a Horse (Ride a Cowboy)."

Hadley has the worst voice Grace has ever heard. The woman is completely tone deaf, with a kazoo implanted in her larynx. It makes Grace incredibly happy. Hadley might look like a million bucks, but her voice would scare off dogs . . . *cats, mice, roaches.*

Miles babbles along. It turns out the kid is a country music fan. And so, even though it is the witching hour, time for his nightly melt-down, he is happy as a clam, gibbering and jabbering along to the music and kicking his feet.

The doctor said eventually the colic would work itself out, and he would stop having fits, but it's been going on so long Grace had given up on it being true. She's not certain if he is simply outgrowing it or if it's the change in circumstances that's triggered the progression. Whatever the case, she is extraordinarily grateful. It's as if a giant burden has been lifted from her chest. Because, though the doctor assured her she was not to blame for her son's misery, it felt like she was, and so, ever since she became a mom, she's felt like a failure. And now, it's as if suddenly she is passing muster.

Dropping the Torellis in Bakersfield didn't work out. Mostly because Grace is an idiot. She missed the exit, and by the time she realized she'd missed the exit, she was so far past it that she just kept going, and she's almost convinced herself it was by accident.

The problem was that at the time she was supposed to be exiting, everyone was asleep, conked out from their predawn start. Hadley was passed out against the window, not twitching or talking. Miles was snoring in his car seat, with Skipper's baseball hat gripped in his little fist. And Skipper was curled on Mattie's lap, Mattie flopped on top of him.

Had any of them been awake, Hadley, Skipper, and Mattie would probably be on a train right now headed for Omaha. But they weren't. They were all peacefully asleep and not being annoying in the least. Then the exit came and went, and it was too late to turn back, or at least that's what Grace told herself, her guilt niggling at her each time she looks at Miles and realizes again the danger she's put him in.

She sings louder, and Hadley matches her as Mattie cries, "Child abuse!"

~

Grace's back aches. The truck's seats have no lumbar support, and the entire drive she's been slouched, causing her muscles to cramp and her back to spasm. They are driving through the mountain town of Mammoth, the radio now crackling with eighties rock and roll.

Miles lets out a loud "Ba ba ba," and she glances at him in the mirror. He babbles a lot now, and it's startling how quickly it has happened, as if he's discovered his voice can be used for something other than screaming.

Skipper stops what he's doing, leans over so he's in front of Miles, and says, "Ball"; then he holds up the baseball they bought at Walmart.

"Ball," he repeats. Miles's face lights up, and he reaches for the white sphere. "Ball, say *ball*," Skipper encourages.

Skipper is determined to make Miles's first word *ball*, and he's been working on it all day, repeating it to him with such frequency Grace is fairly certain he will get his way. Hadley, on the other hand, is just as determined to make his first word *mama*, and she mouths it to Miles every time Grace holds him. "Mama. That's your mama. Say *mama*." Grace pretends she doesn't care, but secretly she does.

All of this makes her think of Jimmy—she's desperate to call him and tell him about all the new developments—and each time, she needs to remind herself what he did that's made that impossible. Over and over she tells herself, *Stop thinking about him,* but it does no good. Ever since she walked in on Hadley and the agent in the archaeological trailer, he has taken up permanent residence in her brain and refuses to leave.

They roll into the downtown, and Grace reduces the speed to the posted thirty-five miles per hour, a creeping crawl through the deserted ski village. They are nearly through when blue and red lights fill her rearview mirror.

"Hadley," she says, the name coming out a croak.

Hadley looks over, notices the light show reflecting off the windshield, glances over her shoulder, and says, "Oh crap. Were you speeding?"

"No. Not even a little."

Without hesitation, Hadley says, "I've got this," and before Grace can answer, Hadley is climbing from the truck with her crutches.

Grace watches in her mirror as Hadley hops toward the police car. The officer is still in his seat and talking on his radio. When he notices Hadley, he steps from his car and, standing behind the door, says something Grace can't hear. She rolls down her window.

"Ma'am, I need you to get back in your vehicle," he repeats.

"Grace, are you and my mom going to be arrested?" Mattie says, her voice tight.

Grace shakes her head, her foot hovering over the accelerator as thoughts of flooring it and leaving Hadley behind spiral through her mind. Her next thought is to throw the truck in reverse and ram it into the cruiser, hopefully disabling it. But Hadley is in the way. *Move,* she encourages, the idea glowing bright.

She also thinks of the gun, Frank's revolver a foot away, in the front pouch of the backpack. She thinks of anything that will stop what is happening from happening, from her being arrested and hauled off to jail, where she will await trial for multiple federal offenses, including firing at a federal officer, stealing his car, and kidnapping him. All of which will put her away for the rest of her natural life.

Miles gurgles, "Geggggg," and her eyes snap to him in the mirror, her mind whirling with panic, and she reaches into the backpack and slides the gun onto her lap.

"What are you doing?" Mattie hisses.

Grace moves it beneath her sweatshirt and ignores the question, her eyes on Hadley, watching as she continues toward the officer.

"Ma'am, you need to return to your vehicle," he says firmly.

Hadley tilts her head as if she doesn't understand, then says, "Oui, the ve-heck-el, that is car, no?" her French accent very thick and very fake.

The policeman, a bald middle-aged man with a thick mustache and wide face, cracks a smile and steps from behind his door. "Yes, ma'am, the vehicle is the car."

Hadley hops backward until she is against the tailgate of the truck. "Now you frisk me?" she says, causing Grace's eyes to bulge from her skull.

"Are you kidding me?" Mattie says, clearly as unimpressed as Grace.

Not only is the act entirely unconvincing, it is also ridiculous. Who, French or not, asks a cop if they are going to frisk them?

Grace's foot returns to hovering over the accelerator, ready to peel away, certain the officer is going to pull his gun and demand to know what drugs Hadley is on.

"No, no, no," the officer says, his hands waving in front of him and his smile now spread cheek to cheek across his face.

"No?" Hadley says. "You not do that here? This my first time pushed over."

"Pulled over," he corrects.

Hadley tilts her head, and Grace cannot see her expression, but she imagines it—her catlike eyes wide and her brows askew as she looks up innocently through them.

"I am *pulling* you over, not *pushing* you over," he explains.

"You not say this a pushover?"

Mattie and Grace guffaw together. "Really?" Mattie says.

Miles answers, "Aa, aa, aa, aa."

Skipper, seemingly as immune to the stress around him as Miles is, holds the ball out and says, "Ball. Say *ball.*"

"Champ, not now," Mattie says.

Obediently, Skipper hands the ball to Miles, and Miles laughs with delight and puts it in his mouth, then drops it, and Skipper hands it back to him.

Grace returns her attention to the mirror. The officer is now a foot from Hadley, his posture relaxed, his large belly jiggling in amusement over something else Hadley has said.

"So why you push . . . I mean pull me over? My friend drive too slow? She drive like old lady. My ninety-year-old aunt drive faster. How you say, nervous ninny? She nervous ninny."

Annoyance bristles through Grace's fear.

"'Nervous Nellie,'" the officer says. "But no, that's not why I pulled you over. Broken taillight." He points to the left-rear bumper.

Hadley hops to stand beside him, slightly closer than necessary, her head tilting as she looks at the offending light. "You give me ticket for that?"

"Technically, I give your friend a ticket, since she's the one driving."

"But it not her truck. It my brother's truck."

"But the way it works is she gets the ticket; then she needs to give it to your brother, and he needs to make sure he gets it fixed. It doesn't cost any money. It's what's known as a fix-it ticket." He explains it very deliberately, as if he is a professor teaching a particularly slow student.

Hadley shakes her head, and her face grows serious. "No," she says. "You cannot give ticket to give my brother." Her voice trembles, full of fear. "You give me ticket. Give me ticket for speeding or whatever. I not care. But you not give ticket to give my brother. He kill me."

Grace has almost forgotten Hadley is acting, her emotions caught up in this poor immigrant woman's plight of getting a ticket she will need to give her ogre of a brother.

"Hey, settle down. You're okay," the officer says, and Grace realizes Hadley might actually have turned on the waterworks.

Hadley's head continues to shake, and she is trembling, her whole body quaking as she says, "Not okay. You not know my brother."

The officer sighs, and Grace nearly cheers, knowing what is coming. "Tell you what," he says. "How about I let this one slide?"

Grace does a small fist pump as Hadley looks up at the officer through her brow with an expression that's a cross between seduction and worship. "You do that? You not push over?"

"Yeah, I do that. I not push you over," he says with a self-congratulatory grin. Then with the tip of an imaginary hat to Grace, he returns to his cruiser, his shoulders pulled back heroically.

As he drives past, he waves, and Grace manages to lift her hand to wave back.

Hadley climbs in, a cat-ate-the-canary grin on her face as she wipes the wetness from her cheeks. "Eight for nine," she says, raising her hand for Grace to high-five.

Grace leaves the hand hanging there, her heart clattering in her chest.

Mattie says, "Eight for nine what?" as she reaches over to slap her mom's hand.

Hadley says proudly, "Your mom has been pulled over nine times, and the only time I got a ticket was when I tried to hit on a woman cop I thought was gay, and it turned out she wasn't."

Grace is irrationally upset, her blood pumping with residual panic and inexplicable anger. She should be overjoyed with Hadley's perverse talent for flirting, acting, and concocting convincing fiction on the spot, but instead her vision is red and her knuckles white on the steering wheel.

"Great lesson you're teaching your daughter," she snarls.

Hadley looks at her, her head cocked to the side. "What's your problem?"

"What's next—you going to teach her how to lap dance her way to a free drink? Or maybe you should just move on to the ultimate lesson and teach her how to marry for money?"

Hadley blinks, and Grace turns from her, throws the truck in gear, and pulls onto the road.

"Seriously," Hadley says, "what's your problem?"

Grace looks at Mattie again, her skin on fire, uncertain what her problem is, only certain of her rage. Finally, she spits, "It's not right," the only words she can think of to describe what she is feeling. "Sex is not a bargaining tool, or at least it shouldn't be. And for most of us, eight out of nine times it doesn't work out. You hear that, Mattie? Unless you look like your mom and master the art of rendering men stupid by sticking your boobs in their face—"

"I did not *stick* my boobs in his face."

"You kind of did, Mom," Mattie says.

Hadley harrumphs, her arms folded over the aforementioned boobs. "I stopped us from being arrested is what I did."

Grace yanks the wheel to steer the truck onto the shoulder and barely gets the door open in time to hurl her dinner onto the street.

The gun tumbles to the ground beside the retch, and she stares at it, her breath coming in gulps and gasps.

Hadley is beside her. She holds Grace's hair from her face as Grace spits the vile taste from her mouth.

Mattie steps from the car and holds out a bottle of water.

"Get her a wipe," Hadley says, her voice full of concern as she rubs Grace's back.

Grace's eyes fill. *Too much,* she thinks. Between yesterday and today and what just almost happened, it's too much. She squeezes her eyes shut and sucks air through her nose.

"No more flirting my way out of tickets. Very upsetting to Grace. Note taken," Hadley says, and Grace manages a weak smile, then bends down to pick up the gun.

"You were going to shoot him?" Hadley says; then, reverting to her fake French accent, she adds, "Perhaps flirting work better, no?"

"Yeah, whatever," Grace says, and she hoists herself back in the truck. And as they continue on, she imagines herself standing in front of a judge with Hadley beside her—the judge smiling down at Hadley as he dismisses all the charges against her, then his gavel coming down hard as he sentences Grace to life.

38

MARK

It's cold now, seriously cold. The wind rattles through the window, along with other night noises. The sun went down an hour ago, and the wind picked up, sending creaks and howls and whipping dirt and sage against the trailer. Mark is too far from the heater to turn it on and, humiliatingly, too far from the bathroom to use the toilet. Herrick left him a bucket, and the stench of his waste beside him makes his stomach curl. He survived worse in the marines, but that was a long time ago, when he was a lot younger, dumber, and tougher.

The fingers on his left hand are raw from sawing at the zip ties for the past six hours with the edge of the zipper pull of the sleeping bag, which he's repeatedly sharpened by filing it on the edge of the desk.

He has managed to cut through two of the three links Herrick tethered to his wrist, the only part of the chain not braided into an impossible rope. But now the tab is ground to a nub and barely makes any headway against the thick plastic.

As he works, his mind wanders, not able to get her out of his thoughts—her scent, her touch, her laughter—mostly her laughter, so much of it, the two of them giggling like schoolkids. He shakes his head to clear it all away, unable to believe he did what he did. Twenty years with the agency, and he's never even come close to crossing that line.

What possessed him?

She did. She possessed him with those catlike eyes, those lips, those hands, and those breasts—silk flesh flowing from the white satin of her bra. His skin prickles with the memory, and he shakes his head against it and presses the heels of his hands to his sockets to blot it away.

When he blinks his eyes open, he returns to his task, sawing frantically, his frustration at critical mass. The blade slips and slices the skin above his wrist, creating a fresh wound around the dozen that already exist. He drops the tab and presses the cloth of the sleeping bag against it, then leans his head back against the wall. *Damn her.* She knew exactly what she was doing, that mischievous grin on her face as she hopped toward him. Then she kissed him, and he wanted to say no; he tried.

But hell, he's human, male human.

He squeezes his eyes shut, wishing he could stop thinking about it.

His mind screamed in a million different directions—worry, alarm, elation, desperation—all of him ready to explode. Then they were laughing again, her giggles running over him and making him believe it was all in good fun.

He was self-conscious and distracted, worried about her ankle, then wishing he had a blanket to put down beneath her, or better yet, a bed. Alcohol to ease the awkwardness. Air-conditioning so he wouldn't be so aware of his smell.

All this spiraled through his head when her fingers closed around him, and then he was no longer thinking at all, his thoughts obliterated as she did things to him that had not been done in such a very long time.

His skin flames with the recollection—he's stunned and mortified, unable to believe he allowed it to happen, unable to believe it happened at all. Terrible and astounding.

He looks down at the cut. The trickle of blood has stopped. He picks up the blade and returns to the task, sawing and trying not to slit himself again.

Women, they make men stupid. She slept with him, messed with his head, then left him tied to a desk with a bucket for a toilet. And women are considered the fairer sex.

He's going to have a serious talk with Ben when he gets home. The kid's only nine, but it's never too early to learn how dangerous women can be, about the power they wield over men, how they can drive you insane and how ruthless they can be after, leaving you bewildered and broken down . . . chained to a damn desk. He won't leave that part out, the part about how ruthless they are. Ben needs to know so he will be prepared.

He switches the grip so he's holding the makeshift blade between his thumb and middle finger instead of his forefinger, which is now bloody and raw.

He was worried about crushing her, his arms trembling as he held himself above her, his focus split between his struggling muscles and trying to make it last, immediately wanting a redo when they were done, a chance to prove he could do better—a bed, liquor, not so much retention . . . his hands not bound together by his tie.

The blade slips again, barely missing his vein, and he squeezes his eyes shut and takes a deep breath.

The after was as amazing as the sex, maybe even more so, her head on his shoulder as she ran her nails over his chest. He was staring at the ceiling. One of the fluorescent bulbs flickered, adding to the strange surrealism of the moment. He told her about his life, and she talked about hers.

I believed in love. In marriage. We were a family, and . . . I don't know, I guess I just sort of believed in the idea that you stick it out—you know, through thick and thin—and that love is permanent, flaws and all. How those words pierced him. It's exactly how he felt . . . feels. It's why he would have stayed with Marcia forever, simply out of his staunch conviction that that's what love is.

He couldn't hold her the way he wanted, but he managed to wrap her fingers in his, his desire to help her building with each second that passed until he felt like he was going to go mad. He tried to talk sense to her, but she wouldn't listen, shushed him each time he started.

Damn woman. He's going to tell Ben that part also, about women not listening and not using one damn bit of common sense, how they think with their hearts instead of their heads. How does she think this is going to end? With her and Herrick riding off into the sunset with Frank's ill-gotten millions?

Frustrated, he yanks hard on the zip tie, and it snaps.

39

GRACE

They are staying at a motel on the outskirts of Lake Tahoe. Grace's exhaustion weighs on her like a heavy cloak, every fiber down to her fingernails done in from the day.

She gave Miles a bath, fed him and changed him, then collapsed beside him. But tired as she is, she cannot fall asleep. Each time she closes her eyes, Jimmy weaves in and out of her restless thoughts. Part of it is the changes Miles is going through and how much she wants to share them with him, knowing how much he would want to hear about it, asking her to tell him again and again and mining for details, begging her to send pictures and videos so he could brag to his buddies.

She looks at Miles sprawled on the bed, his hands above his head like a champion and his mouth hanging open, and she smiles, marveling as she always does in these moments when they are alone, stunned that she's created something so incredibly beautiful and perfect.

Part of it is what happened between Hadley and the agent. All day Hadley has been smirking, silently reveling in a dreamy state of postcoital bliss that has caused a physical ache in Grace so intense it hurts. And now, lying here, staring at the ceiling, the feeling has grown particularly acute, making it impossible to sleep.

Jimmy has always been a snuggler—a wedger, a warmth snatcher. And when they sleep together, he is always touching her in some way, his foot tucked between her calves, his arm draped across her shoulder, his fingers entwined with hers.

It has always bugged her. "Your side, my side," she is always telling him, drawing an imaginary line down their bed before settling on "her side." He pretends to obey, an amused smirk on his face. Then, the moment she drifts off to sleep, he moves in—a toe, an elbow, a hip, some sort of connection somewhere. The problem is she has grown used to it, and now, whenever he goes away, she misses it, and tonight, since she lay down beside Miles two hours ago, she has tossed and turned in search of it.

Finally, giving up, she walks onto the balcony, where she finds Hadley smoking and gazing toward the silhouetted mountains in the distance. The night is cool, and Grace shivers but doesn't return inside for her sweatshirt.

"This the insomniacs' meeting place?" Grace asks.

Hadley scoots sideways to make room, and Grace leans on the railing beside her.

In front of them, old-growth firs reach for the bruised midnight sky, creating black sawtooth shadows against the star-studded night. Shoulder to shoulder they look out at the expanse, the soft rustling of the wind through the trees the only sound.

"Rocking the Walmart blue-light special," Grace says, taking in Hadley's outfit of black velour sweats, blue running shoes, and a cheetah-print blouse.

"I feel like Peggy Bundy. Really? Animal print and velour?" Hadley says.

Grace shrugs and smirks. She might have accidentally purposely bought the ugliest outfit she could find when picking out a change of clothes for Hadley this morning. Though somehow the woman still looks great. Grace swears Hadley could wear a garbage bag and she would start a fashion trend, suddenly everyone sporting Glad or Hefty to red-carpet events. She's just one of those women—the kind who, if you leave her alone with a captive FBI agent who's trying to arrest her, will still manage to seduce him.

"I can't believe you slept with him," Grace says.

"Me either." And even in the thin light, Grace sees her blush.

"You don't need to gloat about it," Grace says.

"I'm not gloating."

"You are. You're gloating all over the place. You're completely covered in gloat."

Hadley's blush deepens, making Grace want to throw her off the balcony. She wants to be gloating. She wishes very badly that Jimmy were here so she, too, could be covered in gloat.

Hadley lifts the cigarette to her lips, the end glowing as she inhales; then she tips her head back and releases the smoke into the air, watching as the feathery gauze drifts away, a smile curling her lips.

"Wow," Grace says. "I knew you slept with him, but I didn't know you actually *liked* him."

Hadley brings her face down quickly. "I don't. I wasn't . . ." She looks away, the words trailing off, and Grace feels bad for teasing her, because it's obvious Hadley really does like him, which makes what happened between them less romantic than tragic. He is an FBI agent. She is a fugitive. Best-case scenario is they never see each other again.

Grace looks back at the mountain scene, watching the night clouds drift across the moon.

"Where's your husband?" Hadley says.

"Afghanistan."

"Army?"

Grace nods.

A moment of hesitation, but Grace knows it won't last. Hadley can't help herself. She's a yapper and a nosybody. She braces for the question as Hadley blurts it out: "So, why'd you leave? Is he a jerk?"

Grace takes a deep inhale of the cool air, then slowly lets it out. "Nope. Jimmy's the nicest guy you'll ever meet."

She can see Hadley looking for more of an explanation, but Grace doesn't offer one. She doesn't believe in talking bad about the people you love.

"That's not fair," Hadley says with a pout. "You know everything about me."

"That's because you like to blab."

Hadley sneers.

"Fine," Grace says. "The short version is Jimmy likes to gamble. It ruined us twice, and the last time, I told him if it happened again, it was over." Her voice sounds matter of fact until the last word, and she needs to work very hard not to show how much the confession hurts, and she is surprised how much saying the words out loud affects her—like pulling the top off a soda pop that's been shaken. Though all she's stated was the simple truth, it feels like a huge expulsion of all the hurt and shame that's been bottled up inside her for years.

Hadley's green eyes grow soft with sympathy, and Grace grows uncomfortable. She's never liked pity.

Hadley looks away, and for a long moment they're silent, until finally Hadley says, "You ever think how different it would be if men were the ones to have the children? Like penguins, reliant on their women to return to the nest to feed them, bring home the bacon or the fish or whatever it is penguins eat, even long after they're no longer the hottest penguin on the beach?"

"Iceberg."

"Iceberg?"

"If they were penguins, they would be on an iceberg," Grace says.

Hadley frowns at her, and Grace shrugs. "I'm just saying it wouldn't be a beach. It would be an iceberg."

"Wow, Jimmy really must be the nicest guy in the world."

Grace sticks her tongue out at her, and Hadley flips her off. It's all very adolescent, and Grace feels a sudden lightening in her chest, the sensation distinctly uncomfortable, familiar yet far away, the vague memory of a time before her grandmother got sick.

"You okay?" Hadley says.

Grace nods, her eyes blinking as her knuckles massage her sternum to clear it away.

"So, what happened today with you and the kids?" Hadley says. "You were gone a long time."

Shrug.

"You're not going to tell me? Skipper's calling you Trout, the most revered name in baseball, and my daughter, who pretty much hates everyone, is following you around like a puppy and hanging on your every word. So what happened?"

"Maybe it's my irresistible charm and personality."

Hadley scoffs and Grace laughs, the moment cut short by a small whinny from inside the room. Grace freezes, then races inside.

She scoops Miles up and jiggles him up and down as she reaches into the diaper bag for a bottle. He starts to cry.

"Stop bouncing him like that," Hadley says, and Grace realizes she's followed her into the room.

Grace switches his position to cradle him in her left arm and sways him back and forth as she continues to rummage through the bag. Miles screams louder.

"For Christ's sake, you're going to give him whiplash. Hand him over."

Grace does as she says, her jaw sliding forward.

Hadley sits on the mattress and drapes Miles over her shoulder. She pats his back as she coos to him in a gentle, soothing tone, and immediately he stops crying.

Grace stares at her.

"What?"

"Nothing."

"Fix his bottle," Hadley says.

Grace grabs the formula and hurries into the bathroom to mix it, then races back and hands it to Hadley. A second later, Miles is in her lap, the bottle plugged in his mouth. He grabs onto it with his greedy little fists, sucking furiously.

"You're fine," Hadley says to Grace's obvious distress. "You'll get the hang of it. It just takes time."

Grace shakes her head. "I suck at it."

And Grace can tell Hadley doesn't mean to, but before she can stop herself, her head moves a fraction up, then down, confirming what Grace already knows, that she is entirely incompetent at the single most important job in the world.

"Sit," Hadley orders.

Grace plops beside her, her hands beneath her rump. Beside her, Miles continues to guzzle, his eyes rolled back in near elation.

"Here, you take him," Hadley says, holding him toward her.

Grace scoots sideways and shakes her head. "He's happy."

Hadley pulls him back, the hand that holds him caressing his foot as he eats.

After a moment, a smile curls Hadley's lips and she says, "Do you know what I'd be doing if I were home?"

It's Sunday night, almost midnight. Grace has no idea what Hadley would be doing, but she knows what she'd be doing. She would be home with Miles, who would be screaming his head off, and she would be trying to comfort him in every way she could think of while praying for him to pass out so she could pass out beside him.

"I'd be doing this," Hadley says. "Without Miles, of course. But I would be sitting on my bed after sneaking a cigarette. Only I wouldn't be enjoying it because I'd be thinking how much Frank hates that I smoke, and I'd be worrying that he might come home and smell it on me. So, I'd be neurotic, sniffing the air and trying to smell my own breath, probably pacing or cleaning. I do that when I get nervous. I clean."

"So, for you, this is actually an improvement?" Grace says.

"A sad statement on my life."

"Your life's not over."

"I'm almost forty."

"Really? I thought you were older."

Hadley's face snaps up, and Grace smirks an "I gotcha" look at her.

"Ha ha, very funny. You just wait until your first wrinkles start winking at you in the mirror. We'll see how much you're laughing then."

Miles has conked out, formula drooling from his open mouth, his hand still holding the bottle.

"Burp rag," Hadley says, and Grace hands her a towel.

Hadley drapes Miles over her shoulder and coaxes several small gas bubbles from him. Grace would have never done that. She would have just let him sleep.

Hadley notices Grace's expression. "You need to get the air out; otherwise it causes cramping." She looks around. "Hand me one of the bath towels."

Grace retrieves a towel from the bathroom.

"Lay it flat on the bed."

Hadley lays Miles on the towel diagonally and folds the bottom corner over his feet.

"He doesn't like to be swaddled," Grace says.

"Of course he does," Hadley says, pissing Grace off.

Grace folds her arms across her chest, waiting for Hadley to finish and for Miles to let out a howl. Since he was born, he has hated the constraints of a blanket being wrapped tight around him.

Hadley finishes and straightens. "There you go, big boy, all set for the night."

He is not howling. Rather, he is sleeping soundly, snug in his cocoon, except for his arms, which are slung over his head like a champion.

"Most boys like to have their arms free," Hadley says, like it's no big deal, like everyone knows that. But Grace didn't know that. No one ever told her that. It's a miracle, the simplest, most remarkable trick in the world. Miles is entirely content, his face not contorted in the least like it usually is as he wrestles himself to sleep. "You'll get the hang of it," Hadley repeats; then she stands and retrieves her crutches. "Well, good night. Another big day tomorrow, hopefully one not nearly as eventful as today."

"Thank you," Grace manages, the uncomfortable feeling in her chest returning.

Hadley tilts her head. "You do realize it's the other way around, don't you? That I'm the one who should be thanking you?"

Hadley is almost to the door when Grace says, "I'm glad I met you."

Hadley turns.

"Regardless of how this turns out, I just wanted you to know that. That . . . this is going to sound really stupid . . . but the last two days, well, they've been kind of fun."

Hadley smirks, tilts her head, then straightens it and says, "Was that painful?"

"Excruciating."

Hadley gives a full-wattage smile, then continues out the door, and for a long time, Grace stares at the spot where she was, knowing how dangerous it is to start liking someone.

She firmly resolves to stop. Miles is her family and her single concern. Hadley, Mattie, and Skipper—they are just people, a random crossing that someday she will look back on with fondness but that tomorrow she needs to leave behind.

She rubs her knuckles against her chest again, rubbing again at the lightness that is terrifying.

40

HADLEY

The highway winds down from the Sierras, bits of daylight peeking through the treetops. On either side of the road, giant pines soar toward the sky, an imposing, glorious landscape that makes Hadley feel small and her problems very far away. She allows herself to get lost in it—no outside world, no worries, no regrets—only the extreme beauty and the sheer awesomeness of it all.

But the moment they hit the highway, a strip of asphalt stretched to the horizon between crust-colored landscapes, her recollection of yesterday and everything that has happened over the past three days slams into her, and her emotions rise—disbelief followed by astonishment:

I am a fugitive from the law. A criminal?

I slept with Mark! An FBI agent I only just met?

She knows she should focus on the first, but her brain keeps getting stuck on the second, Mark's laughter followed by his touch filling her mind and making it impossible to think about anything else.

Her whole life, she has never been a spontaneous person, always worrying so much about doing what's right that the chance to do anything remarkable inevitably passes her by. But yesterday . . . yesterday, it was like all that hesitation and second-guessing miraculously fell away, and for the first time, she was entirely unconcerned about messing up or doing something she might regret—bold and fearless in a way she's never been.

She thinks about how badly Mark wanted to be good, the way he stepped back as she hopped toward him, his bound hands in front of him, and the look of fear on his face, like she was someone to be scared of, the devil out to steal his soul. And maybe she was.

She laughs, and Grace looks over, then rolls her eyes and turns up the radio, as if trying to drown her out.

Hadley turns away and stares at the beige landscape through the window as she replays those remarkable minutes in her mind—*twenty? Thirty? Maybe less?* So little, and yet transformative. Like she is changing. Or has changed. She glances at Grace and wonders if it's possible that some of her amazing courage has rubbed off on her.

So much laughter as they went about it—the fiasco with their clothes, then figuring out how to make it work with his hands tied and the ACE bandage between them. Never has she had so much fun having sex. Usually, it's such a serious affair, or she's taken it that way. But it doesn't have to be serious. It can be fun. And funny.

But also something else. She tilts her head to think about it, define what she's feeling. *Easy,* she thinks, feeling like she's stumbled upon a great secret. Sex with the right person is easy, like finding the perfect match in a ten-thousand-piece puzzle. *Snap. Look at that: we work.* So easy.

Mattie did a report once on seahorses—stunning little creatures that mate for life. They choose a partner to tether their tail to, then float endlessly through the ocean together. But before they make that very important decision, they court, dancing around each other for days to be sure they are compatible, their systems in sync—their rhythms, pulses, and cycles.

That's how it was with her and Mark, like they were seahorses perfectly in sync. She smiles as she thinks how in sync they were.

"Are you kidding me?" Grace says, and Hadley realizes she has giggled again.

She tries to stop thinking about it, knowing this is no time for such happiness. But she simply can't help it. No matter how hard she tries, each time she pushes the thoughts away, Mark marches right back in, smiling and laughing and doing things to her—naughty, horrible, wonderful things—without asking her permission at all.

She is stunned to be feeling this way, like a teenage girl with a runaway crush. But that is exactly how she feels—giddy and breathless . . . perhaps even a little in love.

Could that be? Love? After so little time with someone?

She can't remember the last time she felt this way. Has she ever felt this way? Maybe. Middle school? A crush on the lead singer in a boy band. But not like this, where it is real. Mark is real.

The station switches to a song about doing it better in the next thirty years, and she nods along with the lyrics.

Peanut butter and jelly. Ham and swiss. Fried chicken and waffles. For fifteen years, she has struggled, not understanding what she was doing wrong, all of it so hard. Then, wham, like a shade snapping open, everything suddenly so clear. Chemistry, the simple unique magnetism of two particular organisms toward each other. Yesterday, she and Mark were frothing and fizzing and bubbling all over the place, laughing and having fun and holding each other like it was the most natural thing in the world.

She leans her head against the window and sighs.

His son is Ben. His daughter is Shelly. She imagines the dog he and Ben will choose. She hopes they get a puppy, or at least a dog that's young—the chaos of canine adolescence priceless.

What would it be like to be a part of it? She and Mattie with Mark and Ben and Shelly and a new dog. The idea is far fetched and outrageous, fanciful and delusional, yet also delicious in the way only outrageous ideas can be. Full of charm and possibility, it flutters in her

196

mind like a butterfly, flittering and flickering until it glows so bright her whole mind is filled with it.

She thinks of the likelihood of ever finding that kind of magic again. She is thirty-eight, and this is the first time she's felt it—that's how narrow the odds: one in a hundred thousand, or maybe a million.

"You okay?" Grace asks.

"Fine," Hadley lies, no longer happy at all.

~

They lunch along the Truckee River, a picnic of sandwiches and chips bought from a truck stop a few miles back. The river is beautiful, and they are the only ones on its banks. Miles lies beside her on a beach towel practicing his new talent of rolling over, his adroitness at rolling from his stomach to his back much better than the other way around.

It is Memorial Day. If she were home, she would be at the beach. Every year, the neighborhood gathers in the community's private cove to play volleyball, boogie board, barbeque, and—Skipper's favorite—play Wiffle ball. Frank and Skipper love it. She and Mattie hate it.

This year would have been better than last. The economy is looking up, so her wealthy neighbors would have been slightly less stressed. The wine would be more expensive, the upcoming elections the topic of choice. She sighs thinking about it, glad not to be a part of it, to not be nodding and smiling and making small talk while sucking in her stomach and counting the minutes until they can leave.

She glances at her watch. Frank might be there now. She hopes he is. She hasn't called him since after their dinner at Denny's in Baker two days ago, which means that, even if he is not aware of the trouble she's in or that she stole the money, he knows she is not following the plan. Her brain goes white thinking about it, uncertain what scares her more—being caught by the FBI or being tracked down by Frank.

She pushes the thought away and instead focuses on the moment. She is lying on the edge of a river in Nevada watching Miles entertain himself while Mattie and Skipper sit with their feet in the river playing on their PlayStations as they pop blueberries in their mouths.

Mattie sticks out her purple tongue, and Skipper cracks up laughing. It makes Hadley smile all the way to her spine. It's been a long time since she's seen such joy between them.

Grace lies on a large boulder, napping. She was feeling a bit under the weather this morning but seems to be doing better now. Hadley finds herself worrying over Grace a lot today. She looks very tired and, despite her stoicism, seems a bit lost.

The plan is for Grace to drive them to Salt Lake City; then, in the morning, Hadley will buy a car and give driving a go. Her ankle is slightly better, and by tomorrow, she should be able to bear enough weight on it to press a gas pedal.

The thought of Grace and Miles leaving makes Hadley horribly sad. In the past three days, she has grown incredibly attached. She looks at Miles on the blanket, his legs kicking in the air and his little fists waving in front of him. She is going to miss him . . . miss both of them.

Skipper lets out a whoop of victory, and Hadley looks up and gives Mattie a smile, knowing she let him win, a generosity and kindness Mattie would not have shown a week ago—the moping, angry girl of before replaced with a girl remarkably like her daughter from a year ago.

This morning, at breakfast, she even initiated a conversation, asking Hadley about cars and about the first one she ever owned. They all had a good laugh when Hadley told her it was her dad's old Bentley, a beast of ostentation the size of a semi with a red leather interior and chrome rims. She totaled it a month after he gave it to her, and she swears that was his plan all along.

After Mattie asked about the car, she brought up the preposterous idea of Grace teaching her to drive so Mattie can help out once they're left on their own. Hadley smiles thinking about it, the idea ludicrous. Mattie is only fourteen.

She flexes her ankle again and conceals the wince, concern shadowing her tranquil mood. The drive from Salt Lake City to Denver is nearly eight hours. That's a lot of driving on an ankle that still refuses to bend.

Mattie walks up and plops on the blanket beside Miles, her cheeks flush from the cool air and her hair windblown. Hadley smiles at her. Even her makeup is lighter today, the faint freckles on her nose showing through the brush of foundation.

She lies on her stomach so her face is even with Miles's, who is flailing like an upside-down turtle, trying to unlock the mystery of getting back to his tummy. Mattie gives him a nudge to help him out, and he lets out a squeal of delight, pushes up on his arms proud as a peacock, then promptly rolls himself back to his back and starts flailing again.

Mattie giggles, a light sound like wind chimes, and suddenly her baby is a little girl again—wide eyed and holding her Pooh Bear as she climbs into Hadley's lap to snuggle against her. Time is a thief, she thinks. You believe you have an infinite amount of it, but then you blink and everything that was has been replaced with something else entirely.

"How you doing, baby?" she says.

"Good," Mattie answers absently, her focus still on Miles. A moment later, she says, "Mom, what happens if it doesn't work out?" She is trying hard to sound unconcerned, like whatever the answer, it's okay and no big deal, but her voice wavers.

Hadley forces her own uncertainty away as she sweeps a tendril from Mattie's face and sluices it behind her ear. "Then I'll need you to be stronger than ever."

Mattie offers a brave smile, and Hadley's heart swells with pride, amazed at her daughter's strength and courage, glad she got some of Frank's toughness.

Mattie looks back at Miles and helps him roll over again, with the same overjoyed result; then she mutters, "I hope I do better."

"Better?"

"You know, than before."

Hadley says nothing. She thinks Mattie was doing okay. Perhaps she wasn't as popular as she would have liked, but she got good grades, stayed out of trouble, got glowing remarks from her teachers. Or maybe she's thinking more about her dad and wishing, like Hadley, she'd been stronger or maybe able to change things.

Hadley looks away, hoping she does better as well, that somehow they make it through this so they can start again and she can be the mother she's always intended to be. Her eyes slide to Grace, a mite of a woman, yet no one would mess with her or Miles—no one, not even Frank. He tried, and look what happened. She showed up with her ragged striped bag to take what was hers.

Skipper lopes up and sits beside Mattie, so Hadley changes the subject. "What happened yesterday when you were with Grace?"

"Home run," Skipper says before Mattie can answer. "Over the fence."

"Wow," Hadley says, looking at Mattie for translation, but she doesn't give one.

"Cleared the bleachers," Skipper says to emphasize the point, and Mattie grins.

"You're not going to tell me what that means?" Hadley says.

"What what means?" Grace says, walking up and lifting Miles into her arms.

"Champ says you hit a home run."

"Grand slam," Skipper says, his face lit up, and Mattie and Grace exchange a conspiratorial look.

"Will someone *please* tell me what that means?"

When no one answers, she says, "Really?"

They all just continue grinning, and Hadley pushes to her feet with a huff. "Well, from here on out, no more home runs. From now on, we lie low and don't draw attention to ourselves."

She hops off angrily, hating and loving that she was left out of whatever the four of them shared that was obviously so grand.

~

They drive through miles and miles of high desert, passing through several small towns. A couple of times they stop for potty breaks and to stretch their legs, but mostly they just drive, all of them exhausted and grouchy from the long day of travel, their third in a row.

Near eight, Grace pulls into a barbeque restaurant on the outskirts of Salt Lake City that she says she visited with her husband after they got married. Loud music thrums from the open doors, and people spill out onto the wraparound porch. The smell of meat and barbeque sauce drifts past Hadley's nose, and her stomach rumbles.

Her diet has been completely blown to smithereens the past three days, but surprisingly, it is not as distressing as she would have thought. More a blasé concern. The feeling similar to how she feels about flossing. Each day she thinks about it, knowing that if she doesn't floss, eventually it will catch up with her and she will wind up with gum disease, but when it comes right down to it, the future seems very far off and she doesn't care quite enough to actually get it done.

They settle at a picnic table lined with a red-checkered plastic tablecloth, and Hadley stays with Miles as Grace and the kids go off to get the food. Miles's eyes are wide with wonder as he takes in the music and the lights and the buzz of activity around them, which Hadley agrees really is something.

Pat's Barbeque is a genuine cowboy bar. Across the room, a country band croons from a stage, and in front of it, men, women, and kids decked out in cowboy boots, Wranglers, and large silver belt buckles dance.

Grace plops a heaping plate of tri-tip, corn on the cob, coleslaw, and cornbread in front of her, along with a mug of beer, and Hadley uses her napkin to wipe the butter from the corn and the barbeque sauce from the meat before nibbling at both. Meanwhile, Grace slathers her ribs with extra sauce and drenches her potatoes in gravy, then digs in.

Skipper saws at his steak. Miles babbles and fists a chunk of cornbread into his mouth, some of it making it, most of it landing elsewhere. Mattie gnaws on her ribs, stopping every few bites to ask Grace something about engines or cars, a subject Grace seems to know a lot about and for which Mattie has a sudden fascination.

It's strange, the normalcy of it. The five of them having dinner together, an odd facsimile of family that feels bizarrely right, and Hadley can't recall the last time she's enjoyed a meal so much.

"Dance?"

All of them look up to see a lanky cowboy extending his hand to Grace. Grace blushes, then pushes from the table, and all of them watch in amazement as he leads her to the dance floor and as she expertly joins in a line dance of kicking, stomping, clapping, and twirling that looks like it takes years to master.

The outfit Grace bought suits her—rolled-up faded blue jeans, a white V-neck T-shirt, and knockoff white Keds. She looks spunky and young and full of life, exactly how a twenty-six-year-old should look, and as Hadley watches her, her guilt rises until it strangles her for the danger she's put her in.

"Mom, you okay?"

"Huh? Yeah, fine. Mattie, keep an eye on Miles and Skipper. I'll be right back."

She hops outside on her crutches, leans against the porch railing, and pulls out the burner phone. Tomorrow, Grace and Miles are leaving, which means it's time for her to start thinking about the steps she needs to take without her.

In front of her, a group of bikers goofs off, drinking beers and messing around. She turns away from them and lifts the phone to her ear.

"Ness," she says when her sister answers.

"Christ, Had, where have you been? I've been, like, trying to call you for days. Your cell is like out of service or something. Did you know the FBI are looking for you?"

Hadley's pulse kicks up a notch with the realization that the FBI has called her sister. It makes sense. It's just that, until Vanessa said it, Hadley hadn't considered the possibility, and somehow, her sister knowing makes it all seem so much worse.

"Had, you there?"

"Yeah, I'm here."

"What the hell's going on? They were calling like every five minutes; then they showed up at my hotel—"

"They showed up? In Belize?"

"Well, not them, but some Belizean cops. Two guys came by to tell me the FBI was calling and that I needed to call them back. As if I didn't know they were calling. Tom's totally freaked out."

"It's okay—"

"The hell it is!" she practically screams.

Hadley pulls the phone from her ear. "Ness, calm down."

"Calm down! I can't calm down. Tom is pissed. He was so stressed he ended our honeymoon early."

Hadley has only met Tom once. She joined him for a quick lunch when he had a layover in LA during a business trip. She was not impressed. He is a man who loves to talk, mostly about himself, and he's not all that exciting a subject, his interests limited to mountain biking and his investments.

"Tom's a straight arrow," Vanessa says, "and he didn't sign up for this."

"Ness," Hadley says, working hard to keep her voice calm, "I understand you're upset, but things are fine. Skipper is fine."

Silence.

Hadley feels a prickle down her spine. She looks at Skipper through the window. He sits where she left him, his baseball hat askew and his shoulders slumped as he stares at the people dancing, eating, and talking around him.

After a long minute, when her sister still hasn't responded, Hadley says, "I'm calling because we need to change the plan. I can't bring Skipper to Tom's anymore, so I need you to meet us."

Nothing.

"Ness? Did you hear me?"

"It's been horrible," Vanessa mumbles, and it sounds like she might be crying. "Tom's so upset he won't even talk to me."

It's Hadley's turn to be silent, her skin sizzling as she waits for what's coming, knowing it but unwilling to accept it until her sister says it out loud.

"I can't," Vanessa stammers. "I'm sorry, Had . . . but Tom . . . he doesn't want this . . . I just can't."

A beat later, the line goes dead, and Hadley pulls the phone from her ear and stares at it. She considers hurling it across the parking lot, but the idiotic bikers are still across from her, one of them trying to balance a beer on his head, so she decides against it.

She looks again at Skipper as a woman walking past notices him and smiles. He smiles back, and she grins wider, unable to help herself. Skipper often gets that reaction, a remarkable boy who can't help but be noticed.

Tears well in Hadley's eyes, and her heart aches. Without him, she and Mattie might have a chance. With him, they have none.

41

GRACE

The cowboy Grace is dancing with is named Burt. Tall as Jimmy but with no muscle on his bones, he swirls and twirls and do-si-dos like a cowboy Fred Astaire, and it's all Grace can do to keep up. The old routines return with only a few missteps, and by the third song, she's found her groove and is having a great time.

Hadley disappeared for a few minutes, but now she's back. She sits at the table holding Miles on her lap and guzzling her beer. Mattie is beside her looking bored. Grace grabs Burt's hand and pulls him with her. "Come on," she says to Mattie when they reach the table.

Mattie tilts her head and looks at her like she's lost her mind, an expression just short of an eye roll that says, *Are you kidding? There's no way I'm doing that. I hate country music, and I am far too cool and far too afraid of being uncool to even attempt it.*

Grace doesn't budge. Her hand remains outstretched as she gives a retaliating look that says, *Are you freaking kidding me? You'd rather sit here, bored out of your mind, beside your mom?*

And Grace's look wins, because Mattie's mouth twitches with a smile; then with a grumble, she allows Grace to pull her up and onto the dance floor. Burt shows Mattie the basics, and after a few songs, she has the cha-cha and the wobble down and is smiling ear to ear.

Mattie is curvy like her mom, and the hip-swaying moves suit her; Grace notices several guys' eyes sliding her way. And while she wants to slap their faces for looking at a fourteen-year-old the way they're looking at her, she also feels proud.

She glances at Hadley to see if she's noticing, but Hadley is not looking at the dance floor, her focus on her drink in front of her, whiskey from the looks of it, the pitcher of beer gone. Miles is in his car seat, and Skipper is asleep on the bench. A flicker of concern crosses Grace's mind, but it is distracted by a reed-thin boy who has walked up and is asking Mattie if she'd like to join him for a Coke.

Mattie glances at Grace for permission, which throws Grace off, as she isn't used to having any sort of authority over anyone. Then, realizing there is an awkward pause, she gets it together and offers a nod, the swelling in her chest ballooning as she watches them walk off toward the bar. Halfway there, Mattie throws a smile back over her shoulder, and Grace gives her a double thumbs-up, the swelling growing to near bursting.

"Your sister?" Burt says.

"No, we're not related," she says, though it doesn't feel that way. At this moment, it feels very much like Mattie is blood.

"Darts?" Burt offers.

Grace glances back one more time at Hadley, Skipper, and Miles. They seem fine, so she turns to follow Burt to the game room.

They've taken two steps when Mattie runs up to them. "We need to go," she says, her eyes wide. She shoots a look back at the boy who asked her to join him for a Coke. He sits at a table beside the bar, smiling at his phone.

"He knows who we are," Mattie says. "He's some sort of crime buff, and he saw us on the FBI crime site this morning. He said he wanted to take a selfie; then, as soon as he did, he was like, 'My friends are going to love this. Me and an outlaw.' Then he said the thing about seeing us on the site."

"Frick," Grace says.

"What's going on?" Burt asks.

"Mattie, go to the car." She hands Mattie the keys.

"Something wrong?" Burt says.

"No." Grace paints on a sweet smile. "Everything's fine. Adolescent drama. Thanks for the dance." She walks from him to the kid, who is still smirking at his phone.

She swipes it from his hands.

"Hey," he says.

"You think it's cool to hang with outlaws?" she says, her gaze piercing his. "Here's a tip: don't mess with a woman who has a gun and knows how to use it."

His face blanches.

She looks down at the screen. Snapchat. She deletes the post of him and Mattie with the hashtags #scoringwithanoutlaw, #sizzlinghot, #patsbarbeque. Then she opens his photo library and deletes the photo.

"Did you post it anywhere else?"

His face still white, he shakes his head.

"If I find out you're lying, I will come back here, hunt you down, and castrate you like a newborn bull." She uses her most badass look, the one that is icy calm and that Jimmy says would scare the bejeezus out of anyone.

The kid nods numbly, and satisfied he's sufficiently terrified, she gives him back his phone, pulls a twenty from her pocket, and sets it on the bar. "For the sodas," she says, then walks away. It's always best to leave people liking you.

She marches to Hadley. "We need to go."

Hadley's head is collapsed on her arms, three empty glasses in front of her. She looks up through red-rimmed eyes. "Grace," she slurs. "Hi,

Grace. Are you having fun? You're a good dancer. You should dance more often—"

"Hadley, stop talking."

Hadley stops, her mouth suspended midword.

"We need to go," Grace repeats.

Hadley shakes her head, then drops it back to her arms. "You go back to dancing. I'm just going to take a little rest."

"Judas frigging Priest. Hadley, get up."

"It's funny that you don't swear," Hadley says, looking up through drunk eyes. "It's like you should totally swear because it fits your personality, but then you don't. It's funny."

Grace rolls her eyes. "Hadley. Get. Up."

"Where's Mattie?" Hadley says, looking around Grace as if she might be hiding her.

"She's waiting for us in the car."

"Oh. Okay."

Hadley attempts to stand but immediately falls back to the bench, jostling it and causing Skipper to tumble to the ground. He startles awake and thrashes to a sitting position, his eyes darting side to side to remember where he is.

Grace helps him up as he wipes the sleep from his eyes. "Skipper, do you think you're strong enough to carry Miles to the truck? I need to help your mom."

"I don't need help. I've got this," Hadley says, pushing herself up again and grabbing for her crutches, one of them falling from her grasp to dangle from the bench.

Grace hands the car seat to Skipper, and it takes all his strength, but with great determination, he lugs it toward the door.

"Watch out for cars," Hadley slurs after him.

Grace sighs out through her nose, hoists the backpack onto her shoulders, slings the diaper bag across her chest, grabs the crutch that fell with her right hand, then wraps her left arm around Hadley's waist to support her. They take a step, and the diaper bag falls forward and nearly knocks them to the ground.

"You need to carry the backpack," Grace says.

Slipping from beneath Hadley's arm, she threads the pack onto Hadley's shoulders, adjusts the diaper bag so it's slung behind her instead of in front of her, then picks up the extra crutch again and wraps her arm around Hadley's waist. This time, she manages to drag Hadley toward the door, Hadley's crutch-step motion missing every third stride and nearly buckling Grace each time.

They're almost outside when Hadley stops so abruptly they nearly topple over. "You need to go," she says.

"We are going," Grace says, irritated.

Hadley shakes her head, and her whole body waves with it. "No. Not from here." She uses her crutch to gesture to the room. "From us."

"We are," Grace hisses. "Tomorrow. Remember?"

Hadley shakes her head more adamantly. "No. Now. You need to go, now." She starts to take the backpack off her shoulders. "I have Miles's sweater."

Grace stops her. "What are you talking about?"

"You need to go," Hadley says again, still struggling to pull the strap from her shoulder while Grace pins it in place.

"Hadley, stop."

Hadley does; then her shoulders fold forward and she starts to cry, her body hiccuping with her tears.

"What's going on?" Grace says.

Hadley drops her chin to her chest, and her head shakes back and forth. "We're going to get caught," she mumbles. "I'm going to jail, so you need to go. My sister . . ." The words trail off, swallowed by her sobs as her head continues to sway.

And life begins to make sense. Hadley called her sister, and her sister no longer wants to take Skipper.

"Okay," Grace says. "Let's go."

"But—"

"But nothing. The plan is still the same. Miles and I are going to split but not until tomorrow. For tonight, we're still a team."

"A team?" Hadley says, looking up through her wet lashes. "You and me?"

Grace rolls her eyes.

"Like Bonnie and Clyde?"

"Yeah, like Bonnie and Clyde. Now, let's go."

"Can I be Bonnie?"

"You can be Pinocchio for all I care—just start walking."

She wraps her arm back around Hadley's waist, and Hadley hops along as best she can, still sniffling but no longer distressed.

One catastrophe at a time, Grace thinks. It was one of her grandmother's favorite sayings. She'll deal with the next calamity after she gets through this one.

The cold air slaps them as they step onto the porch, a welcome relief as Grace sweats from the effort of lugging Hadley. She squints into the darkness to see Skipper beside the truck and Miles in his car seat on the ground beside him.

She wonders why he's not inside with Mattie. But only for a second. Her eyes follow her ears to squint into the darkness at a trio of men who have Mattie cornered at the edge of the parking lot. Mattie giggles uncomfortably, and Grace knows that laugh: it's the same laugh she's given when trying to get out of a tight spot without panicking.

One of the men has his arm draped over Mattie's shoulders, and another stands menacingly close.

Grace steps toward them, forgetting she is holding Hadley, and nearly sends them both tumbling down the steps.

"Stay here," she says, unwrapping Hadley's arm from her shoulder and handing her the second crutch.

As Grace walks across the asphalt, her disbelief and anger sizzle as she realizes the three idiots surrounding Mattie are the same bikers who cut in front of her at the gas station three days ago. The fourth biker is to the side, the one who went into the minimart and came out with the doughnuts. He leans against his motorcycle sipping a beer. When he sees her, he tips an imaginary hat. She ignores him, her eyes tight on Mattie.

Mattie sees her and shifts, and the man holding her turns. He tightens his grip, and Grace stops.

"Get your hands off my daughter" cuts through the air behind her, and Grace turns to see Hadley drunkenly crutch-hopping down the steps.

"Whoa, momma," the biker says; then he pulls Mattie closer so he now has her in almost a choke hold, the crook of his elbow around her neck, which forces her to bend. Mattie looks up at Grace, her eyes rounded with fear. "Hey, I know you," he says to Grace. "Where do I know you from?"

Grace is about to say something about leather pants and venereal diseases when, behind her, a gunshot ruptures the air.

Grace whirls to see Hadley holding Frank's gun in the air like she is starting a race. "I said, get your hands off my daughter."

"Hadley—" Grace starts, but that's as far as she gets before the gun fires again.

Grace ducks, and the bikers dive. The one who was leaning against his bike scurries behind it. The two that had been beside the one holding Mattie crawl army-style on their bellies toward a car. And the one who had been holding Mattie now cowers behind a log.

Mattie stands frozen, staring at her mom. Grace grabs her hand and yanks her forward. "Go!" she says, propelling her toward the truck.

"Don't fuck with me!" Hadley roars, waving the gun in the air.

Heart ricocheting in her chest, Grace walks toward her and takes the gun from her hand. "Get in the truck," she says, retrieving Hadley's crutches from the ground and handing them to her.

Hadley hobbles away, still mumbling about not fucking with her.

Grace follows, walking backward with the gun panning in front of her. She has no idea if the bikers are armed, but she's not taking any chances. The bikers behind the car and log stay hidden. The one behind the motorcycle stands with his hands in the air.

She feels the people in the restaurant watching, the buzz of their excitement floating through the door, along with the flashes from camera phones that cause her heart to misfire.

Grace throws the diaper bag onto the seat, then climbs in after it. She stashes the gun in the side compartment, throws the truck in reverse, and peels backward from the spot.

She's shifted into drive and is about to floor it for the exit when the biker who is standing steps toward them. He smiles at her through the windshield and then, for good measure, gives a hip thrust and a wink.

She slams down on the gas and cranks the wheel right. The monster tires kick up gravel as the truck skids sideways, then forward, and the biker leaps out of the way, though there's no need. Grace isn't aiming for him. The ramming bars on the front grille hit his bike first, followed by the satisfying crunch of metal beneath the tires as they roll over the remaining three. The truck bounces back to the pavement, and a second later, they're on the street and racing into the night.

42

HADLEY

Hadley is fairly certain Grace just bulldozed several motorcycles, and she thinks she just fired a gun. Her whole body quakes, adrenaline and alcohol swirling dangerously in her brain.

"Grace, slow down," she says, the trees on either side of them whipping past and the truck wobbling dangerously.

"Why?" Grace spits, pure venom in the word. "You worried we might get pulled over for speeding? No worries—you'll just talk your way out of it. Up your record to nine out of ten. Of course there might be the small, wee little issue the cops might have with the one-way shoot-out you just had in a parking lot. Might be a smidge more difficult to talk your way out of that one."

"Please, Grace, I'm not feeling so good. You really need to slow down." The world is spinning very quickly, Hadley's stomach lurching with it.

"Slow down! Slow down! You do realize that, at this moment, half the cops in Utah are on their way to that restaurant?"

In the back seat, Mattie cries, her soft sobs cutting through Grace's rant.

Hadley turns to comfort her, then quickly turns back. "Really, Grace, I think I'm going to be sick."

The truck squeals, then lurches right, and they bounce violently over a curb, then a sidewalk, to land with a thud in the parking lot of a mall with a movie theater. They skid around an RV parked at one end, and the truck jerks to a stop.

Hadley wrenches open the door and stumbles out. Her ankle buckles, and she collapses to her knees, the contents of her stomach following as she hurls tri-tip, corn, beer, and whiskey onto the pavement. Beneath the undercarriage of the truck, she sees two pairs of feet: Mattie's black Converse high-tops and Grace's knockoff white Keds.

"You're okay," Grace's voice soothes. "Get it all out." And Hadley realizes Mattie is vomiting as well.

Mattie in trouble—her face white with fear as she stood across the parking lot with that man, his arm around her. Then the gun was in my hand.

And BANG!

She was surprised how loud it was and how easily it went off. The twitch of a finger. Then a second time, her arm recoiling with the shock of it.

She shakes her head, trying to straighten the thoughts, certain they can't be right.

Tears drip down her face, combining with the mucus that runs from her nose. She hates guns. Has always hated them. And this is why. They make it too easy to screw up, and to screw up permanently. The man laughed, mocking her as if she were nothing; then he had his arm around Mattie's neck, and something just snapped. *BANG!* And just like that, she made things worse . . . again.

She squeezes her eyes against it, and when she opens them, Grace's shoes are in front of her nose. Mattie is beside her, her arms folded tight around herself. "I'm sorry, Mom," she mumbles, her face streaked with tears.

"You have nothing to be sorry for," Hadley manages. "It's my fault. All my fault."

"What were you doing with them?" Grace asks Mattie.

"The guy asked if I could take a photo of them," Mattie says. She toes the ground. "Then he wanted to take one with me, and I didn't know what to say." She wraps her arms tighter and shakes her head. "He wouldn't let me go; then he started saying things . . ." Her voice trails off, and Hadley cries harder. She didn't even know Mattie was in trouble. How could she not have known?

Thumping inside the truck causes them all to turn, and Hadley tries to stand to go to Skipper so she can calm him, but her equilibrium is seriously off kilter, and all she manages to do is stagger sideways, then fall back to her knees.

When she looks up, Mattie is gone. "It's okay, Champ," Mattie says from inside the truck. "Stop banging. It's okay. Everyone's okay."

The thumping continues.

"Now, on the Saint Louis team," Mattie says, altering her voice so it's wonky, "we have Who's on first?"

Thump. Thump. Thump.

"What's on second," she goes on, reciting the Abbott and Costello skit she and Skipper performed at his talent show this year. "I Don't Know's on third . . ."

"My sister's not taking him," Hadley says, looking up at Grace.

"I gathered that."

"Come on, Champ," Mattie urges. "I Don't Know's on third . . ."
Thump. Thump. Thump.

"It's why I told you to go," Hadley says. "It's over. There's no way we're not going to get caught."

"Look, Miles is smiling," Mattie says.

The thumping stops.

"See, everyone's okay," Mattie goes on. "Miles has never heard us do this. Let's do it for him. I Don't Know's on third . . ."

Skipper's voice, thick with emotion, says, "That's what I want to find out. I want you to tell me the names of the fellas on the Saint Louis team."

Hadley sighs in relief, and Grace exhales as well.

They both listen as Mattie and Skipper continue the routine; then Grace turns back to Hadley and says, "So much for laying low and not drawing attention to ourselves."

"Yeah, so much for that." Hadley looks up through her brow. "Did you really run over those guys' motorcycles?"

A small twitch of a smile as Grace says, "I believe I did."

"I love you," Hadley says as fresh tears spring to her eyes.

"Jiminy Crickets," Grace says, clearly not sharing the sentiment; then she pivots and marches away.

"Where are you going?"

"To get us out of this mess."

43

MARK

Mark is sitting by himself at a tiny table in the front window of Café Bean, an imitation Starbucks on the outskirts of Las Vegas. He stares at the newspaper. The half-page photo on the front page shows a blurry shot taken through the window of a barbeque joint in Salt Lake City called Pat's. In it, Hadley is firing a gun. The photo actually caught the flash from the muzzle, a white splotch that looks almost like a blemish on the dark image. In the background is Grace, four men, and Mattie. Grace and one of the bikers are closest, the others behind them. It's hard to make out the details, but one of the men has his arm around Mattie, presumably the reason Hadley was shooting.

The headline reads, *Real-Life Thelma and Louise Blaze through Salt Lake City.*

He sighs, sets the paper down, rubs his eyes.

Blinking them open, he takes a sip of his coffee, then reads the article for the fourth time, stunned each time with how almost accurate it is:

Like the fictional characters Thelma and Louise, two women have abandoned their suburban lives, hit the road, and found themselves on what appears to be an inadvertent crime spree that has them running from the law. But unlike the movie, these women are not on the run alone; with them are their three children, ages fourteen, eight, and four months.

Hadley Torelli, 38, and Grace Herrick, 26, left their Orange County, California, homes on Friday. It is not clear what prompted the women to leave, but on Saturday, the two eluded officials who attempted to detain them first at a hospital in Mission Viejo, where Torelli was being treated for a sprained ankle, then in Barstow. Why the FBI was pursuing the women is unclear, and the FBI has refused to comment.

Both women left behind husbands. Torelli has been married fifteen years to prominent Orange County businessman Frank Torelli, and Herrick has been married six years to US Army corporal James Herrick, who is currently serving in Afghanistan.

Early Sunday morning, Senior Special Agent Mark Wilkes tracked the women to a motel in Baker, a small city outside of Las Vegas, but before he could apprehend them, the women abducted him at gunpoint, stole his car, and drove him to a closed archaeological site, where they left him bound but with food, water, and supplies. The agent managed to escape late Sunday evening and was unharmed.

If this story sounds stranger than fiction, it is, and it gets stranger. Last night, the women, who had not been seen since leaving the agent, showed up at Pat's Barbeque, a restaurant in Salt Lake City, where the evening ended in a shoot-out in the parking lot with a group of motorcyclists, followed by Herrick using the truck they were traveling in to run over the motorcyclists' motorcycles.

Witnesses say the women appear to be traveling with a substantial amount of money, and everyone interviewed has described the women as friendly, polite, and generous. Nancy Carron, an 85-year-old woman from Mission Viejo who loaned her car to the women so they could drive to Barstow, said this about Torelli: "She was lovely. Poor thing. I could see she was in pain. And that little boy of hers was darling, eyes so light they reminded me of sea glass."

Carron loaned her car to the women in exchange for ten thousand dollars. "They left Pujols, that's what I call my car, right where they said they would," Carron says. "They even left a lovely note. Of course then the FBI got involved. Took the note and the money. Thieves."

Carron is not the only one Torelli and Herrick have been charitable with. The women also gave ten thousand dollars to Hunter Schwarz, a 23-year-old motel clerk who was working at the Wills Fargo Motel in Baker the night the women stayed there. The note penned on the top bill of the bundle of hundreds they left beneath his pillow read, "Get yourself a new smile and a new girl." Hunter explained he has been saving to have two teeth that were knocked out in a fight replaced. He had no idea the women had left the money until the FBI showed up and went through his things.

Unfortunately, neither Carron nor Schwarz will get to keep their gifts. The money has been seized as "evidence," and again the FBI has refused to comment.

Carron has threatened to sue, and unless the FBI has a solid explanation beyond "no comment," she might have a case. When asked about it, Carron said, "Crooks. There was no crime. I made a deal, fair and square, and those bastards took my money." Schwarz seems to agree. "Grace was just trying to help me out. We talked about how hard it is to get going again once you get down on your luck. She was cool, really cool, and she's going to be bummed when she finds out they took the money. It sucks. It really does."

It's unclear what set off the shoot-out outside the restaurant. Witnesses say the women and kids seemed to be enjoying themselves when something happened that caused the group to leave abruptly. No one was hurt in the altercation, and it is unclear whether the shots Torelli took were aimed at anyone or merely warning shots.

The two women and their kids fled in a Chevy truck with California plates.

These women might not be Susan Sarandon and Geena Davis, and there may not be a '66 Thunderbird convertible or an Oscar nomination, but there is no doubt of the similarity in these women's story with the fictional Thelma and Louise's, and we hope for their sake and their children's sakes that the ending is happier than that of the movie.

Mark sets the paper down, puts his elbows on the table, and, for a long time, sits silent, massaging his temples with two fingers on either side. The media storm around this is going to blow up. He can already see a Lifetime Original Movie being made. Hell, the motel clerk, that scrawny kid at the desk who went white as the walls around him when Mark showed his badge, probably has six marriage proposals by now and a dozen benefactors willing to give him a new smile. Every damn person in the article is going to be a celebrity and a hero, while the FBI is being painted as the Big Bad Wolf hunting Little Red Riding Hood and taking money from little old ladies and young men who need dental work.

He pushes to his feet and goes to the coffee station for a refill. A little girl around Shelly's age stands on her tiptoes very carefully pouring creamers into her mother's cup, as if it's the most important job in the world. He sighs. Tonight was supposed to be his night with the kids. Marcia sounded relieved when he called to tell her he wasn't going to make it: one less hassle for her to deal with.

Stan the Insurance Man will be around. He's always around, ever since he became a part of Marcia's life, less than a month after she told Mark she wanted a divorce. He doesn't think they were having an affair. Marcia's too righteous for that. But he suspects a not-so-innocent flirtation that gave her the confidence to ask Mark to leave.

Together they will take Ben to his baseball game, have pizza at Artie's after, then go home and watch *The Simpsons* on the couch together until it's time to tuck the kids into bed. Then, when the kids are asleep, they will go upstairs to have sex in his room, in his bed, his life stolen from him and given to Stan the Insurance Man.

He waits for the familiar fury to wash over him that makes him want to put his fist through the wall or through Stan the Insurance Man's wide-chinned face. Instead, surprisingly, all he feels is strange resignation. Perhaps he's tired. Or perhaps it's because of what happened between him and Hadley. Whatever the case, he just doesn't have it in him this morning to rage.

He rubs the bandaged cuts on his right wrist. Damn woman. What possessed her to shoot at those bikers? *Mattie.* He knows it, and his hate for the bastard in the photo is raw.

The door to the café opens, and he turns to see his boss, Garrett O'Toole, filling its frame. When he sees Mark, he scowls with an expression of disapproval and impatience as if irritated, though he is the one who is fifteen minutes late.

He wears aviator sunglasses propped on his bald head, a cream button-down dress shirt that probably started off white, and brown slacks that ride high on his gut and that are cinched too tight with a worn leather belt.

"Wilkes," he says.

"O'Toole."

Neither man extends his hand.

O'Toole sits down, then leans forward in his chair, the seat straining with his weight. A large man in both height and girth, he uses his size well, intimidating people by crowding their personal space and making everyone he comes in contact with uncomfortable.

Setting his elbows on the table, he leans in a fraction more, his breath surprisingly fresh, as if he's just popped a mint. "A full APB, a roadblock delaying millions of gamblers from reaching their weekend destination, half the Las Vegas police force, and every California and Nevada FBI agent on full alert and pulling round-the-clock shifts—not many agents can lay claim to inconveniencing that many people and costing taxpayers that much money because they were dumb enough to be hijacked by two broads and driven away in the trunk of their car."

Mark holds his ground, his face two inches from his boss's. "Don't worry, Garrett," he says. "I'm fine. Really. But thanks for your concern."

O'Toole grins a toothless smirk. "On the inside I'm dying of worry." Then he leans back a smidge, and Mark leans back as well.

Surprisingly, this is the first time Mark's gotten any grief for what happened. Last night, when he walked into the field office, he was greeted with hearty handshakes and pats on the back, everyone, to a man, relieved he had turned up safe. Guilt lined their faces—confession to their failure to find any lead as to where he was and testament to their waning hope of finding him alive. The only ribbing he got was a few hours later, when a couple of guys joked about not minding being taken hostage by two outlaws as hot as Torelli and Herrick, and wondering aloud if Mark might not have resisted as much as he could have.

But O'Toole is not congratulating him on being found alive or on his escape; nor is he bewitched by Hadley and Grace in the least. "Wilkes, you know what I hate worse than schlepping my ass to Nevada?"

Mark says nothing.

"It's having to explain to a horde of bloodsucking press why the lead agent on the case went Lone Ranger and tried to apprehend two dangerous criminals without waiting for backup."

"They weren't considered dangerous at the time," Mark says, immediately regretting it when O'Toole's face darkens.

"Even better," he says, "to have to explain to a swarm of asshole reporters why the lead agent, a seasoned veteran, who should know better, went after two women holed up in a motel with their three kids, triggering a tornado of mother-bear instincts and causing them to suddenly become armed and dangerous."

Mark's skin turns warm, his screwup impossible to defend.

"You're on thin ice, Wilkes," O'Toole says, his eyes glinting, and Mark feels his glee. Since Mark began working with O'Toole two years ago, there's been no love lost between them. Leaning back, he says, "You're off the case."

Mark tries not to flinch but does a poor job of it, and O'Toole's smile twitches.

"That's a mistake," Mark says. "I know these women and this case better than anyone. Hadley and Grace are not—"

"'Hadley and Grace'?" O'Toole interrupts, arching his eyebrow as if he's caught Mark at something sinister.

Mark exhales slowly through his nose. "Fine. Torelli and Herrick. These women are not your typical criminals. They're two moms who accidentally stumbled into trouble and who are now trying to avoid being caught and ending up in prison."

"Really? My mom isn't real keen on ending up in prison either," O'Toole says. "Then again, she didn't steal millions of dollars, kidnap a federal agent, then go on a shooting spree in a parking lot, not to mention mowing down some very fine machinery."

Mark's skin prickles as his concern grows. O'Toole is the kind of guy who follows the path of least resistance no matter the case, his only objective to clear his desk with as little effort as possible. Combine that with O'Toole's complete lack of empathy, compassion, and common sense, and Mark knows he'll have no problem issuing a shoot-to-kill directive on Hadley and Grace, extenuating circumstances or not.

Realizing how much rests on this moment, he tamps down his emotions and, in as level a voice as he can manage, says, "Garrett, please, these women are not violent, and I can reason with them. I spent time with them, and they trust me. I can bring them in, safely. Taking me off is a mistake."

O'Toole grins, an ugly sliver of malice, and Mark realizes his mistake, whatever chance he had obliterated by O'Toole's long-standing grudge against him. O'Toole knows Mark cares and has been waiting a long time for an opportunity just like this.

"Nothing to reason with," he says. "These women think they're above the law, and they're not. You had your chance. Now it's my turn."

Hadley's laugh and then Grace's smirk fill Mark's brain, and his heart lodges in his throat with fear. With all the humility he can muster, he makes one final plea. "Then put Fitz in the field," he says. "He knows the case, and he can help."

O'Toole squints his beady eyes, and Mark lowers his, praying complete submission will help. If he thought it would do any good, he would get on his knees.

For a long minute, O'Toole studies him before finally offering a nod, like an emperor throwing a beggar a bone. Silently Mark releases his breath. It's not much, but at least he'll have eyes and ears in the field. A feather in a hailstorm, but it's something.

O'Toole glances at the paper on the table. "Our very own *Thelma and Louise*," he says with a chuckle. "Damn, I liked that movie. That Geena Davis was something."

"That movie didn't end well," Mark says.

"Really?" O'Toole says, leaning back and lacing his hands over his wide belly. "I liked the ending." His gaze levels on Mark's, letting him know he would be perfectly fine with Hadley and Grace driving off a cliff—case closed, no messy paperwork, no loose ends.

44

GRACE

The mustard's fallen off the hot dog. It's a Jimmy-ism. Jimmy has a saying for everything, most of them involving food: *Cake can't cure everything. It takes both hands to hold a Whopper. Think outside the bun.* The man loves food.

Grace drapes her arm over her eyes to block out the morning sun streaming through the curtains she forgot to close. Though she barely drank last night, she feels hungover—her head throbbing and her stomach churning.

It's hard to believe how quickly things have unraveled. One minute she was dancing with Burt, laughing and having a good time, and the next, she was dodging bullets and running over motorcycles.

"We need to go," she said to Hadley when she returned from the movie theater, where she'd swiped the purse of a woman lost in a movie about aliens abducting pets to use as hosts.

Hadley was in the exact spot she had left her, the only change being that she had fallen from her knees to her butt, the vomit now beside her.

"Leave me alone," Hadley answered, and Grace considered it. The keys for the truck were in the ignition; the keys to the woman's car whose purse she had stolen were in her hand. The decision was as simple as grabbing Miles and walking away.

"Where are we going?" Mattie said, stepping from the truck with Hadley's crutches and slamming the door shut on any possibility other than continuing on together.

Grace leaned into the truck. "Hey, Skip, we need to go," she said.

He sat frozen in his seat beside Miles, his eyes staring straight ahead and his face pale.

"Listen, buddy, I know this is tough—"

His hands flew to his ears, and his head shook to block her out.

She placed her hand on his shoulder. "Okay, buddy. It's okay." She looked at Mattie. "We need to go."

As if on cue, sirens, thread thin, sounded from somewhere to the left, then grew louder as they traveled closer.

Mattie dropped the crutches beside her mom, then climbed back into the truck beside Skipper. "I hope Posey is catching tomorrow," she said.

Grace watched as Skipper took his hands from his ears, then turned to face her, his eyes flicking left and right, searching for traction.

"He's my favorite," Mattie went on. "You think we'll get to see him?"

Skipper's focus moved in and out, and Grace watched as Mattie searched for the next words. "Plus, he can hit. Posey's a heck of a hitter."

A sideways twist of the mouth as Skipper said, "Posey doesn't catch for the Rockies." And Grace nearly gave a cheer. It was remarkable.

"Well, then, who's catching?" Mattie said, undoing Skipper's seat belt and taking him by the hand to lead him from the truck.

Grace looked at her with awe, and Mattie shrugged like it was no big deal.

"Either Iannetta or Wolters," Skipper said.

"Did you ask Coach about the trade for Wolters?" Mattie said.

"I sent it. Do you have my PlayStation? I need to check."

Suddenly he was frantic again, but not about what had happened at the restaurant, his concern entirely on his fantasy baseball team and the trade he wanted to make.

"I do," Mattie said. She grabbed the backpack from the front seat. "It's in here. We'll check it when we get in the new car."

She led him toward the theaters, and Grace grabbed Miles and the diaper bag; then she kicked Hadley's crutches toward her and walked after them.

Two hours later, they were checked into this hotel under the name Blaire Butz, the name of the woman whose car they were driving, a woman who looks enough like Hadley for Hadley to get away with pretending to be her.

Ten minutes after that, Grace fell into a deep, horrible sleep. And now, eight hours later, she has woken up, and the reality of what's happened has descended on her. She drapes her other arm across her eyes as well, wishing she could return to unconsciousness.

The door to the adjoining room opens, and Grace turns her head to see Hadley in its frame. She is not using her crutches and instead hobbles gingerly on her injured ankle. Her eyes are bruised, and Grace can practically see her hangover pulsing.

"Nice digs," she says, her movements and words slow as she walks toward the bed, as if any sudden movement might rupture her brain.

"Yeah, I figured why not?" Grace answers.

In light of the increasing probability that she is going to be spending the remainder of her life sleeping on a prison mattress, Grace upgraded their hotel to a Sheraton. During her research of hotels that accept cash, she discovered Sheratons are among them, as long as you show ID.

Carefully Hadley lowers herself to the mattress beside Miles. She caresses his thigh and says, "I have a plan."

"Me too," Grace says. "We need to turn ourselves in."

Hadley flinches.

"I mean it," Grace says. "It's our only option."

Grace has thought it through. Because of last night's unfortunate turn of events, the chances of her walking away from this are gone. That kid who posted on Snapchat already knew about them, which means their photos and story are out there. Then, last night, dozens of people witnessed what happened at the restaurant, some even snapping photos. There's no way she is going to be able to just waltz across the border with Miles and start a new life. She wouldn't be surprised if a reward was now being offered for information leading to their arrest.

"But before we do," she adds, "we need to get our story straight."

"What are you talking about?"

"I'm talking about cutting our losses. Look, last night was a disaster. We just went from being everyday fugitives to probably being on the FBI's Most Wanted list, along with warnings about us being armed and dangerous . . . and crazy."

Hadley looks down, and Grace feels her regret. But none of that matters now. Grace is over being angry. What's done is done, and all that matters now is where things stand and how they deal with them going forward.

"The thing is," Grace says, her voice growing tight, "I have a record." She waits for surprise to register on Hadley's face, and when it doesn't, she says, "You knew?"

Hadley nods, and Grace swallows, deeply ashamed, as she always is about her past.

"You, on the other hand, are clean," she continues. "So, the deal is we spin it so it's all on me."

Hadley's head is already shaking. Grace ignores it. She's thought this through. It's the only way. She is going away regardless, but if they play their cards right, Hadley could walk away from this.

"We'll tell them I'm the one who came up with the plan to steal the money, and that I blackmailed you into it—"

"Stop," Hadley says, cutting Grace off. "We are not turning ourselves in, and if we do get caught, I'm telling the truth—"

"You can't. Hadley, you need to listen to me. I know how these things work. The system, it isn't fair. It's not about what's right, and it's not like, if you play by the rules, they reward you. If you play by the rules, you get screwed. The only chance we . . . you . . . have is for us to lie. You're a good liar, and we can make up a story that works. We can negotiate a deal ahead of time, before we turn ourselves in. We'll promise to turn over the money and explain I planned the whole thing. You'll claim you were acting under duress, that I had a gun and that the kids were with me when the agent showed up—"

"No!" The word is a roar. "Stop. We are not turning ourselves in. I told you, *I* have a plan."

Grace grits her jaw shut and waits for Hadley to explain *her* plan, which, knowing Hadley, will involve beguiling border guards with fake French accents so they can sneak into Canada or chartering a private jet to fly them to Spain—some ludicrous idea that doesn't have a snowball's chance in hell of working. When she's done, Grace will continue to explain the best way to spin this. Best-case scenario is Hadley walks and Grace manages to plea-bargain her sentence down to something reasonable: ten years or less. With good behavior, she'll be out in five. She looks at Miles and pushes back the tears that fill her eyes with the thought.

"I know how to get us . . . well, you . . . out of this," Hadley says. "I called Melissa this morning, and it's all set. She's sending her passport to the post office in Omaha, and I reserved a plane ticket in her name to London. You look like her. Well, not your hair, but the rest of you— your height and weight and eye color. She's older than you, but not so old that you can't pretend to be her. From London, you can continue on to wherever you like. The flight leaves Thursday."

Grace blinks, then blinks three more times as she processes the words, shocked to find the idea not only *not* ludicrous but maybe even possible.

Hadley gives a thin, proud smile. "See, I told you I had a plan."

"Melissa could get in a lot of trouble," Grace says. Hadley told her that she reminded her of her friend Melissa, though when she said it, Grace thought she was talking about their personalities.

"If they trace it back to her," Hadley says, "she's going to say I stole the passport and her credit card information before I left. It's why you need to fly out of Omaha, so it looks like we planned it from the start."

Grace stares at Hadley for a long minute, surprised at how well she's thought things through. Flying out of Omaha is brilliant. After what happened last night, it's the last place the FBI will think they'll choose.

"I got to thinking," Hadley says, "after I used that woman's license to check us in, that you could pass for Melissa. So I called her—"

Grace bolts upright, startling Hadley and stopping her. "Melissa fosters kids, right?" she says, remembering this because she was a foster kid herself, though not one lucky enough to land with someone like Melissa. "And you said one was a boy a year younger than Skipper, and the other two are in high school."

"Yeah," Hadley says as she shakes her head, thinking she knows where Grace is going. "I can't pretend to be Melissa. I don't look like her."

"Not you. Me," Grace says, her heart pounding very fast. "I take them. I take Mattie and Skipper with me." The words are out before Grace has fully considered them, and only after she says them does she realize the magnitude of what she's suggesting.

At first, Hadley looks confused, her brows furrowed as if working through a difficult equation; then they arch upward as the puzzle snaps into place. "You take them to London? Without me?"

Her head shakes as Grace nods.

More brow furrowing and head shaking, and Grace looks down at the mattress. Hadley is right. It was a stupid idea. Hadley's known Grace less than a week; she's not going to trust her to take her kids halfway around the world without her.

But then Hadley says, "And I would join you later?" And Grace can't make out if it's a question or a statement.

"Exactly," Grace says. "You have Blaire's license. You have money. And it would be a lot easier if you were alone. And even if they do catch you, you can use the story—"

"No." Hadley cuts her off. "I'm not lying about what happened."

Grace swallows.

Hadley's expression softens. "Grace, if this doesn't work out, I'm telling the truth. You are not going to jail."

Prison, Grace thinks, but she doesn't correct her.

"If they catch me, I'm telling them exactly what happened, except perhaps with a few omissions and embellishments that make you look like the superhero you are."

Grace gives the thinnest smile, and for a long minute, they sit silent as the idea continues to take shape, growing larger and rounder until it fills the whole room and takes on a warm, dangerous glow that terrifyingly feels like hope.

45

HADLEY

Mattie sits on the bed, a towel wrapped around her head. Her face is drawn and her eyes swollen and red from her emotions. On her lap is her book, and though she is staring at it, she doesn't appear to be reading.

Skipper sits on the other bed, looking at nothing, his eyes blank. All of this has been too much for him.

"Baby," Hadley says to Mattie.

Mattie looks up, her sadness radiating across the room, unable to forgive herself for her role in last night's events. A victim. Helpless. Hadley is too familiar with the feeling, and she prays her daughter isn't destined to follow in her footsteps.

"It's going to be okay," she says, the words as pathetic as they sound, and Mattie looks back down at her book.

Hadley's head throbs, like a grenade has blown up in her skull. Tentatively she touches her fingers to her scalp, surprised to find it still feels hard and not soft and mushy like a cantaloupe smashed open. She can't believe she drank like that. Daggers of regret pierce her brain as she thinks of what might have happened had she and Grace not walked from the restaurant when they had. Then another stab of pain as she thinks about the gun and firing it.

Mattie will be better off with Grace. Skipper too. Grace will be a good example for Mattie. She's tough and brave and would never let anything happen to them. Her heart hurts almost as much as her head.

She sits on the edge of the bed beside Skipper and puts her hand on his knee. "Champ, you okay?"

He turns slowly, his eyes so clear they are flat of depth. "I'm not going to live with my mom?" he says. Somehow he must have figured this out during the disjointed events and outbursts of last night.

Hadley shakes her head, concerned how he will take this latest disappointment from his mom. His whole life, Hadley has tried her best to protect him from Vanessa's slights and unreliability, not promising him things unless she was certain of them and softening the blows by making excuses and telling lies. The way she explained him needing to go back to live with her was in baseball terms.

"You were the best pickup of my life," she said the day after Vanessa called with the news that she wanted Skipper back. "A first-round draft pick rookie."

"That was when I was a baby?" he asked.

"Yep, your rookie year, straight out of training camp. Your mom's team lost their coach, so her team was suspended until they could find a new one, and I swooped in and signed you."

He smiled.

"But," she said, "there was this thing called a 'contingency clause' in your contract, and it said that, if your mom's team got a new coach and the team was reinstated, she had the option to sign you back."

"Contingency clause," he repeated. Skipper likes certain words. He doesn't always understand them, but his remarkable mind holds on to them.

"And that's what happened," Hadley went on. "Her team is back in business, and she needs her star player."

She knew Skipper didn't completely understand, but he accepted it. He knows players get traded all the time and that, even though sometimes they don't like it, it's not always up to them, and they don't have a say in the matter.

But now he says, "That's good. She's my mom, but she's not my family." He doesn't say it meanly but rather matter-of-factly, stating it in the straightforward way he has when he's made his mind up about something.

He returns to looking at the wall, and Hadley pats his leg, then, with a heavy sigh, walks toward the door.

As she waits for the elevator to take her to the parking garage, she wonders how she got to this place in her life. She thinks about the gun in her hand and the feeling that came over her as she fired it, such raw rage it was as if she was possessed by it. She thinks of the man's face when it went off: no longer cocky but rather shocked and then scared, his mouth open in panic as he dived to the ground to cower with his hands over his head.

The elevator dings, and the image shifts, and she imagines her aim true, his eyes wide as he looks down to see the hole in his chest. When he looks up, he is Frank, and she fires again, then again and again— *bang. Bang, bang, bang*, the shots ripping across his chest and slicing his body in two.

She blinks her eyes, her heart pounding, then steps onto the elevator and hits the button for the garage.

46

GRACE

Miles is eating, sort of. He sucks on his bottle and chews on the nipple at the same time, a halfhearted effort that's making the process painfully slow. Grace tries not to be impatient, but it is impossible. Yes, he's cute, but these sorts of things do not enamor her the way they do other moms, and it's all she can do not to scream at him to finish already so they can get on with it.

She closes her eyes and focuses on her breathing to keep the sickness that still roils in her gut at bay. *One foot in front of the other,* her grandmother's voice coaxes. *Just keep moving forward, and eventually you get where you're going.*

The idea works in theory but has never actually worked in Grace's life. One foot in front of the other has landed her in a heap of trouble more than once. She squeezes her eyes tighter, all her efforts concentrated on not throwing up.

"What's taking so long?" Hadley says from the doorway, causing Grace's eyes to snap open. Hadley looks at Miles and frowns. "He's playing you. He's done."

Grace looks down at her son, then back at Hadley, then back at her son and feels herself bristle as he gums a smile at her, milk drool spilling from his mouth. The manipulative little imp: a damn charmer, just like his dad. He knows exactly when she's getting irritated and exactly how to disarm her. She pulls the bottle away, and he gives half a protest that's quickly forgotten when Grace drapes him over her shoulder and gives him a mock spanking on his padded behind.

"Up and at 'em," Hadley says. "Daylight's a-burnin'. Burp him, then meet me in the bathroom."

"Why?"

"It's a surprise."

Grace shakes her head as she looks distrustingly at Hadley. Not only does Grace hate surprises, but she's had enough surprises the past four days to last a lifetime.

"Chicken," Hadley chides.

Grace nods, not ashamed in the least to admit she is scared to death of whatever Hadley has planned. As if in agreement, Miles lets out a large belch, and Hadley marches up, swoops him from Grace's arms, and carries him away, as if taking him hostage.

Grace considers not following but knows she's only putting off the inevitable. So, with a heavy sigh, she pushes from the bed and staggers after them. She passes Skipper, who's sitting on one of the two beds staring at the wall in front of him. She follows his gaze to see what he is looking at, sees nothing, and continues on.

Mattie is already in the bathroom. She sits on the edge of the tub wrapped in a bathrobe, her shoulders folded forward and her eyes on the ground. Her white-blonde hair has been dyed russet brown, the deep, warm color of chestnuts, and cut to a bob that stops above her chin. She is not wearing makeup, and the half dozen earrings she normally wears, along with her trademark serpent, are gone. She looks small and young and broken, and Grace's heart twists at the sight of her.

"Mattie, you hold Miles," Hadley says, holding him out to her.

Mattie takes him, and Miles immediately starts to grab for her nose, a favorite game of his. She turns him around so he can no longer do it, and he wriggles against her to get down, so she places him on the bath rug at her feet.

"Leather Black or Midnight Delight," Hadley says, holding up two boxes of hair dye.

Grace shakes her head violently, her skull moving back and forth around her eyes, which are fixed on the boxes. Grace has no illusions about her looks. She is no great beauty. Her only defining feature is her fiery curls, combined with her pale skin and hazel eyes, the startling combination taking her away from ordinary. A stranger once called her coloring "quixotic." She looked the word up when she got home: romantic, visionary. He was wrong, but she liked the idea of it so much that she often says the word out loud when she looks at herself in the mirror.

"Fine. I'll go first," Hadley says, and with no more prelude than that, she sets the boxes of hair dye on the counter, picks up the scissors beside them, and lops off a chunk of her hair.

Grace and Mattie wince together. It's like watching the slaughter of a minx. Hadley's hair is remarkable, a sleek plate of black that belongs in Vidal Sassoon commercials. She chops at it again, the tresses falling to the floor. Snip, snip, snip: she continues to butcher large chunks until all that remains is an uneven helmet of black. She holds the scissors out to Mattie. "You need to do the rest."

Mattie looks at the scissors, sighs, and reluctantly pushes to her feet. Expertly, she moves around Hadley as if she is a professional hairstylist, and again Grace is surprised by the multitude of talents Mattie possesses that she seems to keep hidden. When she's done, Hadley's hair is as short as Ellen DeGeneres's and just as chic.

Grace stares in amazement. It almost seems impossible, but the haircut actually makes Hadley more beautiful, her neck elongated, her cheekbones lifted. She looks like a Greek goddess—empowered, bold, and fearless—like she should be chiseled of marble and holding up a temple.

"Okay?" Hadley says, her eyebrow lifting in challenge.

Grace shakes her head again and backs up.

"Seriously, Grace, are you going to make me hold you down? You look like Melissa, except your hair."

Grace is saved by the unmistakable sound of pooping coming from the floor, Miles's face scrunched up as he does the deed, the smell filling the tight confines of the bathroom.

Grace bends down to pick him up, but Hadley gets there first. "I've got this, and when I come back, I want you in a robe and ready to have your hair dyed."

Grace sits heavily on the toilet and lifts the box of Midnight Delight, cringing as she studies the before and after pictures. She shakes her head, sets it down, reaches over, and locks the bathroom door.

Mattie glances over from where she sits again on the edge of the tub, and her mouth almost twitches with a smile but doesn't quite make it.

Grace shifts to sit beside her, their shoulders touching. Letting out a slow sigh, she says, "Do you want to talk about it?"

Mattie looks at the ground.

"It wasn't your fault," Grace says.

Mattie says nothing.

"But I suppose that's the part that sucks the most," Grace goes on. "At least if it was your fault, then you'd have had some say in it."

Mattie looks sidelong at her, the color of her eyes so like Frank's that Grace needs to make a concerted effort not to react.

"It seems like it happens all the time," Mattie mumbles, looking back at her knees. "It's like the crappy people of the world have all the power because . . . well, because they're crappy."

Grace nods. It's a hard truth she wishes Mattie would never need to learn.

The door rattles. Grace ignores it.

Mattie wraps her arms around herself as she bends over her thighs so her chest is on her knees.

Hadley knocks. "Really? Are you kidding me? How old are you, twelve?"

"I wish I was better," Mattie says so softly Grace almost doesn't hear. Grace rubs her back.

"Like you," Mattie says.

Grace shakes her head. She wants Mattie to be nothing like her.

"Last night, you weren't even scared," Mattie goes on.

Grace rears back. "Are you kidding? I was terrified."

"You were?" Mattie says, her eyes flicking sideways.

"Of course," Grace says. "The only difference between you and me is I'm older, so I know sometimes there's no choice. Doesn't mean I wasn't scared. And when I was your age, I'd have done exactly what you did: tried to sweet-talk my way out of it."

Mattie looks away, and Grace feels her shame. She didn't tell Grace that's what she did, but Grace knows it nonetheless. It's exactly what she would have done at that age if some guy was holding her by the neck.

"You know you have to come out at some point," Hadley says through the door. "I have your son."

They ignore her.

"Grace?" Mattie says.

"Hmmm?"

She hesitates, and Grace waits her out, watching as Mattie sucks in her bottom lip, then eventually blows it out. She pushes her feet out in front of her and swishes them back and forth like windshield wipers. The toenails are painted midnight blue, most of the polish chipped off. Finally, she pulls her feet back in, wraps her hands around her knees, and says, "You ever feel like there's another you?"

Grace lifts an eyebrow.

"You know, like hiding inside you?"

"You mean like behind my kidney or gallbladder?"

Mattie doesn't smile. Her eyes study her knees as her head shakes back and forth. "No. Like there's this really great person buried deep inside, and she really wants to get out, but she can't because you're already this other person, and I don't know, it's like she's in the way or something, blocking the better you from getting out?"

Grace doesn't answer, the question so close to her own thoughts it startles her, though she's always posed the question slightly differently, often thinking of herself as "the girl who might have done something wonderful," wondering who she might have been had her grandmother not died and had she not made the mistakes she made, if things might have turned out differently and if she could have turned out to be more than she is.

"Not someone else," Mattie goes on, struggling to put her thoughts into words, "but a better version of yourself, one who's stronger, and who, you know, does things right?"

"My grandmother used to say, 'We all have a backbone. Up to you to learn how to straighten it.'"

Mattie gives her a thin smile. "I think I would have liked your grandmother."

"She definitely would have liked you," Grace says, and she gives Mattie's shoulder a nudge; then she leans forward, her elbows on her knees, and she says, "I'm going to tell you something, something I haven't told anyone."

Mattie glances over, and Grace holds her gaze for a beat before turning back to look at her hands. With a deep breath, she says, "My name isn't really Grace."

Mattie turns her whole head to look at her.

"My name is Savannah," Grace goes on. "Savannah Grace Swift." She feels a tug at her heart, the name like a ghost, her mother's spirit so close it takes her breath. Growing up, Grace's name was one of her favorite things, one of the few things her mother had left her. *Savannah Swift*. It was just so darn beautiful.

"Savannah?" Mattie says. "That's pretty."

Grace nods. It's been a long time since she recalled that name or the time when she used it.

"There came a point when I needed to let it go," she says. "The name and the girl that went with it."

Grace can tell Mattie wants to ask why, but she doesn't, and Grace appreciates it. It isn't something Grace likes to talk about.

Instead Mattie says, "So you gave yourself a new name?"

"More like a new start. I moved to California, and I began again as Grace."

"And it worked?"

"I suppose. I mean, I was still me, and I still had all the memories from my life before, along with the regret for some of the things I'd done. That stuff doesn't go away. But no one in California knew who I was before, so I was able to start fresh, move past it, and decide who I wanted to be from that point on."

Mattie is listening hard, her eyes narrowed tightly on Grace's. "So, you lied about who you were?"

"Not really. I just didn't talk about it. I kept the parts I didn't want people to know to myself. You'd be surprised how little people ask about your past and how little they pay attention when you answer. Most people are so caught up in their own lives they don't really care about yours."

A long beat of silence passes, Grace looking down at her hands and remembering when they were Savannah's—same hands, different girl.

"You think I can do that?" Mattie asks.

Grace lifts her face. "I don't know. Maybe. I mean, for you it's a little different; your mom and Skipper still know you. But no one else does. It wouldn't be easy. You'd actually have to change. No one can do that part for you. For me, it was all about forgiveness, learning how to let go of all the anger I was holding on to. It was tough. Changing."

Mattie looks away, and Grace watches as she turns the idea in her mind, once again feeling like looking at Mattie is a little like looking at a reflection of her younger self.

"So, I would need to change my name?" Mattie says.

"You don't have to. For me, it helped. Savannah is who I was, and Grace is who I am. Like one of those before-and-after transformations, there's a clear break between then and now, past and future." She pauses, then adds, "What's your real name? What is Mattie short for?"

"Matilde," Mattie mumbles, looking embarrassed. "It was my dad's grandmother's name."

Grace considers it for a moment. "How about Tillie? That's pretty cool."

Mattie doesn't say anything, but Grace feels her rolling it around in her brain. *Tillie Torelli.* Grace thinks it rocks.

Finally, Mattie says, "Do you really think I could pull off being Tillie?"

"I do."

Mattie almost smiles, then pushes off the tub to stand. "You know that boy who posted the picture last night?"

"Yeah."

"He was wearing Superman underwear."

"You saw his underwear?"

"He forgot to zip his fly."

"Too bad you couldn't post that on Snapchat."

Mattie snort laughs, and Grace laughs as well thinking about it: #supermanskivviesloser.

"What's going on in there? Let me in," Hadley pouts, sounding like a toddler who's been left out of a game.

"Should we let her in?" Mattie says.

Grace touches her hair and is about to shake her head, but Mattie is already reaching for the door.

47

HADLEY

Hadley opens her eyes and immediately regrets it. Her hangover has really heated up now, and the light through the windshield works like daggers on her brain. She grabs hold of her head on either side, fearing her skull will actually split in two from whatever is chiseling at it from the inside. She was dreaming of her mom, the sweet memory drifting away before she could grab hold of it—granola and berries, perhaps a dream about breakfast. She's hungry. It's a little past four, and they haven't eaten since their late breakfast six hours ago.

Grace pulls into a gas station with a minimart, part of a small outcropping of businesses with a smattering of houses and cows behind them. It's amazing how many of these small towns they've driven through, communities of a few thousand people in the middle of nowhere, making a living ranching, farming, running a gas station, or who knows what. So little surrounded by so much emptiness, and it makes Hadley wonder how the world can be so crowded in other places.

"Where are we?" she says.

"Laramie."

"State?"

"Wyoming."

Hadley pushes herself up and goes to run her fingers through her hair and hits only air.

She keeps forgetting it's gone, her silky mane now shorn to a choppy pixie cut. She glances sideways at Grace, and just like this morning, the sight of her with straight-ironed ink-black hair makes her smile, mostly because she knows how much Grace hates it and also because of how much it makes her look like Melissa. Though, on second glance, the fierce scowl and piercing glare are 100 percent Grace.

"What?" Grace says, catching Hadley looking at her.

"Nothing."

The scowl deepens; then she turns to the back seat. "Mattie, take Skipper to the bathroom but keep him out of sight. I'm going to pay for the gas and buy some snacks."

Things this morning did not go well with Skipper. While the rest of them had all agreed, however reluctantly, to transform their looks, Skipper would have none of it—not a haircut, not a hat change, and definitely not a uniform change. So, while the rest of them no longer look like themselves, Skipper continues to look exactly like himself: a special little boy in a Dodgers uniform.

This has all been too much for him. He has never dealt with stress well, and the past four days have been extraordinarily stressful. He doesn't understand everything that is happening, but he understands enough to know that yesterday Mattie was in danger, that Hadley was shooting a gun, that Grace was running over motorcycles with a truck, and that afterward, Hadley was throwing up and everyone was arguing and crying.

When it was time to leave the hotel this morning, Skipper refused. His eyes still fixed on the wall, as they had been all morning, he folded his arms and said simply, "No."

Then he said it again and again. The only variation in his continued refusal was the occasional addition of, "I want to go home."

Finally, after twenty minutes of haggling and pleading, Hadley told Grace she needed to physically carry him out. It was the only way, and it was a horrendous ordeal for all of them. Skipper screamed and kicked as Grace struggled with him. Mattie walked behind them trying to console him. And Hadley hopped on her crutches as she gritted her teeth against it all.

By the time they'd made it to the car, they had an audience of several people standing on their balconies of their hotel rooms, watching.

They drove away with Skipper still in hysterics, rocking and crying and kicking the seat in front of him, all of it fraying everyone's already strung-out nerves.

An hour later, Skipper finally exhausted himself and collapsed against Mattie, crashing into a twitchy sleep, and Grace looked at Hadley and said, "He needs to stop wearing that uniform. It's going to be the end of us."

Hadley doesn't disagree. Skipper stands out like a walking billboard advertising that they are, in fact, the ones from the shoot-out last night outside Pat's Barbeque. She just isn't sure what to do about it.

Mattie and Skipper walk back toward the car, Mattie keeping Skipper on the side away from the minimart windows, her body shielding him as best she can. They climb in, and Hadley turns. "Hey, Champ, how you holding up?"

He lifts his face to hers, his blue eyes wide. "I want to go home."

"I know, buddy. I know." Heart twisting, she turns back in her seat.

Grace walks from the store, her face blanched and her shoulders hitched up around her neck. In her hands are a couple of bags filled with drinks and food. Something is wrong, and Hadley expects her to jump behind the wheel and tear away, but instead Grace sets the bags in the back seat with Mattie, then continues to the pump to fill the car.

When she finishes, she climbs in and pulls back on the road, her eyes glued to the two-lane strip of asphalt that stretches endlessly in front of them.

"What's wrong?"

"We made the Fox four o'clock news."

48

GRACE

Renegades, rebels, modern-day Robin Hoods—those are the words the reporter used. She was young, Hispanic, pretty. She stood in front of Pat's Barbeque, the neon sign blinking behind her. The headline beneath her read, *Female Fugitives Still at Large.* The television was above the cashier's head, and Grace watched while the girl rang her up. There were photos and even a short video. It was dark, and it was hard to make out much but the silhouette of Hadley, the flash of the gun firing, and blurry shadows in the distance diving, but it was enough to make compelling television, the five-second clip gripping.

The reporter gave a surprisingly accurate account of what has happened over the past four days, starting with the FBI's pursuit of them at the hospital, then describing the search for them in Barstow and the FBI agent's abduction in Baker, and finishing with the events of last night in Salt Lake City. They even had a map and a timeline.

"All set," the cashier said, causing Grace to look away just as the reporter was introducing Burt, the man she danced with last night.

"Grace was a heck of a dancer . . . ," Burt was saying as she walked from the store.

Renegades, rebels, modern-day Robin Hoods—Grace doesn't feel like any of those things. She feels like a little kid who's accidentally broken a window because she was playing where she wasn't supposed to, and who feels bad and is now desperately trying not to get caught.

"You okay?" Hadley says.

Grace glances at her, then returns her focus to the road.

"You haven't said a word for hours."

"What do you want me to say?"

"I don't know. Something."

"The agent got away."

"Mark? He got away?" Hadley says, clearly excited. Then, realizing she's not supposed to be excited, she forces her smile away.

"It's okay," Grace says. "I'm glad he's okay."

The truth is Grace felt awful leaving him there. It was a terrible thing to have to do. She left his firearm in the trunk of his rental car so he would get it back, and she tried to make him as comfortable as possible, but it hasn't stopped her from feeling bad. He was just a guy trying to do his job.

"This is a bad idea," she says a moment later as she pulls into the bumper-to-bumper traffic eking its way down the exit ramp toward Coors Field.

"We have to," Hadley says with a concerned glance back at Skipper, who is sitting up erect, his eyes scanning out the window to take in the flood of fans.

Grace inches the car forward, her heart pounding.

"Think about it," Hadley says, "this is the last place anyone would expect us to be. And besides, it's the one place we blend in."

She's referring of course to Skipper and his insistence on only wearing baseball uniforms. They stopped at a sporting-goods store outside Denver and swapped his Dodgers T-shirt for a Rockies jersey, and Grace has to admit he looks a lot like most of the kids on the sidewalk.

"I don't like the idea of leaving the money," she says as she follows the parking attendant's gestures to pull into a spot at the far end of a lot the size of ten football fields.

Skipper is bouncing in his seat, the PlayStation that holds his fantasy team and all the stats in his hand.

"Move, First Base," he says to Mattie as soon as the car comes to a stop. "Go. Get out."

Mattie climbs out, and Skipper bounds out after her.

"Well, we can't walk into the stadium with two million dollars," Hadley says. "It might raise an eyebrow or two." She offers an encouraging smile. "Come on, Grace. It will be fine. We'll go to the game, have a couple hot dogs, enjoy a little normalcy for a few hours, then return to our outlaw ways."

Grace, not able to help herself, smiles.

"Attagirl," Hadley says. She climbs from the car, looking nearly as excited as Skipper.

Grace slides Miles into the new front baby pack she bought—one where he faces out so he can see all the action. His legs kick with excitement, and she has to admit he looks very cute in his Rockies onesie, with matching hat and socks.

With a final glance at the trunk of Blaire Butz's Bug, where the diaper bag is stashed with the money and Frank's gun, she takes a deep breath and walks toward the shuttle bus, trailing Skipper, who's yanking Hadley forward as she does her best to keep up without her crutches.

When they arrive at the stadium, Grace leaves Hadley, Skipper, and Mattie at the front gate to go to the ticket window. The air smells of popcorn and beer, and Grace inhales deeply and thinks about what she will eat when she gets inside, her mouth watering with the thought of an ice-cold Coors and peanuts.

Bad as things are, they feel a little less hopeless than they did this morning. Despite the calamitous events of last night, freedom is in sight. Mattie agreed to the plan of going with her to London, and Skipper only wanted to know if they had baseball. And now that she's had some time to think about it, the idea has taken on surprising warmth and brightness, the idea of Mattie and Skipper being with her making her happy each time she thinks of it.

She kisses Miles on the head. "Hey, little man, in two days, you and I are going to be on a plane and headed to London. What do you think of that?"

He kicks his legs and waves his arms.

Her eyes catch on her reflection in the glass of the ticket windows, startling her, then making her smile. There's no way anyone is going to recognize her. She barely recognizes herself—a realization both comforting and disturbing. Without her fiery-red curls, she is plain as rain, entirely unremarkable.

Miles squeals and babbles as they wait for the ticket girl to print out their tickets, clearly excited by the colorful commotion around them, the sidewalk teeming with fans, vendors, laughter, and voices.

The scent of hot dogs drifts past her nose, and her stomach rumbles. She loves ballpark hot dogs. There's something about them that makes them so much better than a hot dog from anywhere else. Closing her eyes, she imagines the first delicious bite, followed by a swig of beer.

She's still relishing the thought when the hair on the back of her neck bristles, a premonition or her sixth sense sending off an alarm. Moving slowly so as to not attract attention, she opens her eyes and turns.

At first, she sees nothing and thinks maybe she was mistaken, but then the man behind her shifts, and the world stands still.

He is a hundred feet away, concealed beneath the shadow of a tree—brown sport coat and white button-down shirt—broad shoulders, thick waist, and cinnamon-blond hair. He is wearing sunglasses, but she can tell by the way he turns his head that, behind them, his eyes are scanning.

"Here you are," the ticket girl says.

Grace glances at her, then back at the agent, then, calm as she can manage, takes the tickets and walks back toward the entrance, her pulse pounding in her ears.

49

MARK

Mark is supposed to be on a plane back to DC. He is supposed to be moving on to a new case involving credit card fraud. He is supposed to be arranging a makeup day with Shelly and Ben. He is supposed to be putting all this behind him.

He almost didn't see her. Had that woman not said, "Look, honey, isn't he cute? The littlest Rockies fan," he wouldn't have turned and he would not have caught sight of Grace's distinct walk as she moved through the crowd with Miles strapped to her chest. Her hair was changed, black and straight, but she still carried herself with a sort of defiance that was unmistakable, her shoulders back and her head high.

He moves quickly to catch up, uncertain if she's aware he's there. Judging by how fast she's moving, he thinks she is.

His instincts paid off. This game was important to Skipper, and the stadium on course to their destination of Omaha. He didn't clear the plan with O'Toole or tell anyone about his hunch, and if this doesn't work out, he will be out of a job, but he's amazed how little that concerns him.

Grace glances over her shoulder, and Mark ducks out of sight. When he straightens, she's turning the corner toward the entrance. His hand goes to the holster beneath his jacket, and he releases the clip and flicks off the safety.

He rounds the corner, then stops in his tracks. Grace is stopped as well, ten feet still between them.

He looks past her to Hadley, whose hair is now short, cropped almost to her scalp. Her crutches are gone, and she stands with most of her weight on her good leg. Her right arm is wrapped over Skipper's shoulder, while Mattie stands slightly behind her.

In front of them, a few feet away, is Frank. Beside him, his brother, Tony.

Mark's mind spins quickly, assessing the situation as he watches Frank say something to Skipper that causes Hadley to tense. Then he leans in and whispers something in Hadley's ear, and Hadley starts to shake her head as she reaches back protectively for Mattie.

She is too slow. Quick like a rattler, Frank grabs Mattie by the arm and wrenches her forward. Hadley reaches out, but Frank's threatening glare stops her. Then he hisses one more thing before pulling Mattie with him through the crowd, his brother following.

Hadley cries out, "No, Frank, please!" and Mattie looks over her shoulder, her face pale.

Hadley steps toward her, but Grace lunges forward to stop her. "No, Hadley, don't."

After that, everything moves in hyperspeed yet slow motion at once: Grace holds Hadley back, the baby between them, as Mattie is pulled through the crowd, then pushed into the back seat of a black car with blacked-out windows parked illegally in the taxi queue. Mark races toward them, weaving through the herd of people that stream toward the entrance, his gun in his hand. "Frank Torelli!" he bellows over the crowd. "FBI. Stop!"

People around him gasp, and someone screams, "Gun!" and Mark realizes a second too late that the gun they are referring to isn't his, the barrel of Frank's pistol swinging around with him and the timing wrong—Mark's shot firing half a second behind.

His first thought is of Shelly, her hand waving as she forgets to sing. His next is of Ben and the dog they were supposed to get. The last is of Hadley screaming as the bullet hits his chest.

50

HADLEY

Grace is screaming that they have to go. "Now," she says as she pushes Hadley from behind. The crowd moves against them, straining to see what is happening—some sort of spectacle. Cell phones glow and are lifted high, trying to capture whatever it is, hoping to be a part of it.

Hadley cranes her head back as Grace continues to shove her forward. Mark is on the ground, people crouched around him, his head turned sideways and his eyes open.

Mattie is gone. In Tony's car.

She stumbles, and Grace catches her by the arm. Miles howls in his harness from being jerked. Skipper has her hand and is tugging at her, tears streaming from his eyes and his face white with panic.

They were having such a good time, discussing what they were going to eat when they got inside. Skipper wanted a foot-long, the same thing he orders every time he goes to a game. Mustard only. A root beer to drink. Mattie wanted to try the Helton Burger, hailed as one of the best burgers in baseball, topped with grilled onions, pickles, and a special sauce.

"Hadley, please," Grace pleads.

Frank. There. Suddenly. He appeared like a magic trick, out of nowhere. Tony beside him. Frank was saying something about a fantasy baseball trade.

Mattie was behind her; then she was gone, being pulled away toward Tony's car.

But then Mark was there as well, almost as if she'd conjured him. And for a second, she thought it was going to be okay. But it wasn't, because Frank had a gun. *Bang.* But it didn't sound like a bang. The sound almost silent. *Pffft.* And Mark fell, his eyes open like he was looking at her.

It all ricochets around in her head, like marbles loose in her skull. Her body jerks, her knees buckle, and she nearly goes down, her legs catching her a moment before she falls.

"Come on, Blue, run!" Skipper screams, pulling with all his might.

Hadley narrows her eyes on the round button on top of his hat and allows herself to be pulled along.

51

GRACE

Grace's breath wheezes in and out, and sweat pours down her face despite the late-afternoon chill. They are in the courtyard of a church, a dozen blocks from the stadium.

Hadley has collapsed on a bench, her tears slowed to a trickle, her mouth slack jawed and her pupils receded to pinpricks. Skipper sits beside her, rocking back and forth, his eyes staring at nothing.

She pulls a blanket from the backpack, lays it on the ground, takes Miles from the baby pack, and lays him on top of it. He kicks his feet in the air and pulls at his purple socks, delighted at the rush of running through the streets.

Grace kneels in front of Skipper. "You're okay," she says, taking his hands.

He pulls them from her and tucks them into his armpits, rocking harder.

She turns to Hadley, puts her hands on either side of Hadley's face. "Hadley, you can't lose it. Do you understand? I need you to hold it together."

Hadley's mouth glubs once, then remains open in a frozen gape.

"Hadley," she says again, the warble in her voice belying her own fear.

Hadley blinks.

"Come on, Hadley, hang in there. Please," Grace says.

Another blink, and then she watches as Hadley, with extraordinary determination, clenches her jaw and nods.

"Good," Grace says. "Good girl."

Hadley turns to Skipper, sees him rocking, scoots close, and wraps him tight against her. She turns back to Grace. "Grace . . ."

"Give me a minute," Grace says, calling on every ounce of will she can muster to keep from falling apart. She focuses on her breathing as she scans around them. They are in a not-so-great part of town, a run-down commercial neighborhood, the sun and heat of the day disappearing quickly.

"He's dead, isn't he?" Hadley says.

Grace turns to look at her, and she wants to lie, tell her he's not, but she honestly doesn't know. She saw him fall but only realized he had been shot after, when everyone was screaming.

"He was trying to save Mattie," Hadley says.

Grace nods. He was. He was a good man trying to do the right thing. The lump in her throat grows, and she turns away so Hadley won't see her distress.

Pull yourself together, she urges, but it's like trying to hold back a tsunami. It's all so awful. *The agent. Mattie.* She takes three shuddering breaths and presses the heels of her palms to her eyes.

When she blinks them open, she looks around again. The stores and businesses are closing up for the night, steel grates being lowered, dead bolts and alarms being set. She shudders from the cold, squats down to bundle Miles in his sweatshirt, then wraps the blanket around him as she lifts him back into her arms.

He reaches for her nose, and she shifts him to her hip. He wrestles against her, not happy about being ignored.

She looks at the church, which not only is bolted tight but also has a chain on the door—a looming edifice rather than a harbor of mercy—and a wave of déjà vu washes over her, so strong it knocks the air from her lungs. Eight years ago, the church was smaller and Baptist rather than Catholic, but the desperation she felt was the same. That day ended tragically, and Grace wonders if history will repeat itself, her life once again unraveled by her choices, and those she loves most ruined by her mistakes.

Miles rails against her, trying to wriggle free. Hadley reaches for him. "Give him here."

Grace hands him over, and Hadley stands him on her lap, where he does little squats, waves his arms around, and babbles, immediately content.

"I'm cold," Skipper mumbles, still huddled against Hadley, his meltdown spent.

Grace realizes Mattie was holding the bag that held Hadley's and Skipper's sweatshirts. She pulls her own sweatshirt from the backpack and hands it to him, then takes a quick inventory of their supplies. None of them are dressed for a night at the base of the Rockies. Grace is in a T-shirt and jeans. Miles is in his onesie and has his sweatshirt and blanket. Hadley wears a skirt and a sleeveless tank. Skipper is in his uniform.

"Hadley, how much money do you have?" she asks.

"I don't know. My wallet is in my bag."

By "bag," she means the canvas grocery sack she's been using as a purse. Grace rummages through it, past the useless contents of gum, cigarettes, a hairbrush, makeup, and Skipper's game console to find Hadley's wallet. It contains sixty-two dollars.

She pulls out her own wad of cash, which she stuffed in her pocket this morning, and curses herself for not thinking to take more money with her. One hundred twelve dollars.

Together they have one hundred seventy-four dollars to get them through the night and to Omaha. Her heart sinks. A hundred seventy-four dollars won't get them out of Denver.

For a long moment, she looks up at the stained glass window of the church, the ruby-and-emerald glass depiction of Christ in his final moment of martyrdom staring down at her.

"Maybe we should go back for the car," Hadley says, her words chattering from the cold.

Grace shakes her head as she continues to look at Jesus, wondering what He is thinking and if He is laughing, finding their mortal predicament amusing.

"Grace?" Hadley says.

"No," Grace says, looking away from the window. "The stadium will be swarming with cops, and I'm sure Frank grabbed the money before he left. He knows it's evidence against him, so he wouldn't have left it. I'm sure he made Mattie tell him where it was and went back for it."

With the mention of Mattie, Hadley's features melt, and Grace watches as she digs deep to realign them, the muscles in her face clenching.

"Stay here," Grace says. "I'll be back in a minute."

"Where are you going?"

"To make a call."

Without waiting for a response, she slings the backpack onto her shoulder and walks to the front of the church. The reception was fine where she was, but she needs to be somewhere she won't be heard.

52

HADLEY

Gone. Hadley blinks. *Mark. Mattie.*

Each time she thinks of what has happened, it strikes like a blow—her mind not able to hold on to it.

Skipper saw him first. "Coach," he said, smiling and pointing.

Hadley followed his finger, her brain a second behind her eyes. *Frank. Tony. Here. In Denver.* All of it registering in delayed time.

Skipper stepped toward him, but Hadley pulled him back, wrapping her arm around him as Mattie shifted behind her.

Frank was smiling. "Hey, Champ." He reached out and tousled Skipper's hair. "I got your trade offer and thought I'd accept it in person. Wolters is yours, but I want Posey in return."

Skipper nodded and held out his hand for Frank to shake on it, which Frank did, and Skipper looked back at Mattie, a wide smile on his face like he did good.

Frank looked up from Skipper to level his eyes on Hadley's. "Hey, babe," he said. "Or should I call you Thelma? Or are you Louise? I've got to say, I didn't see this one coming. You and Grace? Looks like I underestimated that girl."

Ice prickled Hadley's spine, and she hugged Skipper tighter against her.

"Did you really think you could steal from me?" he asked, almost as if amused. "Take my money, my daughter?"

She reached her arm back to shield Mattie, a wasted gesture more instinct than anything real.

He leaned in close, his lips against her ear. "Bad move, babe. You should know better than to screw with me. If you come anywhere near Mattie again, even so much as breathe in her direction, I will hunt you down and squash you like the traitorous roach you are."

She reached back again, but it was too late. Mattie was already gone, being pulled away. Then Grace was holding Hadley back, and Mark was running after them.

And now, here they are, in the courtyard of a church. Mattie, gone. Mark, gone. Her and Skipper, Grace and Miles, here.

A grate being lowered on a storefront makes a great clanging noise, and Hadley startles. Skipper jolts with her, his arms gripping her tight. "It's okay, Champ," she lies.

Miles fusses. It is getting seriously cold now. She wraps his blanket tighter around him as she hugs Skipper closer and shudders away her own chills. A hundred yards away, Grace paces on the sidewalk, the phone no longer held to her ear.

53

GRACE

The phone is tight in her grip. She hung up with Jimmy's brother, Brad, a few minutes ago. He was very calm. She supposes for an ex-marine with shrapnel in his hip and a Bronze Star, a little sister-in-law fugitive action is no big deal. He took down her number, repeated it back, then told her to sit tight.

She's been pacing nonstop since, her arms goose skinned with the cold and the thought of how she's going to explain everything that's happened to Jimmy. Until this moment, none of it felt embarrassing. Horrible as it was, she wasn't really all that conscious of how awful it would be to have to confess what she has done and to own up to the calamity she's made of her life, their life, and Miles's future.

The phone buzzes, and she jumps.

"Jimmy?"

"Grace?"

And with that single utterance, she loses it, all the emotions she's held in check for the past four days spilling out to stream from her eyes and down her face faster than she can wipe the tears away.

"Grace? Please . . . babe . . . tell me you're okay." His voice is frantic, and she feels bad for the panic she is causing him, but there's nothing to be done. Her voice is lost, swallowed by the gulping breaths she's taking in an effort to calm herself.

"Grace, where are you? Tell me where you are." His distress vibrates through the line. "I'm on my way."

"No," she manages, more a grunt than a word. She swallows air and uses her arm to blot away the tears as she pushes down the emotions deep as they will go, burying them in that dark place where all her other demons are tightly locked away. With a shuddering breath, she says, "Jimmy, I need your help."

"Babe, where are you?" he repeats.

"Jimmy, please, just listen, and do as I ask."

"Anything."

"Whose phone are you using?"

"I borrowed it from a trucker who's at the diner where I'm at."

She blinks several times. "You're not in Afghanistan?"

"No, babe. I came home. As soon as the FBI called, I took an emergency leave and came home."

She closes her eyes to process what he's saying. Of course the FBI contacted him, which means he knows most of the story, same as the rest of the world. A wave of relief and humiliation washes over her. At least she no longer needs to explain it.

He says, "I'm sorry, babe. I'm so sorry. I screwed up—"

She cuts him off. "Jimmy, stop."

He stops, and she can see his face—his mouth clamped shut over the words he desperately wants to say, his gold eyes frantic as they dart around, hoping for an idea, some spark of inspiration that will change things, fix what he has done and everything that's come after as a result.

"Is the FBI following you?" she says.

"I don't think so. Though you were smart not to call me on my phone."

"Where are you?"

"Chicago."

She nods. Chicago is where a lot of soldiers fly into when they return.

"I need you to wire me some money," she says.

"I'll bring it to you."

"No." The word comes out harsher than she intended. She softens her tone. "Jimmy, you need to stay out of this. For Miles. You understand?"

"But—"

"No buts. Please, just wire me what you can. Send it to the Western Union on Broadway in Denver. Use the name Blaire Butz. B-U-T-Z. You got that?"

"I got Blaire Butz and I cannot lie," he raps to the "Baby Got Back" tune, the humor falling flat, their old repartee of singsonging to each other like salt in an open wound.

After a long empty pause, she says, "Can you get some money?" Then, not intending to be cruel, but the remark brutal nonetheless, she adds, "Our account is empty."

"I know, babe, I—"

She cuts him off. "I just need to know if you can get some money and send it to me."

"Yes. I can. I will. It will be there when the station opens."

"Okay." A pause. So much unsaid and yet nothing really left to say. "Thanks, Jimmy. Take care of yourself."

"Grace—"

She disconnects and returns to where the others are waiting, hollow as a ghost, as if the wind can move right through her.

54

HADLEY

It was the most miserable night of Hadley's life. The only night that even came close was the night her mother died, but that night was only full of sadness, while last night was full of all sorts of other horrible emotions as well.

Mattie. Mark. Mattie. Mattie. Mattie. Mark. Mark. Mark. Each moment she closed her eyes brought horror and terror. Every sharp noise startled her, her mind thinking it was a gunshot. And as she held Skipper against her and waited for the dawn, she wondered if this would be the new rhythm of her life, a fragile state of unrelenting fear interrupted by extreme moments of regret—every other minute remembering, then forgetting again, because the idea simply won't stick—an endless cycle of torture certain to drive her insane.

She sits up carefully so as not to wake Skipper and rubs her swollen eyes. Grace is a few feet away, Miles in her arms, a bottle plugged in his mouth.

She looks as bad as Hadley feels, her eyes bruised and her hair matted on one side and frizzy on the other. She looks homeless, like she's been living on the streets for months. They all do—the four of them layered in mismatched clothes and blankets bought from a Walgreens two blocks away, gritty with dirt and grime from a night spent huddled in the dark corner of the church's courtyard.

Dinner was peanut butter and jelly sandwiches, and this morning's breakfast will be the same. Grace is oddly adept at knowing how to survive on the street, making Hadley wonder again about her past. She knew exactly which corner would provide the most shelter and how to make the most of their funds, spending it on food that would last and on as much warmth as they could afford. Hadley wanted to buy toothpaste and hand sanitizer, but Grace was adamant they hold on to their money in case Jimmy doesn't come through, which Grace seems to think he might not.

Hadley was surprised when Grace told her she had called him. It was a sign of how desperate things had become. She wanted to ask Grace if she was okay, but Grace made it clear she didn't want to talk about it. So, Hadley let her be, though it's quite obvious the conversation wrecked her, and Hadley has never seen Grace so close to despair.

The bells of the church chime eight times, and Grace turns. "We need to go."

Hadley jostles Skipper to wake him. His response is to curl tighter against her.

"Come on, Champ," she says, her eyes fixed on the purple dinosaur pin on his hat. The Rockies mascot emblem was a purchase Mattie insisted on when they were at the sports store buying his new jersey. Tears pool in her eyes, and it takes all her will to keep them from spilling over.

Skipper blinks his eyes open, wide pools of blue looking up at her, and she forces as bright a smile as she can manage onto her face as she says, "Morning, Champ. Ready to start our day? Trout has a plan."

"To get First Base?" he says, sitting up sleepily.

Hadley tries not to react and keeps the smile plastered on her face. "To get us someplace safe so then we can try to get First Base."

He furrows his brow and nods, his faith in her still remarkably unwavering, still believing she is somehow going to get them through this and that it will all work out, despite all evidence to the contrary.

55

GRACE

They are outside a pawnshop that also serves as a Western Union. The area is seedy, but Grace is not scared. Early morning is the safest time to be awake in a city, the homeless sleeping off their benders from the night before or too done in from hunger and cold to be much of a threat.

Grace spent a precious seventy-five cents on a newspaper this morning, desperate to know what had happened at the stadium after they'd fled, hoping for good news about the agent and Mattie. The story was front-page news. The headline, *Shooting at Coors Field Leaves One Dead*, destroyed her first wish, and the second, smaller headline, *Torelli Daughter Kidnapped by Father and Missing*, destroyed her second.

Beside the blurry photo of the agent lying on the sidewalk were smaller photos of Grace, Hadley, Skipper, and Mattie. The photos of Hadley and Grace were from their driver's licenses and bore little resemblance to what they looked like now. The ones of Skipper and Mattie were their most recent school portraits. Skipper looked exactly the same: the same off-center grin, the top of his Dodgers uniform showing. Mattie, however, looked nothing like the girl Grace knows, and Grace was shocked to see how much she had changed since the photo had been taken at the beginning of the school year. Her hair in the photo was long and brown, her teeth still sporting braces. She was young looking, her smile self-conscious and unsure.

It is difficult to get used to the idea that Mattie is gone. Like she's missing a limb, Grace keeps thinking she's there; then, when she realizes she isn't, it's like this great gaping hole in the middle of everything. Desperately, Grace wants to fix it, her mind spinning and spinning to figure out a way to find her and to get her back, and each time realizing it is impossible.

Grace read the article twice, then threw the paper away before Hadley could see it. She's worried the truth, in Hadley's current fragile state, would be too much for her to bear.

Mark Wilkes—that was the agent's name—is survived by a daughter and a son—the girl six and the boy nine. He also had a wife. Grace tried not to hold that against him. His parents live in Boston, and he has a brother in California. He was a decorated veteran, an ex-marine who served two tours in Desert Storm.

She looks through the window of the pawnshop to check the time. The minutes pass slow as hours as they creep closer to nine o'clock, her faith in Jimmy wavering each second the moment of truth draws nearer. He can borrow a bit from his brother, though Brad won't have much to spare. A dagger of shame pierces her at the thought of asking him again for help. They still haven't repaid him for the loan he gave them to flee LA and get their apartment in Orange County.

Guiltily, she wonders how much Jimmy will be able to send, her concern about the future and their limited funds growing. The plan is still for her to go to London with Miles and Skipper, and for Hadley to figure out a way to join them down the road.

The idea was so much more hopeful when she had a million dollars in her pocket and with Mattie along to help. Now, she wonders how she will survive, a fugitive posing under an alias in a foreign country with no working papers and two kids, one of whom she isn't entirely certain how she'll deal with when things get rough.

At 8:57 a man walks into the pawnshop from the back. He turns on the lights, flips the closed sign to open, then walks toward the door to unlock it.

"Grace."

She is staring so hard at the man turning the dead bolt she doesn't immediately hear someone saying her name. The clock reads 8:59.

"Grace," he says again.

She turns, her eyes blinking as her brain catches up with her ears, to see Jimmy walking toward her, his long strides covering the distance quickly. He wears faded fatigues, his gold hair mussed and his face lined with exhaustion and worry.

Her eyes fill, and she steps toward him; then, realizing what she is doing, she falls back, her head shaking. "I told you not to come," she says as her anger and panic catch up with her.

Her hands wrap protectively around Miles as if Jimmy's presence might harm him. Which it will—not in this moment but in the next day, week, year, lifetime.

"I told you, Jimmy. You need to stay away."

His half smile melts into hurt, and his eyes drop as he says, "I couldn't. I couldn't not come."

Up close, he looks even worse than she originally thought. Even on his worst day, Jimmy is good looking, but this morning, he is bedraggled, his shoulders stooped, his skin parched, and his beard grown out from days of not shaving. But as always, it is his eyes that draw her in, gold like a summer's day and looking at her as if no one else exists in the world.

"Please, Grace, hear me out—"

"We need to go," Grace says, cutting him off and walking quickly past him, suddenly aware that the Western Union man is watching them through the glass. His eyes slide from Grace and Miles to Hadley, then stick on Skipper.

Jimmy looks confused, his head cocking to one side.

"Now!" she practically screams. The man has moved to his desk and is lifting the phone.

Hadley has already stood and grabbed Skipper's hand. "Hadley," Hadley says to introduce herself as she races past Jimmy to follow Grace, who's walking quickly toward the street.

"Jimmy," he says back; then he sweeps Skipper into his arms as if he weighs no more than a sack of flour. "Hey, buddy, how about a ride?"

He is beside Grace and directing her toward a silver Nissan parked at the curb. He pops open the locks, sets Skipper on the ground, and swings open the door. Skipper climbs in, and Hadley climbs in on the other side. Grace, with Miles still strapped to her chest, hops into the passenger seat.

Jimmy's eyes fix on Miles, but Grace snaps him out of it. "Drive," she orders, and a second later, they're peeling away from the curb.

56

HADLEY

Jimmy drives with one hand on the wheel, the other resting out the open window. The guy is damn good looking, like Flash Gordon or Captain America, superhero good looking. Long boned and golden all over, he has honeycomb hair, matching gold eyes, and a crooked smile he uses easily and often.

He wears his army fatigues "to lend credibility," he said with a wink at Grace, who's still very angry with him. Though even through her fury, love pulses.

Hadley sits in the back of the small car beside Skipper, who conked out an hour ago. She stares out the window, seeing nothing, unable to wrap her head around everything that has happened or how quickly.

Unlike yesterday, it is no longer shocking. *Mark. Is. Dead.* Somehow that awful fact has settled in, though it hurts too much to think about. So instead, she obsesses over Mattie, wondering where she is, where Frank might go, and how she can get her back. She has cried so much she is certain there are no tears left. Wads of soggy Kleenex overflow from the side compartment of her door, and her skin is raw and parched.

Today is Wednesday, the day she was supposed to be dropping Skipper off with Vanessa before continuing on with Mattie to start their new life, the notion foggy and vague like a dream from another life.

Everything feels so unreal—Frank is a murderer; Mattie is gone; she no longer has a home to flee from or to run back to—and at random moments, Hadley finds herself so completely lost it feels like she is living in an alternate universe, as if floating outside it all and not really here.

The plan is still for Skipper to go with Grace to London, and Hadley is still supposed to find a way to join them. But how? She has no money, no place to go. And Mattie is still here. How can she go to London when Mattie is still here?

At least Skipper is doing better. In large part thanks to Jimmy. After Jimmy carried Skipper to the car, something changed for him. Like a duckling orphaned from his father, it's as if he imprinted on the first alpha male he found, and Jimmy has gone along with it, perhaps realizing how fragile Skipper is.

It started with small talk about baseball, a sport Jimmy fortunately knows a lot about, but after a while, it turned to the army. Jimmy told Skipper about his job in Afghanistan, leaving out the bad parts and mostly talking about the guys in his unit. He talked about each of them and their nicknames and how they earned them, a topic near and dear to Skipper's heart. Eventually the conversation turned to Jimmy's uniform, and patiently he explained the different "teams" in the army and why each soldier wears what they do. He even took off his fatigue jacket at one point and handed it over the seat so Skipper could check out the different patches and pins as Jimmy explained what each one meant.

Grace pretended not to be listening, but Hadley could tell she was, her jaw clenched hard against it as she tried not to care.

Part of Skipper's change also has to do with what happened with Frank. It took some time for him to process it, but once he did, Hadley's certain he formed his own very strong opinion about it. Skipper has a very defined sense of right and wrong, and though he has a remarkable ability to move past things and is the most nonjudgmental person she knows, he never forgets, and wrong is wrong in his eyes, so he rarely forgives. It's simply who he is.

Hadley asked him how he felt about what had happened when they were walking to the pawnshop, and he said, "Coach shot that man who was in the car with us when I left my uniform at the pool, and he took First Base." Then his face got dark, and he added, "And that's all there is to say about that." Then he marched a few feet ahead, making it clear he didn't want to talk about it again.

Skipper's forthrightness is the reason he still needs to go with Grace. If Skipper is ever questioned, he will describe in remarkable detail what he has witnessed through his crystal-clear lens, leaving out nothing, and everyone will believe him. Skipper never lies, and his recall is extraordinary, a strange gift of memory for places, people, and events. Without meaning to, he would implicate Hadley and he would implicate Grace. He might implicate Melissa, and he would definitely implicate Jimmy. A domino effect of travesty created by his perfect, artless recall.

The car slows as Jimmy takes the exit for North Platte, and a minute later, they pull into the parking lot for a mall.

"Back in a bit," Grace says, stepping from the car with Miles.

Miles began fussing a few minutes earlier, clearly fed up with being strapped to Grace's chest and probably in need of a change. Like a pro, Grace unhitched him from the baby pack and flopped him over her shoulder, settling him down as if it was no big deal, and beside her, Jimmy beamed like she was the greatest mother on the planet. Grace rolled her eyes, but Hadley could tell she was proud, her back slightly straighter as she walked toward the entrance.

Jimmy parks in the shade, then turns sideways in his seat to look at them. And again, Hadley is charmed. Her loyalty bone vibrates, knowing it's a betrayal to like this man who's caused Grace so much pain, but trying to not like him is like trying to not like Superman. He's all muscles and white teeth, and there's something about a man in uniform that makes you believe they are good, even if they've done nothing to prove it. It's like he is cloaked in truth, justice, and the American way, and it makes her want to stand up and salute, or applaud, or knit socks—a swelling of gratitude for his courage, service, and selflessness.

She knows he screwed up. Badly. It's his fault Grace and Miles are in this mess. But now that he's here, smiling at her, his army fatigues undone and his dog tags dangling against his T-shirt, quite frankly she's having a hard time holding her grudge.

"Hey, young man," he says to Skipper. "What do you say we get you your own set of army fatigues? Make you a real private."

Hadley waits for Skipper to shake his head and offer his defiant kneejerk response of "No," the answer he gives anytime anyone suggests he wear anything other than his baseball uniform. But instead, he shocks her with, "That's the starting soldier? Like the rookie?"

"Yep," Jimmy says. "A private starts off with a plain uniform; then he earns the rest."

"And I can wear a private uniform?" Skipper says slowly, his face taking on a look of awe.

"Well, I don't know," Jimmy says thoughtfully, rubbing his chin. "First you need to answer a few questions."

Skipper's eyes get wide, and his face grows serious.

"Were you born in the United States?"

Skipper looks at Hadley, and Hadley nods.

"Yes," he says.

"Have you ever committed any crimes?"

Skipper shakes his head.

Jimmy nods in approval.

"Do you promise to be brave, serve your country, and protect those you love?"

Skipper's head reverses direction.

"Well then, I don't see any reason why you can't be a junior private."

Skipper's face lights up. "When can I get the uniform?"

Hadley blinks in amazement. In less than thirty seconds, Jimmy has managed to accomplish what she and Grace have been trying to accomplish for days.

"We just need to find a store that sells them," Jimmy says; then he winks at Hadley as he turns back in his seat, letting her know he planned this, and her admiration grows.

He pulls back to the entrance of the mall, then jumps out to help Grace with the car seat she's bought. He straps it in beside Skipper. "Private, make sure that's buckled in tight," he orders.

"Yes, sir," Skipper says, responding exactly how Jimmy told him you need to respond when an officer addresses you.

Grace hands Miles to Jimmy, and Jimmy takes a second to hold him at face level and nuzzle his nose. Miles squirms and squeals, and Jimmy does it again and again, his face radiant with love, and the last of Hadley's resistance dissolves. Jimmy might have screwed up, he might even be a screwup, but it's hard to not like someone who glows with so much devotion for his baby and his wife that it hurts to look at him.

57

GRACE

Grace stands outside the restaurant across from the army-surplus store looking out at the barren prairie that sprawls in front of her. Gone are the soaring pines and mountains, replaced with sun-scorched landscape that stretches to the horizon.

Her head aches, her heart too, everything, all of what has happened and is happening overwhelming her. She didn't want Jimmy to come, but now that he is here—solid, real, and certain—it's so tempting to let her guard down and fall into her old ways. To forgive him, give up control, and trust him when he says he is sorry and that it will never happen again. It's the best and worst part about Jimmy, how good he is and how easy it is to put your faith in him, mistakenly believing he will never let you down, a trust that is broken every time. Because, despite his failings—*failing*, she reminds herself, *singular: one single, debilitating weakness*—his love is real. And each time he looks at her with those gold eyes, the ice on her heart melts a little more.

Yesterday, she believed they had a chance, thin but possible. But today, though they continue to go through the motions—driving toward Omaha, pretending she's getting on a plane with Skipper and

Miles—she knows the chances of her going anywhere other than prison are pretty much gone.

Even as she stands here, in the middle of nowhere, she is certain someone will recognize them. Their story is being broadcast coast to coast, all of America watching as the drama unfolds, as if it is great entertainment, gripping reality television without the producers or hype: Two renegade moms on the run from the law with their kids in tow; FBI agents being gunned down in front of baseball stadiums; teenage girls being kidnapped by their crazed dads. All of it juicy and irresistible. Unbelievable, she'd think, were it not happening to them.

Having Jimmy along makes them slightly less conspicuous. No one knows he has joined them, and looking at them, with Jimmy confidently taking up space in his uniform, they look more like a military family enjoying having their soldier home than famous fugitives on the run. But at some point, someone is going to figure it out, and the jig will be up.

Hadley, Skipper, and Jimmy walk from the store, Jimmy bouncing Miles in the crook of his arm as Miles laughs, a great throaty chortle that seems to get more boisterous with each passing day. Skipper struts beside them in his new "uniform," proud as a peacock showing off new plumes. He wears camo pants, a camo jacket, a camo hat, and brown boots. It's very gung ho, super-Rambo, but Skipper's crooked smile and ambling way lessens the severity, and it's hard to take it any way other than a little boy's idolization of a soldier.

Her eyes well with fresh tears as she thinks about how beautifully Jimmy has orchestrated Skipper's change of heart. He's always had a gift for getting along with people—old, young, it doesn't matter. He just takes his time with them, shows extraordinary kindness and patience, and the next thing you know, he's their new best friend.

Hadley walks on his other side, smiling at something he is saying.

Traitor, Grace thinks, while at the same time feeling grateful. It's the first time she's seen Hadley smile since Mark was shot and Mattie was taken away. For the past day, Grace has watched Hadley drift in and out of shock, intermittently despondent and manic, dazed one minute, then chain-smoking and crying the next.

Almost as if realizing she's smiled and is feeling bad about it, Hadley stops, and her eyes dart around to see if anyone's noticed. Grace looks away so she won't know that she did.

She wants to tell her it's okay. Smiling doesn't mean she doesn't care. It's only a symptom of life carrying on, which inevitably it does. No matter how cataclysmic the events, and even in light of the worst tragedies, hearts continue to beat, lungs continue to draw air, and sometimes things continue to be funny.

Some pain changes you, alters you permanently and tattoos your soul. "Forever pain," her grandmother called it, but amazingly you still live through it. And eventually, even forever pain recedes and grows less sharp. You wake up one day to discover it no longer fills every corner of your mind. It's still there, lurking in the background, but it's less present and pronounced, a throb deep within you that almost takes focus to feel.

Jimmy stops in front of her, while Hadley and Skipper continue inside. He steps toward her, and she steps back.

He stops bouncing Miles, looks down at the ground, looks back at her. "Grace."

She shakes her head and wraps her arms across her chest, her heart thumping—love and hurt pounding.

He sighs, looks out at the prairie, then at the toes of his boots. "I'm sorry."

His words tilt the scales, causing blood to race to her face like mercury dipped in a volcano, and he quickly backtracks. "I know that's the wrong thing to say, but I've been trying to think of what else I can say, and I can't come up with the words. I screwed up. Really screwed up."

She glares at him, her nose flaring, so much rage and hurt inside her she's afraid to open her mouth for fear of what might come out.

Miles flails his arms trying to reach Jimmy's nose, and Jimmy pulls his face out of range, but when Miles protests, wriggling and writhing, Jimmy bends down to let his son grab hold and honk his beak. "Beep, beep," he says in a duck voice, his imploring eyes still on Grace.

She looks away, tears threatening. He's right: she doesn't want to hear his words. They are not enough—his apologies, his promises, his vows worthless as dust particles—meaningless, unsubstantial, empty. Atomic dust particles—hurtful, damaging, unforgiveable.

He straightens and runs his hand through his hair so hard it looks like he is trying to pull it from its roots. "If there was something I could do to prove it," he says, "show how sorry I am, I would." He takes another tentative step toward her, and again she backs away. "Grace, please, look at me."

She shakes her head. Looking at him won't help. It will only make things worse: the genuine sorrow in his eyes, the fierce promise in his voice as he tells her he won't do it again, truly believing it, a conviction that has proved false three times before.

Miles squirms and reaches out for Grace.

She takes him, and as she does, their eyes meet. "Grace, I'm going to figure out a way to fix this, to make it right."

She walks past him and into the restaurant, wanting to believe, but plumb out of faith.

58

HADLEY

Grace sits down first, looking about as downtrodden as Hadley has ever seen her, and a moment later, Jimmy joins them. It looks like he might have been crying, his eyes red rimmed and glassy, deep parentheses etched around his mouth, an expression not well suited for his normally happy-go-lucky handsome face.

He pretends to be fine, but Hadley feels the effort it takes, and it makes her horribly sad. While they wait for the waitress to come to take their order, Jimmy shows Skipper the different pockets on his fatigues and what each is used for.

"How'd you get the money?" Grace says suddenly, interrupting them and causing everything to stop.

His hand still on his left hip pocket, he says, "Figured it was time to get rid of the Harley."

Grace winces, a visible flinch. "You sold your Harley?"

He shrugs like it's no big deal, though obviously it is, a great big balloon of big deal now smack in the middle of the table.

"So, this pocket here," he says, snapping closed the hip pocket and moving his hand to his left chest pocket, "this is the most important pocket."

Skipper imitates Jimmy, moving his hand to his left chest pocket, his face very serious.

"In this pocket, you don't just put any old thing," Jimmy says.

"What do you put there?" Skipper asks, and Hadley finds herself leaning in, curious as well.

"This here is the pocket closest to your heart," Jimmy says. "So, that's what you need to keep there, the things closest to you."

"What do you have in there?" Skipper says.

Hadley leans in a bit more as Jimmy unsnaps the flap.

The first thing he pulls out is a photo of Grace in a hospital bed holding a newborn Miles, a wide toothless grin spread across her face. He sets a folded sheet of paper beside it, then lastly digs out a tiny rust-colored feather and sets it on top of the paper.

Skipper fingers the feather, stroking it gently.

"Saved my brother's life," Jimmy says. "The chicken it belonged to, that is. My brother says it was God. I say it was just a chicken. Either way, it was good luck that day when their truck stopped to let the chicken pass and the chicken got blown up by the bomb on the side of the road instead of them. Each soldier in the truck and the one behind them took a feather, and when I enlisted, my brother gave me his."

Skipper pulls his hand away, staring hard at the mystical token, chickens dying and men being spared concepts that are foreign to him.

Jimmy tucks the feather along with the note and the photo back in his pocket.

Hadley wants to ask what the note says, but she knows by the expression on Grace's face that it is personal, the parting words from one lover to another who is going off to war.

It is all more than Hadley can stand, and she wants to scream at Grace to forgive him. *He screwed up. Everyone screws up. Give the guy another chance.*

The waitress appears.

Jimmy orders a cheeseburger, and Skipper, who never orders cheeseburgers, orders the same. Grace orders spaghetti. Hadley orders a salad, no cheese, dressing on the side.

"Really?" Grace says, clearly annoyed. "Are you kidding me?"

"What?"

"We haven't had a decent meal in two days. Today or tomorrow we are probably going to be facing a lifetime of prison rations. And you're dieting."

Hadley feels a blush in her cheeks. She's always dieting. Since she turned twelve. She didn't even think about it when she ordered.

"Who the hell are you trying to impress?"

Hadley blinks, then blinks again, uncertain what she is asking. *No one. Everyone.* She has no idea. Being thin is like having good dental hygiene. It's simply expected.

Embarrassed, she shoots back, "Not all of us are blessed with a metabolism that allows us to inhale infinite calories and none of it sticks."

Grace rolls her eyes, and Hadley has a distinct desire to stick her tongue out at her, but Jimmy's smirk stops her.

She looks from him to Grace, then back to him, then back to her.

"What?" Grace says.

"Oh my God. That's it. The reason you can inhale infinite calories and none of it sticks."

Grace cocks her head.

"You're pregnant."

Grace's eyes bulge, and her head shakes.

"I can't believe I didn't realize it," Hadley says as the past five days cycle through her mind. "It explains it all: the sickness, the bottomless appetite, the constant grouchiness . . . though it's possible that's just your personality—"

Grace's face has drained of color while Jimmy's has brightened, a shit-eating grin spread wide across it.

"Are you really?" he says, interrupting and looking, misty eyed, at Grace.

Hadley feels a bit misty herself and gives herself an invisible pat on the back for figuring it out as Grace slides from the booth and runs for the door.

59

GRACE

Grace's breath comes in short bursts that don't reach her lungs, her mind spinning to calculate the possibility and timing. Her knees go weak, and she grabs hold of the railing as she tells herself it can't be true.

Though it can.

She swallows and shakes her head against it. One time, when Jimmy was home for his mother's funeral and she was too tired to put in her diaphragm. *Only one time.* She looks up at the sky, thinking God must hold a special place in His sadistic heart just for her. She imagines Him looking down and laughing. *Ha, ha, ha, ha. Joke's on you. Just when you thought things couldn't get any worse, look what I can do. Aren't I grand?*

Her right hand moves to her belly as she suddenly notices how taut it is. How could she not have noticed? Hadley's right: it's obvious—the hunger, the sickness, the exhaustion.

The wind has picked up, icy gusts that prickle her skin. On the ground, leaves swirl, and she stares at the dancing cyclones, angry with herself and with Jimmy and with God. It's one thing for Him to allow her to bring a child into the world when He had no idea how inept she would be as a parent, but to allow her to bring in a second, knowing how badly she has failed, is wrong and entirely irresponsible.

The door opens behind her, and she looks back to see Hadley limping toward her. "Congratulations?" she says, more question than statement.

Grace turns away and looks back at the swirling leaves.

Hadley steps beside her and bumps her shoulder. "Come on, it's awesome. Miles will have a brother or sister."

Grace shakes her head.

"Okay, so maybe the timing's not ideal—"

Grace's scathing look stops her.

Hadley sighs, straightens, and says, "Well, anyway, your pasta's here." She takes a step, stops, and, unable to resist, adds, "And you'd better come eat. After all, you *are* eating for two."

60

HADLEY

Hadley watches as Grace slides into the booth. Jimmy reaches out to wrap his arm around her, then reconsiders. He lowers his eyes sheepishly, but it is an act. Pride and joy radiate like the sun's glow around him.

"Champ, put that down and eat," Hadley says to Skipper, who's playing on his PlayStation.

"But First Base is talking to me," he says, not looking up.

Hadley's fork freezes halfway to her mouth.

"Who's First Base?" Jimmy asks.

Hadley snatches the game from Skipper's hands, and Grace leaps from the booth to lean in beside her so she can see the screen as well.

champ i need to talk to blue

"How do I do this?" Hadley says, flipping the device back and forth as if looking for a hidden keyboard.

Jimmy takes the device and gives her a demonstration, showing how you get to the touch screen keyboard.

mattie im here where r u, Hadley types.

i got away in a town called mccook

Hadley types, how, her heart beating triple time and her hands shaking.

i took uncle tonys car when we stopped for gas and dad and uncle tony were in the store

u drove

yes

Grace fist pumps the air, and Hadley looks at her, confused, then turns back to the small screen.

where in mccook

parked behind giant silos

stay put im on my way i love u

i love u too

"Where's McCook?" she says, her eyes still fixed on the screen and Mattie's words.

Jimmy flags down their waitress and repeats the question. "Have you heard of a town named McCook?"

"Sure. It's about three and a half hours south of here."

"Can you pack our food to go?" Jimmy says.

Hadley looks at him, tears of gratitude filling her eyes. Then she looks at Grace, and Grace nods, causing Hadley to lose it, the tears escaping to stream down her cheeks.

"Thank you," she croaks.

"I love her too," Grace says, her hand absently going to her stomach, betraying her fear despite her brave words.

"We're going to get First Base?" Skipper says, his face lit up, feeling like a bona fide hero at having had a part in it and looking like one in his uniform.

"That's right, Private," Jimmy says. "Time to roll."

Skipper practically leaps from the booth.

"The private and I are going for supplies," Jimmy says with a wink at Grace. "We'll meet you soldiers in the car."

"Where are you going?" Grace says, uncertainty in her voice.

Jimmy's eyes flick to the army-surplus store across the street. "Need to pick up some hardware. Don't want to greet Hadley's husband and her brother-in-law without any firepower."

Grace shakes her head.

"Babe, trust me."

Grace says nothing, and Jimmy turns to leave.

Hadley's skin prickles. "Jimmy, wait." Jimmy turns back. "Grace, what is it you're not saying?"

It's weird seeing Grace around Jimmy. As strong as she is, she defers to him in a way Hadley can't get used to, her southern roots showing like a bad dye job.

"Spit it out," Hadley says. "I know you have this whole he's-the-man-and-he's-my-husband thing going on, but something's on your mind, and since you're a heck of a lot smarter than your husband—" She stops to look at Jimmy. "No offense, Jimmy, but she is." Jimmy nods. "You need to stop acting like the good wife and tell us what it is."

Grace kind of scoff chuckles, like Hadley got her with a good one, but her cheeks flush, either embarrassed at being called out or angry. Hadley can't be sure and frankly doesn't care. Mattie is three and a half hours away, and this is no time for worrying about bruised egos.

"It doesn't feel right," Grace says, her mouth setting in a thin line.

"What doesn't feel right?"

"How do we even know it's Mattie who's talking to us?"

"Good point," Jimmy says. He holds out his hand for the PlayStation. "What's something only Mattie would know?"

Hadley looks at Skipper, and the answer comes to her. "What did Skipper save from under Mattie's bed?"

"A spider," Skipper contributes excitedly.

"Good job," Jimmy says as his thumbs fly over the screen. "Bad luck to kill spiders."

Spider pops up almost instantly on the screen.

Hadley lets out a whoop. "It's her. It's her."

Grace still looks uncertain.

"What?" Hadley says, irritated and impatient. "It's her. She just proved it."

"I still don't trust it."

Hadley wonders if she doesn't trust it because she's scared and wants to back out, the balance shifted with the new life inside her.

"Here's the thing," Grace says slowly, as if still working out the thoughts as she says them. "McCook is probably the size of a postage stamp, right?"

All of them nod, even Skipper. Every town they've driven through since leaving Denver hasn't been larger than a few blocks wide.

"And Mattie's been trying to reach us for hours, sitting in a black muscle car with out-of-state plates behind some silos."

"Yeah, so?"

Jimmy's the one who answers. "So why hasn't anyone asked her what she's doing there?"

"Exactly," Grace says. "I grew up in a small town. And there's no way the foreman of the silos or a security guard or a nosy neighbor wouldn't have called the local sheriff to tell good old Bob, Joe, or Hank that some tricked-out mafia car is hanging around."

"So what are you saying?"

"I'm saying I don't trust it. They know she's there."

"Who?"

"The cops? The feds? I don't know."

"But then why haven't they picked her up?"

"That's the question."

"Because they're waiting," Jimmy says.

"For what?"

"For us."

61

GRACE

It was an excruciating drive, the tension ratcheting up with each mile until, by the time they reached the exit for McCook, Grace felt like her head was going to explode. As the sun went down, the clouds closed ranks, and now a steel wool sky conceals the stars and the threat of rain looms. Jimmy drives carefully down the main street as Grace scans the town, suspecting every car and van of holding agents lying in wait.

Jimmy holds her hand. He took it when they pulled off the highway, and she was so distracted she didn't think about it, and now it is too late to pull it away, his long fingers curled around hers, both reassuring and disturbing at once. Things always seem so promising when Jimmy is around, yet they never seem to work out.

Everyone is silent, even Miles, as they creep along at the posted twenty-five-mile-per-hour speed limit.

The town is small and typical—fast-food restaurants, a few mom-and-pop stores, a gas station, and a Walmart—the stores mostly buttoned up for the night, though it's just past nine.

"Turn here," Grace says, directing Jimmy to pull into a motel called the Chief Inn. Her eyes slide to the motel across the street, then travel left and right, surveying again for trouble. "Park in the back."

Jimmy does as she says, and Hadley steps from the car to check them in with Blaire Butz's license. Grace watches as she works to control her limp, though the effort it takes is obvious.

A few minutes later, she returns, two keys in her hand, and Grace feels Jimmy's concern over their dwindling funds. He would have preferred they frugally shared one room, though he says nothing.

He thinks the money from his Harley is all they have to start their new life. Grace knows it's not. Mattie's game console was in the diaper bag with the cash in the trunk of Blaire Butz's car, which means Mattie has the cash. But the last thing she wants is for Jimmy to know that, so she keeps it to herself.

Hadley hands Jimmy a key, then takes the car seat with Miles from his hands. "You two need some time alone," she says with a wink, then, not waiting for an answer, marches away.

Grace glares at her meddling, irritating back. Ever since they left the restaurant, she could practically hear Hadley's thoughts: *He's a good man, Grace. Look what he's doing for Mattie. For me. Not to mention good looking. Icing on the cake, but still, very nice icing, you have to admit. And he loves you. So much. And Miles. Look how he adores his son. Christ, Grace, what do you want? He screwed up, but he's trying so hard to make it up. We all screw up. You need to forgive him. Damn it, get over yourself, and just forgive him already. The guy deserves a chance.*

Skipper looks back and gives a crooked smile and a thumbs-up, and Jimmy gives a thumbs-up back.

Dang conspiracy, the two of them ganging up against her. Three of them, if you count Miles, who is as smitten with his dad as Skipper and Hadley are.

Jimmy smiles an infuriating I-had-nothing-to-do-with-it smirk, and she opens her mouth to tell him exactly what's what, and that, despite him charming the pants off everyone around them, it doesn't change things. But before she can get the words out, he has closed the distance between them and his lips are coming down on hers.

~

It is almost midnight when they return to the motel. They've been driving around McCook for hours, memorizing and rememorizing every street and every possible route. The town is laid out in a typical midwestern grid of letters and numbers. The streets travel in both directions, and alleys divide the lettered streets.

Grace rubs her tired eyes as Jimmy opens the door to their room. They stagger in, and she falls into his arms, hooking her thumbs in the back pockets of his fatigues and leaning her head against his chest. He leans down and kisses her hair, his strong arms wrapping around her. Under her ear, his heart keeps time, and she listens to its comforting thump.

The plan has changed, and the terror of what they are doing eliminates any concern she had about his gambling and has erased her anger over the past. All they have for certain is tonight, and she is not going to waste it. Jimmy is hers, flawed but perfect, and if they make it through this, she will never forget that again.

He leads her to the bed and lies down beside her, and when he opens his mouth, she puts her fingers to his lips to stop him.

All night, they cling to each other, their lovemaking frantic and desperate, then gentle and slow. She shushes him each time he apologizes, and he kisses away her tears when she breaks down and weeps. For hours, he lies with his head on her stomach, and they talk about the new life inside her and what they should name him or her. Jimmy doesn't argue with Mark for a boy, but he has a real problem with Virginia if it's a girl.

"Do you realize how much grief she's going to get in middle school?"

She lifts her eyebrow as if to say, *Really?*

"Virginia the virgin. Virgin Virginia. We're setting her up to be a slut, simply to disprove her name."

Grace laughs. "Seriously, you think she's going to get teased because the word *virgin* is in her name?"

"I guarantee it."

"Fine. We'll call her Ginny."

"Great, she'll end up a drunk."

"I won't let her become a drunk," she answers, a hint of sadness in her voice.

62

HADLEY

It is the longest night of Hadley's life. The minutes tick by like hours when she knows Mattie is so near and that she can't go to her. Grace's plan is dangerous and, if they pull it off, brilliant. But so many things can go wrong it terrifies her to think about it.

She sits on the edge of the bed, stroking the gentle slope of Skipper's jaw. Miles sleeps beside him, swaddled tight, his arms over his head like a cactus. *Her boys.* Strange how quickly she has come to think of Miles and Grace as family, but unquestionably that is what they are—a part of her, people she would stake her life on and risk her life for.

An ache balloons in her chest as she thinks how she has endangered them and continues to do so, her debt so large she knows in a lifetime it will never be repaid. With a deep sigh, she stands and walks to the window. Parting the curtains, she stares across the parking lot at the bright marquee of the motel across the street, her vision blurring as she thinks about tomorrow and what they need to do.

When the morning finally brightens enough to turn the room gray, she gets the boys up and takes them to the dining room beside the lobby for breakfast. Skipper eats cinnamon oatmeal as Hadley spoons small bites into Miles's mouth. Miles gurgles and spits with delight, and the sight is almost enough to unclench the panic strangling her heart.

Grace and Jimmy arrive a few minutes later, Grace tense, Jimmy relaxed. Grace leans down and kisses Miles on his head, her lips lingering. Jimmy rests his hand on her back. The hurt between them is gone, dissolved into a new perspective that no longer allows room for old wounds, and watching them is like staring into the sun, warm and blinding and painful.

For the millionth time, Hadley searches her brain for an alternative, some other way to get through this.

"It's time," Grace says, her voice raspy from a night of emotion.

Jimmy lifts Miles from his car seat and flies him around like an airplane before depositing him in the baby pack Hadley has strapped to her chest. Hadley also holds Skipper's hand. Jimmy carries the empty car seat. Grace carries nothing.

Jimmy kisses Miles gently on his head, kisses Grace passionately on the lips, then strides away, his head held high, his gait long and sure—a bona fide hero—not the illusion of a uniform but the character of the man who wears it.

Grace watches him go, her chin thrust out. "Let's go," she rasps, going for bold confidence but failing.

Hadley follows her through the lobby, hobbling as quickly as her injured ankle will allow, and Skipper hustles beside her, aware of how important it is for him to keep up.

They walk outside. The sky is a soup of dark clouds that weighs the air and makes the morning dim.

They reach the street, wait for the traffic to clear, then jaywalk to the motel on the other side.

"Hurry, Champ," Hadley encourages. "Faster."

"Private," he corrects her as he picks up his pace, all of them almost running now.

Hadley's eyes dart around the parking lot for the Economy Suites. Tony's car is parked in the third spot, exactly where Mattie said it would be. Four spots away is a green Fiat with no one in it. Other than that, the lot is empty. *Maybe Grace was wrong?* she thinks as she continues to race for Tony's car. *Maybe they're not here?*

Daggers of pain shoot through her ankle, but she doesn't slow, the car now only twenty feet away. She glances at the window of the second room on the bottom floor. In the lower-left corner is a two-inch square of yellow—a Post-it Note placed there by Mattie signaling that the plan is a go.

She lunges for the back door of the car at the exact moment the door to Mattie's room opens, and tears fill Hadley's eyes at the sight of her baby running toward them.

Hadley pulls Skipper with her into the back seat as Mattie yanks open the passenger door.

"First Base!" Skipper yells as Mattie throws the striped bag on the floor and leaps in after it.

"Hey, Champ," she says, turning back to look at him.

The car is rolling before her door has closed.

Miles squeals and kicks in his pack against Hadley's chest as they drive over the curb to bounce onto the road. Half a second later, Hadley crouches over him and reaches out to brace Skipper as they're thrown sideways when Grace whips around the next turn.

When she straightens, she cranes her head to look behind them, and her heart misfires when she sees a gray sedan racing behind them.

"You were right," she says in disbelief, staring at the blue swirling light in the windshield.

Grace says nothing, her eyes tight on the road as she continues to gun it down the street.

Hadley can't believe it. Until this moment, she didn't actually believe anyone could predict so much based on so little. But Grace did. She said the feds were waiting, and they were.

The car skids into an alley, then banks sharply onto a side street.

"Seat belts," Hadley yelps at the exact moment Skipper yells, "Red!" and Hadley looks up to see them charging toward an intersection with cross traffic moving steadily through it.

"Grace!" she screams.

Grace doesn't hit the brakes. She doesn't even slow. The car flies toward it at breakneck speed, and Hadley squeezes her eyes shut as she pulls Skipper against her and bends tight over Miles.

The car swerves and horns blare, but miraculously, when Hadley sits up, they are past it.

She looks back to see the sedan two football-field lengths behind them and counts the seconds between them. Four. Grace estimated they would need at least six for the plan to work.

They travel in the general direction of north, circumventing the town in a haphazard pattern that appears random but that Hadley knows is planned. They pass from the town into a residential neighborhood, then come out the other side into farmland, the fields recently cropped, leaving nothing but miles of stubbled gold around them—no place to run and no place to hide.

Grace floors it down the laser-straight two-lane road, and a moment later, the abandoned silos come into view, six massive concrete drums reaching for the sky.

"Seat belts off," Grace says.

Hadley unhitches her belt and grabs Skipper's hand as her other hand moves to hover above the door handle.

"Ready?" she says to Skipper.

He nods, a soldier set for battle. They practiced last night, pretending the bed was the back seat of Tony's car.

The silos seem to take forever to get closer; then suddenly, like a time warp, they are upon them. Hadley's heart lodges in her throat as the car bumps from the road onto the gravel of the site. The tires kick up dirt, creating a dust cloud behind them, and when Hadley looks back, she can no longer see the sedan.

Grace cranks the wheel right, sending them skidding around the office building; then she yanks it left, and they slide the other way so the car is now aimed for the narrow space between the silos. At full speed, she barrels toward it, and a second later, the shadows of the drums swallow them, and a second after that, the car slams to a stop.

Hadley throws open the door and yanks Skipper with her as she dives toward the loading dock to her left. Pain shoots through her ankle as she lands, but she manages to scrabble into the corner and wedge herself in tight as she hugs the boys against her.

She lifts her head barely in time to see Jimmy leap into the driver's seat, taking Grace's place.

He peels away, and three seconds later the sedan races past. She stares after it in disbelief, unable to believe it drove right by.

She doesn't move. Neither does Mattie, who squats in the shadows across from her, or Grace, who lies flat on the ground beneath the ramp beside them.

Only when the dust has settled and the taillights have disappeared does she run across the dirt to pull Mattie into her arms, tears streaming down her face even though she's smiling, her emotions too big to hold inside, her whole body trembling with relief.

63

GRACE

Grace stares at the diminishing dust cloud until there is nothing left to see. Tears brim in her eyes, and her hand goes to her belly, the skin taut like she has eaten a big meal, though she hasn't put anything in her stomach since the pasta she ate the day before. *Your dad is really something,* she says silently to their child. *And he loves you. Someday, I'll tell you just how much he loves you.*

"We need to go," Hadley says, sounding like Grace usually sounds.

Grace takes one last look into the distance, then turns away, unable to believe it worked, relieved and heartsick at once. She knew their only advantage was the element of surprise, to do something so daring and unexpected the feds would be caught completely off guard.

Grace spent a long time thinking things through. The moment Frank shot Mark, an APB would have been issued on Tony's car. The local police would have spotted the car at the silos and called the FBI.

The reason they didn't apprehend Mattie was because she's a minor. Had she been an adult, they could have taken her in and coerced her into cooperating. But because she's only a kid, the moment they engaged her, they would have needed to call social services. And, as Grace knows from experience, social services is real particular about how kids are treated, and there's no way they would have let the feds use a fourteen-year-old as bait. So instead, they let her be, using her as a carrot without having to involve the mother-bear agency.

"Wow," Mattie says, stepping up beside her. "They really were watching me. What if I was like in serious trouble?"

Grace wraps her arm around Mattie's shoulders and nuzzles her head with her chin, the relief of her being safe and beside her overwhelming.

"If you were choking on your tongue, they might have stepped in." She nuzzles her again. "You did good."

"I did good too," Skipper says. "Out like a bullet. Duck and cover." He puts his hands over his head to demonstrate.

"You did, Champ," Mattie says. "You did real good." She holds out her hand for him to high-five, which he does as he says, "I go by Private now."

Mattie nods her approval as her gaze runs up and down him, taking in his new duds. "I like it. Very heroic. And I go by Tillie now, but you can still call me First Base."

Hadley steps up beside them. "Where'd you learn to drive?"

Grace winks at Mattie, and Mattie winks back, and Hadley frowns, pretending to be upset but not pulling it off even a little, her relief at having Mattie back completely destroying the act.

As a group, they walk toward the edge of the lot to the Nissan, which is parked where Jimmy left it, beside the maintenance shed and out of sight from the road.

Originally, it was supposed to be Hadley who drove away in Tony's car, leaving Grace and the kids behind to go to Omaha, and then on to London. Then, last night, Jimmy changed the plan, coming up with the idea of him doing it instead. He was adamant and unwilling to take no for an answer.

"My way to make things right," he said. "Please, Grace, let me do this."

And so she did. And now, here she is with Hadley and the kids while he is driving Tony's car on a two-lane highway that stretches through Nebraska, then South Dakota, then North Dakota, then all the way to Canada.

He won't make it that far. The car will run out of gas somewhere in South Dakota, but hopefully it will buy enough time for Grace and the kids to get on the plane to London and for Hadley to put some distance between her and McCook.

The illegal tint on Tony's windows, which is so dark it is impossible to see through, along with the rain forecast for later this morning, should make it difficult for anyone to realize a man is behind the wheel instead of her and that he is alone. She is counting on that as well as all the media attention to keep the FBI on their best behavior. If they think there is even the slightest chance that children are in the car, they will be cautious, and Jimmy is going to drive very safely. His goal is to draw this out as long as possible. "A nice long drive in the country," is how he put it.

～

Fifteen minutes after leaving the silos, they are back in town and parked in front of the Amtrak station. The timing was planned down to the minute. The train to Omaha is already on the track and scheduled to depart in ten minutes.

Hadley pulls Mattie into a fierce hug. "I love you," she says, the words strangled.

Mattie pulls away. "We're going to be okay," she says.

Hadley manages a nod.

Mattie toes the ground and looks back at her mom, and Grace watches as she fights to keep the tears in her eyes as she says, "Thanks . . . you know . . . for what you did . . . for all of it. You were amazing."

Grace sees how the words affect Hadley, her eyes going glassy as she studies her daughter for what might be the last time for a long time. She places her hand on Mattie's cheek. "Be good."

"Not too good," Mattie answers with a wry smile; then bravely she turns for the train, and Skipper, unaware of the significance of the moment, bounds after her.

"Do you want me to get him?" Grace offers.

Hadley shakes her head. "Let him be. As long as Mattie's with him, he'll be okay."

"You sure about this?" Grace says, her eyes trailing after them.

Instead of answering, Hadley says, "Listen to Mattie when it comes to Skipper. She knows what he needs: his medical issues, his allergies, the condition with his heart. She can help you, but you still need to take him to a doctor when you get settled. She's a good girl, a good big sister, but don't let her get all motherly on you. She does that, thinks she's Skipper's mom sometimes, and uses it as an excuse to not make friends of her own."

Miles pushes off Grace's chest like he is trying to break free.

"You can't push her," Hadley goes on, "but if you encourage her, she'll surprise you."

"I'll keep that in mind," Grace says, a lump lodged in her throat.

Miles kicks harder, protesting being left behind by Skipper and Mattie. Hadley takes hold of one of his little fists, then leans in to drop a lingering kiss on his head. Stepping back, she levels her gaze on Grace's and says, "You can do this. You're going to be fine."

Grace looks down at Miles, then back at Hadley and lets out a heavy sigh. "Of course I can. Easy peasy."

Hadley's lips almost curl. "Okay, let's not get cocky."

"Three kids and me, international fugitives living under false identities in London? No problem. I've totally got this."

"And, don't forget, one on the way." Hadley nods toward Grace's belly.

"Right," Grace says. "And one on the way." *Easy peasy.*

64

HADLEY

Hadley watches as the train disappears into the gray haze and, for a long moment, stands silent as a light mist falls around her. Only when the whistle blows to signal a new train arriving does she climb back into the car, her eyes dry and strangely at peace. Her family is together and safe, and she feels calm in a way she has never experienced before.

On her way out of town, she stops at the post office. As she drops the package in the mail slot, she hopes Mark's wife will respect her wishes and keep it private. But if she doesn't, oh well. It will be what it will be. Again, the odd apathy—carefree or careless, as if none of it any longer matters. A shutting down or a release, whichever, she simply no longer has the energy to give a damn, her emotions plumb worn out, with nothing left to give.

As she drives, rain spits on the windshield, and she sends a silent prayer that the camouflage will keep Jimmy safe. Her wipers swish back and forth, and she finds the rhythm of the blades hypnotizing. Lost in a trance, she is thankful to Grace for planning out what Hadley needs to do, her movements switched to autopilot.

Her ankle throbs as it presses the accelerator, but she pays it no mind, her eyes scanning from the road to the speedometer to the gas gauge as her mind calculates. Jimmy drives north. She drives east. She should be halfway to her destination and the kids and Grace safely in the air when Jimmy runs out of gas.

The radio is on, and she listens intermittently as the news reports on the progress of the pursuit. The reporters use their names—Hadley, Grace, Skipper, Matilde, and Miles—as if they know them, and they talk about them as if they are truly concerned, their smooth voices full of worry as they discuss how traumatic this must be for the kids and whether they are hungry and how they will go to the bathroom.

Hadley finds herself caught up in it, fretting along with them, until she remembers it isn't real, that they are talking about them—her and Grace, and Miles and Skipper and Mattie—but that they aren't in the car; Jimmy is.

On and on they go, interviewing neighbors and friends and experts, anyone who might have some added insight on the story—Skipper's teacher, a neighbor of Grace's, one of the parking lot managers, a lawyer, a child psychologist. For the most part, everyone says nice things. Even the random strangers who are interviewed and asked their opinions are nice. Almost all of them blame the FBI and say they bungled the case. "Mother-bear instinct" gets thrown around a lot, along with "backed into a corner" and "fight or flight."

Everyone prays for them and hopes for a peaceful resolution, one in which no one gets hurt, especially the kids.

The story is rehashed again and again, dissected from every possible angle: not only what is happening but everything that led up to it, the last six days analyzed endlessly. They get the details surprisingly right. The only parts they get wrong are not realizing that Grace and Hadley never planned to team up and that Jimmy is now a part of it.

The child psychologist discusses the long-term effects this could have on the kids, which distresses Hadley, especially when the woman talks about trust and abandonment issues.

A slew of lawyers debate the legal trouble she and Grace are in, and all agree that Grace, with her history, is in serious trouble. Her record, combined with her more significant role in the crimes, puts her at much higher risk for a long-term sentence than Hadley, who none of them seem to be able to agree on in terms of what kind of punishment she will face.

At one point, a car expert comes on to discuss the make and model of Tony's car and to predict how long it will take for it to run out of gas. His estimate is roughly the same as Grace's. If Jimmy continues to maintain the speed limit and started with a full tank, he will be able to drive approximately seven and a half hours.

An ex-FBI agent has been on several times, and each time he reassures the reporter and audience that the pursuit will continue in the manner it has, the police following at a safe distance and proceeding with extreme caution. The primary objective is to bring the women in safely without anyone getting hurt.

The reporters go back and forth about Hadley and Grace's motives for not surrendering, the consensus being that they are prolonging the inevitable in order to spend as much time as possible with their kids. They play up the nobility of it, making her and Grace sound heroic.

Each of the reporters goes on and on about what they would do with that precious time if they were in the same position, what they would say, and the wisdom they would impart. They ask callers to call in and contribute, and they do.

It's all very dramatic and tragic, and Hadley finds herself playing along, thinking about all the things she would like to say to Mattie and the things she still wants to share with Skipper.

A family lawyer discusses what will happen to the kids after the women are arrested. Mattie and Skipper will most likely end up living with Vanessa, Hadley's only living relative, though it's possible Frank's parents could make a case for raising Mattie. The thought is very upsetting. Frank's parents are not nice people, and Mattie hates them.

Miles, of course, will end up with his dad, Corporal James Herrick, who is currently serving in Afghanistan.

There's a lot of talk about Jimmy, an outpouring of support for the heroic soldier whose life has been turned upside down by his wife's recklessness. It's strange how much support there is for Hadley and the kids and how little there is for Grace.

Hadley has already listened to two women callers phone in and offer to marry Jimmy if Grace doesn't make it or if he decides to divorce her for what she's done, which you can hear in their voices is what they think he should do.

Hadley feels bad for how Grace is being portrayed, the blame for anything criminal or unscrupulous put on her because of her past and because they do not like the way she looks. Several times her scowl is mentioned, and once a reporter even commented on the way she walks: "Like she's cocky or has something to prove." Hadley hated the woman instantly. None of these people have any idea what they're talking about.

The way they talk about Hadley is laughable as well. Melissa made the mistake of saying Hadley was trusting, and the press took that and ran with it, making Hadley out to be a gullible victim who got caught up in Grace's harebrained scheme because she was naive and desperate to escape her abusive marriage.

Of course Frank is the real villain, the sinister monster who tracked down his wife, kidnapped his daughter, and shot down an agent in cold blood amid a crowd of families. An abuser, a wife beater, a devil without a soul, he's nothing but evil and deserves to be strung up by his toenails and horsewhipped. As she listens, she hopes Mattie is not listening. To some extent we all believe ourselves to be products of our parents, and no one would want to be a part of the person they're describing.

She waits anxiously for updates on Frank and Tony, knowing they're still out there. The reporters hypothesize they were making a run for Mexico when Mattie escaped, and they might be right. But she knows

Frank will not be heading there now. Cruel as Frank is to Mattie, she is also his progeny, and he won't leave without her.

She looks again at the gas gauge. The needle hovers halfway between empty and full. Grace and the kids should be in Omaha now and on their way to the post office to retrieve the passports, and in another three hours, they will be in the air and on their way to London, away from the FBI and away from Frank.

Her heart keeps rhythm with the wipers, her hands tight on the wheel and her eyes tight on the road. In the distance, lightning flashes. She drives toward it, hardly paying attention now to the radio as it continues to jabber on about her family, all of it far away, like a distant dream she is chasing that continues to move away and get farther out of reach.

65

GRACE

Grace is at Eppley Airfield with Miles, Mattie, and Skipper, her eyes glued to the television over the bar in the restaurant beside their departure gate. The coverage of the car chase has been nonstop. For two hours, Grace has joined the rest of the world as it watches Jimmy driving, first in Nebraska and now in South Dakota, a battalion of cop cars behind him.

It is strange to see. The fascination. As if their story is the most important thing in the world. It seems to her that there must be other more vital things to be concerned with. Somewhere in the world people are starving, children are being abused, nations are being besieged by national disaster. Yet, all day, every news channel has shown nothing but a helicopter view of a black car driving steadily down a two-lane road in the rain.

On either side of the car are fields. It looks like corn but might also be wheat or barley. It's hard to tell in the dim light and blur of the rain. The headlights are on, though it's only three o'clock, the storm obscuring the sun and making the world dark.

Behind the dozen police cars that trail Jimmy, dozens of other vehicles stretch out in a sort of haphazard parade. There are media vans, the kind with extendable antennas and satellite dishes on the roofs, along with everyday cars with people in them. Grace isn't sure what to call them. *Fans* seems like a strange word, but that's sort of what they are: spectators caught up in the spectacle who want to witness it up close and be a part of it.

When Jimmy drove through North Platte, people huddled alongside the road waiting, holding umbrellas in the downpour to watch him drive by. Some waved signs of support with sayings like **STAY FREE** or **GO MAMA BEARS**. It was strange to watch, and Grace wondered what Jimmy made of it. She imagined him smiling and waving, though it's doubtful any of them could see him through the gloom and the rain and the dark tint of the windows.

There's been some speculation that a man is driving the car, but the FBI has dismissed it, restating several times that two agents witnessed Grace and Hadley, along with their three kids, get into the car in McCook and that the FBI has been following them since.

The FBI seems irritated by all the attention, and Grace can't really blame them. They have not been painted in a good light, and the circus following the pursuit is a recipe for disaster. They have repeatedly asked people to stay away so they can do their job, but their pleas have been mostly ignored, the nation captivated by the drama.

Grace turns from the coverage to look at the tarmac through the windows and at the planes taxiing up and down the runway. Skipper kneels with his nose pressed to the glass, his hands on either side of his face. Mattie—Tillie now—sits on the stool to her left. And Miles is asleep in Grace's arms. She leans down to kiss the soft skin of his cheek, warm and moist like dew.

Grace can't believe they are here. The three passports were waiting at the post office just as Melissa promised, and no one blinked an eye when they checked in or went through security.

A woman a few seats away points excitedly, and Grace turns her attention back to the television. An Asian newscaster fills the screen, the words beneath her reading, *BREAKING NEWS!* The shot switches from the newsroom to a helicopter view of the pursuit.

The car is stopped, its headlights shining into the rain. The police cars behind it have stopped as well, and she watches as people flood from their cars and as the police race to form a line to contain them. Like a swarm, they press forward, straining to see, and Grace feels herself leaning in as well, practically lifting off her seat toward it.

The PA system announces their flight, and Skipper, who's been listening intently for their number, leaps to his feet. "That's us," he says. "One one five nine. We need to go."

Grace doesn't move, her eyes glued to the scene above her. On the television, a large man dressed in a white shirt and brown pants hitched high on his waist walks without an umbrella toward Tony's car. Several officers, guns drawn, follow.

Skipper takes Grace's hand and tugs at it. "Trout, we've got to go."

Mattie pulls him away. "Hold on, Private," she says.

"But they announced our flight. One one five nine. That's us."

The driver's door of Tony's car opens, and a second later, Jimmy steps out, his hands raised in front of him. Grace feels her blood stop as she watches the spotlights shift to target him, his body lit up against the storming afternoon.

Miles squirms, and Grace realizes she is gripping him too tight. She loosens her hold as her nose pinches tight and her jaw slides forward.

"Trout, *come on*," Skipper says as the PA system announces that their flight is now boarding.

The large man with the too-high pants walks past Jimmy, bends to look inside the car, straightens, then slams his fist on the roof.

Skipper breaks away from Mattie, grabs hold of Grace's hand again, and tugs at her. "Trout, come on."

Her eyes still on the screen, she allows him to pull her toward the gate. Her last glance is of Jimmy being led toward the waiting cruisers, reporters, and crowd. He turns to face the camera, and a thin smile crosses his lips as his eyes look directly into hers.

66

HADLEY

Despite the earlier rain, the night is clear and relatively warm. A few vagrant clouds drift in the midnight sky, the stars beyond them bright. Hadley's seat is tilted back, angled so all she sees is sky. For a long time, she gazes at Orion, the only constellation she knows. She learned about the star warrior on a field trip she took with Skipper's class last year, surprised to learn the three bright stars in a row that she always believed to be part of the Big Dipper belong to another constellation altogether and that she had spent her whole life being wrong.

The hours pass in silence, save for the occasional passing big rig on the highway to the west or the caw of a night bird—an owl, or perhaps a bat. In and out of consciousness she drifts, though mostly she is awake, her thoughts vacillating between hate and love and how both have led her to this place in her life. She thinks about how much she hates Frank and how much she has grown to love Grace and Miles and Jimmy.

You were amazing. Mattie's words repeat in her head, and each time she thinks of it, profound sadness chokes her and makes it difficult to breathe. How did she allow herself to become so lost or to let things go on as long as they did?

Pffft. Frank didn't even react as he pulled the trigger, his face blank, as if Mark were nothing more than an annoyance, a gnat buzzing around his head. That is who she was married to, who she allowed her children to be raised by.

She lights her third cigarette of the night and lowers the window so the smoke will not fill the car. When she's done, she turns on the radio. It cackles with more news about Jimmy. They can't get enough of him: his sacrifice, his return from Afghanistan to save his wife and son . . . and unborn child. She smiled when she heard this new juicy tidbit had been revealed, knowing that, despite everything, Jimmy couldn't help but boast about his family.

When her eyelids grow too heavy to keep open, she turns off the news, closes the window, and tries to rest, time passing slowly, the minutes ticking like hours, until finally the dawn rises and her ankle feels strong enough to continue.

The storm of yesterday is a memory, and the morning sky is cloudless. She wonders how they are doing—Grace, Mattie, Skipper, and Miles. She imagines them in London, Mattie pulling Skipper along as he staggers behind, wide eyed with wonder, and Miles kicking and babbling, excited by all the commotion.

The miles slog by, and she focuses on the road and on staying awake. It feels like she hasn't slept in a year, her exhaustion lulling her dangerously toward sleep, the sound of the tires like a lullaby. Several times her eyelids flutter closed, and she snaps them open a second before driving off the road.

A little before dinnertime, a sign welcomes her to Grand Portage Chippewa Reservation. Her stomach is hollow with hunger, but she ignores it. She drives straight to the lodge, walks to the front desk, and asks to speak with Dennis Hull, the name Grace told her would get her across the border.

"Mrs. Torelli?"

She turns. The man talking to her is in his twenties and not Native American. His skin is white, his eyes gray. He wears comfortable shoes and a suit that looks new. She sighs, as relieved as she is disappointed. She is so tired.

She will confess, protect Grace as best she can, serve whatever sentence they give her, and move on with her life.

"My name is Kevin Fitzpatrick."

"Fitz," she mumbles, and she feels a small smile on her lips, glad it is Mark's friend who is arresting her.

She staggers sideways, and he reaches for her, catching her by the elbow to steady her.

"Whoa," he says. "Dizzy?"

Hadley nods.

"What do you say we get you a bite to eat?" he says, his accent pure Brooklyn.

Hadley blurts out, "I want to confess."

"Okay, but how about we feed you first so you don't pass out during the confession?"

She allows him to lead her by the elbow toward the dining room.

He's not very tall, perhaps her height, and thin, his suit loose, like he doesn't quite fill it out.

"You're a field agent now?" she says. "Mark would be so happy for you."

"He recommended me," Fitz says proudly but also sadly.

Mark told Hadley about Fitz, how he was the one who spotted them on the surveillance tapes the night they took the money. "Smart kid, with a good head on his shoulders but a soft heart," he said. "And that doesn't work in the field." She could feel his worry, how much he liked Fitz and wanted to protect him. At the time, she didn't understand, but now she does. Fitz is more concerned about her fainting than getting a confession from her.

As the hostess leads them to a table, she scans around her, looking for more agents. "Where are the others?"

"Just me. I'm actually supposed to be on my way to South Dakota, but I came here instead."

Hadley collapses into the booth, and Fitz slides in across from her. He pushes her water glass toward her.

She takes a sip, and her body responds with a surge of thirst. She guzzles it down, realizing only after she's finished that she has not put anything in her body since she left McCook.

Fitz orders a cup of coffee and a cup of soup, and Hadley does the same.

"How'd you figure out where I was?" she says.

"You might say I'm a bit of a detective nerd. For a year, I've been working the desk on the case. My job was to relay information to Mark and to keep the case file up to date. It's not the most exciting job, but it does give you a sort of wide-angle view of things. Things got interesting when you and Herrick took the money."

"That's one way of looking at it," she says, that night so far away it seems like another life altogether.

"Did you plan on teaming up?" Fitz says.

Hadley shakes her head.

"I didn't think so." He sounds almost excited. "It was just too random. Remarkable."

Hadley says nothing. She would hardly describe anything that has happened over the past week as remarkable. Tragic, awful, regrettable—all better-suited words for what has happened.

"Herrick is extraordinary," Fitz goes on.

Hadley nods.

"She only made one mistake."

Hadley lifts an eyebrow.

"The burner phone."

"Her phone?"

"I realized she had one when Jimmy turned up. I figured out that Jimmy's brother was the go-between, checked the phone records, and traced the phone back to the Walmart in Barstow." He is animated as he talks, excited by his brilliant detecting. "I checked the surveillance tapes, saw that Grace used the computers, did a history search, and bam, there it was, ways to sneak into Canada."

"Oh," she says. Mark was right. Fitz is very good.

She looks down at the table, staring at a scratch in the table in the shape of an *S*. She wonders what made the mark as she thinks how disappointed Grace would be to discover her mistake.

"Why did you come alone?" she says finally.

"I wasn't sure I was right, and O'Toole, he's my boss . . . and he's . . . well, he's . . ."

"A jerk," Hadley says. "Mark told me."

"Exactly. And I didn't want to lose my promotion in case I was wrong."

She nods again.

"And as it turns out, I was only half-right."

Hadley says nothing.

"Herrick has the kids?"

She traces the scratch with her finger, rubbing at it as if she can wipe it away. "None of this is Grace's fault," she says. "I want to tell you what happened, but I want to start by saying that I'm willing to cooperate, but not in incriminating Grace. Because none of this, and I mean none of it, is her fault. Grace was only at the office that night to check on the uniform order—"

The waitress sets the coffees and soups down in front of them.

"She caught me looking for the safe—"

"Stop," Fitz says. "Eat."

Hadley looks down at the steaming bowl of corn chowder, then looks away from it. "But I need to tell you what happened."

"Eat," Fitz says again. "Please. You don't look so good . . . I mean you look great . . . you're a good-looking lady . . . I mean . . . crud. Please, Mrs. Torelli, eat your soup."

He blushes, his embarrassment plain on his young face, and Hadley thinks Mark was right to like this kid and to worry about him. He's a little how she imagines Skipper might have turned out had the placenta that nurtured him not detached before it was time.

She takes a bite of her soup and, despite her current state, closes her eyes as it melts on her tongue and as its warmth spreads through her body. Neither of them speaks while she finishes.

When she's done, she pushes the bowl aside and looks up at him.

"Better?" he says.

"Yes. Thank you." Then, with a deep breath, she starts again, weaving a fabulous story in which she held Grace at gunpoint and ordered her to cooperate, then held Miles hostage to force Grace to drive them to the hospital, then Barstow.

"Mrs. Torelli," Fitz interrupts.

She looks at him.

"We have you on video. At the office, at the hospital, and at the mall."

"Oh," she says, a blush rising. Then, almost desperate, she says, "But you have to believe me: Grace had nothing to do with this."

"Okay. Well, then, how about you start again, and this time you tell me the truth."

Hadley looks down at the napkin she is shredding and shakes her head. "Because then Grace will go to jail."

"Prison," Fitz corrects, and Hadley flinches.

"Sorry," he says, holding out his napkin so she can wipe the tears that have sprung to her eyes. "I'm not trying to upset you."

She shakes her head, no longer wanting to confess, afraid anything she says might be used against Grace.

"Start with the money," Fitz encourages. "Did you know it was dirty?"

Hadley shakes her head. "I was just trying to leave. I had no idea Frank had that much stashed away."

"And where is it now?" Fitz says, and Hadley feels her blood go cold, wondering if that's the real reason he's here. But when she lifts her eyes, all she sees is sincere concern on his face.

"Grace has it."

"Makes sense," he says; then he leans back, considering this new information. His eyes flick back and forth as he puzzles it out. "The car switch happened somewhere in McCook, probably at the silos. Then you and Herrick split up. She takes the money and the kids, and you hightail it to the border . . ." His eyes grow wide. "Because Herrick had another way out!" His face lights up. "She got out! And the kids were part of her cover: three kids instead of her and a baby." He seems thrilled by the idea, and she realizes he is rooting for them. "Brilliant. A truly remarkable mind." His grin fills his whole face, smiling as if he has a celebrity crush, and Hadley wonders if that is a thing, criminal admirers.

"None of this is her fault," she repeats.

"Maybe," he says, "but she might have a tough time convincing a jury of that. After all, she did shoot at a federal agent."

"She didn't shoot *at* him," Hadley says. "She was warning him not to go for the gun I dropped."

Fitz frowns, and Hadley realizes she just did what she swore she wouldn't. She just incriminated Grace. She drops her eyes and returns to shredding the napkin.

"It's good she got away," Fitz says. "Hopefully far away . . . far, far away, like a nonextradition country. Is that where she went?"

Hadley says nothing, though that was the plan. Once Grace gets to London, she will decide where to go next. She was considering Dubai or a country near South Africa. Once she gets there, she'll get word to Melissa, and Melissa will pass the information on to Hadley.

"With her past," Fitz goes on, "things won't go well if she gets caught."

Hadley nods, seemingly unable to stop herself from confirming his theories and making things worse.

"For you, it's different," he says. "You have more to lose and less at risk."

She tilts her head.

"You don't have a record," he says. "So long as you make it clear you had no idea Mark was an agent when you pointed the gun at him, the charges against you won't be so bad."

She says nothing. She knew perfectly well Mark was an agent, and Fitz knows it.

"Sometimes it's all in how you present the facts," he says, sounding a lot like Grace did when she was trying to convince Hadley they needed to turn themselves in.

"Why are you helping us?" she says.

His face pinks, and he looks uncomfortable. "I just don't want to see you in more trouble than you need to be."

"But why?"

He looks down at the table, then back at her. "Ironically, for the same reason Mark was always getting on my case." He smiles sadly, and Hadley can tell how much Mark meant to him. "Mark was always saying I cared too much."

Hadley nods. It's exactly what he told her about Fitz.

"And I suppose because of the note," he says.

"What note?"

"The one you left for that lady who loaned you her car."

"Nancy?"

"Yeah. Nancy."

Hadley remembers the note, a thank-you card she bought at Walmart and left on the dash for Nancy to find.

"Mark got mad at me," Fitz says, "when I told him the card you left was nice."

"He didn't think it was nice?"

"He didn't like that I called you Hadley and Grace instead of Torelli and Herrick when I told him it was nice."

Hadley smiles, unable to help but be amused by the idea of Mark setting this young man straight for calling her Hadley.

"He was always telling me I needed to toughen up and disengage." He pulls his shoulders back and imitates Mark's bluster, then relaxes and slouches forward in his oversize suit. "Then he did it. After he escaped from the archaeological site, he called the office, and when he was telling me what happened, he slipped up and called you Hadley."

She laughs, the sound escaping like a yip and causing Fitz to smile.

"He didn't even realize he'd done it. But it struck me because he'd never done anything like that before. And so, I don't know, after he died, I kind of felt like I owed it to him to try to figure out what was what before O'Toole got involved. I mean, while I get what the whole thing looks like, I also get why it happened, and I think Mark did also. It's why he went to Coors Field to try and stop you before things got worse. He wasn't supposed to be there."

"He wasn't?" she says.

Fitz shakes his head. "O'Toole had taken him off the case."

"Oh," Hadley says, her emotions surging forward as she is reminded that Mark died because of her . . . *for* her. She bites down on her lip to hold back the tidal wave that threatens to overwhelm her.

"Let's face it, Mrs. Torelli," Fitz says, "you're not exactly a hardened criminal. You took money you believed was yours. You ran from men you believed were working for your husband. You shot a gun in the air because some jerk was harassing your daughter. Most juries are going to sympathize with you. So long as you convince them that you didn't knowingly pull a gun on a federal agent, I think you'll get off pretty light, possibly only probation."

"And I'll miss out on years of my kids' lives," she says. Each time she's considered this moment, this has been the part she can't quite get past, knowing how much she will be missing. Desperately, she wants to be there for Miles's first steps, for Mattie getting her license, for Skipper learning to ride a bike, for the birth of the new baby, and the thought of missing those milestones destroys her.

Fitz looks away, sympathy plain on his young face.

"It's okay," she says, feeling bad for him. "I know you have a job to do, and I deserve what's coming. I appreciate you trying to help. I do."

He nods, but she feels him struggling. "At least if you serve your time," he says, "you won't have to abandon your house and the business."

Hadley drops her eyes and shakes her head. "That's why I took the money. Frank won't ever let me near any of that. He'd see it all burn to the ground before he'd ever give me a cent."

"You don't know?" Fitz says.

She looks up.

"Frank is dead."

The words float. She heard them—*Frank. Is. Dead*—but can't quite make sense of them.

"They found him holed up in a motel in Red Willow," Fitz says, "a town east of McCook. He came out firing and was killed."

"You killed him?" she says.

"I wasn't there," Fitz says carefully.

She stares.

Frank. Dead.

Like Mark.

"He's dead?" she says, the words whistling thread thin.

"Mrs. Torelli?" Fitz says.

The quake starts at her chin, a small tremor that grows and spreads outward, down her neck and to her spine before moving to her arms, her legs, her fingers, and her toes.

Fitz moves to the seat beside her. "Mrs. Torelli, I'm sorry. I thought you knew."

She wraps her arms around her gut as sobs spill out of her in great hiccups and heaves. She feels Fitz's hand on her back and hears him saying words that don't reach her brain.

A week ago she was whole; her family was whole. Frank was alive. He was buying baseball cards for Skipper and talking about lineups. She didn't know Mark or Grace. Mark was a continent away, being a father to Ben and Shelly. Grace was making a life for herself, her past safely behind her. Then, like making the wrong move in Jenga, she pulled out the wrong brick—made a single horrible wrong move that sent three worlds tumbling.

"Shhh, Mrs. Torelli, you're okay," Fitz says. "He's gone and will never hurt you again. You're safe now."

He's got it wrong. He thinks she is sobbing with relief. He couldn't be further from the truth. She doesn't want Frank to be dead. She wants him home, worrying about the tick in the Mercedes, bragging about the pizza oven to their neighbors, laughing with her about the neighbors' dog and whether he might indeed be half sheep because of his strange bark. She hates Frank for what he did, for who he was at times and for how difficult he made their lives, but she also loved him. For fifteen years, she loved him. Then she did what she did, and it sent all of them over the edge.

She keens against it, wishing she could turn back time.

"Mrs. Torelli, what can I do?"

Aware of people staring and of how uncomfortable she is making Fitz, she stammers, "Please . . . can I . . . I need to . . . is it okay if I go to the restroom? I'll leave the key."

She pulls the Nissan key from her pocket, sets it on the table, and staggers away. Her ankle nearly gives out, but she makes it to the women's room, locks herself in a stall, and collapses her head to her knees as sobs continue to spill out of her.

A minute or an hour, she has no idea, but eventually her tears run dry, leaving her hollowed out and empty, and shakily, she pushes to her feet to return to Fitz and face whatever is to come.

She walks into the restaurant to find him gone, three dollars tucked beneath the saltshaker on the table for a tip and the Nissan key on top of a napkin. The note scrawled on it reads: *On my way to Bismarck. Send my regards to Grace. F.*

She stares at it for a long moment.

"I understand you're looking for Dennis Hull."

Hadley turns to see a raisin-skinned man with a black ponytail talking to her.

EPILOGUE

GRACE

The ball rockets back and forth, and Skipper's eyes dart with it, a smile chiseled on his face. Today he wears his favorite football ensemble—a red-and-gold-striped soccer shirt, white shorts, and a black Nike headband with a red Swoosh.

Deon Hotto is his favorite player, though Benson Shilongo is a close second. He has also become a huge fan of cricket and rugby and golf, and his uniforms vary with the seasons.

The tickets to the Africa Cup of Nations final match cost a small fortune, but Jimmy insisted it was worth it. Their family's anniversary was worth celebrating, he said. That's what he calls it—June second, the day their remarkable family was formed. Grace always reminds him they were together on that day less than three seconds, and that Jimmy and Tillie didn't actually meet until months later, but that kind of reasoning does nothing to discourage Jimmy or his romantic notions. June second was the beginning—the day that, in his mind, it all worked out.

He holds the baby against his shoulder, burping him after his bottle—Mark James Herrick, born five months ago. The kid is a carrot top, his hair so orange it nearly glows in the sun. Skipper has taken to calling him Newbie, which has kind of stuck, except with Hadley, who still insists on calling him Mark.

Hadley fusses with Miles, who is now more than a handful. He got his walking legs at eleven months and has not stopped toddling into trouble since. At the moment, he is trying to climb over the railing and onto the field, inevitably to get the "ball," which, much to Skipper's delight, was his first word.

Each day he grows to look more like Jimmy, his pudge thinning into muscle and his smirk growing more and more mischievous. Hadley says that, though he looks like his dad, his personality is Grace's, and she warns them that they are in real trouble, that he will be either the next great hero or villain, depending on how they raise him. A great responsibility.

Hadley chomps hard on her gum. She showed up smoking a pack a day and immediately tried to wean herself from the habit using the patch, meditation, and hypnotism on tape. When none of that worked, she went cold turkey, and she's been struggling on again, off again, ever since.

She was a bit of a mess when she first showed up. Grace thought it impossible for Hadley not to be beautiful, but the woman who arrived on their doorstep a month after their own arrival in Namibia was not the same woman they had left in the States. She was drawn and gaunt, her skin was sallow and pale, and there was a vacancy about her that was terrifying.

Shell shocked, Jimmy said. He had seen it before. Soldiers, who in battle ran on adrenaline and then, when it was over, crashed, as if suffering a delayed response to the traumatic events that they had experienced. Not so much PTSD as a shutting down, an almost comatose state of debilitating moroseness, like they had been anesthetized.

Slowly, she has gotten better, the kids seeming to provide the antidote she needs. But every now and then, Grace still catches her staring off into space, her thoughts far away, as if thinking about something or trying to puzzle it out, a confused expression on her face, like no matter how hard she tries, she can't quite make sense of it.

"They won!" Skipper exclaims as the game buzzer goes off, sealing the game. He knuckle knocks each of them, even walking around the seat to fist pump Mark, who is still draped over Jimmy's shoulder.

Grace stands and gathers their bags. She still uses the diaper bag she carried on their fateful journey a year ago, the bag a reminder of all that happened and where it led. Hadley rolled her eyes when she pulled it out to pack it as her hospital bag. The Kmart-purchased pouch was ratty and stained, the handles threadbare and the front pocket torn.

Grace is pretty sure Hadley had her eye on a bag from the new Gucci for Babies line. They could have afforded it. They've done well with their money. Windhoek, Namibia, is one of the fastest-growing cities in the world, and providing parking in the congested downtown has turned out to be a lucrative business. They started off subleasing lots from businesses and now own two parcels of their own and are in the process of buying two more.

Grace runs the business side of things. Jimmy runs the day-to-day operations. And Hadley rolls her eyes a lot, offers far too many opinions, and takes care of the domestic life—a three-way partnership that works remarkably well.

As they make their way from the stands, Jimmy talks to Tillie about the upcoming stock car race at Killarney. "I'm putting my money on Frikkie," he says.

"That's because you're a fool," Tillie says. "McGrath has it this year."

Tillie has become an avid racing fan. She loves cars, racing, and anything to do with cars and racing. Her dream is to become the next Danica Patrick, though she wants to drive Formula One, not NASCAR.

"You can't pick a winner based on how cute the driver is," Jimmy protests.

"Put your money where your mouth is."

"Fine," Jimmy says. "A hundred grand."

Grace smiles.

"Two hundred," Tillie shoots back.

Jimmy shakes his head. "Too rich. I'm still broke from the last race."

"Fine. A hundred. But if you lose, you're taking me to the Rallycross Championship."

Jimmy spits on his hand and holds it out. Tillie spits on her own hand, and they shake.

Grace makes a mental note to order more Monopoly money. Jimmy is going to lose, and he is going to need a loan from the bank. She can already see it coming.

Jimmy has adapted remarkably well to life outside the army. She did a jig when she discovered Jimmy's sentence for his involvement was only six months in prison. The charges were eluding police in three states and aiding and abetting known criminals. He was given leniency because of his military service and because his lawyer did a brilliant job defending his crimes as a heroic act of passion for his pregnant wife and child.

A week after he was released, he boarded a plane to Africa using his brother's passport, arriving a week before Mark entered the world.

Grace chose Namibia because it is one of the most stable nonextradition countries in the world and because the national language is English. They have found living here is a lot like living in America, except they are a minority, and every once in a while, a zebra, rhino, or giraffe will stroll across the road.

Before Jimmy even unpacked his bags, Hadley had him enrolled in Gamblers Anonymous. There is no program in Windhoek, so he attends online meetings, and Hadley is all over him about not missing them.

Jimmy has learned quickly that enduring an hour-long meeting is preferable to being harangued for the next month for not holding up his end of the bargain. Grace pretends to be on Jimmy's side when he complains, but secretly she cheers Hadley, knowing that the reason she's being a pit bull is for her.

So, nowadays, the only gambling Jimmy does is with Skipper and Tillie using play money. Tillie leads, with close to six million in the bank. Skipper is a distant second, with two million, refusing to bet on anyone but his favorites. And Jimmy is always broke, a reminder that he sucks as a gambler.

As they walk, Grace watches them—her family, so perfect and fragile it terrifies her. Jimmy assures her it will be okay, but it all feels tenuous as a butterfly's life, and it takes constant convincing for her to believe him, his optimism warring against her paranoia that something so perfect can't last.

"Grace, are you on vacation or are you going to give me a hand?" Hadley says, breaking Grace from her thoughts.

Grace scoops Miles into her arms, and immediately he wriggles to get down. She raspberries his belly, causing him to squeal and distracting him long enough for Hadley to open the stroller.

"No stwrollewr. No, no, no," he protests.

So Hadley pushes the empty stroller as Miles dodges and darts and stumbles his way in his drunk toddler way through the crowd. Tillie follows him, huddling over him with her arms held protectively around him like a human bumper. She mutters *sorry*s and *excuse me*s as she goes.

Each day she grows to look more like Hadley, stretching taller and her features growing more refined—a shorter, younger replica of her mom, except her eyes, which are still entirely her dad's.

Grace isn't sure how she feels about Frank being dead. Hadley's pretty broken up about it, but each time Grace thinks of him being gone, she can't help but feel relieved. Frank wouldn't have stopped until he'd tracked Hadley down, and part of her is thankful they don't need to worry about it.

Miles face-plants on the sidewalk and lets out a wail. Tillie scoops him up. He is fine and pulling away before she can even check for a scratch.

Mark smiles at her from over Jimmy's shoulder. He is so different than Miles was as a baby, or maybe it's Grace who is different as a mother. His beginning was so unlike Miles's. He came into the world surrounded by devotion and smothered with love.

A strange family—the seven of them—all of them using Melissa's last name of Jenkins. Hadley's false papers add three years to her age, making her a whopping forty-two, and Grace takes every opportunity to tease her about it. Hadley makes the appropriate faces of annoyance and acts suitably offended, but Grace can tell it's an act, her vanity no longer as important as it once was. During that fateful week, something was lost that has not entirely been recovered, in its place ennui that Grace worries is permanent.

A week after they escaped, Mark's ex-wife did an interview on *60 Minutes* as part of a segment they were doing on Hadley and Grace's great escapade. Her name is Marcia, and she is a handsome woman, blonde and well put together.

She talked about Mark and the day of his death and the package that arrived a few days after. In the package were two letters, one for each of the kids, to be opened when they turned eighteen. It also contained a hundred thousand dollars with a note attached that said, *College fund.* Attached to the money was a Post-it that said, *Please get your son a dog,* and Marcia endeared herself to the world when a floppy-eared beagle puppy bounded onto the set.

A lot of the interview focused on the call Mark made the morning of the day he died. Marcia didn't come right out and say that it was as if he knew he was going to die, but she did say that, looking back on it, it seemed as if he knew things were no longer going to be the same. She cried, and Lesley Stahl handed her a tissue; then she went on to explain how difficult their separation had been. She told Leslie how Mark had resisted the divorce, but then how, on the morning of the day he died, she felt like he had made peace with it.

At that point, she broke down completely, and it was a full minute before she was able to go on, to explain that she thought it was because he might have met someone.

The assumption by the world was that it was Hadley, and the juicy tidbit stoked the already raging fire of fascination with their story.

Since the episode aired, rumors have been floating around about a movie being made. Grace cringes at the idea, certain someone like Angelina Jolie will be cast to play Hadley, while some actress who looks like Nanny McPhee will play her.

Jimmy folds the double stroller into the back of their minivan as Hadley straps Miles into his toddler seat. Tillie and Skipper climb in beside him, and Grace nuzzles Mark's nose before putting him in his car seat. She climbs into the passenger seat as Jimmy slides into the driver's seat. She still can't get used to the left side being the passenger seat, and Jimmy finds it endlessly amusing how she startles each time he makes a turn.

"I get to choose the music," Tillie says, reaching over the center console to switch the radio to a Namibian grunge station that only plays songs that sound like trash cans being run over by freight trains.

"That's not music," Grace protests.

"This coming from a woman who could win a gold medal for worst playlist."

"Bruce Springsteen is the Boss."

"The boss of what? Tone-deaf musicians?"

Screeching guitars blast from the speakers, and Grace rolls her eyes, a hidden smile on her face. Jimmy pulls into the traffic waiting to exit the park, and Grace glances back at their almost full van. A single seat remains, a spot between Hadley and Mark in the last row. *Perhaps one more?* she wonders. *Or is that asking too much?*

She turns forward again, the sky ethereal blue and eternal through the windshield, and her thoughts spiral back to the moment that started it all, marveling as she often does at the likelihood of two women being in the same spot at the same time to commit the exact same crime.

Coincidence is not something Grace believes in, and the chances of what happened that night are too infinitesimally small for her to simply write off as happenstance. No, it seems to her that some hidden connectivity existed in that moment that profoundly influenced their lives, intertwining their fates and bringing them to this remarkable place and time.

Her eyes burn with the cerulean intensity. *Maybe a girl,* she thinks, *to even things up? Annabelle?* Her grandmother's name.

Might even have already happened. She has been feeling a bit green lately.

Everyone will call her Annie, except Hadley, who will insist on calling her Annabelle. And who knows what Skipper will call her.

She smiles, fully covered in gloat.

AUTHOR'S NOTE

Dear reader:

I am often asked where the ideas for my stories come from. The answer is: never the same place. The idea for *Hadley and Grace* came from my enduring love for the movie *Thelma and Louise*. I wanted to write the same sort of exciting road-trip adventure that also had an underlying theme of self-discovery and empowerment.

As it turned out, I couldn't actually tell the story as it was originally conceived by the talented Callie Khouri. Fortunately for us, times have changed, and sending a big "screw you" to all the misogynist men of the world for being oppressive twits who bully women while women sit back and take it no longer works. We've come a long way from gawking truck drivers, bar-thug rapists, and patronizing do-gooder cops as typical male stereotypes. So, while the plot is similar—two women on the run who become accidental outlaws—the story needed to change.

I knew I wanted children involved, and I knew I wanted Skipper to be a part of it. I had just finished reading the real-life Skipper Carrillo's biography, *Have a Home Run Day!*, written by his sister, Alicia Rowe, and his clear-eyed, pure-hearted vision of the world inspired me. So, I started with Skipper and went from there.

Grace is a character near and dear to my heart. While she is not me, she is the closest I've come to writing a version of myself. I told my son the other day that if I could give my younger self one piece of advice, it would be to realize that the energy you put out is the energy you get back. If you are defensive and closed off, then life will be harder than it needs to be. There might be good reason for you to be that way, as there was for Grace, but as soon as she allowed Hadley, Mattie, and Skipper in, her world changed. During that fateful week, while Hadley became tougher, Grace actually became softer, her heart opening, an evolution that was both wonderful and terrifying to witness. I didn't realize that was going to be her journey until after it happened, and it was a beautiful discovery, one that resonated with me personally.

I hope you have enjoyed this wild ride as much as I enjoyed writing it.

Suzanne

ACKNOWLEDGMENTS

Enormous thanks to the following people, without whom this book would not have been possible.

Skipper Carrillo. This story started with you, and I could not have created the character without the man. It is rare in this world to meet a person who shines so bright and with such special light it changes the way you view the world.

Alicia Rowe and the entire Rowe/Carrillo family, for allowing me to use the real-life Skipper's indelible spirit and love for baseball as the inspiration for the fictional Skipper in this story. While the real Skipper inspired the character, I want to make it clear that this story is a work of fiction, and that the character's circumstances and family are entirely a product of my imagination. Skipper Carrillo's mother and father were loving, devoted parents and bear no resemblance to any of the characters in this story.

My family.

Kevan Lyon, my wonderful agent.

Alicia Clancy, my editor, for her invaluable insight and feedback.

The entire team at Lake Union, including Bill Siever, Laura Barrett, Riam Griswold, Ashley Vanicek, and Kathleen Lynch, for once again turning a humble manuscript into the beautiful finished work it has become.

Sally Eastwood and Lisa Hughes Anderson for reading the story when it was ugly.

Skipper Carrillo at our restaurant, Lumberyard, celebrating his eightieth birthday after taking an "Angels" photo in front of artist Colette Miller's Global Angel Wings, which are painted on the wall of our other restaurant, Slice Pizza and Beer. As legit an angel as there ever was.

DISCUSSION QUESTIONS

1. In the beginning of the story, both Hadley and Grace believe they are failing their children. How did you feel about them as mothers at the start of the story?

2. Frank is a dangerous man. How do you feel about Hadley leaving the way she did? Jimmy has a gambling problem that endangers Grace and Miles's future. How do you feel about her leaving the way she did?

3. Skipper is a special boy who sees the world with a unique perspective. How did you feel about him as a character? Have you ever met someone like him?

4. Grace has an ongoing relationship throughout the book with her dead grandmother. Have you ever lost someone yet still felt their presence in your life? Do you think that presence is real, a memory, or a conscience?

5. Hadley and Grace take close to two million dollars from Frank. Do you think it was right for them to take the money? What if Grace had just taken the amount Frank owed her? Would that have been right?

6. Do you believe in karma? How about coincidence? Grace and Hadley end up at Frank's office at the exact same time to rob him, which sets in motion a series of events

that alters their destinies. Do you think a hidden connectivity exists between us that often dictates our lives?

7. There is a remarkable synergy between the characters. Grace has street smarts, and Hadley has charm and is a gifted liar. Grace connects with Mattie. Mattie has a special understanding of Skipper. Hadley has a way with Miles. And, by the end of the story, they all would lay their lives on the line for the others. For Skipper, biological affiliations hold no weight. How do you feel about that? Do genetics dictate a family, or does something more powerful than blood tie people together and make them a tribe?

8. Grace and Hadley are accidental criminals. How accountable should they be held for their crimes? Do you think they deserve to be punished? Go to prison? If they were caught, do you think Grace's punishment, because of her past record, should have been more severe?

9. Mark and Hadley share an incredible moment. How do you feel about what happened between them? Do you believe in natural chemistry, or, as Hadley put it, "the simple unique magnetism of two particular organisms toward each other?" Do you find what happened between them romantic or tragic?

10. Jimmy, against Grace's wishes, shows up to help. How do you feel about Jimmy? Do you think Grace did the right thing in forgiving him?

11. At what point did you figure out Grace was pregnant? Were you happy for her, or did you feel sorry for her? Do you think maternal abilities are natural, or can they be learned?

12. An underlying theme of the story is about each of us having a better self within us hidden under strata of fear. Do

you ever feel that fear stops you from being the best version of yourself? Grace tells Mattie the story of how she started over when she moved to California, and Mattie decides to become Tillie. Do you think making a clear break like this is helpful in changing? Or do you believe we are hardwired to be who we are and incapable of true transformation?

13. Who was your favorite character? Why?
14. Movie time: Who would you like to see play each part?

ABOUT THE AUTHOR

Photo © 2015 April Brian

Suzanne Redfearn is the bestselling author of four novels: *Hush Little Baby*, *No Ordinary Life*, *In an Instant*, and *Hadley and Grace*. In addition to being an author, she's also an architect specializing in residential and commercial design. She lives in Laguna Beach, California, where she and her husband own two restaurants: Lumberyard and Slice Pizza and Beer. You can find her at her website, www.SuzanneRedfearn.com, on Facebook at SuzanneRedfearnAuthor, or on Twitter @SuzanneRedfearn.